LOST

IN THE

SURF

LOST

IN THE

SURF

HARRY SLACK

H. Slack Jr. Books

This is a work of fiction. Names, characters, organizations, places, events, and incidents are either products of the author's imagination or are used fictitiously.

Published by H. Slack Jr. Books, Bandon, Oregon

Edited and designed by Girl Friday Productions
www.girlfridayproductions.com

Cover design: Emily Weigel
Project management: Katherine Richards
Editorial: Bethany Davis
Image credits: cover © Shutterstock/nito (texture), Shutterstock/ Juuso (boat), Shutterstock/margo_black (surf)

ISBN (hardcover): 978-0-578-90471-9
ISBN (paperback): 978-0-578-90472-6

Library of Congress Control Number: 2021911319

Dedicated to the Bandon coastguardsmen

IT COULD HAVE HAPPENED

PART I

CHAPTER 1

SEPTEMBER 1939

Kenji Kosoki sat on a flat gray rock while easily leaning back against another rock. The slight wind warmed his face, but Kenji was not dozing. The chum salmon and sockeye salmon were running up the Tokachi River. It was the most important time of the year for Kenji's family. He was watching his family's gill nets, which were stretched out at four places halfway across the river. The flood tide had just started coming in, and with it, the salmon. The glass floats holding the nets bobbed and jerked, and some fish were thrashing in the top of the nets, throwing water in all directions. In thirty or forty minutes, the action would settle down, and his work would start. He would signal for his family to help pick the entangled salmon from the nets. It wasn't a bad job if the weather and surf were calm, but if it was windy and the surf rough, it was very difficult. The income from salmon sales was substantial, however, and gave Kenji's family some small affluence in the Ōtsu hamlet.

Yet Kenji's mind wasn't on fishing either. While the nets were bouncing to life, Kenji's thoughts drifted from family to fishing to the navy. It might be the last season he would do this, which bothered him slightly, but sitting on his behind waiting to work one of the gill nets was not his desired future, nor was living with his family in Ōtsu for the remainder of his life. He loved his family, but it was late summer 1939, he was nearly eighteen years old, and the Japanese military was taking all the enlistments it could get.

Kenji knew some things about recent Japanese military history thanks to school, but most of his favorite war stories came from his grandfather Maki. Maki Kosoki had been eighteen when he'd enlisted in the Imperial Japanese Navy as a candidate for an officer's commission, and earlier this year, he had retired to Ōtsu after reaching the rank of commander.

Kenji was fascinated by his grandfather's naval adventures. His stories of great battles ended in glorious victories, and they filled Kenji's heart and soul with pride and a love of his country. Grandfather was at his best when recounting the defeat of Russia in the Russo-Japanese War. The Russians had built up a large fleet at Port Arthur and Vladivostok and then sailed that fleet toward Japan's home islands. At the Strait of Tsushima, the Imperial Japanese Navy surprised the Russian fleet and caused thirty-four of thirty-eight Russian warships to be sunk, scuttled, captured, or interned. More than ten thousand Russian sailors were either killed or captured. Grandfather always proudly stated, "Japan lost three torpedo boats, three warships were damaged, and one hundred and ten Japanese sailors were killed—four on my ship—but the battle ended that war."

Kenji never tired of hearing these stories. He marveled at the skill and power of the Japanese Navy. He wanted to be part of it.

At age fifty-three, Grandfather Maki, as commander of his own ship, had landed Japanese invasion forces on the shores of China. It had never occurred to him, he'd told Kenji, that the conduct of the Japanese soldiers in China would eventually earn his contempt and the disgust of the remainder of the civil world. This disappointment had contributed to his retirement, but hadn't tarnished his view of the navy at all. In fact, Maki said that made him revere the Imperial Japanese Navy. The officers and enlisted men of his acquaintance were professional and honorable. Their training at the various naval academies had been superb.

While there was no love lost between Maki and the Japanese Army, Kenji couldn't imagine he would have the slightest hesitation in assisting Kenji in entering one of the Japanese naval academy programs.

And there Kenji would flourish; he was an exceptional young man. He was physically more powerful than most of his peers, he was a good student, and he never shirked a difficult task. He was five feet, eleven inches tall and somewhat dark in complexion. He had been in a few fights that were not of his making, and he had been criticized for severely battering a couple of his antagonists. His respect for his parents and siblings was absolute.

Yes, Maki would help him. Kenji would talk to him—soon.

As the annual six-week salmon run continued, Kenji's constant companion was his dream of a career away from the fishing business. Finally, one night, as he and his grandfather were alone mending a gill net, Kenji confessed his desire to leave to his grandfather. He relied upon Maki nearly as much as he relied on his mother and father for answers to personal concerns, and he couldn't discuss this with his parents, who knew nothing of his desire to leave home. Kenji saw a look of care come over Maki's face. His grandfather put his mending needle down on a box and looked at him.

"Kenji, I have told you stories about my experiences in the navy. You need to know that those stories painted the glorious and heroic events in my life. The suffering and dying were not included. I also left out, for your mother's and sister's benefit, the sight of sailors lying on a bloody wooden deck with horrible and sometimes fatal wounds. Nor did I say anything about being at sea for months in crowded conditions on short rations of food, or taking orders that made no sense, or having seasick men around you, or the low pay, or being skipped over for a promotion. You need to know and consider all of these things now."

Kenji slowed his net mending as Maki continued. "You will miss your family and friends, and in wartime, the risk of being killed or wounded is great. And even though the Imperial Japanese Navy is the greatest naval power on earth, there are no guarantees—though the war with China should soon be over. Kenji, do you understand what I am saying?"

"I think I understand what you have told me, and I thank you for telling me," Kenji said. "I have thought about some of those things concerning the navy, but it does not change my mind."

Grandfather Maki nodded and picked up his mending needle again.

That evening, before falling asleep, Kenji pondered what his grandfather had said about the dangers and uncertainties of life in the navy. But it was what he wanted. He would let Grandfather Maki know that, and maybe he would help him.

The next day, Kenji was back to minding the nets and thinking of escape. He would soon be unable to conceal his melancholia from his mother, who knew him well. He would reveal to her his vision of a different life. With difficulty she would accept Kenji's vision as would Kenji's father. Their family had done this before.

Many years ago, when Maki Kosoki had left Ōtsu and joined the Japanese Navy, it had been against his family's wishes, but it hadn't been long before Kenji's great-grandparents had seen the value of their young son pursuing his dream. Maki's happiness had been obvious in his letters, and no fewer salmon had been caught.

Kenji had considered what his absence would mean to the family's fishing enterprise. They could hire a seasonal employee to replace him. Ōtsu had many fishermen. It was situated at the mouth of the Tokachi River on the southeast coast of Hokkaido, approximately twenty kilometers from the larger inland town of Toyokoro. Landscapes were always green, from the highest hill to the river's edge. It was a pleasing and alluring place to live and work, and he would miss that part of it, but it was not in Kenji's makeup to stay.

His friends—and sometimes his father—had admonished him a few times for what his father called hostile, combative behavior, though scuffles after school were the only episodes of such conduct that Kenji could recall. His father had counseled him that his personality was partially beneath the surface, and that while the 95 percent on the surface was very good, he just needed to control the other 5 percent. Kenji didn't see it that way. He knew what he was doing when he was confronted or when he was trying to resolve something that didn't meet with his sense of fairness.

That toughness had not prepared him, however, for breaking the news of his desire to leave to his family. The fishing season continued, and Kenji kept thinking only of escape while playing the dutiful fishing son every day. He watched the nets as always until they stilled, then he called for his family.

His father, mother, two brothers, and one sister would help him haul the heavy, fish-laden nets over the rails of their fishing skiffs. Each net floated on the surface by way of glass balls, or floats, attached to the top line of the net. Frequently a glass float would break off the net and float away. Hemp, cotton, linen, and other natural fibers were used to make the nets and to fasten the glass balls to the top line. These fibers chafed and rotted easily, so the floats were lost. They were only ten to fifteen centimeters in diameter, easily held in two cupped hands, and once lost, they headed to sea. Sometimes if the wind and current were right, they washed ashore near the area where they broke free.

On this particular day, Kenji hauled the net vigorously into the boat, paying little attention to the floats. When one ripped off on the outside of the gunwale, he heard his father sigh in frustration as it drifted away, probably gone forever.

"Be careful," he said to Kenji. "Each float is worth the price of a salmon."

Kenji didn't need the reminder. Trips to the glassworks cost time and money. Net repair and mending, which included retying the floats, was also time consuming. For all fishermen, but particularly for Kenji, it was a miserable job.

Removing the fish from the nets was a physical but nearly mindless task. As he continued working, dropping the fish in the bottom of his skiff, his thoughts were elsewhere. Kenji's mind spanned the Pacific, charted the drift of the ocean, and soared in the direction of all those disappearing glass balls. He knew that North America was to the east; China was behind and somewhat to the south of the Japanese isles. Were the floats lost at sea? Were they struck by boats, broken, and sunk? Were they scooped up in nets and returned to the float merchants? Kenji knew little of the other fisheries onshore and offshore of the Japanese isles; sometimes their glass floats washed up near his home. Floats of all sizes were used around the country, each for different kinds of fish and fishing. The largest floats, fifty to sixty centimeters in diameter, had the highest buoyancy and were used for tuna longline fishing, where a single line was laid out for miles. Medium-size floats were used in other fisheries, and the smaller floats were used in salmon gill net fisheries.

Another glass float broke loose, and Kenji thought of his trips with his father to the glassworks. There was a family glass float manufacturing plant in Toyokoro, where all sizes of glass floats were handblown. Once blown to size, the floats were sealed with melted glass, the seal was stamped with the maker's trademark, and the floats were placed inside a firebrick furnace to evenly reduce their temperature. This Toyokoro maker's trademark was a squiggly, double-crossed T—the same mark Kenji had seen on the glass ball floating away from him.

The nine or ten other glass float manufacturers in Japan had huge capacities for producing any and all sizes of floats for the Japanese fisheries. Kenji had heard his father and the man at the glassworks say that up to half of the floats in these larger operations were lost every year. The image of all of those glass floats at sea, careening toward a new life away from their tiny fishing villages, filled him with hope.

"Kenji! Kenji!" his younger brother yelled. He was sitting next to Kenji in the skiff and raising his voice over the sound of the waves. "Are you going to pick fish from the net, or are you going to act like you're not even here?"

Kenji looked at his brother and said, "I was thinking about tossing my annoying brother over to follow these glass floats!"

His brother laughed, and Kenji immediately went back to work. But his thoughts were never far from the idea that being aboard a warship would be better than sitting in this skiff covered with fish slime.

With each haul of the net, the salmon kept coming into the skiff. The floor of the skiff was now awash with flopping, bleeding, and dead and dying salmon.

"This is a good day to be a salmon fisherman," his father said. Kenji just nodded.

Such news was not uplifting for Kenji, who was fishing by rote now, with only his motor functions on the task and his mind fixed on a private vision of himself as a sailor in the Japanese Navy. How would he get out of this? These fishing sites had been owned and fished by his family and ancestors for more than a hundred years. They were excellent sites and were coveted by nearly every salmon fisherman in the community. Fishing for salmon was his family's life. It would greatly offend and disappoint his father, mother, brothers, and sister to declare that he wanted to leave and make a life in the navy. There had never been a word spoken or a conversation held about any of them giving up salmon fishing. Was he, Kenji, the only member of his family who wanted to exchange commercial fishing for a different occupation and another way to live? Was life at Ōtsu, where the great Tokachi River entered the Pacific, inevitably to become part of his past? How could he leave?

CHAPTER 2

SEPTEMBER 1941

The old Ford school bus rolled down the dusty, one-lane road. As it made its inevitable approach toward the long gravel drives east and west, its brake lights flashed red. The bus slowed to a stop where two metal mailboxes perched together on a fence rail. Two boys and a girl in pigtails leaped out of the bus. One boy ran around the front of the bus, looked up and down the road, and dashed up the east driveway to a house just out of sight. The other boy ran up the driveway to the west with the girl behind him yelling, "George, wait for me!"

George Williams's unzipped jacket and his elbows flapped at his sides. When he reached the house, he leaped over the small stairway to land on the front porch. With one more maneuver, he opened the screen door and was in the living room, where he dropped his book and lunch box. His mother was sitting by a rear window, sewing in the late-afternoon sun. George hurried to his room upstairs and immediately returned with his .250-3000 caliber varmint rifle and a pocket full of cartridges. His mother turned to say something to him, but he instantly headed for the back door in the kitchen, opened it, and broad-jumped over two steps to sail through eight feet of air and into the backyard. But after three quick steps toward the wooded area, he heard his mother, who was also fast on her feet, say, "Stop! Not again today—you find something else to do."

Deflated, he yelled, "But, Mom, David and Henry are waiting for me. Deer season opens in a couple of weeks, and today we're going to finish sighting in our rifles. We need the practice."

With a stern voice, she said, "You've practiced enough. I have a few chores for you."

He pleaded, "Come on, Mom. There's been a west wind blowing for three days. Nobody's been on the beach, and there are surely some Japanese floats there—you know I can sell the small ones for a dime and the larger ones for more."

Annoyed, his mother told George he could go and added that his father would be speaking with him that evening.

George walked across his lawn near some brush to meet his friend Henry Johnson, who lived slightly to the southwest. Henry was standing casually, holding his rifle to his side, balanced with one hand grasping the breech. Henry and George and been the best of friends since before the first grade. They each had a love for the beach, hunting and fishing, and generally fooling around; the latter included everything from helping themselves to the neighbor's ripe cherries to siccing the dog on stray cats.

They lived only a quarter mile from the Pacific foredunes, with George's house somewhat closer to the ocean beach. The thirteen-mile stretch of foredune land south of the town of Bandon, Oregon, was a boy's paradise. The inland side was heavily wooded with shore pine, fir, red alder, salal, huckleberry, and other brush. Although the land features were surprisingly consistent—the same topography, timber, and brush seemed to stretch on and on—an occasional small stream emerged from the vegetation and cut through the foredune to the sea, and the area was frequently crossed by sandy, beaten paths. A path to the beach near George's house had been hacked through the brush and low-hanging tree limbs until it merged with sand. The path was George's family's handiwork.

Ocean beaches in this area were generally open expanses of sand. With a low gradient between the high- and low-tide lines, it was not uncommon for two-foot minus tides to leave a large swath of beach exposed for beachcombers after nine-foot-high tides had replenished the ocean's treasures. However, in two sections of this long stretch of beach, the gradient was very steep, so the area of beach exposed between extreme high and low tides was minimal. In these spots, the steep slope of the beach guaranteed that washed-up glass floats would not stay onshore but would roll back into the sea with the outgoing tide. George and his friends had seen Japanese floats in the water in these steep areas. Sometimes the boys had waded into the sea to grab them, but more often the floats simply could not be reached.

George and Henry looked down the beach side of the foredune. Standing on a slight rise in the sand dune was their buddy David Harris, holding up a gunnysack.

"I'll bet the son of a bitch has some glass balls in that sack," George growled, "and I'd say he came onto the beach just ahead of us and scoured the beach for them."

When they caught up to David, he was sitting on a piece of driftwood with his rifle in one hand and three glass balls in his sack in the other. Before George or Henry could voice their opinions about David reaching the beach ahead of them, David said, "My mom wouldn't let me bring the rifle unless I promised I wouldn't shoot any seagulls."

Everyone who knew David knew he was death on seagulls, which were technically protected game, not legal to shoot. George had little patience. "For Christ's sake, David, you dumb shit. If you don't stop it, you're going to be in big trouble with the cops."

Henry chimed in. "You've got to stop that seagull crap or you'll get *all* of us in trouble. Maybe we only have one game warden in Coos County, but you never know where he is or what he might do. He gave his own mother-in-law a ticket for too many trout, and he'd sure as hell give you a ticket for shooting seagulls. Besides, they're all guts and feathers!" Then, staring at David's rifle, he blurted out, "Hey, this isn't your rifle!" In fact, David looked to be holding a .300 Savage.

"It's my father's gun, but he said I have to buy my own ammo," David replied, standing up.

The three boys strolled down the oceanside slope of the sand dune and onto the beach. The west wind had cleaned the beach of seaweed and other debris and deposited it at the high-tide mark. The boys looked up and down the beach, hoping to spot a glass float.

Henry, who was looking down the beach to the south, said to David, "Let me check out your rifle."

David handed it to him. "There's nothing in the chamber, but be careful anyway."

Henry put the rifle to his shoulder and checked the beach ahead with the telescopic sight, suddenly handed the gun to David, and ran south as fast as he could.

"That sucker sees a glass ball," George said softly to David.

George was right. By the time they caught up with him, Henry was holding a glittering twelve-inch glass ball. The receding high tide had left the prize stranded on a slight hump on the shore in dry sand, where the boys all took a seat. A float that big was worth at least seventy-five cents or a dollar, and Henry now had it in his hands, thanks to the telescopic sight on David's rifle.

They all sat there for a while, with David and George looking up and down the beach for a glimpse of another green jewel. George got up and walked to a large driftwood snag, where he sat down again, while the other boys lingered nearby. They talked about the amount of junk the high tide had left on the upper shoreline: pieces of old boats, bottles, a shoe, single gloves, and some dead birds. Anything that could float in the ocean might be there.

David got quiet, and when George looked over, he was in a prone shooting position. A hundred yards distant, at the surf's edge, was a seagull. David fired, and a brown bottle exploded in the surf twenty yards beyond the bird. George was happy the seagull lived to fly away.

"That was one hell of a shot," he said.

"My dad and I can drive nails with this gun," David said.

"Think you can do as well, George? I do," Henry said. George agreed to try, so Henry found two small bottles in the drift line, walked down the beach about a hundred yards, and set them on a piece of driftwood. He said, "OK, let's see if you two are as good as you think you are."

George's prone shot hit one bottle, and David's hit the other. They were ready for deer season.

It was getting late, and it was time to be home. The three boys walked northward on the beach, talking and occasionally kicking some unseen object in the sand. When they came to the steep ocean beach, they saw a small glass ball in the calm of the deep water.

"We're not going to get that one," George said, and the others agreed.

Henry said, "See if you can hit it."

"Sure I can," George said, "but David should take the first shot."

David shot and missed.

George shot and sunk it in a hundred pieces. "The trick is to wait and fire only when it's at its lowest point in the trough of a wave, and do that regardless of the size of the wave." He lowered his gun. It weighed seven and a half pounds and fit George perfectly. The stock was precisely the correct length, as was the drop at the comb, and when George raised the gun to his shoulder and laid his cheek on the comb of the stock, his shooting eye fell squarely on the center of the eyepiece of the telescopic sight, all without any adjustment. He added, "My father taught me that when we were hunting seals and sea lions." The state of Oregon paid a good bounty for seal and sea lion scalps, and George's father had collected a few. The purpose of the bounty was to protect salmon stocks. The problem was that the hunter rarely found the fatally injured seal or sea lion to scalp for the bounty, but that was OK with the salmon fishermen. One less seal or sea lion meant many more salmon.

George said, "David, what do you do when you're out here by yourself? The seals, sea lions, and seagulls aren't safe with you around, are they?"

"You'll never know, George."

They walked on and came across two decomposing seagulls. George and Henry gave David a glancing look of condemnation as he shrugged his shoulders in innocence. Then they split apart to walk back to their own homes, where family and homework awaited.

CHAPTER 3

NOVEMBER 1941

Henry, George, and David, whose activities were mostly outdoor activities, were indeed fortunate to live in Bandon, a small coastal community of 1,500 people. The entire town had been destroyed by fire five years earlier and was in the process of reconstructing itself. Many of the historic merchants and businesspeople had either moved away or lacked the funds to rebuild, but Bandon's lumber mill still employed 150 men, and the town had several motels, a movie theater, two hardware stores, a dry goods store, and a variety of small businesses. The beach and the Coquille River still made it an attractive community for families. Bandon was a lumber-exporting port as well as home to a commercial salmon-packing industry. The United States Coast Guard lifesaving station was new, as was the Bandon Cheese Factory.

George, David, and Henry were in the same eighth-grade class at the newly rebuilt Sunset Public Grade School. They were all good students, but George was the best. They attended classes in three different classrooms, each with a different teacher and different seating assignments. Front-row seats were saved for the unruly, and Henry and David qualified from time to time. History and geography courses interested all three boys, arithmetic and reading less so. It seemed that the girls were the better students; they were starting to be of some interest to the boys.

Mr. Meyers taught American history. One bright October Friday, toward the end of class, Mr. Meyers announced that they would be starting their discussion of the reasons for the American Revolution that week. "Among the many causes were the taxation of goods produced by the colonists, the prohibition of the sale of cotton and other agricultural products to any nation except Great Britain, and the denial of freedom of speech as well as freedom of the press. One of the most grievous issues was the billeting of British soldiers in private residences without the consent of the homeowner."

George raised his hand and asked, "What do you mean, 'billet'?"

Mr. Meyers explained, "For example, let's say the Japanese invaded the West Coast of the United States and occupied it. They could order a homeowner or anyone in a house—maybe you and your parents—to provide food and lodging, without pay, to Japanese soldiers. They could even evict you from your own home and take your belongings and personal possessions—everything in that home. It is easy to see why some colonists would despise the British."

George held up his hand and asked, "Why did you use the Japanese soldiers as an example? They're on the other side of the world."

"Well, I could have used German soldiers, George, you're right. That might have been a little more realistic."

Jason Gleason, the new student from Portland, held up his hand, then said, "Wait—the Japanese example was perfect."

Henry, sitting beside George, said in a low voice, "Oh shit, a big-city smart-ass."

Mr. Meyers looked at the clock on the wall. He said, "Jason, do you want to add something?"

"According to my father," Jason said, "the Japs have invaded China, and we've embargoed oil shipments to them, and they are flashing their sabers, so who knows what they might do."

"That's gross speculation," Mr. Meyers said, "and enough of that for now. Tomorrow we'll talk more about this and about the Bill of Rights, and how those rights arose from British rule of the colonists. Class dismissed."

Mr. Meyers's class was the last of the day. George and Henry made their way to the school bus loading area, where David stood talking to a couple of girls. Though they were in the same grade, David was nine months older than the other boys and often bragged about being more mature; he was already more interested in girls than the others were. When he spotted his friends, however, he headed straight for them. "Well, we have the whole weekend. So what'll we do?"

"There's nothing left to do. No ducks around, and no more deer," George said. They each had bagged a buck with their father's assistance.

David said, "We could shoot seagulls."

"Christ," Henry said in disgust, dismissing the notion. "You knothead."

Jason walked by, and Henry glanced over. George could see he was still charged up from class and thought Jason was a show-off. "Hey, what's with the Japanese bullshit? Are you afraid of them?"

"No way," Jason said.

"So you were just buttering up Mr. Meyers."

"Baloney," Jason said. At least he was staying pretty calm. "What do you guys do around here besides go to school and make stupid comments?"

Henry looked at Jason and said, "Maybe we can show you some of the things we do, but I doubt you can do any!"

George, trying to get Henry to knock it off, asked more kindly, "Do you have a .22-caliber rifle, or a deer rifle, or a shotgun?"

Jason said he had all three. "So what do you guys want to do, start a war against Germany? Or Japan?"

George and David looked at one another as if to agree that this Jason guy from the big city might not be so bad after all.

Jason waved to his new acquaintances as he jumped onto the school bus and said, "See you guys around, and keep your powder dry."

The boys decided to catch a ride home later so they'd have a minute to talk. David, watching a girl nearby, said rather absently, "You know, Henry, you've always had a big mouth, and it's caused you some trouble—a fat lip here and a sore cheek there. I even saved you once. Remember that?"

"Hey—" Henry started, but George intervened.

"He gets provoked sometimes. It's not always his fault." Turning toward Henry, he said, "But he's not far off base. You do have a smart mouth, and you do make problems for yourself with it. This Jason fellow seems to have good big-city manners and thought better of getting cross with you."

David said, "Look, we know each other as well as anyone could, so we kinda need to look out for each other, and, Henry, that's all I'm doing for you, OK?"

"Yeah, I know."

George gave Henry a friendly nudge with his shoulder. "You and I have been friends forever, and the three of us can spar and make fun of each other, but to do that to guys we don't know, newcomers, isn't so good."

"Yeah," Henry acknowledged.

"He seems alright to me," George said. "Guess we know nothing about him or what he thinks of us."

Henry looked upward and said, "OK, now that we have that settled, I suggest we find a way home."

George arrived home after his sister and before his father. His mother was in the kitchen preparing for dinner. He sat at the small kitchen table and said, "There's a new boy in school, Jason Gleason. His family moved here from Portland, and I think his dad is a superintendent or something at the big mill in Coquille. Could we have Jason for dinner sometime?"

George's mother, Mary, said, "Of course, but it might be nice to have his mother and father also. I'll talk to your father about it and maybe call them."

A week later, Mark and Gloria Gleason graciously accepted the Williamses' dinner invitation. Before and during dinner, the two families learned some basic facts about each other. Joe Williams was the shop foreman and chief mechanic at the Ford automobile dealership in Bandon. Their home had been spared by the fire, but the dealership hadn't been so lucky. After the big fire and before the car dealership was rebuilt, Joe had worked as a mechanic in the lumber mill where Mark Gleason worked now.

Jason had moved with his family from Portland to Bandon in late August. When Mark and Gloria had visited the area the previous March, they'd found that Bandon suited them best, even considering the eighteen-mile commute to Mark's work as the new manager of the large Smith Wood Products mill in Coquille. Mark was a graduate of Oregon State College with a master's degree in forestry and logging engineering with minor studies in business administration. He was an experienced mill manager responsible for the entire operation, including managing the raw timber and logs that kept the mill operating three daily shifts. The Gleasons were honestly circumspect, if not humble, in relating their work, educational, and social experiences, and thus no social divide reared its head between the two families.

Dinner was almost over when George's mother appeared with pumpkin pie. George, sitting next to Jason, had eaten too much and moaned in stuffed agony but still started eating the dessert.

When he was finished, he asked Jason's father, "What exactly does your mill do besides make two-by-fours and stuff like that?"

Mark mulled over the question. "Well, George," he said, "the mill produces all the types of dimensional lumber necessary to build any wooden building—including two-by-fours, as you mentioned. We also manufacture plywood, materials used in venetian blinds, and, most importantly, battery separators."

George asked, "What are battery separators?" Mark explained that they were an integral part of every storage battery used in cars, trucks, and almost anything with a gasoline or diesel engine, including airplanes and submarines.

The military angle piqued George's interest. "So what exactly is a battery separator? What's it look like?"

Mark described the separator as a thin piece of wood, made from Port Orford white cedar. "It's about three-sixteenths of an inch thick, and in a regular car battery, it would be about six inches square. It sits upright in the battery between the lead plates, separating them and preventing them from fusing together and destroying the efficiency of the battery. Separators in truck batteries, especially those in large diesel trucks, are much larger. The separators in submarine batteries are even larger than those in trucks.

"They can only be made from Port Orford cedar because only the Port Orford cedar has the correct chemical composition *and* lends itself to a viable manufacturing process—a slicing machine that creates a smooth, accurate product. Composition and accuracy are especially important in the manufacture of separators for large submarine batteries. Some of these separators are shipped worldwide—except to certain nations, such as Germany and Italy."

Mark continued, "The interesting thing about the separator business is that southwestern Oregon, where we live, is the only place in the world that grows Port Orford white cedar."

George said, "I guess we're lucky to have all the white cedar in the world right here."

"That's one of the reasons I'm here," Mark said. "It will be even more important if we get into a war with Germany and Italy."

"What about the Japanese?" Jason asked.

"Yes, the Japanese could be a problem now that they have aligned themselves with Germany and Italy," Mark said. "We've exported white cedar to them in the past, and they've been storing it, probably to use for military purposes."

Joe added, "Even when I was working at the mill, there was talk by the workers and the loggers about the Japanese log buyers operating in this area. The way things are going, with President Roosevelt having stopped the sale of oil and scrap steel to Japan, it's no wonder the Japanese want cedar logs from us."

"The Port of Marshfield is the exclusive port for shipment of these logs to Japan, and it's been good business for everyone, from the timber owners—and the United States government is one of the timber owners—to the longshoremen who load the vessels. The Japanese use the white cedar for various purposes, including finish work in house construction and in personal and public shrines, but they're also storing some logs, apparently, for their military." Mark shook his head. "Now they're doing terrible things in China and claiming we're not treating them right, but they've nothing to gain in a war with the United States—and they're too smart to try. But who knows what they might do."

George, who was ever curious about mechanical things, wanted to talk more about the cedar battery separators. "Surely some other material or product could be used for a battery separator."

"Well, other substances are being developed," Mark said, "and certainly the Germans have found something, but it's not information that's been shared or published." He explained that the white cedar wood was somewhat porous when cut thin. It had an insulating quality and worked well between the positive and negative lead plates. The porous nature of each separator allowed electrical currents to flow between the plates while preventing short circuits.

It appeared to Mark that Jason was a little overwhelmed by the explanation. Mark said, "You still with me? It's a lot, but it's also kinda interesting. Would you like to hear more?" The boys nodded yes, so he went on.

"OK," Mark said with a smile before continuing. "This is going to bore the socks off everyone. Powdered lead and sulfates are added to the lead grids to make positive and negative grids. Each positive plate or grid is paired with a negative plate or grid, with a separator between. The battery is filled with electrolyte—or battery acid—a mixture of sulfuric acid and water. Without the electrochemical separator, there would be no battery, and I guess it would follow that there would be no diesel-electric submarines."

This did, as Mark predicted, end all interest in further conviviality, and everyone politely left the table and headed for the living room. Gloria and the boys helped Mary with the cleanup.

The next morning, Jason's phone rang. It was David. "You wanna do something?"

"Sure thing. Gonna start a war or something?"

"No," David said, "but George and Henry and I are going for a hike on the beach, and you're invited. We live near George on 101, so you could either ride your bike or have your mom or dad bring you. And bring your big rifle and some ammo with you for some target shooting." He gave Jason the directions, and Jason knew the area.

"OK, if I'm not there in an hour, I'm not coming," Jason said.

He was at David's house inside of thirty minutes. David invited him in and introduced him to his mother, Lucy; his sixteen-year-old sister, Jan; and his father, Robert Harris. Following some get-acquainted conversation with David's family, David and Jason walked away from the house, rifles in hand. The boys arrived at George's house and David said, "We'll ask George to take his dog, Luke, with us. It's fun to watch him romp and hunt for stuff, and he probably needs a run on the beach anyway." George called Luke and he came running. The black Lab came from good hunting stock and was a skilled retriever as well as an excellent pheasant dog. He could smell a dead fish five miles distant and a dog in heat eight miles distant. Luke was leaping straight up and down and looking at David eyeball to eyeball at the height of his jump, probably excited by the prospect of some hunting.

As soon as David and Jason met with George and Henry, they walked on a clear path toward the beach, and Luke leaped ahead, nose to the ground, hunting anything that was huntable.

Before long, David and Jason heard gunfire. In a few minutes, they saw George and Henry shooting at something at the edge of the surf. They were actually shooting at small rocks approximately ninety yards distant, and they occasionally hit one. Jason had thought he was a crack shot, but these boys definitely had superior shooting skills.

"I brought Jason along to help undo his big-city problems and hang-ups," David said, and all of the boys laughed.

They strolled south along the upper level of the beach, with the surf crashing on the steep shoreline peculiar to this beach area. The November day was clear and cold with no wind.

As the four of them wandered south along the surf line, George gradually worked his way to the line of debris left by the high tide. Suddenly he yelled something unintelligible. They all ran to him and found him on his knees, crouched over a huge round object enmeshed in rotting seaweed and old rope. A careful look through the mess revealed green glass.

"It's a monster!" George cried.

"Is he nuts?" Jason asked, wondering why anyone would be so excited about a glass ball.

Henry explained the situation to Jason. "That one may be worth five dollars," he said admiringly.

George scraped away most of the seaweed but couldn't cut the rope off with his dull pocketknife. He thought it would be easier to carry the object with the rope intact.

While George was busy examining his find, his friends set up pieces of driftwood on a drift log, and each demonstrated his shooting skill. George soon joined them. They were all expert marksmen. Jason had his Model 94 Winchester carbine, a 30-30 with a peep sight. At the hundred-yard range, he was good, but not as accurate as the boys with the telescopic sights. They were impressed with Jason's shooting, though, and David asked if he wasn't just having a lucky day. Jason put his rifle to his shoulder and shot a can on the upper beach at about sixty yards. The can jumped six feet in the air and fifteen feet backward.

Jason said, "Who are you guys, anyway?"

"You're one of us!" David said.

Jason gasped in mock alarm. "Oh shit!"

They all laughed and walked on down the beach, with George dragging his treasure in one hand and his rifle in the other.

As the afternoon wore on, they sat down in a wide depression in the dry sand area rimmed by green dune grass. They built a fire, and after they had all stared into the flames for a while, Jason asked, "Do any of you smoke?"

David said, "Well, we've tried it. We smoked some coffee grounds in a corncob pipe we bought for ten cents. Then we tried dried dock seeds and some baby shit off Indian arrow wood. We even picked up some cigarette butts and used the tobacco, but we gave it up. It was crap!"

Jason couldn't believe what he heard but asked no questions about David's statement. They all agreed that the coaches didn't want any of their players to smoke, so it must be bad stuff. Jason told them that he didn't smoke but that some of his Portland friends did, and he was happy to get away from that temptation, if that's what it was. The conversation revealed that Jason's experiences, for all his thirteen years— except for the weird smoking part—paralleled those of his newfound acquaintances. Jason knew by now that his new friends were boys who loved the outdoors and outdoor sports. He learned from George that Henry's grandparents, Sven and Mabel Clausen, commercially netted salmon on the Coquille River. Jason told them that his father had taken him fishing for salmon on the Willamette River near Oregon City, and they had caught a few fish.

"Do you have a girlfriend?" Henry asked.

"No," Jason said.

"Neither do any of us," Henry said, "but we're thinking about it."

"Speak for yourself!" David said, and the boys laughed.

David, staring into the fire, asked, "Do you guys hate Germans?"

Henry answered by saying that the Germans were terrible and added, "On my birthday last June, my mother read me a newspaper article about the Germans invading Russia, killing Russian farmers and civilians. So, yeah, besides all the other stuff they've done, I hate Germans."

George thought that invading France was awful, and Jason allowed as how he hated the Germans, but especially the Nazis and Hitler. Henry said, "They invaded Norway, and that's where my grandfather Clausen was born. Sure I hate 'em."

"Well, if Hitler came walking up the beach," David said, "would you shoot him?"

Their first collective answer was that they would shoot him, but after challenging each other, they decided they couldn't kill anyone, including Hitler. But they could capture him, kick the shit out of him, and give him to the British. Having solved that problem, they agreed that it was time to head for home. They started back up the beach, George with his prize glass ball in tow.

As they walked, each of them was mulling over the question about killing someone. George thought it would be awful to kill a person—but what if you had to do it to save your own life? He guessed he could if he was a soldier in war. He decided, *Oh well, I'm not going to have that problem,* and his thoughts turned to how much money he might get for his glass ball.

Jason's thoughts were on doing something with his new friends that was more constructive and worthwhile than hiking on the beach. He didn't know what that might be, but he would work on it.

CHAPTER 4

DECEMBER 1941

In the past decade, the Japanese nation, although a secretive nation, had advanced itself among the world powers, both industrially and militarily. The Japanese military was in charge. Japan had made the decision to emulate the dominant nations of the world and become imperialistic, and it had set its sights on nearly all territory in the western Pacific. It lacked, however, the raw materials for its industrial and domestic growth, and the United States had cut the flow of exports and demanded that Japanese forces withdraw from China.

The Imperial Japanese Navy of 1941 was second in strength only to the greatest naval force on the planet, the British Royal Navy. The British had built Japan's first naval vessels during the early twentieth century. Eventually Japanese yards were designing and building ships of extraordinary architecture and capability, while Japan's naval academies—in particular the Etajima academy—produced highly competent naval officers to run them. Etajima was located on an island in Hiroshima Bay, a part of Japan's Inland Sea and due south of the city of Hiroshima. The city of Kure, with its naval shipyards and immense arsenal of naval weapons and supplies, was to the east and even closer to the academy, which had been designed as an exact copy of a British

Royal Navy academy. This area of the Inland Sea was the home port of the Imperial Japanese Navy.

Kenji's grandfather Maki had graduated from Etajima. It was inspirational for Kenji to see the great warships of Japan and their movements; to be a part of it was precisely what he wanted in life. Nothing could be better than to be in command of one of those warships.

Kenji had left Ōtsu by bus in January 1940 and enrolled at Etajima. The drill and work was hard, but Kenji had mastered it. He knew he had taken the right path, one that had been cleared by Grandfather Maki and his former acquaintances in the navy and colleagues at the academy.

Kenji had prospered at Etajima over the past two years. He had been admitted to the officer training regimen, and his instructors were soon aware of the first-year cadet's proficiency in navigational studies, as well as his outstanding physical strength and skill. Discipline in the Japanese Navy was ironfisted, and an officer candidate who demonstrated a mastery in administering as well as accepting discipline was likely to advance.

The Japanese Navy also needed skilled men who could act in advance of general military operations to carry out covert and secretive functions. Thus, at the behest of the commander of Etajima, Kenji had accepted a move from the four-year officer training course to a two-year intensive training program with the promise that, upon the completion of certain assigned duties, he would be readmitted to Etajima. After finishing the intensive training, he would be granted the highest noncommissioned officer rank and would be placed immediately on active duty. Kenji didn't ask what his duty would be, and he wasn't told. The duty he wanted was that of a commissioned officer aboard a large naval fighting ship, and the actual nature of his duty was unimportant to him.

Kenji rested on the steps of the main academy building, viewing the grounds before him. The two-story redbrick buildings housing classrooms and administrative offices sat on either side of a vast expanse of well-mowed green lawns. A few old military guns and cannons were placed here and there. Many deciduous trees still held their gold and amber leaves. It was early December; the sky was clear and blue, and there was a chill in the breeze, a reminder of home. Cadets in white uniforms were milling about, and some were hurrying across the grass, probably to a class. Kenji wondered if he had done the right thing this time, sidestepping the long route to a commission and a degree of value in favor of seeking future advancement.

He had talked to one of his instructors, retired commander Yamaguchi Tamon, about the abrupt change in his naval education. Tamon had said, "You need to do what your two years at the academy has taught you. If a superior officer wants you for a special purpose, there is a good reason for it, even though you may not now know what that duty is. You have been a superior cadet, and you have greater strength and are more athletic than most. That may give you some clue as to why they want you."

Kenji supposed he was right. Nevertheless, his biggest concern was what his grandfather Maki would think. Maki had given much of his time and some of his money to get Kenji enrolled in the academy. Travel by bus, car, ferry, and train from Ōtsu had been long and difficult. While the journey had been interesting for Kenji, who hadn't been more than twenty-five kilometers from Ōtsu before that trip, the distance meant that he was now not able to discuss his decision in person with Maki. There was no phone service to rural areas on Hokkaido. He pledged he would write to his grandfather and explain the circumstance of his abrupt change in academic direction. Perhaps he could ask an officer who knew the circumstances to include a note of explanation. In any case, he would eventually return to complete what he had started and what his grandfather had envisioned.

The next day, a messenger came to Kenji's room and handed him an envelope. It contained an order for Kenji to be at the submarine pier at the academy wharf with his gear at 1700 hours. The order revealed nothing else.

What he wasn't told was something that only the admirals, the emperor, and a few generals knew, that late in November, large attack formations of the Japanese Navy had sailed for the Hawaiian Islands, the East Indies, and Indonesia, and were poised to sail across the South China Sea to invade the Philippine Islands.

Kenji obeyed. That evening, he showed the order to the sailor at the gangplank, who motioned to Kenji that he should board the sub floating there. By that night, Kenji was on a Japanese submarine.

They traveled on the surface of the water at night and under the surface during daytime, first on the Pacific Ocean and finally on the South China Sea. They were headed in the direction of the Philippines, a territory of the United States of America.

Kenji had makeshift quarters with the radio officer; his gear and equipment were stored elsewhere. He was trained to act alone, without help, and without any more provisions and supplies than he could carry. He had no idea what his assignment would be, but he had pledged to fulfill the assignment even if it cost him his life. He could only wonder at the circumstances that might bring about such a sacrifice. The samurai class, symbolized by the sword, had been abolished by the end of the nineteenth century. However, the samurai ethical code of Bushido—stressing warriors' strengths, such as loyalty to one's master; self-discipline; and respectful, ethical behavior—was alive and thriving in the officer class of the Japanese military. It was this code that made Kenji accept as possible his own sacrifice.

One day, the executive officer came to Kenji's quarters, if the cramped bunk space could be called that. In Kenji's presence, he opened a brown envelope, read the contents to himself, and then handed the paper to Kenji.

Kenji scanned it, looked at the officer, and said, "So, this is finally it, is it?"

"That's it. I will go inform the captain, who will bring this vessel to the east shore of Luzon at a place called San Fernando. You will be dropped off in a one-man rubber raft with your provisions. We will depart immediately. You will not see us again." The officer made a few notes on a small piece of paper and left.

Kenji remained seated, studying his instructions. Obviously Japan was attacking the Philippines. Kenji was not yet aware that Japan's navy had struck Pearl Harbor, devastating the United States Navy's Pacific fleet, nor was he aware of Japan's attacks made and planned for Indonesia, but he knew the Philippines were a territory of the United States. He wondered what else was going to happen and where, but that was not his concern. His concern was the official directive he held in his hand.

He was to proceed ashore with a radio, have no contact with Japanese military forces already ashore, and generally stay between the Japanese forces and the Filipino and American forces. When he noted the strength or declared movements of the American and Filipino forces, he was to radio that vital information to a designated Japanese warship that would be offshore but within radio-signal distance. He had been furnished a simple code for the job. His rather large back-pack held a battery radio with a hand-generator battery charger, some food, first-aid supplies, a handgun, and a belt knife. He would carry extra cartridges for the pistol, packaged rice, and other field rations in small containers. He was to be on his own until the Philippines were in Japanese control, and then—and only then—was he to make contact with the Japanese forces ashore.

There was not enough food to last more than ten days. He would be required to forage for food and had been trained in what to eat and what to avoid, but he knew he might also have to kill someone to obtain food. Kenji decided he would make every effort to avoid that method. He made up his mind that he would not kill someone just to take his food, but he might kill to get to a larger supply of food. Whatever happened, he could not afford to do anything that would reveal his presence.

Over the next few days, he prepared his supplies and tried to wait patiently. At night, Kenji attempted to sleep, but the submarine was noisy, hot, and smelly. Such inconveniences and the willpower to endure them were part of his military life. He had never been subject to such annoyances in Ōtsu.

After a few nights, the executive officer appeared suddenly and said, "Get your gear ready. We'll be sending you ashore in your raft in approximately thirty minutes."

Kenji looked at his wristwatch. It was midnight.

The officer reported that Japanese forces had, the day prior, landed on Luzon. He paused, and then added, "The Imperial Japanese Navy has defeated the United States Navy at the Hawaiian Islands in the central Pacific."

The significance of this additional information was not readily apparent to Kenji. He had an immediate job to do, and he would do it. He gathered his stuff and went up the narrow ladder to the bridge.

The crew had his raft ready beside the submarine. The sea was calm, and there was enough moonlight coming through the thin cloud cover that he could see a very narrow surf line and above it trees silhouetted against the sky. Kenji stepped into the small raft with his equipment, picked up the paddle, and headed for shore.

CHAPTER 5

DECEMBER 1941

It was Sunday. At school on Friday, David, George, Henry, and Jason had agreed to meet at David's place after Sunday lunch to decide what action they would take to make their small domain on the Pacific coast safe from a Japanese invasion.

The Japanese sneak attack on Pearl Harbor on December 7 had made their hatred and fear of the Japanese like a visible thing before their eyes. One week had elapsed since the attack, and so far, they had done nothing at all. Doing nothing was unacceptable. And to the best of their knowledge, that's exactly what everyone else in the community had done too.

So they gathered at David's house in his living room to brainstorm. David's family was at home, but their conversation about beach patrol was no secret. Their other ideas were.

"We could lie about our ages and join the army or navy," Henry said.

"Yeah, I know a guy in Portland that makes fake IDs, and he could make us some fake birth certificates," Jason chimed in.

The other two replied at once that the idea was crazy, no one would believe them—and besides, their parents would veto the idea.

"For God's sake, we've got to do something!" Henry said.

"What do we even know about the Japs, anyway?" Jason asked.

"The only thing I know is what I heard my mom and dad say—mostly what a rotten bunch of yellow rats they are," David said. "My father wants to join the army, and my mother wants him to stay home. They argue about it all the time. I don't know what will happen."

George knew David's father; he was a foreman in the cedar division at the same mill Jason's father managed. He tried to imagine Robert Harris at war but couldn't.

Jason said, "My father told us that the production of battery separators would be declared an essential war industry and that neither he nor any of the cedar plant foremen would be taken by the military. So, David, that should settle the difficulty between your mom and dad. He just told my mother and I that yesterday."

Each of them had heard much adult conversation about the war as it evolved to include Japan, Germany, and Italy. None of them had paid much attention to the newspapers until the war started for the United States. Now they read the front page news daily in the *Coos Bay Times*, an evening newspaper delivered around the county. Occasionally they also read the *Oregonian* and the *Daily Journal*, both published in Portland and distributed throughout the state. George was riveted by news photos of airplanes, warships, and tanks, as well as shots of war wreckage and carnage. Most news items dealt with losses and damage sustained by the United States and its allies, Britain and Russia. Nothing good seemed to happen, and the dearth of positive reports was troublesome to them all. They had to do something, but what?

"We should talk to my dad," David said. "He might have some ideas." The other boys agreed.

Robert Harris was thirty-eight, a native of the southern Oregon coast. David's parents had lived in Port Orford when he was born, moving to Bandon when Robert's logging contractor employer went out of business. Robert had been hired by the Bandon sawmill and later by a larger diversified mill in Coquille. George respected Mr. Harris and knew his parents did too. He was a levelheaded and practical man, and the perfect person to go to for advice on the war effort.

They sought him out and found him in his garage sharpening an axe. They wanted to help win the war, so what could they do? Harris was staggered a little by the question, but the boys were obviously serious.

"If you and your friends are driven to save us, then you should do something that won't adversely affect your families," Harris said. "It should be something you are experienced at or something you could easily learn. For instance, you guys walk the beach all the time, so maybe you could patrol while you're out there. You might even try to organize beach patrols to include others. There's no one watching the beaches around here, as far as I know, so it'd be a valuable service." He paused and then almost smiled. "But assuming you choose to do something like that, you better understand that it can't interfere with your chores around here, nor can it interfere with your schoolwork."

David's sister, Jan, who had walked into the garage, said, "I hear an airplane lookout group is being formed. You could do that."

George looked at the others. "How would we do that?"

"They give you instruction in identifying planes," she said. "I've heard they're supposed to find places where the visibility is good, and then they give you a phone to call in suspicious planes."

"I'm not doing that unless they give me a .50-caliber Browning machine gun so I can shoot down any Jap plane I spot," David said. "You and your girlfriends could go spot Jap planes."

David's mother had also walked into the garage and, hearing some of the conversation, interceded. "That's enough on this subject," she said. "David, you and your friends can work this out yourselves, alright? But right now, it's time for dinner."

The other boys headed home. George thought only about the beach patrols as he walked. It was a good idea. They'd even be able to keep packing their rifles with them. They'd have to talk about it more at school tomorrow, he decided. He just hoped the other guys felt the same way.

The next day at school, most of the conversation was about the war and how the Japanese were invading the Philippines and Indonesia. But rumors did not spare the Oregon coast as a potential site for invasion.

Mr. Meyers cautioned his American history class against rumors of the Japanese invading the Pacific coast. "Some of the teachers have been asked to address our classes on this subject," he started. "The United States is engaged in sea and air patrols over the eastern Pacific, and nothing unusual is being reported. There will be ample warning in the event of an ordered evacuation, and even that's a very long shot. The main thing is not to overreact—especially to rumors and other gossip about what would and would not happen. Just go about your schoolwork and other activities like normal. Of course you can't help but think about the war, but don't let it disrupt your lives. Less than six years ago, the people of this community weathered the fire that destroyed the town, so surely we will deal successfully with a war that is raging now eight thousand miles away."

Mr. Meyers's words and similar admonitions from other teachers seemed to have a salutary effect on the students, and conversations throughout the school returned to normal for most kids, but not for the four boys.

During the noon recess, David, Jason, George, and Henry gobbled down their lunches in the school cafeteria while deeply involved in serious conversation. They were considering Robert's plan of beach patrols. David's sister, Jan, and George's sister, Lisa, walked near to the boys' table, and Lisa said loudly, "Oh, they're plotting the destruction of the Japanese Empire. I just hope they all survive."

"Ignore her," George said.

Jason leaned across the lunch table, stretched, and said, "Mr. Meyers gave us a pretty good lecture, and I hope he's right, but my father says that there's no way we can know everything that's going on out there in our ocean. There can be subs and other stuff in broad daylight, in the dark, or in the fog. How many patrol planes have we seen?"

"None."

David nodded. "And just look at the Coast Guard. About ten sailors and two boats—and one with oars only. Mr. Meyers is a good guy, but he can be wrong."

Henry, gazing raptly across the room, said, "Watch!" They followed his stare to an older boy, Ben, who was tossing a tomato up in the air, getting the feel of it for a good throw at another boy, Dewey, who clearly felt menaced. Suddenly, Dewey dashed for the exit door, but Ben stood up and caught him square in the back with the tomato. The school principal, lunching at the other end of the cafeteria, saw the entire display of bad table manners. Ben would be sweeping the cafeteria for the next ten days.

"Wouldn't Ben be great with a hand grenade?" Henry said.

George said, "Let's get serious about this beach patrol business. We've got to get organized if the job is to be done right. It will take a dozen or more boys to do a decent job. We need to patrol in fours in case we run into trouble."

"Come on, George. We're not going to run into anything that one or two of us can't run for help on," David said.

"Who knows for sure? Besides, it will be more fun with four on the job," Henry said.

"OK, but I'm not going out there when it's raining or when the wind is blowing a gale," David said.

"Right. When the weather is rotten, nothing's going to happen anyway," George said.

They all agreed to this and decided to start their patrols as soon as possible.

CHAPTER 6

JANUARY 1942

Mark Gleason sat behind his desk at Smith Wood Products in Coquille. Before him were three superintendents—one each for the day, swing, and graveyard shifts—several of the mill foremen, the millwright, the engineer in charge of the mill generator, the bookkeeper, and the office manager. Robert Harris was also present. Those management personnel that could not be spared from their work or who were not available during the day shift would be briefed at a second meeting. Mark announced that he had called the meeting in light of the manufacturing plant's designation as essential for the war effort. Security issues, particularly as they related to the cedar division and its production of battery separators, were now in the spotlight.

"I want you to give the security of our mill serious consideration," he said. "Between now and next week, I'd like each of you to present me with a written statement of your security concerns and any recommendations for implementation of solutions." Mark's sober tone guaranteed compliance. "For the present, does anything jump to your mind that flies in the face of good security?"

One of the foremen in the plywood division, John Merchant, spoke up. "Well, I can remember that for the past nine or ten years, our log buyer, Steve Clinton, has asked me to show those Japanese log buyers our mill. I've given them tours of everything, from the log rafting on the river to the headrig, to the power plant, to the battery-separator operation, even the railcar shipping operation."

Mark asked, "Has that happened since I've been here, John?"

"Yes," he said. "Last year."

"There can be little doubt, then," Mark said, "that someone in Japan knows all that's needed to get to the separator operation and destroy it."

Sam Mack, the tough, hardworking foreman of the retail lumberyard, was known as a man who spent less time on the barroom floor than his bloodied opponents and who saw things in black or white. He now jumped up and said, "Those rotten, slant-eyed sons of bitches! The retail lumberyard is not an essential war industry, and I'm joining the fuckin' navy and helping kill some of those yellow bastards!"

Someone shouted over the group's laughter for Sam to take it easy.

Mark said, "Well, I imagine that's how a lot of people feel, whether they work in this mill or not, but we need to be rational about this. So to start, we will be taking security measures based on what we know and the recommendations that I have requested from each of you. Japan is halfway around the world from here, giving us plenty of time to protect ourselves." He described a few starting security measures they'd have to take in the meantime: blacking out the windows and turning off outside lighting were mandatory, except for light needed on the river to allow the men to move logs from water storage. "I'm interviewing some additional employees to work as night watchmen," he said. "One more thing: don't panic and start running through town screaming that the Japs are coming. We are a lesser war industry than most, and compared to what our fighting men will be going through, we are ninety-nine percent safer. We are in a war, and we will support the United States the best we can—and we will let no one believe we will do anything less than Sam Mack wants to do!"

The meeting broke up, and Mark wondered to himself if his words were true. Everything was subjective at this point, and mill management and employees didn't know how much danger they actually faced. The mill was near a highway, a railroad, and a well-trafficked river. It stood in plain sight of all three, with not even a fence to protect it, and there were no armaments or even a single gun inside. The only phone was in Gleason's office. They were essentially sitting ducks.

He made a note to find out where the military authority for the area was located; he'd contact them as soon as possible to see what was happening security-wise. Maybe they could send someone to tell them what to do.

In the meantime, he hoped Sam Mack would stay on the job. He'd like to put him in charge of plant security, but that would keep him out of the navy. Gleason decided he'd talk to him as soon as possible. They needed all the security they could get.

CHAPTER 7

FEBRUARY 1942

The war had been going on for nearly two months. George, Henry, David, and Jason had patrolled the beach south of town only eight times in January, being kept off the beach by storm after storm. Even in fairer weather, the tides were higher than usual, with the wind pushing the ocean waters eastward and far on the shore, making for miserable walking. The only consolation was the discovery of several glass balls. It had become, clearly, a task too big for just four boys.

George suggested they make sign-up sheets as written notices that would possibly shame more people into helping. All of the guys agreed to make signs that evening and bring them back the next day. Henry wasn't sure what his would say, but he promised to work on it.

At home that night, Henry first read the evening newspaper. It contained a chronology of what the Japanese had done to the United States so far. He read it out loud to his mother, who pretended to be listening: "December 7, Japanese attack Pearl Harbor—December 10, Japanese invade Philippines—December 23, Japanese take Wake Island—January 2, Japanese take Manila—January 11, Japanese invade Dutch East Indies at Borneo."

Henry's mother, May, had already read the paper. She was happy that, since the start of the war, Henry had begun reading it every day.

She knew that Henry liked the pictures of warplanes, tanks, and war-ships, but more than that, he had discovered a need to know what was going on in the world and especially how the war was progressing.

May was an educated woman. She had met Henry's father, Bill Johnson, at the University of Oregon in Eugene. They had both grad-uated in the class of '26, with degrees in business administration. In early 1937, Bill and May purchased a commercial lot in downtown Bandon. They cleaned up the debris of the building that had burned and started construction of a wood-frame building to be the home of their men's and women's clothing and dry goods store. The business thrived under the name "Johnson's Emporium," and they now ran the store together.

While Henry read the paper, May was concentrating on the goods and prices in a wholesale order catalog for the store.

"Mom, we're losing the war. Isn't anyone doing anything about it?"

"Of course they are," she said. "What seems to be the problem?"

Henry tried to explain to her that he saw no one in the commu-nity doing anything, that he and a few of his friends tried to patrol the beach but couldn't get any help, and that no adults were looking after the beaches, either north across the river or south of town. "The Coast Guard still has the same number of sailors, and all they do is watch the bar for boats in trouble," he complained. Then, looking over at her, he asked, "Is Dad going to go into the army?"

"No, you know the army and navy wouldn't take him, with his arm." Henry's father had fractured his arm near the elbow when he was ten years old, and his old family doctor had failed to set it properly. The arm had healed badly, leaving him slightly crippled. "It troubles him greatly, but for us, it might be a blessing."

Henry wasn't sure he saw it that way. "Anyway, Mom, I need to make a sign or notice to pin on the school bulletin board that will make people want to help with the beach patrol. Do you have any ideas?"

"How about, 'Help defend your country, patrol the beach for invad-ers, and save your families and friends.' Will that work?"

"Sounds OK to me."

Henry wrote it out and placed it with his homework. He had no idea what his buddies would conjure up.

The next morning, Jason was waiting at the school for the bus to stop when the three other boys jumped off, anxious to get their notices posted and revive the beach patrols.

"OK, guys, what did you come up with?" Jason asked.

Henry showed them his idea of a notice.

George said, "Your notice is good, but maybe not exciting enough to arouse real interest."

He then pulled a folded piece of paper from his coat pocket and handed it to Henry. The notice read, in big letters: DON'T LET ROTTEN, FILTHY, MURDEROUS, RAPING JAPS COME ON OUR BEACHES AND KILL US AND LIVE IN OUR HOUSES. JOIN THE BEACH PATROL. SEE GEORGE, DAVID, HENRY, OR JASON. P.S. MUST HAVE GOOD RIFLE.

"Sounds good to me," David said, and the rest agreed.

David slipped a paper from one of the books he was carrying and handed it to George. It stated, DON'T LET STINKING, YELLOW, LICE-RIDDEN JAPS INVADE AND MURDER US. SEE DAVID, GEORGE, JASON, OR HENRY ABOUT JOINING OUR BEACH PATROLS.

They all agreed that David's notice would also inspire mass enlistments.

Jason then produced his notice, written in large black-crayon letters: HELP STOP JAPANESE SOLDIER RATS FROM LANDING ON OUR BEACHES AND COMING INTO OUR HOMES AND STABBING, SHOOTING, MAIMING, AND TORTURING US TO DEATH. JOIN THE BEACH PATROL. NEED GOOD GUN AND KNIFE. SEE JASON, HENRY, GEORGE, OR DAVID.

The group decided that the notices were all so good, they should all be posted.

Henry asked, "Do you think we should ask the principal for permission to post the notices?"

They decided that asking permission would just delay things; besides, what could be the objection to what they were trying to accomplish? So they posted all four notices, each on a different school bulletin board. Obviously the only result would be a stampede to join up. Their organizational skills would be challenged by the response, and in the end, their community would be much safer.

The first important product of the notices was a summons from Principal Ernest Smith to George. George went obediently to the school office, where he handed the summons to the secretary. She looked at George while shaking her head, then pointed to Principal Smith's office with a sharp red fingernail.

Jason, Henry, and David were already seated in the small office. Two of them were holding their small summonses in their hands. Mr. Smith carefully looked them over and in a calm, civil voice said, "I admire your devotion to your country and your willingness to sacrifice your time and energy to that end, but why in the hell do you want to lay the groundwork for fear and panic among your fellow students? Think about what 'rape' and 'killing' might mean to some of the children who have little or no reasonable knowledge of what you are talking about."

David said, "We didn't think about those things. We've had no luck getting guys to help us, and we thought we needed to stir things up to make them see what we're doing."

Mr. Smith acknowledged that he knew what the notices were about. "But," he added, "they are in such bad taste. Don't you understand that the Japanese soldiers and sailors have mothers, fathers, brothers, and sisters at home, and that those people are not killers and rapists? One of the many reasons you get an education is to be able to see the whole picture so as to avoid saying and writing uninformed things. Now, don't misunderstand me—I despise what Japan did to us at Pearl Harbor, what they have done in China, and what they are continuing to do in the Pacific and Southeast Asia. Japan is ruled by wicked men, and they have not taught their soldiers and sailors restraint or fair play. I do wish you success in your endeavors to save us. Just don't cause panic in our school's hallways."

The boys stood up, and the principal continued, "By the way, I did leave one notice posted. I'm guessing that one of your parents wrote it for you. Now go back to your classes. You'll hear nothing more from me, as long as you post no more inflammatory notices in the school."

The boys walked out of Mr. Smith's office single file, each looking at the secretary with a smile that said, "We won that one."

The boys added a sign-up sheet to Henry's tamer notice, and in short order, twelve boys had signed their names. They all said they'd obtained permission from their parents, and each boy had a rifle or the use of one. This enlistment surge meant that sixteen boys were now available.

The boys went back to their original plan: four boys to a single patrol (mainly because there was a good chance that only two or three might show up). They also decided that there would not be a patrol every day, and there wouldn't be any patrols after school in the winter and early spring because the days were so short. "A few patrols are better than none," George said, and the others agreed. On weekends, a full patrol could be made.

The beach patrols were organized to include Jason, George, Henry, or David with three new members. At first, weather—and the other volunteers' short attention spans—conspired to make it sometimes two weeks between patrols during the winter, which was discouraging. But after two months of poor weather and short days, the temperature began to warm and the days grew brighter and longer. By the middle of April, the four boys decided that more frequent patrols were in order. Unfortunately the novelty of the operation was gone, and their recruits were losing interest fast. They were complaining to anyone who would listen about how tough a job it was and how nothing was ever going to happen anyway. Patrols in the rain and walking in soft sand when the tide covered the beach were the chief complaints.

By the first day of May 1942, the beach patrol corps had dwindled to eight. Some other students seemed to doubt their effectiveness. At the school bus stop, Jan and Lisa would from time to time be heard to say, "There are the killers now."

The boys continued their patrols. They ignored the girls' taunts, and there seemed to be few if any taunts from the boys. Sometimes they had help, but it was inconsistent. Sometimes only two of them would patrol. At times, they were discouraged, but what was at stake gave them just enough will to continue the patrols. They received a small dividend, because in the spring, the west winds were bringing a good number of glass balls to the beach. Summer was approaching; they hoped more help would come their way.

CHAPTER 8

APRIL 1942

Kenji had been on Luzon since the middle of December 1941 and had diligently carried out the duties assigned to him. Kenji had moved about in the Philippine jungles and along major and secondary roads with much success. He was constantly on the move because the invasion was proceeding down the island with great speed. He had been put ashore near Lingayen Gulf and had conducted his mission north of there for two weeks. He was now operating south of the gulf. He had been sleeping on the ground, in palm huts, in sheds, under wrecked vehicles, and, once in a while, in an abandoned house. He ate native fruit, caught a few chickens that ran at large, and, three or four times, he had butchered a pig. Generally he was hungry all the time. He wondered how long his job on Luzon would last.

In order to foil the efforts of Filipino scouts, his instructions were to stay away from everyone until the enemy surrendered. No one was to know with whom he was connected. The only direct contact he had with the army was when he picked up fresh batteries in person for his radio from pinpointed locations.

Still, he had had plenty of radio contact with the Japanese Army. In the beginning, reporting the locations of American and Filipino troops was not difficult and brought devastation to those troops. Not only did

Kenji's messages summon naval artillery fire, to his surprise fighter aircraft joined the fray and soon turned battles into routs. One time, Kenji had radioed for what he thought would be a naval barrage, but none came. Instead, a dozen light bombers devastated the coordinate area. Bombs dropped near him and so damaged his hearing that for ten days he could not hear to send or receive a message.

He often wondered why the Americans had not caught on to him. They had to realize that bombardments of such accuracy had been called by a ground observer. They must have noticed that the Japanese knew where the weak points in the American defenses were, where the American flanks could be assaulted, or where the Americans had retreated to establish new defensive lines. But the Americans had little time for intelligence activities when they were being overwhelmed by the better equipped, better trained, and more numerous Japanese forces.

As the war continued, however, the Americans and the Filipinos, despite great odds, were able to focus their defensive efforts and slow the Japanese Army. This concentration of forces had made Kenji's task more dangerous because he needed to be closer to the fighting to make accurate broadcasts. Kenji had been discovered on five separate occasions by non-uniformed Filipino fighters. His backpack, with radio antennas thrusting skyward, told his discoverers that he was not friendly. By the time they realized who they had found, he'd killed them, either with his automatic pistol or with his long-bladed knife. He never liked what he had to do under those circumstances, but—always—it was his life or someone else's life.

On April 4, 1942, Kenji received a message from General Nakayama's command center that he was to report to the general immediately. Kenji thought that the war in the Philippines was probably over, because the order conformed precisely to his initial instructions: he wasn't to have in-person contact with his army until surrender was imminent. He would hike to Nakayama's camp, and that would take time. Perhaps he would soon have leave to go home and be with his family.

Kenji stood at attention before a lieutenant at Nakayama's command center. Kenji's clothing was dirty, torn, and bloodstained. He hoped the dusty navy cap and the backpack with radio antennas sticking out of it told the lieutenant that this was not a man to admonish for any reason.

"Warrant Officer Kenji Kosoki reporting to General Nakayama by his request, sir," Kenji said without emotion.

"We'll see about that," was the lieutenant's response, and he left.

Kenji relaxed and looked around to see if any real food was in sight. None was.

The lieutenant reappeared and said, "Follow me."

Kenji did so across a compound filled with trucks and supplies into a wood-frame structure that might have a commissary. General Nakayama was seated at a desk with another officer. The general was of medium height, a little overweight, with a pleasant round face. He had a demeanor that told Kenji that this was a man who cared a great deal about his soldiers. The general's and the other officers' uniforms were neat and pressed, but their posture was casual.

Kenji stood stiffly at attention and saluted, and Nakayama motioned for him to sit down. Kenji couldn't imagine himself sitting in front of an admiral, but decided perhaps generals were different.

Nakayama said, with considerable praise in his tone, "So you're the one that has helped us stay on course. I can't begin to tell you the value of your work to the soldier on the ground."

Kenji bowed his thanks.

"I see by what's left of your insignia that you are a noncommissioned officer. You can expect a promotion in rank."

Kenji bowed again.

"The reason I've called you in is that we are now receiving overtures of surrender from the Americans, and we can't tell whether they are surrendering in full or only piecemeal. The officers proposing surrender claim they have no authority over all of their forces in the Philippines. I want you to go back into the field, behind their lines, and find out what is going on. You are not required to go very far. If one sector held by the Americans is in disarray, they are probably all in disarray. Can you do that?"

"Yes, sir," Kenji said.

"What will you need?" asked the other officer seated at the general's desk.

"I would like a decent meal, a bath, a haircut, some clean clothes, and some new shoes, plus a good night's sleep. Also I will need a way to get where I'm going. I can walk long distances, but thirty or forty kilometers in the jungle won't be quick."

"Your requests are granted. You'll leave first thing in the morning," Nakayama answered, and then Kenji was dismissed.

The next day, Kenji was driven by truck and set afoot in an area that appeared to be void of people. There was no gunfire, there were no natives, and nothing indicated a war was raging. He'd been directed to head due south about six kilometers, which he did, until he saw non-Japanese soldiers. They were walking south, some without fire-arms. From his high vantage point in a tree, he could see only a few vehicles, and through his binoculars, he saw no artillery. Some soldiers looked to be wounded, and no one appeared to be in charge. When he moved farther south and then to the west, he saw a similar situa-tion, except that these soldiers were destroying munitions and heavy guns. He had gone far enough. He walked back to his pickup point for retrieval.

The evening of April 8, Kenji met again with General Nakayama, reciting what he had seen. Nakayama told him, "We have won a great victory. Tomorrow I meet with the American General King, who is in charge of all the enemy forces on Luzon, and negotiate unconditional surrender."

That was exactly what happened. King got none of the conditions he wanted—surrender was unconditional. Kenji's job was done. On April 15, 1942, he was taken to a Japanese destroyer waiting offshore, the *Hamakaze*.

Not long after, Kenji leaned against the railing on the rear. The *Hamakaze* was one of nine destroyers of the Imperial Japanese Navy's first battle fleet and strike force that had attacked Pearl Harbor. The state-of-the-art destroyer was laid down in 1940 and completed June 30, 1941. Kenji had been informed by his bunkmate of the ship's prior service record and of the significance of its design. The ship's name,

Hamakaze, meaning "beach wind," focused his thoughts on home and the endeavors his family might be engaged in at that very moment. After four months' absence, he could now contact them, but what would they think of their country's military actions? What would Grandfather Maki think of Kenji's absence from the naval academy?

As Kenji looked about the ship, he felt and heard the power of the vessel. This was why he had entered the naval academy at Etajima. Not to crawl around in some strange jungle to come face to face with persons who would kill him if he didn't kill them, but to ultimately command a ship of the Imperial Japanese Navy. Once he saw his family, he would, if he could, make every effort to return to the naval academy. The *Hamakaze*'s home base was Kure, on Hiroshima Bay, in Hiroshima prefecture, only a few kilometers from Etajima. He would contact them from there.

CHAPTER 9

MAY 1942

David, George, Henry, and Jason were seated in Mr. Meyers's American history class. They had just finished a test and everyone had handed in their answers. With fifteen more minutes to the bell, Mr. Meyers addressed his class. "Well, how is the war going?" Looking straight at George, he continued, "I notice that some of you are trying to participate."

Many of the boys in Meyers's class had developed a significant interest in the machinery of the war—particularly airplanes and warships—and, in feeding their interest, had soaked up plenty of information about what was happening on land and sea around the Pacific. They had, in their hatred of Adolf Hitler, learned from their parents' newspapers that the Germans had invaded Russia, that London was being bombed, and that ships were being torpedoed in the Atlantic.

Jason held up his hand and reported that Japan was winning the war.

"Wait a minute," cautioned Mr. Meyers. "We haven't had time to mobilize our army and navy. When we do, it will be a different story."

Jason objected. "General King surrendered the Philippine Islands to the Japanese, and that was after General MacArthur fled to Australia. Not only that, the British have lost Burma, and the Japs have captured everything in the Pacific. They're whipping the Chinese, and our navy is sunk. I'd say they're winning, Mr. Meyers."

"You must all understand the difference between a battle and a war," Meyers said. "The United States is in the middle of a war, and this war will be won right here in the good old USA. As a matter of fact, we have already begun to win the war. Can anyone explain what I'm talking about?"

A girl spoke up. "We are starting to build more airplanes and ships and guns, and the army and navy are drafting men, including my father. Unless something stops us from making ships, airplanes, and guns, nobody can beat us."

"Exactly," Mr. Meyers said. "So let the Japanese win some battles. It will do them no good in the end. By the way, David, how's the beach patrol coming? Have you encountered any invaders?"

Ignoring the uncomplimentary remark, David said, "The beach patrol is alive and well, no thanks to a lot of people. Just four of us have the job, and it's getting done when the weather is good. It seems to be too much trouble for most people."

A voice from the back said in a disparaging tone, "What would you do if you saw a Jap? Would you shoot him?"

"It depends on what he was doing and what he was carrying," Henry said without turning his head.

Mr. Meyers said, "We're getting off the track now. Class is dismissed. I'll see you tomorrow, but think about what has been said here today. We may revisit the subject again."

The four boys met near the bus stop after school. David was the first to speak. "I'm really pissed off at Meyers and that history class. Who do they think they're dealing with, a bunch of nuts?"

"And that girl in the back of the room, Susan Buttinski or whatever her name is, wanted to know if we'd shoot a fuckin' Jap," Henry said, clearly disgusted.

"You're damn right we would," David said. "It's a good day for patrolling, so can everyone go? We'll fix a sandwich and stay until dark."

Jason said he couldn't go but would make up for it later on. The others agreed to meet on the beach just south of George's house. All their recruits had given up, and the four boys had resigned themselves to being the only beach patrollers. That was the way it had been for nearly a month, and that was the way it would continue.

That evening, after they joined forces on the beach, the three boys walked south with Luke, the black dog. They removed their shoes and socks, rolled up their pants, and forded a small creek that crossed the beach and emptied into the ocean.

While sitting on a drift log putting his shoes back on, David saw a flash of bright-green glass in the drift line. Luke's black form came between David and the glass, and when Luke passed by, the glass appeared to have moved. But it had not. David knew it was a float, and as soon as his shoelaces were tied, he made a dash for it. It was about ten inches in diameter, and on the glass weld sealing it, there was a squiggly double-crossed *T*. He walked back to his buddies and showed them his prize. He said, "I've seen a few other floats with a mark on the seal, but this is the first one I've found with this specific mark. I wonder who put that mark on it and where it came from."

Henry said that after he started bringing the glass balls home, and after asking his mother question upon question about the origin of the floats, she'd told him to go to the public library and find a book on the subject so he could learn about the floats from an expert. "I did exactly that, and I can tell you anything you want to know about these glass balls. For instance, did you know that glass balls have been used in fishing nets by Russians, Norwegians, Chinese, Koreans, and Japanese? They're used to float and mark fishnets, and they're superior to wood because they never rot or get waterlogged. They're held to the nets by rope that wears and deteriorates, and if they don't wash ashore where they are used, they get caught up in ocean currents and away they go."

"Henry," David said, "you're just full of information. I may have to stop shooting the floats I can't reach if they're such a prize."

Henry said, "Well, if you don't want to hear it, just say so. The floats we find are mainly Jap floats that have gotten into the Japanese current that flows around the Pacific Ocean to our shores. The current flows along the coast of Japan, then east across the North Pacific. It contains all sorts of debris and crap that is deposited on the beaches it touches. Some of the glass balls wash ashore, and some continue for years, maybe forever, floating in the Japanese current. Where they can all end up nobody knows."

"Good grief, do you suppose there are bodies and stuff from the war starting to float around in that current?" David asked.

Henry ignored him. "The experts think that around forty percent of all the glass fishing floats lost by Asian fishermen are still in the Pacific Ocean. The Jap glass floats are made by big float manufacturing companies, but also by small family businesses. These ones with marks are usually floats made by small operators. Fishermen may have them returned to them if their mark is recognized. Anything else you want to know?"

"Jeez, Henry, you're smarter than I thought," David said.

"I sure would like to see a glass ball made," George said. "And better yet, meet the guy that made it, just to see what a Jap looks like and what kind of a guy a Jap fisherman is. He might be OK, but we might have to shoot him."

At six o'clock, they all sat in the dry sand above the drift line, leaning against a large log, to eat their sandwiches. Luke sat directly in front of them, staring at their food and drooling, minutely scooting closer and closer. George told him to back off, and he heaved a sigh and moved away. He sat again, stared at the food, and drooled some more.

David said, "What do you think about what Susie Buttinski said about shooting a Jap? Could we do it?"

They sat looking at the sand and then at their sandwiches without saying anything.

Finally, Henry said, "If I saw a Jap soldier coming at me with his rifle or pistol in his hand, I'd probably run for cover and disappear someplace. If I was trapped and couldn't run and hide someplace, I guess I'd shoot the bastard before he shot me."

"Well, I'd shoot the son of a bitch," George said.

David asked, "What if the son of a bitch was running away from you? Then what would you do?"

"I'd shoot the son of a bitch in the back," George said.

"What if he was carrying a white flag and held up his hands to surrender? Then what would you do?" inquired David.

George, refusing to be backed into a corner by David, said, "I'd motion for him to drop the white flag and to put his hands down, and then I'd shoot the son of a bitch!"

"Well, you're a bloodthirsty peckerhead if I ever saw one," David said.

George had listened that very day at breakfast to his father read an article in the morning paper that listed the sailors from Oregon that had been killed in the attack on Pearl Harbor. Sam Caspar was listed. Sam was a Bandon boy, born and raised there; the Caspars still lived in Bandon, and the Caspars and Williamses were good friends. George was very upset about it, but the other boys so far knew nothing of Sam's death. He decided not to tell them because they were having a good time.

By now, the other boys were laughing, mainly at each other, because none of this stuff was going to happen anyway. Henry said that he wished Susie Buttinski could hear George, because if she did, she'd probably wet her pants.

"OK, wise guy," George said, looking at David, "what the hell would you do if a Jap soldier came walking at you with his rifle in hand?"

David allowed as how he might first shit his pants and then think about shooting.

"You're not answering the question," George said.

"OK, if I couldn't run for help, I'd probably shoot him."

"You would run for help? Where in hell are you going to find any help around here?" George asked. "We are out in the middle of nowhere. There's no Coast Guard patrol, no United States Army, and no United States Navy. Coos County has one sheriff and no deputies, and the city has one policeman with a car that runs—sometimes. So, we really need to know what to do if we see a Jap soldier or sailor or saboteur on the beach. Do we shit our pants and run for cover, run to my house and call for nonexistent help, or take cover and shoot the sons of bitches?"

No one spoke. Each thought to himself: *This isn't ever gonna happen, so what's the big deal? But wait—what if it does happen? Maybe we should have a plan.*

David suggested out loud, "We should each think about the problem, and maybe the next time we are on the beach, we can make our plan."

Late spring showers kept the boys off the beach for five days, so their plan of attack remained unresolved. Numerous schoolyard suggestions yielded nothing. The first good day for a long and conscientious patrol was a warm, calm Saturday, but George and Henry both had family obligations. George and his family were traveling to Coquille to a Saturday matinee. It was a double feature, *All Quiet on the Western Front* with James Cagney and *The Dawn Patrol* with Errol Flynn. George couldn't miss either one. On Sunday, Henry had to attend his grandfather Sven's sixtieth birthday party.

Sven and Mabel Clausen lived in a small village on the south bank of the Coquille River, about five miles upstream from where the Coquille entered the Pacific Ocean at Bandon. The Clausen house, situated between the county road and the river, rested on cedar pilings about 150 feet from the riverbank, in an area that was marshy or sometimes flooded by freshets in the winter. A wooden walkway on small posts extended from the unpainted wood-frame house, and a hinged wooden ramp ran from the end of the walkway down to the surface of the dock, completing the house-to-dock connection. Sven, a lifelong commercial salmon gill net fisherman who had come to the Coquille River in 1908 and had worked in the river's shipyards, kept his fishing boat moored to the riverside of the forty-foot wood-planked dock.

Henry thought his grandfather Sven was the best grandfather anyone could have, and Sven thought Henry was an extraordinary grandson.

The day of Sven's party, Henry was sitting on a box on his grandfather's dock watching Sven tinker with the engine in his boat. Henry knew they would be called to midday dinner soon, and it would take his grandfather considerable time to wash the grease and oil from his hands and arms.

Henry said, "Do you remember the time you took me all the way to Coquille in that boat? How far upriver is that?"

"About twenty miles."

Henry loved going on Sven's boat because he always learned a lot of good stuff. From that trip, he remembered the large rafts of logs tied to pilings along both banks of the river, the many docks with boats tied to them, and the tugboats towing the rafts of logs to the mills. From the river, Sven had pointed out the mill machinery at work, including the huge conveyor taking logs from the river to the mill to be sawed into lumber. A big crosscut saw cut logs into eight-foot-plus lengths in the water, while a hoist lifted them into the part of the mill that made plywood. It was one of the first plywood mills in the world.

Henry had been fascinated by the huge white cedar logs that were intermittently hauled up the big log conveyor. They were so uniform in size, with little or no taper. He thought about the fragrance of the cedar when you sawed a board or whittled on it. He recalled his grandfather pointing out the part of the mill that manufactured battery separators and venetian blind slats, and how most of the mill was built on pilings twelve feet off the ground to keep the mill above winter flood level.

Remembering the adventure suddenly made him want to see the mill operation from the inside. Maybe Jason's father or David's father would take them sometime.

His fantasies were interrupted by his father's call from the house that dinner was ready. Henry ran up the board walkway to the house. He hoped Sven's birthday cake was chocolate with chocolate frosting.

On Monday, George, David, Henry, and Jason met after lunch and sat on the lawn in front of their school. They had agreed that they were tired and disappointed in the lack of interest their schoolmates had shown in the patrols.

"Should we abandon the patrols?" Jason asked. "If we do, there will be no beach watch."

That didn't sound like a good idea. "Maybe we should visit the Coast Guard station and talk to the guy in charge," David suggested. "They should be watching the beach anyway. Maybe they could spare a guy or two to help out."

"Yeah," Jason said. "Maybe they could give us some kind of authority—you know, some way to convince the other guys they have to patrol."

"That'd be great," Henry agreed.

"We'd have to go during the day," George said.

"Well, the school year's almost over," Henry said, and that seemed to settle it. Soon, the four of them would be free to make a daytime visit.

Their trip to the United States Coast Guard lifesaving station surprised them. First they were asked if they wanted a tour of the facility. They thought that was a good idea so that they might know what they were dealing with. After touring the machine shop, lifeboat storage, crew quarters, and the recreation hall overlooking the river, David asked, "Who's the captain in charge?"

"Master Chief Petty Officer Spears."

"Right, we want to see whoever is in charge," George said.

"Follow me," ordered their tour guide, and they were marched to a small office. Master Chief Petty Officer Art Spears presided from a chair behind the desk.

"Please be seated, and tell me why I have the pleasure of your company," Spears said.

They all started talking at once but stopped when the officer held up his right hand. "Now, one at a time."

Jason told him about their beach patrols and how difficult they had become, and that without some help they would have to quit. If they did that, the beaches would not be patrolled.

David jumped in. "What we need is a coastguardsman or two to help out," he said, but seeing a scowl on Spears's face, he continued, "They'd only be needed once in a while, probably."

"Actually," Jason interrupted, "what we would really like would be for you to let us work for the Coast Guard, and kinda be under your control, and maybe give us some authority to force some of our classmates to patrol with us. You could also loan us some real equipment, like binoculars, and maybe a couple of those new automatic Garand rifles. We are all crack shots with our own rifles, but they don't hold much ammo and might not be powerful enough."

Henry, having swallowed up Jason's suggestions, eagerly said, "Yes, and maybe we could come here and hang around once in a while to get a better idea about how to guard the beaches."

Master Chief Petty Officer Spears seemed to be enjoying the meeting, and he relaxed in his swivel chair. "You're pretty enthusiastic," he said. "You remind me a little of myself at thirteen."

The friendly reception was an invitation to the boys to keep talking. "Do you know what we really need?" George asked. "What we really need is a signal gun with some shells for it. If we saw something and needed help, we could fire that gun. Maybe one for each of us would be fine."

Spears leaned forward and with elbows on his desk said, "OK, I get the picture. We've known for some time about your beach patrols, and you are to be commended for taking action. By the end of this year, we'll have more men stationed here. Instead of thirteen or fourteen men, we may end up with ninety or a hundred. We should also have some horses and four-wheel-drive vehicles for beach use. So don't worry; we'll take care of the beach. In the meantime, you're sure as hell not walking out of here with any automatic rifles or flare guns. Your parents would come down here and scalp me if I did that."

"Then I guess we can't have a Thompson submachine gun either," Henry said.

Spears looked angry for an instant but then laughed, and the boys with him. "Once we start our regular beach patrols, you'll have to stop yours. We won't be closing the beaches, but we want as few people out there as possible, particularly on those remote beaches north and south of here. What you can do for now is continue your patrols as you like, and if you see anything weird or suspicious, come and see me. I don't care if you want to stop by here once in a while; just don't make a nuisance of yourselves. And whatever you do, don't be making up any strange tales about what you think you see or what you think you know. If we have to run down a bunch of goofy stuff created by you, you'll be off the beach. Now, is there anything you don't understand about what I have said?"

No one spoke.

Spears stood, as did the boys, and after goodbyes were exchanged, the boys left.

Out on the sidewalk again, Jason said, "I don't think we accomplished a goddamn thing, except we know him and he knows us. At least he knew who we were and what we've been doing. He had no problem with it, but he won't help us. And Henry—a Thompson submachine gun! Where in hell did you come up with that?"

Art Spears continued to sit at his desk, swiveling and leaning back in his chair and staring out the window at the coastline across the river. He could see seven or eight miles of flat beach, with the white surf washing ashore beneath a thin fog of surf spray. There was no one on that beach. Moreover, there was no guard or patrol on that beach—or on any beach on the Oregon coast, either north or south from where he sat. Little did those four teenage boys know the gravity of the situation.

When the Coast Guard was ordered to operate as part of the US Navy on November 1, 1941, it had become privy to information regarding the Japanese threat to the Pacific coast and the US Army and Navy preparedness to meet that threat. The truth was that they were not prepared, even now, nearly six months after Pearl Harbor. A present-day defense of the western coast of the United States was nearly nonexistent. And the military authorities knew it.

Wishful thinking in the military had it that the Japanese were too occupied in the central Pacific to attack US western shores. Spears had known months ago that soldiers from West Coast army posts, some of them only partially trained, had been rushed to various points along the coast of California to prepare defenses against invasion and that some of California's beaches were strung with mile upon mile of barbed wire. Yet to his knowledge, there was not a beach on the Oregon coast similarly defended. The air defenses were a joke. The Second and Fourth Air Forces, located in the Western Defense Command when the war began, were primarily training units. On December 7, 1941, they had had a combined strength of 100 bombers and 140 pursuit planes, many of them obsolete. There had been some expansion of the air defense by early 1942, but it would be ineffective against a large-scale attack or an invasion. The Army Air Forces had been severely criticized in January 1942 for lack of radar on the West Coast.

To make matters worse, Japanese submarines had been operating in coastal waters and had torpedoed several merchant ships. Larger groups or attacks couldn't be far behind. The detection problem on the Pacific coast was complicated by fog. The prospect of a Japanese carrier force sailing in behind one of the normal succession of storm fronts that moved from the northern Pacific toward the West Coast was sobering indeed.

Spears knew Captain Roger Avery, who was stationed at the head-quarters of the 13th Coast Guard District in Seattle, and he decided to call and check on the status of things.

"Good to hear from you, Art. Things aren't like they were a year ago, are they? What the hell do you want? We're busier than hell up here trying to figure what to do, with nothing to do it with."

"That's what I'm calling about. I still have only thirteen men here, which gives me only two or three men to a watch—and that's only if no one's sick or injured. There's no navy and no army here, so what does the admiral want me to do, conscript the townspeople? For God's sake, I now have four teenage boys patrolling a part of one beach south of here on a part-time basis, but no other beach patrols. Tell the admiral that I furnished each of the boys with a regulation Thompson subma-chine gun and plenty of ammo."

"Art, have you lost your fuckin' mind?"

"Come on, Roger, I'm joking. But I'll tell you one thing, those boys would take guns like that on their patrols."

"Look, here in Seattle, we're protecting one of the West Coast's largest seaports, and vital defense industries are located here. This is where they make most of the B-17s, remember? There's no defense industry in your area, and no port of interest, so you'll stand down when the goods are handed out. I'm sorry, but that is the way it is, at least for now."

"Lumber is a necessity for the war effort, and we have the only two battery-separator manufacturing plants in the country," Spears said.

Avery reminded him that before the year ended, the Bandon Coast Guard station was in line for some horses, jeeps, and more men, then proceeded to diminish the Japanese threat to the West Coast. The battle in the Coral Sea in early May had slowed the Japanese march toward Australia, and the Japanese appeared to be more interested in taking south and central Pacific territory.

Spears stopped Avery. "I know all of that," he said, "but the threat's still pretty great, considering our lack of defenses."

"You know I agree," Avery said, "but that's the way it is."

After Spears set the phone aside, he leaned back in his chair. *Those four boys and their beach patrols*, he thought, *are doing more than the*

US Coast Guard in my neck of the woods. They're the only thing we have going on the beach, and even then, it's only in good daylight.

He stood and walked to a window looking out over the river and miles of ocean beach to the north, sighed in slight disgust, and walked toward his quarters at the other end of the building. The reinforcements couldn't come soon enough.

CHAPTER 10

JUNE 1942

Jason, George, David, and Henry were enjoying their summer vacation. They had been out of school for almost three weeks and had managed not to get in trouble—despite helping themselves to ripe cherries and early transparent apples from neighbors' trees, and shooting cormorants off river pilings near the mill and docks. They had also raided gardens at night, caught more than the legal limit of trout from small streams, killed a deer out of season, and peeled numerous sacks of chittum bark from trees on the property of unknown owners. They had shot a few seals and sea lions, and had sneaked into the movie theater without paying.

There were many distractions for thirteen- and fourteen-year-old boys in a small community. They frequently hitched rides on Highway 101, getting dropped off at a point where they could hike to a small lake for swimming. The lake was at the extreme southern range of their beach patrols, which had dwindled to two days a week or less. But today was a good day to patrol the beach. Everyone could go, including Luke.

The four boys wandered along the beach, looking over the newest beach trash but not finding much. Occasionally one of them would shoot at some object floating in the surf. They had not neglected their shooting skills—proceeds from the sale of chittum bark had given them plenty of money for ammo. At one point, they came across a huge, dark, sticky mass of thick oil mixed into the sand, probably a hundred feet long by twenty-five feet wide.

"Must've come from a ship torpedoed by the Japs, the rotten sons of bitches," Henry said, and the others agreed.

They rested in a low spot in the dune next to the beach. It was one of those places where the beach was steep to the surf and the water was deep. There was little wind. They talked about the fact that they would all be in high school this coming year.

David said, "It'll be a great change. We'll be able to play basketball and football. And guess what? All the pretty girls are in high school!"

"Yeah, but do you suppose we'll have to go to dances and stuff?" Henry asked.

The others ignored Henry. George commented that there was a girl going into junior year who was so pretty he couldn't look at her.

"What are you saying?" David asked.

"I'm saying I can't look at her, because if she caught me looking at her, she would think I'm some sort of pervert and would have me killed," George said.

"That has got to be the stupidest thing I ever heard," David said.

Henry promptly proclaimed that he would look at her the first day of school and sacrifice himself for all of them.

His generous offer put an end to the topic of school and the opposite sex. It was late in the afternoon, and they decided to head back soon. None of them were watching the ocean except George, who wanted to shoot a sea lion. A light fog had begun to move toward the shore but seemed to linger near the surf line as if something were pushing it back from the land.

George suddenly yelled, "Holy shit, look at that! What is it?"

They all stood up to see a large black ship resting perpendicular to the beach. It was beyond the surf, and no one could be seen on what appeared to be its deck—if it was a ship at all. The object started to move as if turning around, and as it became parallel to the shoreline, they could see the outline of what looked like a large gun.

As the fog lifted slightly, David exclaimed, "It's a fuckin' submarine!"

Then Jason said, "Holy shit, it's got a Jap flag painted on the side of its conning tower!"

"Jesus, get down," David ordered. They all hid in the small sandy depression and watched as men began to appear on the deck of the submarine.

"What're we going to do? What're we going to do?" Henry demanded. They were all scared and frightened. Henry said, "Let's get the hell out of here!"

David insisted that they wait to see what was going to happen. "You've got your rifles to protect yourself, so be prepared," David said. He didn't budge an inch, and neither did the others. "Because even though you may shit your pants, you may need those guns."

Each boy put his rifle to his shoulder, not to shoot, but to observe every detail and every person they could see through the telescopic sights. They were on their bellies behind the small dune, which hid them—barely.

"Maybe they're just scouting out the place and nothing is going to happen," George whispered.

"Oh yeah. But then they might be scouts for an invasion force. Or maybe there's a bunch of saboteurs aboard," Henry said.

"Maybe we better get the hell out of here and report this to the Coast Guard, and do it before we get our asses shot off," Henry further pled.

"Just wait until we see what the bastards are gonna do. Besides, they're three hundred yards out there, which means we have plenty of time to leave if they start to come ashore," David said.

"Jesus, David, I hope we know what we're doing. I think one of us should run for it and tell someone what's happening. Then, as you say, once we know what they are up to, we can all go," George said, sounding a little calmer than anyone felt.

"Sounds good to me. Is that OK with everyone else?" David asked. They all seemed to agree, but no one moved.

From their hiding place, the boys could see through their rifle scopes that nothing was happening on the submarine, except that the sailors, if that's what they were, seemed to be gathering on the deck. David looked around and saw that, if he and his friends kept low to the ground, the four of them could slip away to the scrub shore pines behind them and make an escape. He also thought that if any of those

Japs—and he was sure that's who they were—wanted to come ashore at this place, he and his friends could also disappear into the countryside.

The four boys looked at each other, not as shaken now as they initially had been.

"I wish to hell I had that Thompson submachine gun," Henry muttered.

"Come on, guys," David whispered, as if the men on the submarine could hear, "you must know, we've got to do the right thing here. Running now would be the wrong thing. We've got to keep our heads, find out what those bastards are up to, and then leave."

They all nodded in agreement and continued to observe through their telescopic sights and binoculars. They could now see an object beginning to appear on the afterdeck of the sub. Men moved quickly on the sub's narrow deck, and some objects were brought to the afterdeck.

Henry, in an excited but low voice, said, "Let's get the hell out of here."

David quickly said, without looking up from his rifle, "We're a beach patrol, remember? Just hold on a few minutes more, then we're goin' for help."

"Holy shit, they're putting a raft in the water—and look, there are guys getting in the raft. Crap, the bastards are coming ashore and probably right in front of us. We better get out of here now," George said. For a moment, watching the submarine had fascinated him so much that he had lost touch with the danger of their predicament.

As the soldiers brandished paddles, the thin fog line thickened and dropped, first concealing the sub and the raft. But a late-afternoon offshore breeze shoved the fog back, and the raft could be seen headed away from the sub and toward shore. They all managed to make out that there were four men in the raft before the fog closed in again.

The boys were starting to frighten and maybe reaching the panic point, but David said in a collected voice, "Just a few minutes longer to make sure we report this correctly, and then we're out of here."

Henry said, "I hope to hell you're right, because if you're not, we're in deep shit!"

The fog persisted.

"OK, let's go," David said.

They stood up with their backs to the ocean, each mentally figuring out an escape route. They certainly could not walk back up the
beach. Before they turned for one last look, rifle fire exploded from the
ocean, and there was the thump of bullets hitting the sand in front
of their little dune. They saw the raft about 175 feet from shore. The
breeze had blown an opening in the fog, and the boys fell behind the
protection of their dune.

Henry screamed as another report of rifles was heard. "I've been
shot!" he cried, and fell on his face in the sand. Blood was coming
through his shirt from his right shoulder.

Jason pulled Henry down into the depression for more protection
and yelled, "Henry's shot! God Almighty, God Almighty, what are we
gonna do?"

Now they were in no position to run without fully exposing themselves. Henry was crying, "I'm gonna die, I'm gonna die, I want my
mother, my mother, oh God."

George looked him over quickly and said, "You're not bleeding
much. We'll get you out of here."

"We're going to shoot those bastards, that's what we're gonna do.
We have no choice," David said. He was already drawing a bead on the
lead paddlers in the raft, and Jason and George took up position.

David fired and missed.

Jason fired and missed.

George fired and missed.

David yelled, "Be calm! Settle down! Just pretend they're seals and
squeeze the trigger!"

The raft was now at the outer edge of the surf. They did calm down
a little before again firing, and the lead paddler slumped over the soft
round side of the raft. The boys fired again. To their surprise, the raft
exploded. The blast was so potent that it blew the raft and everything
in the raft to bits and pieces and into the sea. Sea water and small bits
of debris fell on the boys.

The fog lifted, but there was nothing to be seen in the ocean. The
sub had disappeared, and so had the raft and its occupants. The occupants were now Dungeness crab bait. When the seagulls returned,
they would clean up the beach. It would be as if there never had been a
submarine or a raft with men in it.

Momentarily dazed by all that had occurred, the boys had for-gotten about Henry. Jason knelt beside the wounded boy and rolled him over. Henry's eyes were half open; he was bleeding from his right shoulder, but he was breathing.

"I'm going to die," he said around a sob. "I'm going to die."

"No, you're not," Jason said as he looked under Henry's shirt, checking the injury from the front and the back. There was a small entry wound just below Henry's collarbone and a slightly larger exit wound on his back. "You've got a clean wound, and you're not bleeding too badly. We're getting you to a doctor as soon as we can." Jason took off his own T-shirt, tore it in half, and pressed the cloth against the bullet's entry and exit wounds under Henry's shirt. David and George made a boson's chair by interlocking their forearms between them. Jason helped Henry to his feet and placed him in the chair. As the boys headed up the beach, Jason ran ahead as fast as he could. George's house was the nearest, and it was more than a mile away.

After walking two or three hundred yards, David and George were exhausted. They sat on a large drift log and eased Henry off their arms. Henry wasn't as big as the other boys, but he weighed 125 pounds, too much for David and George to carry much farther without tiring.

"How are you doing, Henry?" David asked.

"I don't know," he said. He wasn't gaining any strength, but he also didn't seem to be getting worse.

"Jason ran ahead for help," George told him, watching the sun sink into the ocean. "Someone will come for us soon."

CHAPTER 11

JUNE 1942

Four days had passed since the rifle fire on the beach and the explosion. Henry was still in the tiny Bandon hospital, a single-story wood-frame building in the downtown area, across the street from the river's edge. He'd fallen unconscious shortly after George and David had rested on the drift log, and they had decided not to move Henry any farther. Instead, they had waited for help to arrive, in the form of the town's volunteer firemen. They had carried Henry the rest of the way up the beach and listened to the boys tell their stories. Other than their parents, they were about the only people the boys had talked to, but it seemed all of the citizens in and about Bandon had heard something about the event on the beach south of town. Only a few had the details. Speculation and guesswork and old-fashioned gossip were running their course.

The boys hadn't yet been allowed to see Henry, and they weren't sure why. Their parents had asked them to stay close to home for a while, to avoid people for a while, and to give the community a chance to come to grips with what had happened. They'd explained that they did not want their sons examined and re-examined by people driven by malicious motives.

So far they had been spared. A few of the rescuing firemen had asked questions, and George and David had given them some of the highlights of the clash of rifle fire. The chief of police had sauntered into the Johnsons' downtown store and talked to Henry's parents. He'd said maybe it was a case for the Coast Guard, and the boys agreed. They were starting to feel a little wounded; four days had passed, and so far no one had suggested that they were heroes.

They'd mostly stayed home to avoid questions and having to repeat the story, but they were restless. Finally, on the fourth day, George grew frustrated. He called Jason and David and told each of them, "We are going to see Henry now, not tomorrow or the next day, but now, come hell or high water!"

The boys met at the hospital, but the nurse told them that Henry was resting and should not have company. The boys walked to the confectionery store, knowing without saying it they were going to return and see Henry.

At the small confectionery store, they ordered a milkshake each and one for Henry. The store had a twenty-foot-long bar with round, leather-covered swivel seats in front and a half dozen small tables with cheap wire seats on the small open floor. Two of their friends from school, Kyle and James, were there, seated at a table. They exchanged hellos. "How's Henry?" Kyle asked, but his tone was strangely guarded.

"He's fine," Jason said. "He'll be home soon."

The other boys nodded but made no effort to join them or keep talking.

In a low voice, George said to his buddies, "You guys wonder why they don't say anything to us about what happened? You'd think they would want to hear the bloody details of every bloody thing that happened to us. We've told very few people. I'll bet those firemen that helped rescue Henry didn't believe us."

Kyle lived in town and usually had a pretty good grip on what was going on. His father was a cheese maker and his mother a grade school teacher, so he was privy to a lot of gossip. George called, "Hey, Kyle, come on over here. We want to ask you and James some stuff."

The two boys joined the other three. George asked, "Can you guys tell us what's being said about Henry and us?"

Kyle and James looked at the table for a moment, and then Kyle looked at George. "Well, if you really don't know what is going on and what is being said, I guess we should tell you. Everyone appears to have something to say. A lot of people seem to think that one of you guys accidentally shot Henry. Trouble is, most people don't know you guys. Some people think that you really shot some Japs and that they shot Henry."

"Jesus," David muttered. "Wouldn't you know it?"

"My father is a volunteer fireman," James said, "but he didn't help rescue Henry. He's heard the other firemen talking, and they doubt there were any Japs around. Some of the firemen who were there walked on down the beach and said they couldn't find anything on the beach to confirm your story. They found a few small pieces of fabric that could have come from anyplace, and that was it."

"It was almost dark when those firemen arrived," Jason said. "They would have needed a good flashlight to find anything worthwhile!"

"James and I know you guys," Kyle said, "and we always thought you were straightforward and truthful. Most people who know you don't think you could make up a story like you told the firemen. The problem is that most people really don't know what to believe. We don't have any decent reason not to believe you guys, and yet it is one hell of a wild and crazy story."

"Look, just to clear the air and get it straight from the horse's mouth: Did some Japs in a landing party shoot Henry? And did you guys shoot the Japs or blow them up, or what?" James asked.

"We did exactly what you just said," David said. "It's a long story, but just know there was a Jap submarine on the surface and it launched a raft with four Japs in it. We started to leave, but they shot Henry. We fell back and shot one Jap, and then we must have hit some explosives or something because the whole damn raft blew up. When the dust settled, we got the hell out of there." The boys had just finished their milkshakes when the waitress came to their table with Henry's milkshake.

Jason thanked Kyle and James for talking to them. As they stood to leave, Jason said, "We hope our story has cleared the air for you guys. You now have the truth, so please keep telling it that way."

The boys headed back to the hospital. David said, "That ugly nurse, I don't think she likes us." The others agreed. When they arrived at the hospital, the "ugly nurse" was not in sight. They were told they could pay Henry a short visit and that the milkshake was OK.

Each boy had his own story to tell Henry about all the questions that they had been collectively and individually asked. Henry could recall little or nothing, at least nothing in a lucid manner. "What the hell happened to me?" he asked.

"Well," Jason started, looking around the room to confirm that the boys were still alone, "we saved the fuckin' day, but I think people may not believe us."

"Come on, Jason. Stop the crap and tell me what happened. Yes, I remember the submarine and the raft and all that very clearly, but what happened after I was hit?"

Jason then related how the Japs had kept firing, how he, George, and David had fired back, first missing, then hitting one Japanese, and then how the whole raft had exploded into a zillion pieces. "Jesus, Henry, don't you remember the blast from the explosion? It almost got us, and might have if we hadn't been in that hole behind the sand dune." Jason continued to tell Henry about carrying him, and the firemen coming and taking him to the hospital.

George said, "We have been trying to get in to see you since the day this happened, and they wouldn't let us in. If you had died, we would have known it, but since we hadn't heard anything like that, we figured you were going to make it, and you did!"

"Jesus, George, you don't need to be so fuckin' crude about dying," Jason said. They laughed.

George added that he was glad that they had left Luke at home that day or those dickheads might have shot him too. They weren't shooting too straight, what with their bullets hitting all around the boys.

David said, "Those Japs were bobbing up and down in the waves and didn't do too bad. What the Japs don't realize is that everyone in this country has at least one firearm, and usually a half a dozen, and that most of us can shoot the eyes out of a rat at a hundred yards. The problem is there is not a trace of those bastards or the horse they rode in on!"

Jason said, "And if people here don't believe us, how in the hell do we explain how Henry got shot? Henry knows how he got shot, and so do we. A lot of people think one of us accidentally shot him. That's why so many people have questioned us. Think about that for a while."

George added, "Not only have our parents—and particularly Henry's parents—questioned us, but the chief of police, a deputy sheriff, and a state police officer have grilled us. Our stories have all been identical. I think that they wanted us to stay away from Henry to see if his story was the same."

"Let's not be making up trouble. Our job is to get Henry well and get him out of here," David said. "Besides, there is little or no reason for people not to believe us."

"Can we bring you anything else, like maybe another milkshake or a hamburger?" George asked, quickly adding that the three of them had, in the past two days, peeled and sold about ten dollars' worth of chittum. "And you know they've upped the price, so they're paying twenty cents a pound for wet and forty-four cents for dry. We were in a hurry, so we sold it wet, but we have some money to buy you stuff to make your stay here easier."

Jason then said, "I would like to know, if you can tell me, what that bullet did to you? On the beach, it seemed really bad, so what saved you?"

George said, "For God's sake, Jason, what a lousy question."

"It's OK. I asked Dr. Rankin the same thing," Henry answered. "I couldn't understand what he was saying, so I asked him to write it out for me, and he did." He leaned over, slipped a piece of paper from his nightstand, and read the doctor's words aloud: "The bullet passed above the lung, below the scapula, passed through the supraclavicular area, missed the backbone, missed major blood vessels, missed the ribs, and passed through soft tissue."

Henry explained, "Dr. Rankin told me that he had treated gunshot wounds when he was an intern in Portland, and after he started practicing in Coos County, he treated a couple of gunshot wounds caused by hunting accidents. He said that my wound was different in that it was so clean. Nothing was really torn up. He said that the bullet must have been a non-expanding bullet, one that doesn't mushroom like the bullets we use for deer hunting."

Henry asked if the boys had been to see Officer Spears at the Coast Guard. David told Henry that they had been there, but Spears was on leave and wouldn't return until that day or the next.

George said, "We talked about seeing someone else at the Coast Guard station, but Officer Spears made it clear that he was the one we were to report to. We're going over there when we leave here."

Henry wanted to know what their parents were saying about the shooting. The boys reported that their parents were horribly upset that Henry had almost been killed and horrified that their sons had killed four people. Henry was uncertain what his parents thought about the incident; they just talked about how happy they were that he was alive and that there would be no permanent damage to him. Henry did have a sense that his parents didn't want to deal with anything but his recovery, that anything else was neither here nor there.

He said, "My father and mother told me that they had talked to Jason's mom and dad, and they agreed that the less talk about what happened to us the better."

Jason said, "My parents told me about that conversation and that there was already too much speculation and gossip as to what happened. They also told me we'd be in the news sooner or later, and if a reporter approaches us, we should tell him to come by when the whole family is home, not try and talk to him ourselves."

George then added, "I did hear my father say, 'It seems obvious that we parents are all solidly in the boys' camp, but we will be tested.'"

David said, "There are some that won't believe anything, but screw 'em. I just want the Coast Guard to believe us."

A nurse entered Henry's room and without saying hello to the boys told them that their visitation was over and they needed to leave.

David said, "We've only been here ten minutes or so. Give us another ten minutes."

The nurse immediately responded, "Haven't you done enough already? You need to let Henry rest now."

"Let's get going," Jason said. "We'll be back, Henry."

The boys walked out of Henry's room. They passed two nurses, both of whom looked at them with what the boys interpreted to be disapproval.

The boys then silently walked on the sidewalk west along First Street past storefronts, a hotel, and some small houses to the Coast Guard station. They were deep in thought about the events of the past few days.

David stopped walking, and the others stopped with him. He said in an agitated tone, "Did you see the way those nurses looked at us? Particularly that fat, ugly one?" David had never let anyone bully him, and as a result, he'd engaged in a few fistfights and wrestling matches with his peers. He was well liked and avoided intimidating anyone, but he would not be bullied, verbally or otherwise, by anyone, even an adult who questioned his integrity. He said to his buddies, "Look, there are some people who have no idea what our ordeal was like or how it happened, and I'm here to tell you, we're not taking any shit off them! OK?"

George added, "Those nurses had seen and heard us in Henry's room and said nothing. There is no reason for them to be so unfriendly."

"OK," the others said.

David added, "I'm not saying that we need to walk around with a chip on our shoulder. I'm just saying that we always say exactly what happened to us and that we just be ourselves. That's pretty much what my parents told me, and I agree."

Jason told them that that was the advice his parents had given to him, but not in the same words. According to Jason, his parents had told him that many people would try and ask questions. "If we don't want to talk, tell them that we don't want to talk about it, or ignore them, depending on who it is."

The three of them wandered west on First Street toward the Coast Guard station. The street was paved with sidewalks on each side, and the river was close and visible to the north along the way.

Officer Spears had returned, and the boys sat before him. "I was not here when you drove the enemy back into the sea," Spears said, with a tint of levity in his tone.

David, remembering the conversation in the confectionery store, bristled. He looked at the officer, and then at his two friends, and rather coolly for an almost-fifteen-year-old, stood up and said, "You need to know that we did your job for you, without any help from you, and probably in spite of you, and if you think we're gonna take any shit from you, you're mistaken. You're the last person we expected to joke about what we did and what happened to us."

Before David could continue, and he wanted to, Spears said, in a patronizing, superior manner, "Please sit down. I want to hear it from you boys as to what exactly happened."

David was still smarting from the way the nurses had looked at him and what Spears had just said. He was also brooding about the way others had questioned him and what Kyle and James had told them in the confectionery. David looked at Spears and said, "You may be older and smarter than us, but I can tell by the sound of your voice that you question what happened to us without hearing us out and that you think we should be humble. Well, that ain't gonna happen. You either take us at face value, or you don't take anything from us!" David was surprising himself as well as George and Jason, but he was not going to let anyone make light of what had happened.

Officer Spears was now leaning on his hands with his elbows resting on his desk. He had a small corner office with windows facing north at the Coquille River and facing west at the river's entrance to the ocean. There was barely room for four guest chairs. He seemed to have decided that these small-town country boys had backbone and character and he wasn't going to antagonize them further. Just maybe what he had heard was fact. "Alright, I'm ready to listen," he said.

George said, "OK, we'll tell you what happened, exactly the way it happened, and if you start doubting us before we finish, then we're done here and you can patrol the beach with nothing." Now George surprised himself. Maybe killing four human beings had made him a stronger, more direct person.

Jason said, "I'll start to fill you in on the details. First, the submarine was around three hundred yards offshore. We used our rifle telescope sights—mine is ten-power—and we saw Japanese on the sub's deck, two giving orders, or at least that's what I thought they were doing. They had gold markings on their caps. We saw them inflate the raft and launch it. We saw them load supplies in the raft, and four soldiers got in the raft with rifles. They headed for our shore." Jason looked as though he didn't want to say any more, so George stepped in and related the remainder of the story.

Art Spears did not interrupt but instead waited until George had finished. "That is pretty much the story I have heard," he said. "The explosion must have been terrific."

George said, "It was. There was nothing left of those men or their raft or their stuff, and our ears were ringing for days afterward."

"I notice you didn't take any notes on what Jason just told you," David said. "Do you mind telling us why?"

Spears ignored the question. "I've been out of town, but not on leave," Spears said. "As soon as I heard about this matter, I contacted the vice admiral in Seattle, who commands this Coast Guard district, and he contacted General DeWitt's headquarters in San Francisco. General DeWitt is the commanding general, Western Defense Command, and among other things, he is Fourth Army commander, who receives and deals with all sabotage threats. Based on what happened to you boys, the 13th Coast Guard District—my district—sent him a sabotage alert, and that is what I have been dealing with during my absence. Fortunately I was able to catch a navy plane to and from Marshfield. For your information, a navy air base is in the works for Marshfield."

"So what does all that bullshit have to do with us?" David asked.

"It means that if you boys did what you say you did, it was the most significant thing to happen on the West Coast since Pearl Harbor, and it makes you all first-class heroes. But there is one big problem— General DeWitt has received orders from the Defense Department to bury the story, and I have received orders from my vice admiral to bury the story, and that's what I'm going to do. It never happened, do you understand?"

David stood up. "I heard what you said, but I don't understand, and I certainly don't agree and we will not agree. You have no idea of the silent bullshit we're getting from people about this. I don't think they believe us, and the hardest part is getting them to believe how Henry was shot. If the fuckin' Japs didn't shoot him, who did? Us?"

"What's the big deal? Why cover it up?" Jason asked. "There's no reason for the army to do this to us, and I, for one, will not lie about anything, and neither will my friends. So screw all of you and the horse you rode in on!"

"I've never known boys your age that used such profane language," Spears said.

"You haven't heard a fuckin' thing yet," George said. "When my father hears about this, he'll be all over your ass!"

"Now wait a minute, you haven't heard the reason for keeping this quiet," Spears said. "The reason is simple: we can't risk alarming the people on the coast. They're engaged in essential war industry. The Port of Marshfield ships more structural lumber than any port in the world, and the armed forces of this country need a lot of that lumber. Also plants in Coquille and Marshfield manufacture essential battery separators. The Japanese attacked us six months ago, and we have little or no defenses established here. If the populace realizes that Japanese soldiers have tried to come ashore, people working in those industries may flee the area. We can't have that. Even though we just whipped the Japs so bad at Midway Islands that they probably can never mount another major offensive, such as invading this West Coast, the people here may not be convinced of that. Our citizens will be safe; we just want to keep the workers working here."

George asked, "Has the Coast Guard examined the beach where this thing happened?"

Spears said no and added, "Why should we? This thing didn't happen, and we don't want to prove to anyone that it did happen, at least that's what the army and navy want."

The boys looked at one another, and David said, "Give us a minute to ourselves." Spears stood and left the room. David said, "I understand what he said, but I think it's a mistake. What he wants to do is make liars out of us! To hell with him, we did our part. Now let them do their part and do it honestly. Our parents will back us up." George and Jason agreed.

After a while, Spears returned. David said, "We don't agree with you. When our parents and our friends hear about this bullshit, you'll have to walk up the back alleys in this town. Come on, guys, we're out of this place. Coast Guard, my ass," he said, and they walked away.

The boys headed back to the hospital and went through Henry's street-level window into his room. In Henry's room, they talked quietly. Henry was sitting up, his right arm in a sling and his right shoulder bandaged and exposed.

David said, "You can't believe the horseshit that we've been listening to. First, Officer Art Spears, supposedly our friend, had a long chat with us. We think he believes what happened to us, but the son of a bitch won't say it. He says it's important not to alarm the local public for fear they'll leave essential wartime jobs. He says some of his superiors want him to say nothing about what happened, even though it makes liars out of us. Basically the four of us are going to be taking a lot of shit."

George stood up, frustrated at Spears, and with a little anger seeping in, said, "You know, I think that maybe the Coast Guard guy, Spears, might believe us, but what he tells us his superiors are doing is plain stupid. We are so used to people not believing us that maybe we automatically think the same about Spears. Maybe he'll come around, but I say it's a waste of time arguing with him. So to hell with him."

"I'm getting out of here soon," Henry said. "My wound is healing. I sure as hell know how I got it, and I'm not taking any bullshit about it."

Henry's statement surprised his buddies, who looked at one another. Henry might be a little tougher and older because of the beach fight too.

"Look, guys, if I can get shot by a fuckin' Jap and live to tell about it, I can sure as hell put up with people who don't believe us," Henry said. He asked if they knew if anyone had been down to the beach where the fight took place. No one knew the answer to that question. Henry said that he remembered finding a pretty good glass ball just before they saw the Japs, and he wondered what happened to it.

"Jeez," David said, "who cares?"

"Well, I care. Not only do I want that glass ball, but I had it when the shooting started. It should be there in that little depression in the sand dune that saved our asses. It will mark the place if it's still there."

George nodded in agreement with Henry and suggested they find out who had been to the place where they saw the sub and if they had found anything. They decided they would go back when Henry had recovered. In the meantime, maybe someone would come up with some solid evidence proving what had actually happened.

The heavy events of the past few days had made the boys weary but sensitive to all that had transpired. Each of them had recounted in their minds a hundred times the events that had occurred on the beach. They had each thought about the killing of the four men, but those men had been shooting at them, they were Japanese soldiers, and they'd been up to no good. Grieving over them was unnecessary.

George and David had also given further thought to the families of the men killed, but the events of their 1942 summer vacation overshadowed even that. With all that was happening to them, they weren't going to spend any time worrying about those men or their families. George was at David's house sitting on the edge of the back porch. George said, "We've got to continue the beach patrols. Not only is it necessary, but it tells people that we are serious and honest about it, and in spite of what they believe, we will finish the job knowing we are right."

That night, Jason's father and mother asked how he was feeling about things and how the other boys were feeling.

"Each one of us is starting to feel like we've done something wrong, and we haven't," he said. "Most of our friends are OK, but others don't seem to act normal around us. Some adults don't seem to be as friendly as before. But we've all agreed, we are going to go about our business as usual. We are not going to change. The truth is on our side, and maybe someday everyone will know it."

When the phone on his desk rang, Master Chief Petty Officer Art Spears picked up.

"This is Captain Roger Avery's office with the 13th Coast Guard District in Seattle," a voice said. "Hold for Captain Avery."

Soon, another voice said, "Art? How are things going down there?"

"Did you get my new report on the submarine and shore party?"

"We did," Avery said. Spears's recent report had more information than his initial report had contained, including his meeting with the boys involved. "Your take on the matter troubles us—not me so much, but Vice Admiral Wayne Barkley was greatly upset."

"You mean to say that the truth upset him?" Spears asked.

"No, no, it was your assertion that suppressing the matter was wrong. Besides, substituting your opinion for his, who's to say what happened or that it did, in fact, happen? The Coast Guard is no different than the navy—all critical matters have to be confirmed, and you have made no independent investigation of your own. At least we know of none."

"What if I conduct an investigation of the beach area and come up with some concrete evidence supporting the boys' story? Will I have to bury that too? Has the admiral made an investigation? No, of course not, and further, he has ordered none," Spears said. "Does he want an investigation, or is that irrelevant to the demand to entomb the story?"

"Art, listen to me," Avery said. "Are you aware of what the Japanese have done on the West Coast in the past two weeks?"

"Of course I am," Spears said. He had read the reports. A Japanese submarine had surfaced and attacked the freighter SS *Fort Camosun* near the Washington coast recently, damaging the ship but not killing any crew. Just after that, a submarine had fired seventeen rounds from its deck gun at Fort Stevens, near Astoria, Oregon. The shelling hadn't caused much damage but had alarmed the public.

"Well, add to these attacks the attack you described, with Japanese soldiers coming ashore on a remote beach. Jeez, Art, do you want to cause an exodus from the West Coast?"

"Don't you see the difference, for Christ's sake?" Spears asked. "Those incidents haven't been suppressed, and they shouldn't be. I guess it's easy to sit up in Seattle and make liars out of four teenage boys, but it's OK not to make liars out of a few people who saw Fort Stevens being shelled or for the few people on a freighter. I'm not buying any of that crap. Besides, people are not going to flee. These folks down here are just as pissed off at the Japs as anyone. If I know them, they are no different than these four boys. They'll stay and fight; they will not run." He paused to let his argument sink in, then sighed in exasperation. "Come on, Roger. What am I supposed to do? I've been interviewed by the local daily paper, and I told them the matter was still being investigated and couldn't comment. They'll be back after they interview the boys and probably their parents. I'm not good at lying, and you better tell Admiral Wayne that."

Avery seemed to know the conversation was going badly and getting worse by the minute. "You know that the admiral is going to question me about how things are going on the south coast of Oregon and especially how you are handling it. Right now, I don't know what the hell to tell him, and you know he's going to ask!"

"Tell him that I am puzzled by what he is asking and that I would like a written order signed by him instructing me precisely how to handle the situation. I want him to include in that order a recitation of the facts upon which the order is premised," Spears said.

"He's not going to like that," Avery said.

"Well, just tell him that I have to live with myself, now and in the future."

CHAPTER 12

JUNE 1942

Dr. Rankin released Henry from the hospital with instructions to take it easy for a while and not lift anything too heavy with his right arm. The days were now long, with daylight until nearly nine p.m.

Henry's mother brought him home, and he spent the remainder of the day on the living room sofa. His shoulder was sore, and if he moved his arm too much, it made matters worse. Barely a week had passed, and his wounds still needed tending. They were to heal from the inside to the outside to better avoid infection. His mother would dress his wounds daily until they healed. Dr. Rankin was to be visited frequently, but Henry was out of any real danger and he would soon heal.

The Johnson family had eaten dinner together, and now Bill was reading the *Coos Bay Times* while May finished cleaning the kitchen. There was a knock at the door, so Henry eased himself off the sofa and answered.

A middle-aged man carrying a notebook asked, "Is this the Johnson residence?"

Henry's father came to the door. It was still plainly daylight. Bill Johnson looked the man over. The man was dressed in slacks, a white shirt with tie askew, and a tweed sports jacket. He had a nice smile on his face; he seemed harmless but interesting. The car behind him in the driveway was of a decent vintage.

He introduced himself as Linus Rink, a reporter for the *Coos Bay Times*, and he asked to interview the Johnsons on the events reported to have occurred on the beach south of town about two weeks before. Bill invited him in. Henry returned to the sofa. He was apprehensive but wanted to hear what a newspaperman had to say.

Linus Rink said, "I talked to Officer Spears with the Coast Guard and learned little or nothing. I know this is probably a very sensitive subject to discuss, but our readers—and there are plenty of them in this area—do not know what to think about the situation because they have few, if any, facts on which to form an opinion. I am definitely aware that there is some sort of division and unrest in the community as to what happened, and that is chiefly because the four boys have made no real public statement. I can understand that. But it is time to publish, through me, your version of what happened."

Henry said, "My version of what happened? I have no *version*. My story is not a *version* of what happened." Henry's agitation was obvious, and he could see that his parents were surprised. In the past two weeks, his maturity had started to surface thanks to his experience on the beach and the attitude of the US Coast Guard and the Western Defense Command of the US Army. He'd spent his time in the hospital deciding that he'd challenge anyone who cast any doubt about his integrity.

Henry stood up, took his shirt off, and pointed to the scar of the bullet's entry wound. "This is my *version* of the Jap bullet's entry wound." Turning around, he said, "This is my *version* of the Jap bullet's exit wound. What is your *version* of my wounds?"

His mother said, "Now, Henry, you need not be rude to Mr. Rink," but his father seemed amused.

"You must understand," his father said, "that my son and his three friends see the beach fight and the shooting in black and white. There is no gray area. The only question that the boys have is: What were those Japanese in that landing party up to?"

The Johnsons invited Rink to sit. Henry's father turned to him, holding the *Coos Bay Times*. "I just finished reading a feature article you wrote, and it's quite good. Any commentary faulting the moving of Japanese Americans from the West Coast has great human interest to me. I believe the whole thing is a disgusting violation of their constitutional rights. You obviously feel the same. This is the first day that I have noticed an article by you in this paper. Are you new to the paper?"

"Yes," Rink said. He then told a bit about himself. He'd moved to Marshfield from San Francisco about a year ago and only recently had found a job with the paper. He told them about his job with the *San Francisco Chronicle*. He did not tell them of his difficulties with one of the editors. It seemed that his editor had asked Rink to do a little less drinking and to spend a little more time on the job and that he had wanted to do more drinking and spend less time on the job. Rink had received a praiseworthy letter of recommendation in exchange for his resignation.

Rink said, "I think I know a good story when I see one. Truth and fair play might even be involved in this one."

"And you think this sounds like a good story?" Henry asked.

"Well, I don't know yet," Rink said. "Maybe you could tell me a bit more about what happened."

Henry described the whole fight that he had seen and heard up to the time he was hit. He told Rink about the submarine and what appeared to be officers giving instructions to others on the sub's deck. He mentioned the gold markings on their hats and the hats' distinctive shape. He told Rink how he'd watched them load stuff into the raft and then watched the four soldiers get in the raft and paddle toward shore.

"Soldiers?" Rink asked.

Henry explained that their uniforms were completely different from the others. Even their hats were different—they were like short-billed baseball caps, which, like their uniforms, were a tan color.

"We were ready to leave to notify the Coast Guard when the fog closed in," Henry said. "When we looked back as we started to leave, we saw the raft and I felt a blow to my shoulder." He paused. "I don't remember much after that."

He told Rink what Dr. Rankin had said about the wound, that had it hit a little to one side or the other, it would have been fatal. He also told the reporter and his parents what Dr. Rankin had said about the special kind of bullet. "Dr. Rankin didn't say that the bullet that hit me was a military bullet; he only said that it must have been a full-jacketed bullet. But I've heard that military bullets are really the only full-jacketed bullets around."

Rink seemed fascinated by Henry's story. "Has the Coast Guard combed the scene of the fight in an effort to confirm the event?"

Bill answered, "We don't know what has been done in that respect. You would think there would be some pieces of something lying around down there, and maybe, by now, something has washed up on the beach."

Rink appeared puzzled by the apparent lack of interest by the Coast Guard in ferreting out the truth of the boys' stories, but he didn't give away—as far as Henry could see—how he viewed the situation. As he left, though, he handed his business card to Henry's father and said, "I'm going to try and write as accurate an article as I can. I just hope people will talk to me."

Henry wondered exactly what that meant.

Rink left the Johnson house knowing one thing for sure: he'd have to go and see the beach where Henry was shot soon.

It took him almost an hour and a half to drive Highway 101 back through Coquille to his home in Marshfield. During the trip, he pondered the probabilities inherent in Henry Johnson's story. He knew it would be an error to jump to conclusions before any story was fully investigated. But what if Henry's story was true—and it might be. The event would mark the first time an enemy soldier had attempted to set foot on United States soil since the War of 1812. He knew he might be on the threshold of a great story, and he would convince his editor to turn him loose to find the answers. He would have the boys take him to the scene and describe the event. Even more important, he would search the beach for evidence of the gunfight. Sooner or later, he would interview the Coast Guard officer again and find out about the Coast Guard's response, or seeming lack thereof.

Before he reached Coquille, a large billboard loomed for a few seconds in his headlights. Displaying a skull and crossbones, it read: DEATH RIDES WITH A DRUNKEN DRIVER. He was hankering for a drink, but thought to himself, to hell with it. He worried his wife enough as it was.

CHAPTER 13

JULY 1942

Henry had healed, and talk of the beach adventure had diminished slightly as the summer wore on. Each of the boys had been questioned by their peers, who were usually more vigorous in their demand for details than the adults. Some of their friends and acquaintances wanted to know why they hadn't shot at the sailors on the sub, and some wanted to know where the Japanese soldier had been hit. Some wanted to know if the water had turned bloody, and some wanted to know what had happened to the blown-up soldiers: Were there any bits and pieces of them lying around, and didn't they have any souvenirs, and what had the Coast Guard guy said? Some asked the boys if they would continue their beach patrols. Some believed the boys, and some did not believe them.

The boys grew accustomed to all the talk. There were the believers and the nonbelievers. Soon, they were dismissing rumors, questions, and innuendos about what did or didn't happen on the beach.

The boys were starting to get the feeling that many adults were passing the whole thing off as a firearm accident. The attitude seemed to be that, since the boy who had been injured was going to be just fine, what the heck, forget it, there's a war on!

Several days had passed since the reporter for the *Coos Bay Times* had visited Henry and his family. Henry had told David, George, and Jason about the visit and most of the questions asked and the answers given.

The four boys were seated in the confectionery each having a Coke. It was a warm summer day, and the place was busy with customers, some seated at tables, others on stools at the bar.

Their demeanor and their conversation style were returning to normal. Jason said, "It's funny the reporter didn't visit all of us."

After some discussion about what Rink might do or report, they decided to visit Officer Spears. They agreed that now was the time to see if the Coast Guard had investigated the beach area where the gunfight had occurred, and if so, what had they found and what were they going to do.

George said, "If anyone was going to investigate the beach, they should have done it immediately. Right after the shooting, there were some huge high tides and big run outs. A tremendous movement of water."

Jason added, "They would need to go there with garden rakes and screen sifters to find stuff, and they weren't going to find anything the crabs and seagulls couldn't eat."

David added that maybe they should go back to the scene and look around after they visited Spears.

At the Coast Guard station, they immediately headed up the steep indoor stairway to the office area. A coastguardsman met them; he had only a single chevron on his upper sleeve. "Where are you going? What do you want?" he asked.

"We want to see Officer Art Spears," David said.

The coastguardsman looked surprised and said, "Officer Spears is no longer here. He was transferred to Louisiana a week ago."

"Then we want to see whoever took his place," Jason said.

"No one has actually taken his place. Captain Roger Avery from headquarters in Seattle is filling in until Officer Spears's replacement arrives," the coastguardsman said. "What do you want to see him about?"

David blurted out, "We want to see him about the fuckin' Japanese that shot him," he pointed at Henry, "and that we blew up, OK?"

At that, the coastguardsman walked down the hall and knocked on a door before opening it. He stuck his head into the other room for a few seconds, then returned to the boys. "The captain will see you."

When they walked into the office, Captain Avery did not get up. They were in Spears's old corner office where they could see the river entrance from the corner window and the river from the north-facing windows. After asking them to be seated, Captain Avery said, "I know who you boys are and what has happened to you. Officer Spears told me all about it."

David looked at Avery and said, "Would you mind telling us who you are and why Art Spears isn't here?"

"I'm from the Seattle office of the Coast Guard," Avery said. "Spears has been transferred to New Orleans to work with guarding and watching the heavy ship traffic there."

David wanted to say, "I'll bet," but didn't. Instead, he said, "Well, what is the Coast Guard going to do about what happened to us? It's going on a month, and we haven't heard a thing."

George added, "We all had the feeling that our friends were joking about us patrolling the beach. We did it because no one else was doing it, not even the Coast Guard. And as we understand it, you are still not patrolling the beaches, north or south. Have you made a search of the beach to find some proof of what we say? We're here to find out what has been found out and what you are going to do about it."

Avery said, "We have not made our investigation, and we really don't know of anyone who has. Basically we are not going to spend any time finding out whether the event happened or didn't happen. The point is this: the vice admiral in charge of this district has made the decision that the public need not be alarmed by the story. In addition, the army headquarters in charge of the Western Defense Command has reached the same conclusion. The lumber industry is an essential war industry, and we don't want workers leaving the area because of some story about Japanese soldiers coming ashore near their community. It's too bad, boys, but that's the way it is and that's the way it's going to be. Spears told me that he told you this very thing. I am not about to say anything different, and I'm asking you to go along with us."

"So some admiral in Seattle and some general in San Francisco are afraid we'll cut and run?" Henry asked.

"This is such a bunch of horseshit!" David said. "And you guys think the people in this community can't handle a story about some little pissy-assed Japs trying to land in a raft. Well, they can and they will."

"By the way, you still have only a dozen or so men at this station? Maybe you just don't care what goes on down here. Well, we care!" Jason said. "You guys in charge better change, because we're not about to, and you're going to hear plenty from us. When we let people know what you're doing or not doing, there's gonna be hell to pay."

Avery stood, suggesting that the meeting was over, and then said, "I'll deny that this conversation ever took place, and that won't make you look good."

"Let's get out of here before I throw up," David said, then he stopped himself. "But wait—we wanted to ask about Officer Spears. So tell us why he transferred. Did it have anything to do with us?"

In a condescending manner, Avery said, "That is Coast Guard business and not yours."

"Officer Spears was well respected and liked in the community," David continued, "and we really don't know anyone that spoke poorly of him, except maybe us when we were in his office. All the Coast Guard 'boys'—that's what our parents call them—are well liked, and most of them have friends here. It bothers us that we seem to be the only ones in the area who are having trouble with you guys. Can't you say why Officer Spears left? Did you and your admiral have him transferred?"

"It doesn't matter how he got there."

At that remark, the boys left the small office and continued silently down the stairs and out to the sidewalk, where they stopped for a moment. George looked up at the second-story windows of the station and said, "That bastard. I'm glad the rest of them are not like him."

"We need to sic Linus Rink on him," Henry said. "Part of the time, Avery was talking down to us, and part of the time, he was acting high and mighty, as if we were nothing. Come on. Let's get the hell out of here!"

The boys walked back downtown, where Henry's father waved them all into the dry goods store. It was a large, open store with clothes and clothing articles displayed on tables and clothing racks, big south-facing windows helped light the store, as did numerous fluorescent lights hanging from the ceiling. A counter and a fancy cash register were located in the center of everything.

They saw Linus Rink talking to Mr. Johnson. Henry introduced the reporter to his friends. Rink was wearing an old gray tweed sports jacket, a clean but unironed white dress shirt, and a nondescript tie. His gray flannel trousers were threadbare at one of the knees.

"I've been looking for you," Rink said. "I'd like you to take me to the place on the beach where the shooting occurred, if you have the time."

"Sure, we do," George said. They were all ready for some action after the showdown with Avery.

The boys piled into Rink's 1940 black Ford sedan and headed for George's place. Jason recounted their conversation with Avery and the fact that Spears, who had been there for about five years, had been transferred to Louisiana days after he interviewed them about the beach fight.

"Maybe the Coast Guard thought Spears wouldn't handle the situation as they wanted him to," Rink said, then he shook his head. "That's OK, boys. It only makes for a better story. Shoving good honest stuff down a rathole never makes sense; all it does is piss off the rat."

Rink drove his V8 Ford into the Williamses' driveway, and Luke barked from his front yard territory. "Just how far am I going to have to walk?" Rink asked the boys.

"About a mile, maybe closer to two," George said.

As soon as the boys alighted from the car, Luke recognized them and quit barking. He greeted all of them, including Mr. Rink, with a dog smile and a wagging black tail. George's mother and his sister, Lisa, appeared on the front porch, and George made the introductions. "Mr. Rink is a reporter for the *Coos Bay Times*, and he is doing a story on our fight down the beach," he told them.

Rink asked, "Mrs. Williams, are you aware of anyone else coming past your house to go to the beach area where the shooting incident happened?"

"No, and I'm here most of the time. This is one of the few places for beach access to the south," she said.

"Do people drive their vehicles on the beach over there?"

"Sometimes we see tire tracks," George said, "but only once or twice a year. We really don't know who it is. We know that some people search for the glass balls on this beach, but it's a long walk from the access points north of here, and there aren't any good beach access points south of here."

Rink mumbled something almost to himself about wishing he could drive down the beach. George sized Rink up. The man was probably overweight; the walk would likely do him some good, he thought. "We better get going."

Rink and the boys walked west to the beach and then south, with a northwest wind at their backs and Luke running and sniffing ahead.

"How many times did the Japs shoot at you?" Rink asked.

"We really don't know, but their bullets were thumping in the sand in front of us," David said. "It looked like only two of them had rifles, and they were the ones doing the shooting. We're glad they were bouncing around in that raft or they might have shot better."

"How do you know that there were four?"

"We saw four soldiers get into the raft at the sub's side, and we watched while they stowed stuff in the raft that was handed to them," George said.

They continued walking down the beach. Rink complained about being tired, so they rested a couple of times, but they finally arrived at the scene.

"This is it," George said.

Rink said, "How do you know 'this is it'?"

George immediately started looking around in the depression behind the little dune and soon saw the top of the glass ball that Henry had found. George proclaimed, "This is the place! See that glass ball? It's exactly where we left it. That's where Henry dropped it when the shooting started."

"OK. That's a good start. Now tell me where you think the Jap bullets were hitting."

"Right here in front of us, but we wouldn't know exactly where," David said.

"Let's start looking for a bullet. Just one—that's all I need," Rink said.

All of them, including Rink, dropped to their hands and knees and started digging and brushing the sand away. When Luke saw the digging, it excited him. He commenced digging furiously next to George, throwing sand to the wind as well as on Henry and Rink. The four boys each thought to himself that this was a needle-in-the-haystack job, and even though there must be some spent bullets around, they were not going to find any. Rink told them that a bullet would not penetrate sand to any depth, and there was no need to dig down to the wet sand. "Just look close to the surface."

Fifteen minutes of digging and scratching around produced nothing but a few old crab and clamshells.

Rink stood up, brushed himself off, and said, "Let's come back to this later. In the meantime, we can walk down the beach and see what we can find. Maybe something washed up that will tell us something."

They all stood, and David said, "Look there." He was pointing to the sandy area immediately behind the front of the little dune that had protected them when the shooting occurred. There were three or four empty brass shell casings left from the boys' gunfire. "No question this is the place where we saw the sub," David said. "Unless you don't believe we really saw it."

Rink didn't answer, just looked at the casings.

After the five of them and the dog had walked farther south down the beach along the drift line for two or three hundred yards, they spotted a few bits and pieces of tan cloth among driftwood, bird feathers, and rotten seaweed. They picked up some of the tan cloth and discovered a thick, multilayered, sewn piece of what appeared to be the same tan fabric. This latter piece looked as if it could have come from some kind of hat or other reinforced material. They walked on south, speculating about the fabric and what it could have come from. Then they saw a few pieces of black rubberized fabric and decided that it could have come from a rubber raft. They soon found a piece of dry brown leather that might have come from a belt or strap, and then discovered what appeared to be a piece of shoe with one eyelet intact.

Rink and the boys had walked on down the beach approximately one-half of a mile beyond the place of the shooting and ultimately ceased finding anything else worth collecting. They discussed their finds on the way back north and decided that the explosion had reduced everything in the raft, including the soldiers, to very small bits and pieces, most of which must have been pulverized beyond identification.

As they walked, Rink mentally reviewed some of the criminal cases he had worked and reported on when he was employed by the *Chronicle*. Those cases, according to his cronies in the San Francisco Police Department, had had fewer pieces of credible evidence to start with than the pieces of fabric, rubber, leather, and the shoe part he now had in his pocket, plus what he otherwise knew about the case at hand. The San Francisco cases had eventually been solved and convictions obtained.

He told the boys, "With your story and what we have gleaned from this beach, I think we have the foundation of a provable story. But we are going to keep all this to ourselves until we have more solid stuff, OK? We don't want people picking us apart before we are ready."

The four boys all agreed and arrived at the area of their initial search when they saw that the wind had blown the dry sand almost smooth where they had been digging maybe an hour ago. Henry walked over to find and pick up his glass fish float. Pointing to a spot in a mound of sand they had dug up in their search for bullets, David stopped and said, "Look here." The wind had blown and made smooth the clumps of sand, exposing two copper-clad bullets. The nose of each bullet was slightly bent and blunted from hitting the sand.

Rink, wishing he had his camera, carefully picked up and examined each bullet.

"They don't look like anything we've ever seen!" George said, and the others quickly agreed.

"They're even a weird diameter," David said.

"What I said about keeping this stuff to ourselves still goes," Link reminded them as he pocketed the two bullets. "A little hard work and perseverance will most always have its rewards."

On the way back to George's house, nearly exhausted, he told the boys that he had not decided exactly how he wanted to handle the situation at this point. His chief interest was to confirm the truth of the boys' story for their benefit. At the same time, he added, he wanted to publish a good, accurate account of a boyhood adventure to beat all boyhood adventures. He let them know that he would take all the pieces of evidence they had found and keep them safe—plus, he had heard of a gunsmith in Marshfield who could probably determine what exactly those bullets were. After returning to George's house with Luke, they said their goodbyes, and Rink left with Jason, David, and Henry in his car.

The final words Linus Rink said to the boys were, "Remember, boys, there's always the likelihood that other bits and pieces of evidence will turn up."

That evening at dinner, George's mother asked him, "Did you boys and Mr. Rink find anything on your hike down the beach?"

At first, George didn't know how to answer. He hadn't given such a question any thought or he would probably have had a ready answer.

"We found some dead birds, and rotten seaweed, and the glass ball Henry found on the day of the shooting. It marked the place where it all happened," George said.

His sister, Lisa, interrupted. "I'm taking a lot of ribbing from my friends about you and your friends," she said, "and no one believes what you boys said happened because there's no proof of anything except that Henry got shot."

"Things happened exactly the way Henry and David and Jason and I say it happened, and you and your stupid friends, who were not there, know nothing! Besides, we don't have to prove anything to anybody. We know what we saw and what was done. The truth is the truth, whether you and your friends believe it or not!"

George's father broke in. "Please, that conversation is old business. I have something important to tell all of you. I've already talked to your mother about this. I have enlisted in the US Navy."

George and Lisa both gasped, saying, "Oh no, you can't! We want you here."

Joe Williams held up his hand as if to kindly silence them. "Hold on a minute and let me finish. I'll leave within a week or so. I quit my job, but I'm assured I will have that job when I return after the war. I'll be able to come home from time to time, but not very often after I ship out, which will likely be to the Pacific someplace. I'll write often and let you know how I am doing. You need to know that the navy is a safer place than the army or marines."

George and Lisa had stopped eating. They were stunned. How could their father leave them? It just wasn't fair. Lisa got up and threw herself in a big overstuffed chair in the living room. She was sobbing, and George felt like doing the same. They both implored their father not to go. He might not come back, and what were they going to do without him? There would be no one who could really take care of their small farm.

George's mother said that she had been offered a job at the cheese factory in Bandon and that her income, plus the military allotment she was to receive for herself and her two children, would enable them to make it just fine. She added, "Your father doesn't want to leave us any more than we want him to leave. But he is like many men in this country; he feels, and rightly so, that it is his patriotic duty to fight for his country and that he must go. I tried to talk him out of it, but came to realize that it was right for him to go. He's still very young and will make a good sailor. Besides, he will eventually come home, and we'll have him the rest of our lives."

George's father looked at him and said, "You've done more for the war effort than I have, and I can't let you get the better of me on that score. I do want you to help with the two acres of cranberry bogs we have. You must see that the water system works at all times. You know how to do that. When harvest time comes, you might have trouble hiring enough pickers. Just post a notice at your school announcing that you're paying twenty-five cents a box and you should get enough help. School pickers may come from as far away as Coquille and Myrtle Point, so don't be afraid to have notices posted in those schools. Other cranberry growers will be doing the same thing."

Before the evening was over, and following the initial shock and gloom of their father's announcement, George and Lisa began to understand the firmness of purpose in their father's actions. They reluctantly became resigned to his enlistment in the navy. No amount of protest on their part would change matters.

George asked, "Are you going to be on a battleship or aircraft carrier or what?"

"I have very little choice in the matter, and I'll go wherever they put me, but I'll let you know as soon as I can, if I can."

After dinner, George walked over to the beach with Luke. As he sat on the sand with his dog, the amber sun crept closer to the ocean. He thought about how his life would be without his father. There would be no more deer hunts or duck hunts unless someone invited him. But worst of all, his dad just wouldn't be there. He looked down between his knees, and a few tears fell, making round, wet spots in the dry sand.

The next day, George walked across the county road and up the slight hill to David's house, where he found David and his older brother, Michael, sitting on the top step of their front porch. George sat on a lower step and told them about his father joining the navy.

Michael said, "It's too bad, but I guess the navy needs more than high school boys to run a ship. With his mechanical experience, your dad is probably just what the navy wants. It's guys like him that are really gonna help win this war."

"I guess you're right, but we're really going to miss him. I miss him already, and he's not leaving for a week," George said.

David said, "Maybe we should call Jason and Henry and start walking the beach again. I don't think anyone else is doing it, and, you know, the Jap submarines are still out there. It's only been about three weeks since they shelled Fort Stevens and attacked that freighter off the Washington coast."

In a skeptical tone, Michael said, "You guys can do what you want, but leave me out. I'm going into town," and he got up and left.

George and David didn't move. They decided not to call Jason and Henry. George didn't feel like doing anything, and besides, he'd heard that a few more coastguardsmen were now stationed nearby, maybe enough to patrol the beaches.

Things were not going well for the four-boy beach patrol. Henry had been shot, and now George's father was leaving home for the navy. They had told Linus Rink, the reporter, everything, but was he really going to set the record straight for them?

CHAPTER 14

LATE JULY 1942

Linus Rink parked in front of the only sporting goods store in Marshfield. A tiny sign in the front window advertised that a gunsmith was on duty. Rink had called him ten minutes before. Rufus Goodman had been recommended to Rink by several men in his newspaper office who said Rufus knew everything there was to know about guns. Rink walked into the store, then walked to the back where Rufus worked and took a seat. The walls were lined with guns of all types of shapes and vintages. Two tables had some handguns on them, and the shelves were full of glass jars with parts, springs, nuts, bolts, little sights, and anything else that might be part of a gun.

Rink introduced himself and laid the two copper-jacketed bullets in front of Rufus.

Rufus picked one up and said, "What the hell am I supposed to do with this?"

"You can tell me what the hell it is and where the hell it came from."

A grin spread across Rufus's face as he said, "It sure as hell didn't come from around here. It's really a strange size, and it's not meant for huntin', but if you wanted to shoot someone in a war, these would work."

"What I really want to know is what kind of a gun these bullets came from," Rink said.

Rufus opened a drawer and produced a set of calipers marked in micromillimeters and measured the diameter of each bullet. Then he weighed each bullet on a tiny set of scales before setting them down and pulling a large paperback catalog from a cluttered shelf. He sat down in a chair at the table with Rink and then thumbed through the encyclopedia-like book until he came to a page that he studied for a while before turning the page to study further.

Finally he looked up and said, "I don't know where you got these bullets, but they are 7.7 millimeters in diameter and weigh a hundred seventy-five grains. More specifically, they are 7.7-by-58-millimeter Japanese Arisaka Type 99 rifle bullets. The Japs have had this rifle around for some time, but in 1939, they remade it slightly to accommodate the 7.7-by-58-millimeter cartridge, a replacement for the original 6.5-millimeter cartridge. I suppose one of the newer-model Arisaka Type 99 rifles could have gotten over here, but that's highly unlikely. So, Mr. Linus Rink, where did these bullets come from?"

"You and everyone else will soon see an article in the *Coos Bay Times* that will fully lay out the story of these bullets, and will you be surprised," Rink said. He gave Rufus a five-dollar bill. "Is that enough for your services?"

"OK with me," Rufus said.

As Rink was leaving, he turned to Rufus and asked, "By the way, may I use your name in my story, identifying you as the expert who identified these bullets?"

That, too, was OK with Rufus. Rink left the store walking very lightly, with almost a skip to his gait and a smile on his face. He thought as he drove back to his office that those four kids in Bandon were real bona fide heroes, and nobody knew it except maybe old Linus Rink.

The big question was: What were those Japanese soldiers up to? He started to give the matter careful thought. "Those bastards had all those explosives. They were going to blow something up—so what the hell could it be?"

When Rink returned to the *Coos Bay Times* building in the center of town, he immediately went to the office of the publisher, Marvin Hackett. He asked Hackett to call in the newspaper's editor, Red Carson, to review an important and difficult story that should be published at once. When all were present, Rink laid the story before them. Carson said he had heard rumors of the episode with the four boys at Bandon but had dismissed the story like nearly everyone else who had heard it. Now he was extremely interested, as was the publisher. To them, it appeared that the story was true and that Rink had good verification—but could there be other explanations?

Rink said, "Let's ignore that for now and ask ourselves this: If it is true that there was a Jap shore party, what were they doing with a large cache of high explosives? What is there around here that would be important enough for them to want to destroy? What about ships in port, dock structures, bridges like the bridge across the bay and the Southern Pacific railroad bridge? There's the Highway 101 bridge across the Coquille River at Coquille, and it's the only bridge across that river that will hold a heavy vehicle. The loss of that bridge would stop all traffic on Highway 101. There are a lot of mills in the area, but the men couldn't carry enough explosives to blow up more than part of one mill. So what the hell were they doing?"

"Maybe they were trying to somehow get aboard a large freighter and sink it in the shipping channel," Red said, "but if they were going to do that, why come ashore south of Bandon?"

They all agreed that there were so many shipping docks in the area, including the Moore Mill dock at Bandon, that destroying one dock would be meaningless.

Marvin said, "You know, I've noticed that the Evans Products mill near Marshfield has been flying one of those new *E* flags beneath the American flag. The *E* means 'essential industry,' and, what's more, that mill has recently blacked out all of its windows. Someone needs to go to the other mills in the area and find out if they are flying that *E* flag. Don't call them—go to the mills, including Smith Wood. Then, Rink, you find out from the mill or mills flying that *E* flag what it's about, and we'll hold the story until then."

Red added, "And even then, we may not want to speculate as to what we think those Japs were up to. But the thing is—and this is most important—the Coast Guard has got to get its head out of its ass and figure this thing out. Rink, do you know anyone down there at the Bandon Coast Guard station?"

"I don't know anyone there, but the boys do, and I haven't yet told you about the Coast Guard's response to their story." He told them about Captain Avery taking over for Officer Spears and about their accusation that the Coast Guard was burying their story. "I think Spears argued with his superiors about their instruction. The boys told me that Spears was transferred to Louisiana for duty, and that happened right after Spears interviewed the boys and relayed the story to the Seattle headquarters."

"This is getting to be one hell of a story," Red said, "and we should get to the bottom of it as soon as possible. I want Rink to interview the Coast Guard before we publish, but there is no sense in involving the Coast Guard here in Marshfield or in any other place. This is the Bandon station's baby!"

"So there we have it. Any more ideas?" Hackett asked. "If not, Rink, you're off to the mills and then to the Coast Guard in Bandon."

Later that day, Rink conducted a windshield survey of the lumber mills and flagpoles in the Marshfield area, as well as the large mill in Coquille. Only the Evans Products mill in Marshfield and the Smith Wood Products mill in Coquille flew the blue-and-gold *E* flag. He walked into the mill's main office, which was located in a portion of a huge wood-frame structure that housed the plywood and battery-separator operations. The dimensional lumber manufacturing operation was in an adjoining structure. Small divided sectional panes made up each large wood-frame window, which overlooked Southern Pacific railroad tracks. The entire mill was located on the north bank of the Coquille River. Linus Rink asked to see the manager. He was ushered into the office of the general manager, George Smith.

"I'm a reporter from the *Coos Bay Times*," Rink said. "I'd like to ask you about that *E* flag your mill is flying."

Smith responded, "The flag is directly related to the manufacture of cedar battery separators, an essential component of every storage battery. There are only two such manufacturers in the country, Evans

Products and Smith Wood Products. Battery separators are an integral part of every storage battery. Every vehicle, every airplane, every ship, and every submarine needs them."

Rink asked, "Where did the *E* flag come from?"

"From the Defense Department," Smith said. "Unsolicited, but it does make us mindful that we have an important facility here. Our daily production of battery separators usually fills a railroad boxcar, and that's one hell of a bunch of battery separators. I don't know the production numbers for Evans Products, but I'm sure it's substantial."

Smith kept filling Rink in on the details of the battery-separator business, and finally asked Rink if he would like to see the separator operation. Rink nodded that he would, and Smith called Mark Gleason's office in the separator plant. Gleason's secretary said that he was in the plant but would be back soon and return the call. Smith invited Rink to wait in Smith's outer office for Mark's call.

As Rink turned to leave, Smith said, "Tell me, why are you making these inquiries? Is there something I should know about our mill operation that concerns you?"

Rink told Smith the salient parts of the boys' encounter on the beach near Bandon and that their story was probably the truth, regardless of what the public might know at this time. Then, with a serious and grave look, Rink scrutinized Smith's face and said, "Some of us—and I won't tell you who, and it isn't any part of the military or the Coast Guard or otherwise—have deduced that those Japs with their high explosives may have been after these separator plants or the large bridge across the bay." Rink fudged a little on the "some of us" part, but he knew that would be the general deduction once his colleagues knew about the separator business. He added, "If you have a security problem here, you'd better fix it. This war ain't over yet!"

Smith quickly replied, "Yes, but those stupid bastards wouldn't try it again."

"Who knows? For us, the war is only about eight months old, and except for Midway, we're getting our butt kicked. You better not figure that they won't try another time."

Smith's secretary announced that Mark Gleason was on the phone, and Smith invited him up. When he arrived, Smith introduced him to

Rink, and Mark asked if Rink was the *Coos Bay Times* reporter that his son, Jason, and his friends had been talking to.

"I'm the guy," Rink said.

Smith said, "Mark, I want you to give Rink a tour of the separator plant. When you're finished, I want you to come back here at once."

Mark and Rink headed to the point where the separator manufacturing operation began. They first walked out of Smith's office to a wide wood-planked driveway between buildings and then into the battery-separator building. Rink noticed the entire area was on wood planking resting high on wood piling. He also noticed a vehicle-refueling area next to the building that housed the separator plant. Lumber carriers and a log truck were refueling while a pickup truck waited its turn.

Rink followed Mark into the plant where at least a dozen separate machines, each operated by a woman, were producing cedar battery separators. Each machine had a small carriage that moved up and down at a forty-five-degree angle, moving a block of white cedar through a slicing mechanism. Each movement up and down produced one separator.

Near the west side of the building, Rink could see daylight through the twelve-inch-thick floorboards. *This place is susceptible to sabotage of the simplest variety,* Rink thought, *and if the Japanese had talked to any of those cedar log buyers that Smith had mentioned, they knew it.* He wondered what was going on over at the Evans Products plant. Was it a sabotage setup like this place?

Mark then took him to the railroad loading platform on the north side of the building. Forklifts were busy loading pallets of paper-boxed finished cedar separators into a boxcar. There were at least nine boxcars lined up and waiting to be loaded. It crossed Rink's mind that maybe the railroad bridge across Marshfield was the Japanese target. But then again, even if the bridge was gone, trucks could haul the separators from each plant to a railroad siding on the other side of the bay to be reloaded in boxcars, so that couldn't have been the target. Even if the bridge across the bay were knocked out, there was a way around it on the road skirting the north side of the bay and across another bridge, thus reconnecting to US Highway 101 with maybe a twenty-five-minute delay. Therefore, he thought, it had to be these separator plants. It had to be.

Interrupting Rink's quiet calculating, Mark said, "Well, that's about it. Do you want me to walk you back to the main office?"

"No," Rink said, "I can find my way."

He stopped again at George Smith's office, and the secretary told him to go on in. Rink said to George in a serious tone, "Would you call the manager of Evans Products, whoever he is, and tell him about the conversation I've had with you? It will save me a lot of time. Incidentally, I don't know much about sabotage and blowing stuff up, but your separator plant has got to be vulnerable to about anything anyone would want to do to wreck it. Evans Products is probably not much better off."

"Yes, I'm going to ask Mark Gleason to come talk about security with me," Smith said, and Rink agreed this was a good idea.

Rink thanked Smith for his hospitality and left. As he walked to his car, he had a feeling that he had done nothing more than cause George Smith to think that he, Rink, was selling red herring for the sake of newsprint.

Meanwhile, Luke was sleeping in one of his favorite spots beside George's house, partially in the shade and partially in the sun. The sun was getting uncomfortably hot, and he stirred. He lifted his black snout and tested the breeze for interesting subjects. He sorted through scents of a cat, another cat, a ground squirrel, something dead, the garbage can next to the garage, and maybe a ruffled grouse. Nothing reminiscent of a beautiful dog in heat, no duck or pheasant scents, but there was the smell of the ocean. He hadn't been over there since the trip down the beach with George and his friends less than a month ago. So what the heck, he thought, he'd go for a hike on the beach. He rose, stretched, yawned, stretched again, and trotted westerly. After a couple of side trips, he reached the beach and headed south on the drift line, checking out anything and everything that smelled or looked interesting. He cooled himself in the surf a couple of times, then continued south, beyond the area where he had helped the boys dig in the sand.

A black rectangular object was lying flat on the sand near the drift line. It looked like something people would have, and it didn't smell too bad. He picked it up, and decided he'd call it a day and head for home.

Mary Williams was sitting on the front porch when Luke walked up and handed the black rectangular thing to her just like any good retriever would do. Mary examined the object. It looked like a big vest-pocket-type wallet, only bigger: four inches wide and about ten inches long. It was tightly wrapped in some sort of waterproof paper or fabric. She opened it. It was damp, and the papers inside were stuck together and to the interior leather of the thing. What immediately caught her interest was the strange gold printing on the exterior. Was it Japanese writing or what? She thanked Luke for the gift, although it was nothing unusual for him to bring stuff home and deliver it to whomever was present. Mary placed the object on a shelf in the partially enclosed porch. It needed drying. She would tell her husband, who hadn't yet left for the navy, and she would tell George, when they were home. Until then, Mary returned to sitting on the porch.

Linus Rink sat at his desk in the *Coos Bay Times* newsroom, which was also occupied by all of the newspaper's other writers, the classified department, the business office, and the editor, to whom Rink was waiting to talk. When Red got off the phone, Rink walked over and sat down at Red's desk. Red looked hassled, and his thinning red hair was in disarray. A veteran newspaperman, he was very busy and liked every minute of it. He was anxious to hear what Rink had learned.

"We need to discuss our next move," Rink said. He told him about the area's lumber mills and about his visit with George Smith and Mark Gleason. "Red," he said, "I've come to the conclusion that the two battery-separator manufacturing plants in this county are what the Japanese want to destroy. To the best of my knowledge, there is no other facility in the area that could interest those little bastards. As active as they have been, in rather stupid ways, on the western shoreline of this country, there is no reason to believe that they won't try again. They have the naval capability and the incentive, as long as our western shores and seas remain unprotected. So what do you think?"

"You may be correct," Red said, "but we must be careful not to create some sort of an invasion panic syndrome among us. They need to know what happened south of Bandon, but we need the Coast Guard on board on that score. Their disavowal of the boys' story can't stand." Red stamped out his cigarette in a dirty ashtray, threw his pencil on his desk, and rubbed his face in his hands. He looked at Rink and said, "I think we need to put the pressure on the Coast Guard. They don't know about the bullets matching those of rifles in use by the Japanese military, and they must not have thought about the battery-separator business. And you haven't told them about the fabric you found on the beach." Red's phone rang and he didn't answer it; it kept ringing. When he finally picked up the phone, he listened briefly, then said, "Tell the son of a bitch he can't do that!" and hung up.

Rink thought, *What the hell was that? Best not ask.*

Red pondered the call for a minute and said, "What was I saying? Oh yes, I think that maybe you should round up some of the boys' parents and go see captain what's-his-name at the Coast Guard in Bandon. Be careful not to impugn the Bandon Coast Guard generally. They have an excellent reputation in the community. It is only this Captain Avery and apparently his boss at Coast Guard headquarters in Seattle who are stonewalling this matter. I guess the army is too, since they've all kept their mouths shut about it. The Bandon community has no idea what's going on with them or this case."

Rink agreed and returned to his desk. He made plans to get to Bandon as soon as some of his other work at the newspaper would permit. Writing articles about serious vehicle accidents, noteworthy lawsuits about important people, and buildings burning down were now a distraction.

Two days later, at the Williams house, Mary spoke up at dinner. "Mr. Rink from the newspaper called, and he'd like one of us to go with him to the Coast Guard station to talk with Captain Avery," she said, serving Joe more mashed potatoes. "He said he'd be calling the Harrises and Johnsons and Gleasons too, so we can all go in a group."

"Mary," Joe said, "I'm trying to wind things up before I leave for the navy, so why don't you go with him? If you don't want to do it, don't; it will be OK. I had hoped this whole business was behind us."

"You know, talking to Rink reminded me of something," Mary said. "Several days ago, Luke brought me a very interesting object that he must have found on the beach. Just a minute and I'll get it." She hurried from the table and returned with the folded black leather object, which she handed to Joe. George's attention was instantly focused on the black object.

Joe looked it over. The exterior was obviously black leather that had been wet, and it had some salt crystals on it. The leather was finely stitched together. Joe said, "My God, I think that's Japanese writing on the cover." He began to fiddle around with it and carefully tried to open it. Inside, he saw folded paper with printing and lines in color. The paper seemed to be a heavy paper, and it was still quite damp. One page could be separated from another page, but it wanted to open in two different directions, like a road map.

George excitedly arose from his chair and leaned over his father's back. "Mom, why didn't you show this to me? It's gotta be from those Japs in the raft! Good ole Luke."

Joe now had the leather case fully open and was trying to open the enclosed papers. When it was about half open, they could see that it was a highway map of Oregon. As Joe unfolded it, the paper started to dry out a little. Soon, Joe had the map fully open; it was the kind of map handed out for free at service stations. This particular map was issued by the Shell Oil Company. A close inspection of the map, which was written in English, showed a couple of pencil markings. One marking started at a point on the coast just south of Bandon and went from Highway 101 south of Bandon to Coquille; another penciled line went from Coquille to Marshfield. What seemed to be Japanese writing with an X appeared on the map at Coquille and at Marshfield.

"This is either terribly real and important, or it is nothing. If it is real, it may have something to do with the mills in those towns. What should we do with it?" Joe murmured.

"Come on, Dad, this has got to be something carried by those Japs that tried to come ashore. They musta dropped it overboard in their panic," George said.

Joe was careful not to argue with George and suggested that they find someone who could read Japanese, if that's what it was.

Mary suggested that they call Rink, who might have better information, and it was agreed that she call him in the morning. In the meantime, the map would continue to dry.

After dinner, George called Jason and told him about the map that Luke had dragged in. Shortly thereafter, Jason's father called, and Joe picked up. Mark asked if he could see the map, and Joe invited him over.

When Mark arrived, the Williams family was sitting around the living room anxious to hear and join in the conversation about Luke's find.

Examining the map, Mark asked, "Where did you say this map came from?"

"Luke, our dog, showed up with it a couple of days ago, and we think he found it on the beach," Mary said.

Mark looked over the black leather case that had enclosed the map, carefully examining the gold lettering on it. He thought the lettering was Japanese, but said they should find out for sure. Mark then told the Williams family about Rink's visit to his mill and the meeting he'd had with his manager, Smith, after Rink left. Smith had told him about Rink's supposition that the Japanese military may have had their sights on the battery-separator plants. "We thought there might be something to it, but with this map and the Japanese writing on it, there may be more to it than speculation."

The parents compared notes and learned that Rink had already called the Gleasons about accompanying him to the Coast Guard station. "Since it looks like I might be directly involved in his story, I figure I had better go with him. And I'd guess Robert Harris will want to, too, since he's got a similar stake in the matter."

After listening to the conversation between his parents and Mark Gleason about their suspicions and what Mr. Rink was thinking, George left the living room for the phone in the kitchen. He excitedly called David and told him the recent developments. He didn't care who heard him. David was excited, too, and proclaimed, "The Coast Guard is now gonna get theirs!" George hoped he was right.

Linus Rink received the phone call from Mary Williams the following morning. He was excited to see Luke's map; he wanted to have the writing on it and on the leather case translated. He just had to find a translator, since the few Japanese in the area had all been removed from the West Coast. He asked around and found a woman in Marshfield who was Chinese but had studied Japanese, so he immediately drove to Bandon, picked up the map, and took it to Tami Wing.

After careful inspection, Tami pronounced, "The lettering and writing is Japanese. The words on the leather case say 'Lieutenant Ushi Seiko,' and the writing on the map says 'battery-separator plant' at the mark on Coquille and at the mark on Marshfield."

Rink thanked Tami Wing, gave her five dollars, and left. He was both optimistic and concerned. The puzzle was now solved, but the confirmation of a plan for a covert military operation by the Japanese on the northwest shore, which could destroy a vital industry and kill many people, was not pleasant. He and the Bandon boys would have to convince the Coast Guard of the reality of the situation, and now he was primed to do that. All he needed was an appointment to see the patriotic but misguided Captain Avery and put the evidence before him. If the captain didn't respond appropriately, Rink would send a torpedo from his newspaper that would sink Avery and his superior's ship. One way or another, the boys would be redeemed and the beach would get its military patrols.

CHAPTER 15

AUGUST 1942

Kenji had landed, finally, back in Kure at the naval base. It was bustling with activity. Kenji had taken it upon himself to explore around the naval headquarters, and on occasion had walked onto the docks that were close by. One day, as he was headed to headquarters for a meeting, he walked into an unusual scene. There were people—men, women, and children—under heavy guard alighting from a ship. These people looked Asian, if not Japanese, in some respects. He asked one of the guards who they were.

The guard said, "These are prisoners taken from Adak and Attu in Alaska, the islands we took at the time we bombed Pearl Harbor in the Hawaiian Islands." These people were in tattered clothes, some fabric and some animal skins. It made no sense to Kenji. He headed on to his meeting.

The Japanese naval headquarters was built to the east of the shipyards. It was a three-story gray concrete building with small, square, uniform windows. Standing in the window of a small conference room, in full white uniform, was Lieutenant Commander Mikasi Nomuro, a veteran of the Japanese marine landings in Borneo and Bougainville.

He looked first to the northwest, where he could see seventeen armed naval vessels and support ships at anchor, then to the southwest, where ship after ship was under construction. Keels were being laid down, cranes were lifting turrets onto warships, and other new ships appeared ready for launching or their dry docks ready for flooding. When his eyes focused on a huge warship moored to a pier that extended far into the bay, he knew at once that it was the *Yamato*, the world's largest battleship. It had just been launched and was now being outfitted and supplied. He was standing on the grounds of the world's third-largest shipyard and in the headquarters of the world's second-largest navy.

He knew that Japan had attacked the United States of America for good reason, that the Japanese military would prevail, and that he would be a part of it. He had never underestimated his importance, and the meeting he was about to lead would be a demonstration of his military skills. Nevertheless, he was not exultant over this assignment. It was beneath his seasoned knowledge, and it seemed to be some sort of worthless foray engaging the use of a valuable ship, material, and supplies.

His job was to outline and order the strategic action for a five-man expedition to the West Coast of America to demolish some unessential lumber mill. There were two good things about it: the plan was not his, and he didn't have to go. It didn't matter. Japan would win the war it had started, and he would play a major role in it, missions like this notwithstanding.

A door opened and uniformed Japanese naval personnel entered. There were submarine naval officers; four noncommissioned sailors; Lieutenant Kenji Kosoki, a newly commissioned naval officer; a civilian; and one other naval officer. They had all been summoned by a high-ranking covert naval operations officer who was Nomuro's superior. Some milled around, taking in the powerful views from the windows, and some sat at the large conference table. A tall man in civilian dress took one of the many chairs against the windowed wall.

Nomuro remained standing and moved to one end of the large table. He introduced himself, then said in a lofty, forceful voice, "I am here to lay out and describe a covert naval operation that will occur on the West Coast of the United States of America. You will not mention the operation to anyone not in this room. It is an operation nearly identical to one set in motion about two months ago that failed. This operation will not fail. It will be an exclusive navy operation, and it will be planned and shaped in detail. Its blueprint will be marked on your minds."

He outlined the plan: five of these men would board an I-15 class submarine in Kure, supplied with an inflatable rubber raft, 440 kilograms of high explosives, personal handguns, and foodstuffs enough for ten to fourteen days on land. They would be put ashore for the purpose of destroying two battery-separator plants and would return to the point of shore entry to be taken aboard the submarine again. "For the benefit of you who are not in the submarine service, your submarine is *I-25* with a length of 1,168 meters and with a cruising range of over fourteen thousand miles. It can be replenished at sea if needed. You will not know your date of departure until the day you board that sub.

"I would now like to introduce to you Milo Sabonu. He has spent many years in the area you'll be entering, and he has been to each of the mills you are directed to attack. He knows how and where you must place your charges to inflict the most damage. He also knows the roads, rivers, and cover you must use for travel and concealment. Listen very carefully to what he will tell you. Being on foot in a foreign land is not easy. Your job would be difficult even on familiar ground, and you need every advantage that knowledge will give you."

Milo Sabonu rose and informed the group that he had been a buyer of Port Orford white cedar logs for several mill owners in Japan and that his job had taken him to the only place in the world where the white cedar grew. He explained the use of the white cedar wood in storage batteries and how every vehicle, airplane, and war vessel used the batteries.

A sailor raised his arm and said, "If they have all the cedar for battery use, then we must have developed a substitute for use in the batteries, and surely the Americans have done the same thing. So what's so important about these two mills that we are ordered to destroy?"

Lieutenant Commander Nomuro said, "We use the same cedar. Our mills have been importing the Port Orford white cedar logs for years, and we have enough of the logs stored in log rafts in our inland bays and ports to supply us with battery components for nine or ten years. We are developing a substitute, but it is not perfected. The Americans are doing the same thing, but they continue to rely heavily on the cedar separators. Manufacture of the separators is an essential industry to them and to us."

Milo Sabonu continued, "I am handing each of you a road map that I picked up at a Standard service station on my last trip. The Americans hand them out at no cost. Open the map. You can see I have marked a spot south of the town of Bandon and traced one line on the highway marked 101 to Bandon and then to a place on the Coquille River five miles upriver from Bandon. I have also traced a line on the highway marked 101 from the same point south of Bandon to the city of Coquille and, from there, to the city of Marshfield. It is my understanding that three of you will make your way to Marshfield, and two of you will make your way to Coquille."

Sabonu went on to describe the Smith Wood mill, making it sound particularly vulnerable. "The mill is of wood-frame construction, and there is little fire-suppression equipment in place. Once on fire, it will destroy itself. I haven't been there since the war started, but there were never any security personnel around the place, and, knowing the Americans, they believe they are isolated from the war. There probably isn't much security in place now." He also described the area around the Evans Products mill but couldn't give as much information on its destruction, choosing instead to leave that to the experts charged with the mission. "Any questions?"

Two or three tried to speak at one time, asking variations on: How do we get to these mills?

Nomuro stepped forward, then looked over the room and the faces staring at him. "Mr. Sabonu, I thank you for the most valuable information that you have given us; however, I must ask you to leave now."

After Sabonu left, Nomuro sat down and said, "There is a person in this room that you may not have met. The man sitting to my right is Lieutenant Kenji Kosoki. He was a cadet at Etajima when we interrupted his naval training and career and sent him behind enemy lines on the invasion of the Philippines. He operated there for more than three months, furnishing our army and navy with vital information on enemy troop movements and installations. He came face to face with the enemy on more than one occasion and survived each encounter—some in a most violent manner. He was a noncommissioned officer during that action, but after General Nakayama interviewed him at the time of the surrender of the American forces in the Philippines, the general recommended that the navy give Kosoki a commission, even though he had not completed his education at Etajima. And now, again, we have taken him from the naval academy for this special force operation on enemy shores. He is now Lieutenant Kosoki, the only lieutenant who is also a cadet in the Etajima naval academy. I learned of Kosoki's work when I was on the destroyer *Hamakaze*, which returned him from the Philippines to Etajima.

"Now, the question asked was: How do you get from the beach in Oregon to your objectives, the mills? By using these maps, your good sense, and your experience, you will plot a course—two of you to Coquille, three to Marshfield—on foot to the mills. You will stay clear of houses and other habitation and travel only by night. It may be necessary to steal a motorized fishing boat to reach the mill in Coquille, but you should try to avoid killing anyone, as a body will attract all sorts of attention. Silence and stealth are your friends; anything else is your nemesis."

Kenji stood and asked, "A motorized fishing boat. What are we talking about?"

Nomuro said, "Milo told me that he had seen them many times. They belong to the commercial fishermen. They are wood planked, usually about seven meters long, with an automobile engine for power and sometimes with a tiny cabin."

One of the recruits asked, "Should we not also take a car instead of going on foot?"

"Not to the Coquille mill," Kenji said, inspecting the map. "We can attack the mill only from the river. For the Marshfield mill, a car will be OK. You heard Milo tell you about the Coquille mill and the fact that it's supported off the ground on pilings. A motor vehicle approach is out of the question. An approach from the front without detection would be difficult, and even if it wasn't, we couldn't just walk in with our explosives and place them for detonation. The surest way to get under the mill is from the riverside. Besides, if you take a car, it will be missed, and if you take possession of it directly from the owner, you need to silence the owner, possibly creating more problems. The fewer cars taken, the better. The boat is the way; there is no other decent option.

"The mill in Marshfield seems a different matter," he continued. "If you follow this Highway 101, it will be approximately sixty-three kilometers, and for the last part of that route, you could take a car. Do so at night to be less visible, of course, and according to Milo, you will need a car to get into the Marshfield mill. It is actually in the town, and there are many cars going in and out and around the place all the time. You must give the Marshfield party time to arrive and determine how and where to set their explosives. We don't have many details on that mill. But each party should detonate their explosives at about the same time. If you do that, there will be no chance of a warning communication between the two mills. You can figure that out about the time you get to Coquille. There are many uncertainties here, and we must make the final details on the ground."

Nomuro then continued the briefing, giving general directions to both groups, but he left the plans of attack up to them to decide. "I don't want any suicidal attacks," Nomuro said. "I want you all to return. Your present experience, plus this new experience, will add up to an invaluable asset to the Japanese naval forces. But do not let yourself be captured. You will be wearing clothes recognizable as military uniforms, so if captured, you should not be shot as spies."

Nomuro moved over to the window, looked out for an instant, then turned back to the seated sailors. "A mission nearly identical to this one was initiated about six weeks ago, with army officers composing the landing party. Nothing came of it. We don't know what exactly happened. The officers and crew of the submarine that put them ashore heard and felt an explosion shortly after the raft was deployed and the sub had submerged. Our man in Portland, Oregon, reported only that the two mills were not attacked and they are still running. The army shore party was in full field dress uniform, and some even carried rifles." He shook his head at this ridiculous lack of planning. "You will not be in dress uniforms but uniforms that will make it difficult to see you in Oregon's green landscape. I don't need to say any more. You can draw your own conclusions."

The lieutenant commander walked back over to the conference table and said, "There is one more thing you must know. We are putting you ashore in exactly the same spot that the previous expedition went ashore. We are doing this for the simple reason that this particular beach area is still not patrolled. It is isolated and as close to the target mills as we can get you. The ocean has good depth at this point, almost to the shoreline. If the Americans do know that we came ashore at that place, they will never believe that we would be so stupid as to try it again in the exact same place. That's where they are wrong. We are not stupid, and they will make a huge mistake by thinking we are!

"Again, I want to emphasize: If you encounter anyone on your beach landing, you are to quickly and permanently dispose of them. If you have any questions about materials and supplies, ask Lieutenant Kosoki. You will be notified of your boarding time in due course. That is all. You are dismissed."

They all exited into the wide corridor. Kenji could hear the other sailors were brimming with questions.

"They're taking us halfway around the world and dumping us on a beach in the United States. How can it work?"

"They'll never come and get us."

"I've never been on a sub. Is it as awful as some say it is?"

"Why don't we just bomb those mills?"

Kenji decided to answer what he could. "We will do what we are ordered to do and make every effort to do it the best way we know. I've been on a submarine and a warship, and you will like it better than living by your wits on land in the midst of your enemy."

Kenji stepped in front of the sailor who doubted they'd be picked up after their task was complete. "If you are worried about not returning for any reason, get out of this unit now. If you think you're a born hero, get out now. I want no hesitancy and no heroics. We have work to do, and that's it."

Grading separators. Image from Coos Historical and Maritime Museum.

Battery separator manufacturing. Image from Coos Historical and Maritime Museum.

Coos Bay, Oregon. Image from Coos Historical and Maritime Museum.

Packaging separators. Image from Coos Historical and Maritime Museum.

Image from Coos Historical and Maritime Museum.

Smith Wood aerial view. Image from Coquille Valley Museum.

CHAPTER 16

AUGUST 1942

Coast Guard Seaman Ronald Freeman and apprentice Seaman Sam Gibson drove down the long driveway to the Williamses' residence and parked the new Coast Guard jeep near an outbuilding. Mary Williams, standing on the porch, greeted them. She was surprised but also happy to see that the Coast Guard was possibly taking an interest in what had happened to her son and his friends.

After introducing themselves, Sam asked, "Is it alright if we park there while we take a walk to the beach?"

"Sure," she said. "Mind telling me what you're doing? I think you are the first coastguardsmen to be on our beach."

"Captain Avery sent us down here to walk the beach to the south for a couple of miles to see if we could find anything unusual," Ronald said.

"You may as well know," Mary said, "one of those boys was my son, George, and my husband and I have no reason to doubt his word. I hope you find something that will convince your superiors that my boy is telling the truth."

Sam said, "I hope we do too, ma'am."

The two seamen hurried to the beach trail. Ron, sounding annoyed and a little distressed, said, "You know, Captain Avery instructed me, in case we found something of interest, not to say anything to anyone about it and to report directly to him on our return. I don't get it. The truth is the truth, and I don't like keeping something to myself if it hurts someone else."

"Yeah, but orders are orders, and we'll follow 'em," Sam said.

When they reached the beach, they headed south, kicking junk on the sand as they progressed. Sam saw a round, greenish object rolling up on the beach with each little wave and then rolling back into the water. He ran after it. It was a glass ball. He had never seen one; both men were originally from Kansas. "Suppose this is what the captain is lookin' for?" he asked.

"Beats the hell out of me," Ron said.

Sam carefully placed the glass ball high on the beach and planned to pick it up on the way back to the jeep.

They paused to look up and down the beach. It was desolate, not another person in sight. There were old and new, large and small pieces of trees high on the beach. Some were half buried in the sand, some were not, and one large tree without limbs but with the root wad still attached was stuck partially in and partially out of the surf. A thick growth of shore pines, salal, alder, and other brush arose behind the slight foredune. Coarse faded-green grass covered the land side of the foredunes and extended a short distance to the tree and brush line.

It was an unusually pleasant day for August without the wind. The captain had given them specific instructions to look for a Sitka spruce windfall and then inspect the area around it. They continued south about three miles before they decided to turn back.

"What the hell is a Sitka spruce, anyway?" Sam asked. "And how would we see it around all those trees?"

"I don't know," Ron confessed. "Guess we should have asked the captain for more details. But I suppose it's a good idea to walk a little closer to the tree line."

After walking a ways, they saw a massive bunch of tree roots standing on edge. As they came closer, they found a huge tree lying flat on the ground in the brush.

"Maybe this is it," Sam said. "It's the biggest damn tree I've ever seen anyway."

Figuring they'd reached their goal, they walked over to the area where the dune grasses met the clear sand of the beach, then strolled around, kicking the sand and any object sticking out of the sand.

"Nothing but a little junk," Sam said.

"Yeah, but wait," Ron said. "Look at this." He pointed to some empty brass from two or three different types of rifle cartridges. He picked up all the brass he could find and put it in his pocket.

Sam was standing and watching Ron when they both noticed what appeared to be a segment of canvas-like cloth partially buried on the wet beach. "Well, looky here," Ron said, pulling a piece of black rubberized fabric from the sand. It was roughly seven or eight inches square, and it had writing on it. He could see some kind of marks that looked Japanese or Chinese.

Ron said, "Could be from a rubber raft, maybe a Jap landing raft."

Sam put it in his pocket. They searched the area for anything else unusual and found nothing. They returned to the jeep at the Williamses' with the glass ball.

Sam said, "I hope Avery is satisfied with what we found, which is almost nothing."

As they were getting into the open, gray-painted jeep, Mrs. Williams came out of the house.

"Find anything worth mentioning?" she asked.

Sam replied, "This is the only thing we found." He held up the glass ball. The men started the jeep and left.

Twenty minutes later, they parked on the concrete apron at the east end of the Coast Guard station and walked upstairs to Captain Avery's office.

Standing in the hallway outside the door, Ron said in a low voice, "You know a captain is one grade below a rear admiral in the Coast Guard, so this business with the boys and their Japs must be pretty important for them to send a guy down here that's almost an admiral."

"On the other hand, what's so goddamned important about a kid's story unless they think there's something to it?" Sam asked. "Anyway, let's go in and tell him what we came up with."

Ron knocked, and the men were invited in.

Sitting at his desk in the corner office, Avery asked, "You find anything?"

Sam produced the glass float. "That's the most interesting thing," he said.

Avery shook his head and said, "These things are found all up and down the coasts of Washington and Oregon. Did you find anything else?"

Ron took the shell casings out of his pocket and put them on the desk in front of him, and Sam did the same with the rubberized fabric. "We found these on the beach too," Ron said.

Avery examined the lettering on the face of the brass. "This is all American brass." Then he picked up the fabric and bullets and examined them. "Thanks, boys. Did you find anything else?"

"No."

"Dismissed."

While Ron and Sam were leaving, Sam said, "We know that fabric is from a rubber raft. It has that lettering on it, and it supports the boys' story. Let's go back and tell Avery what we think."

"Forget it," Ron said. "Chow's almost ready. Let's go eat."

As soon as the seamen left his office, Captain Avery made two calls: to the rear admiral in charge of his Coast Guard District 13, and to the office of General DeWitt, the commanding general of the Western Defense Command. He told both executive officers about the empty shell casings and the black rubberized fabric with the lettering on it, as well as about the rumors he had been hearing about a regional newspaper's interest in the case. He took care to remind them of the Japanese naval activity on the West Coast and that maybe the boy Henry had been shot by a Japanese landing party.

Seattle headquarters told him to ignore it, but Western Defense Command said they'd immediately send an army officer to Bandon, though they wouldn't say for what reason. General DeWitt was still firm in keeping a lid on the incident at Bandon.

A few days later, Linus Rink was back on Highway 101 driving to Bandon. He had arranged to meet with the captain today. Some of the boys' parents would be there also, and Avery had said Major Allen

Carlock from the Western Defense Command in San Francisco would be present. It was a long, narrow, crooked highway. He wished this whole thing had happened in the Marshfield area.

When he pulled up in front of the station, the boys were already there, as well as their fathers; only George's father wouldn't be joining them, but his mother was there. They met Captain Avery and Major Carlock in the station's recreation room. It had a wonderful view of the Coquille River entrance to the Pacific Ocean and the coastline for miles to the north, but today wasn't a day to enjoy the view.

Rink introduced himself to the two officers, and then he introduced the boys and their parents. "I want you to know up front, I'm ready to print a story about the boys' adventure on the beach with the Japanese," he started.

Major Carlock interrupted. "Well, we can't have that!"

Rink sized up Carlock as a blustery man lacking leadership sense. "If I may continue," Rink said, "we have a situation that you, the military, have basically ignored, probably hoping that it would go away. The problem has been exacerbated by your apparent refusal to apprise yourselves of the facts of the case."

The boys looked at each other, and smiles crossed their young faces.

"Now just a minute—"

Rink held up his hand. "Major, don't interrupt me." Though not prone to confrontation, Rink could be aggressive when needed. "We have all afternoon for you to say what you think you have to say. When I finish, you will have plenty to respond to, thus giving each of us an opportunity for an orderly, cogent presentation."

Mark Gleason, looking at Avery and then Carlock, said, "Look, we're here to see that the right thing is done for our boys and to make certain that you understand what happened."

Rink continued laying out his case, including the boys' account of what happened, Dr. Rankin's statement about Henry's wounds, the witnesses to the sound of an explosion, the recovered pieces of fabric and the Arisaka-type rifle bullets recovered from the beach, and finally the map holder and map.

"Gentlemen, based on what I've just laid before you, and since nearly everyone present is vitally involved in the story and anxious to have your response, could you, Major Carlock, and you, Captain Avery, tell us your response now?"

"Mr. Rink, I insist that you not publish any story on this matter," Major Carlock said.

George's mother gasped and blurted out, "My God, he doesn't get it, does he?"

"Why, Major Carlock, you can't order me to do anything," Rink said. "My story, minus the events of this conference, is ready for publication, all with the blessings of my editor and publisher. If you even look like you might try to obtain some official order from your superiors blocking publication, a phone call from me will put the story in today's edition, and when tomorrow's edition is printed, it will contain a near-verbatim account of what was said and done here today—and your idiotic request not to publish."

Major Carlock's face turned red, and he looked to Avery for help.

Rink looked at Avery, too, and quietly said to him, "You're standing in the same bucket of shit as the major, but none of us here wants to impugn or blemish the otherwise excellent reputation of the Bandon Coast Guard. Transferring Master Chief Petty Officer Art Spears was a gross error by you and your vice admiral Barkley, but the community knows nothing about what you have done or not done about this case. You're shorthanded and we know it. And as far as we are concerned, that is the way we'll leave it." Rink was guessing about the mechanics of Spears's transfer, but he knew the rest was true. "Of course the major here and his superiors don't know jack shit about what's going on up here because they turned their heads and refused to investigate. They should be blamed for not investigating an obvious hole in their defense of the West Coast."

"We need time," Avery said. "We need to review this information. Trust me, though, we'll give you a response tomorrow."

Rink shook his head. "The problem is, I don't trust either one of you. Your superiors can order you to do the opposite of what you may agree to," he said. "But if I have your promise in writing not to do anything that would interfere with the publication of my story, then I can withhold publication for a day or so to give you an opportunity to put together your written statement to be published with my story. This way, you have time to come to your senses, we will affirm the truth of these boys' stories, and the populace will be on guard for any future incursion by the Japanese."

Mark Gleason offered that he was the man in charge of the battery-separator plant in Coquille and that he was eager for his security personnel to know what had happened down here. "And I'll tell you, the general manager of the Coquille plant has seen that map too, and I've already told the manager of Evans Products."

Avery looked at Carlock, thought about his vice admiral's initial response, and said, "That should've been our job."

While Mark was talking, Rink drafted an agreement on his yellow pad for Avery and Carlock to sign. When finished, he shoved it in front of Avery, who sat bolt upright in his chair.

"Don't be alarmed," Rink said. "When your superiors know what actually happened here and have all the evidence of it as well as the reaction of the battery-separator mill personnel, they will commend you for your decisive action." Rink shoved a pen at him, and Avery signed and dated the agreement.

Though he hesitated, Carlock seemed to see no help in the room. He signed and dated the form, too, looking resigned. After having a Coast Guard typist make a copy for their own records, the men departed.

Outside on the sidewalk with Rink, the boys and their parents agreed that the meeting had gone well, and Rink was thanked. The boys were exultant, believing the truth would finally be told—and in the newspapers.

They did not realize, nor did anyone else, that it would become national news.

Two days later, at nine a.m. sharp, a gray military jeep pulled up and parked in front of the *Coos Bay Times* building. A coastguardsman stepped onto the sidewalk with a brown envelope in hand, walked into the paper's front office, and handed the envelope to the receptionist. "This is for Mr. Linus Rink."

That evening, the lead story was headlined, "Bandon Boys Stop Japanese Landing on Bandon Beach," and the full story was finally recounted. Contained in the body of the article was the statement from the US Coast Guard, Bandon station:

The United States Coast Guard, with the assistance of its headquarters office in Seattle, Washington, has, following an extensive investigation involving the interview of numerous persons and the collection of considerable hard evidence, determined that, in fact, the Japanese attempted landing a small party of soldiers on a beach south of Bandon. Four Bandon teenagers witnessed a submarine launch a raft containing four soldiers. Shots were exchanged and the raft exploded, killing the four aboard. One boy received a gunshot wound but survived. The Coast Guard asks that all residents along the coast and near the beaches continue to be vigilant. Within the next seven months, the number of personnel at the Bandon station will increase substantially, and dog and horse patrols of the beaches will commence.

By the next day, David, Henry, George, and Jason were having difficulty deciding whether they liked the situation better with folks not believing them and questioning them or with everyone telling them how wonderful they were. Nearly every word of congratulations or praise included a request for a private account of what had occurred, with frequent interruptions for more exact and precise details. Some people even wanted to know what the boys would have done if confronted by the landing party already ashore.

"So what's a guy to do, go glass ball hunting every day from dawn to dusk to avoid people and their questions?" Henry asked one afternoon when the boys had met at the confectionery for milkshakes.

"It'll die down," Jason said. "Soon, it'll just be back to normal."

"Well, the bastards are still not patrolling the beach," George said. "So for a while anyway, we can still look for glass floats and do a little patrolling while we're at it."

"Might as well kill some time on the beach," David said. "School will be starting September first, only a couple of weeks away."

"Jeez, David, don't go mentioning school. You'll wreck my day," George said. "Up until a day or so ago, we've all had an awful summer, and now you want to remind us that school is about to start and ruin the rest of it! Just keep that bullshit to yourself, thank you!"

For a few minutes, they stayed busy sucking on straws to capture the last drops in their milkshake glasses. Then George said, "So my dad's leaving for the navy tonight on the five p.m. Greyhound bus to San Francisco. It'll be at least six months before we see him again."

No wonder he's in a bad mood, David thought. "Sorry, George," he said.

"He'll be safer there than in the army or anything, at least," Henry said, and Jason agreed.

George wasn't appeased and got up to leave, still brooding about his father's planned absence. He wanted to head home to be with his family for the last few hours before his father boarded the bus. The others rose too.

When they walked out of the confectionery store, Henry headed home, while Jason and David started for the hardware store to see if there were any new guns. They'd made no definite plans to meet at the beach anytime soon, but in each of their minds, they knew that with a phone call or two, the beach patrol would resume.

David thought, *There are still glass balls to find and sell, and besides, the beach patrol is our job, and we're good at it.* All of the boys assumed that the Japanese would never try another landing, particularly on their beach.

Jason and David walked up to the gun counter in the hardware store. Immediately two of the store's customers, mill workers in their fifties, came to them. The boys knew them but not their names.

The one with the dirty baseball cap said, "You know we're all proud of you boys. A bunch of the fellows at the mill wish they'd been there to help with the shooting. We're all happy that the Johnson boy is OK."

The other man said, "You gonna keep patrolling the beach?"

David replied, "I think so. The Coast Guard isn't ready yet."

The men asked a few more questions and then left. After a little more browsing, David and Jason soon headed home.

CHAPTER 17

AUGUST 8, 1942

Kenji Kosoki lay flat on his back on his assigned bunk. In six days, they would be standing on the Oregon coast of the mainland of the United States of America.

Ten days ago, the call had come to board *I-25*, and he and four veterans of the Japanese Special Naval Landing Forces had gathered at one of the Kure submarine piers, dressed in a greener version of the Imperial Japanese Army uniforms but with a navy anchor on their caps. While they waited for permission to board, they had watched in surprise as a crane loaded torpedoes into *I-25*. They hadn't heard about any other operations or missions.

They asked the warrant officer overseeing the loading operation what was going on. He looked them over and wanted to know who they were and what were they doing there.

"We've been ordered to board *I-25*," Kenji said.

"Oh yes, we've been expecting you," the officer said. "As soon as these torpedoes are aboard and secure, you may board. Have any of you ever been aboard a sub?"

"No," said one of the other navy men, "which is why we were wondering about those torpedoes."

"All I can tell you," the officer said, sounding pleased, "is that if the captain gets a chance, he'll use them."

Kenji sensed that the warrant officer was very proud of his rank and present task. He thought he could get more information from him. "I had no idea torpedoes were so large," he said.

"Of course," the officer said. The torpedoes, he told Kenji, were Type 95, the best torpedoes available to date, and the only ones that used oxygen to burn kerosene for propulsion, giving them three times the range of their Allied counterparts. It also reduced their wake, making them harder to notice and avoid. The Type 95 had, by far, the largest warhead of any submarine torpedo.

As Kenji lay on his bunk, he thought about how different *I-25* was from the destroyer *Hamakaze*. The talkative warrant officer had informed him that nearly all Japanese submarines were larger and speedier and had much greater cruising ranges than the submarines of any other nation, though their hulls were not as strong as their German counterparts and they could not dive as deeply or survive such rough treatment.

Though *I-25* was a huge submarine by world standards, its crew of ninety-seven made for cramped quarters, and the lack of clean bedding made things even worse. Exercise for Kenji and his troop of four was essential, and as the ranking officer, he required twice-daily calisthenics. Open spaces in passageways accommodated this exercise routine, but once complete, the men had nothing else to do—and no way to clean up. The more time spent in the submarine, the greater the stink and the more Kenji longed to be off the sub.

The sound and the barely noticeable vibration of the submarine's engines had, at first, kept Kenji awake; now they were like an anesthetic to him. As he was falling asleep, he again thought about his family in Ōtsu. They were probably fishing the early part of the salmon run. Who had they found to take his place? There were barely enough family members, even with him present, to work the gill nets. Maybe he would have been better off not to have joined the navy, but alas, he would have been drafted anyway. These thoughts kept creeping into his mind. He had joined the navy to live and fight on a warship. It wasn't happening. He was fighting land battles, and tiny ones at that. He had been promised a return to Etajima after the Philippine venture, but here he was again going ashore from the deck of a submarine. *Maybe,* he thought, *I should not be so proficient with my onshore work.*

But the war couldn't last forever, he reasoned, and he would eventually get home. He might even stay home if his career in the navy didn't place him aboard a warship, but, of course, the navy would not allow it until the war was over.

The next day, Kenji and his colleagues were invited to the officer's galley to enjoy lunch with Captain Hiro Toshi, the veteran commander of *I-25.* He had taken the sub to the fleet for the Pearl Harbor attack, and now he was en route to the West Coast of the United States to patrol the area from San Francisco to the Columbia River.

They sat down to a lunch of rice and canned salmon. Kenji wondered where the salmon came from.

Captain Toshi was formal but friendly. "Did you notice the hangar just forward of our conning tower?" Toshi asked as the men ate. "There's a floatplane housed in it. We did reconnaissance flights over Kodiak Island in Alaska in support of an attack and invasion near Dutch Harbor in the western Aleutian Islands. From there, we sailed southerly along the Alexander Archipelago to the coast of Washington State where, in June, we attacked a freighter, and on the next day, we shelled a fort near the Columbia River. On the way back to our base in Yokosuka, we sank a US submarine that was surfaced in broad daylight."

Captain Toshi was obviously proud of his achievements, and Kenji was impressed. Still, Kenji did not like the submarine service, and he knew his colleagues didn't either. Though they were sitting at ease, Kenji could tell they all felt trapped. He wanted to be on the surface, always. The tiny galley where they were meeting was adequate, but the light was poor and all the walls were gray. He wondered why they hadn't painted the interiors white at least.

Kenji said, "We have been on this sub a long time. Surely you came across ships that you could have torpedoed. Why didn't you?"

"I'll tell you why. The main reason I called you here for lunch is to tell you that our first mission is to put you ashore. We are under orders not to engage in any action whatsoever, except self-defense, that would betray our presence in US waters. As you know or may have guessed, it was *I-25* that put the other unsuccessful party ashore. No one seems to know what happened, but after we launched the raft, we immediately left for the open sea. About the time we were fully submerged, we thought we heard and felt an explosion of some kind.

"We intend to put you ashore in the same place because the ocean is quite deep almost to the shore and there is a lighthouse just south of the spot that aids in navigation. We also believe, as you probably have been told, the Americans will never suspect we would come ashore in the exact same place.

"We would like to put you ashore in the dark, and we will do so if the weather permits. We can even wait for good weather by resting this sub on the ocean floor, but for a limited time only. I notice that we stowed almost four hundred kilograms of your high explosives; you must be especially careful in the raft. An accidental discharge of a sidearm could be lethal, and so could the mishandling of your detonators. Do any of you have any questions?"

"What will happen if the weather is bad? Can you get us close to shore or what?" asked Hideke Sato, Kenji's partner in the Smith Wood separator plant operation.

Toshi said, "I can't say for certain what we will do, but I will tell you this: We will get you ashore as safely as we can and in the designated spot. Your raft is large enough to get you onshore with your materials even in thirty-knot winds and five-foot seas. If we set you off under those conditions, we will not do so in darkness but instead at dawn's first light or at dusk. It is unlikely that anyone will be on the beach under those conditions. If the surf is heavier and the winds stronger, we will wait it out by surfacing at night to charge our batteries and rest on the ocean floor during the day until the weather improves."

Kenji wanted the mission to go as planned, even though his belief in the validity of the project was lacking. The target was so far away from Japan, and his party so small, and his sparse amount of equipment and questionable transportation to the mill were handicaps. His melancholy carried into his voice as he spoke. "I wish we knew much more about the land and terrain, the vegetation, the wild animals if any, outlying houses, secondary roads, and the routines of the people that we do not want to encounter. I know that what we've been ordered to do may sound simple, but nothing like this is simple, especially when dozens of questions must go unanswered."

Captain Toshi said, "I suppose if four or five thousand troops were involved, we'd know the answers to all those questions. This operation involves five men who might be considered expendable."

Kenji looked for any reaction on his colleague's faces and found none. "I think all of us came to that conclusion some time ago," he said. "We were not asked to volunteer for this mission, suicide or not—we were ordered to do so. But we have all vowed to return to this sub, and we intend to keep that solemn promise. We fully expect you, Captain, to be here for us." He met the man's eyes. "Please don't get this submarine in any trouble in our absence."

Toshi appeared mildly affronted by Kenji's declaration and frowned at Kenji, but he didn't seem to be annoyed by it, and the men parted company on amiable terms. Kenji and his landing-force friends returned to their bunks and their boredom.

CHAPTER 18

MID-AUGUST 1942

David, George, Jason, and Henry had spent substantial time with their families since the Linus Rink newspaper article was published. Their notoriety around town had been more than fleeting, but it was finally fading away, as was the event that spawned the story and the foolishness that followed. Now the beach patrol that mainly concerned the boys was the search for Japanese glass floats. That is what they talked about, but beneath it all, they each clung to the belief that guarding the beach was a good thing to do. They still carried their rifles, but only because there was always the possibility of shooting a sea lion, seal, or cormorant from the surface of the ocean. Sea lion scalps were still worth three dollars apiece.

Lying beneath the surface in each boy's mind was the fact that the Japs had come to the boys' beach and there was nothing to stop them from coming again. And if they did come again, would simply seeing them put the boys to flight? Would they stand their ground? Just what would they do? George had, from time to time since their encounter, urged the continuation of their patrols. Even through all the questioning and explanations, they managed to make numerous patrols, some with help from other classmates.·

The Linus Rink newspaper story had caused the Coast Guard to increase its pleas for more personnel and equipment, mostly for beach patrol, but to date, nothing had arrived except a few additional personnel. The beaches were still basically unpatrolled. A true patrol would mean continuous patrol twenty-four hours per day seven days per week.

The boys had decided to get together this day because there wasn't much else to do, and no one else was really guarding or patrolling the beaches. The weather had settled down after a stout west wind that might have brought some Japanese floats to shore. They all biked to George's place, as usual, with their rifles in slings, or in Jason's case, held crossways on his handlebars. No one who saw them ride by seemed to give them even a second glance.

They started their search late in the afternoon because the wind had died that morning and the tide would be receding, possibly leaving a few glass balls high and dry. They had walked this beach innumerable times, as had Luke, who was far ahead of everyone, busily sniffing everything sniffable.

When the boys passed the place of Henry's wounding and the death of the Japanese soldiers, David said, "I guess we made this place famous, but no one really knows exactly where it is."

"People came to our house and wanted us to bring them here," George said, "but we wouldn't do it."

Jason told the others that a coastguardsman had talked to him and told him that he and a coworker had found a piece of black rubberized fabric with some Japanese or Chinese lettering on it down here someplace, and that they had turned it over to Captain Avery. "The guy's name was Ron Freeman, and he told me that they had given the fabric to Captain Avery a couple of days before the newspaper article was published."

"Wonder if that had anything to do with the way Captain Avery and the army major caved so easily," David said.

"Well, it couldn't have hurt anything."

They walked another mile or so before heading back. As they passed the site again, Henry said, "Let's stop here and rest. I know it's getting late, but I told my mom I might be late."

They all sat down and reclined on the steeply sloping side of the little sand dune. The sun was starting to gather a little red on the horizon.

Jason said, "You know, guys, this is really crazy. I'm resting here thinking about another sub surfacing and unloading another raft with guys in it. What the hell's the matter with me?"

"You're nuts, and I must be nuts, because I'm thinking the same thing."

George agreed. "I've known you were nuts all along, and finally you guys admitted it!"

"We'll all remember that day as long as we live," David said, "and I doubt that anything that important will ever again happen in our lives. To realize that we killed some guys, even though they were Japs, and even though it might have been an accident that they blew up that way, is something we won't forget." The sun sank lower and became redder, and the sky dimmed. "We should get the hell out of here," David said. No one moved.

The fifteenth day of the voyage of *I-25* was nearing an end, and Kenji and his crew were all talking about how difficult life must be for the submariner. They were commiserating with the galley crew when the captain ordered all hands to their surfacing stations. Submariners were hurrying fore and aft to their positions when the captain ordered Kenji and his men to stand by. He spoke over the intercom and announced that they were standing off the shore of the state of Oregon, that it was eight p.m., and that they were going to surface to check on the weather conditions. If favorable, they would approach the shore.

Kenji ordered his men to prepare to land, and they gathered their things.

When Kenji and his men appeared in the control room, Captain Toshi told them the tide and weather conditions were perfect, but there was still some daylight. "I have looked through the periscope. The beach appears deserted," the captain said. He told Kenji and his men that the risk of detection was greater even in the dimming light, but because they would have some light to navigate by, it would be much safer getting through the surf. "Being thrown out of a broaching raft in the surf very far from shore could mean death in the near-freezing water." This was what the captain thought would be his final word on the subject.

Kenji agreed with this. He'd experienced a broaching craft several times before, being caught coming ashore with a skiff full of salmon. The ocean was the same temperature at Ōtsu as it was here, he knew from the briefings at Kure, and too cold to survive for long. But he still thought darkness provided necessary protection. "I thought my men and I were going ashore in the dark. It is only hour 2000 and still daylight."

Toshi said, "We are precisely where we should be, and we don't have the depth beneath the keel that we had two months ago. Bottom sands shift close to shore. The tide is on the ebb, and it's not getting any better. If we wait until dark, we will be too far from land, and we will increase the risk of detection of my ship. The surf conditions are excellent, and you'll make it."

Kenji agreed with the captain's plan, and the captain ordered the crew to surface *I-25*. When Kenji heard the order to surface, the hackles on his neck rose. He thought, *Now it starts, but who knows how it ends?*

Shortly thereafter, the captain and several officers scrambled up the conning tower ladder, opened the hatch, and stood on the deck searching in all directions through their binoculars. Kenji followed and found the scene just as empty as the captain had said.

They climbed back into the sub, and the captain ordered the deck crew to inflate and ready the raft. Kenji directed his crew to gather their supplies, and soon, they were on deck near the raft loading their equipment and supplies aboard it. The low profile of the submarine provided secrecy from the shore or surface vessels while they loaded. "With the sun low in the sky behind us," the captain said, "a person standing on the shore a thousand yards distant would, with the naked eye, have great difficulty, if not total inability, to see our submarine without powerful magnification."

CHAPTER 19

AUGUST 14, 1942

David was lying on his stomach on the back of the little sand dune, trying to get a bead on a very active sea lion just beyond the surf. He wasn't about to waste a cartridge, and he was waiting until the animal surfaced in the trough between waves and stopped bobbing up and down and was otherwise holding steady before he squeezed off a round. The sea lion would not cooperate, though, so he looked for another target.

Henry was urging them to leave. "Come on, button it up. It's going to be getting dark."

David didn't answer. Instead, he fixed his aim on something. "Jeez Christ, look out there," he said, voice anxious and excited. "It's another fucking sub. Those bastards are at it again!"

"You're shittin' us, David," Henry said. "Let's go."

"No! Those fuckin' Japs are coming here again! Look!"

They all threw their rifles to their shoulders and looked through their sights. Then they knew. Sure as hell, the Japanese were there again.

"What the hell are we going to do?" George yelled.

"Let's beat it the hell out of here and get help," Henry stammered.

David took charge. "Henry, you were shot once doing this, so you run for help. The rest of us will stay here and do what we did last time. Jason, George, you got that?"

Jason and George looked at one another and agreed to stay. David's father and Jason's father both worked in the same separator plant that the other Japanese landing party had wanted to destroy, and George's father was in the navy, so they had every reason in the world to stay.

Henry left on a dead run, keeping as low and as concealed as he could. He knew that his friends needed to surprise this shore party as they had the other.

"This is unbelievable. It can't be happening to us again. Are we stupid or are they stupid?" George spoke without realizing it.

David opened the breech of his rifle to make certain there was a shell in the chamber, then urged his friends to do the same and to make sure their magazines were full. They each again looked at the sub through their sights. The sun was directly behind the higher structures on the sub, shielding the rays from the boys' position, but they could make out the rising sun flag painted on the conning tower and the marking *I-25*. Their telescopic sights gathered light, making the flag and the lettering plainly visible.

"My God," George said, "that's the same friggin' sub that was here before. You don't suppose they're going to try the same stuff again?"

David, in the sternest voice a fifteen-year-old could muster, said, "Now listen to me, if they come in here, and it looks that way, we cannot miss on the first shot. If they get in close, we'll each pick out a target so that we're not shooting the same son of a bitch. By the time they get in here, Henry should have help on the way. George, are you OK? Jason, are you OK?" David asked.

"We're OK," they responded.

"Stay down and we'll give 'em hell to pay."

Most of the crew had left the submarine's deck, but a few officers, including the captain, were scanning the shore with their binoculars. "We see nothing," the captain told Kenji. The raft was alongside in the water with all equipment in it. Kenji and his men slipped aboard and headed for the beach. Kenji was the last man in the raft. He and the captain saluted. The men paddled a safe distance from the sub, and soon, the *I-25* used its twin screws to turn ninety degrees seaward and headed due west in a slow submerging mode. The landing party was alone.

Two separate inflatable rubber tubes formed the entire raft. If one tube lost air, its occupants could still cling to the other tube. Kenji sat on the front of the raft's right tube and positioned Hideke Sato on the front left tube, with the others behind them. All five had paddles, and they began the slow, awkward trip to shore. Kenji had handled many a wooden skiff under similar conditions, but never a raft. He cautioned his crew they would have to keep the raft perpendicular to shore to prevent a wave from tipping it over. The action of the surf was greater than he'd anticipated. It would test their skill, but it still looked feasible. Kenji wouldn't want to try this in truly rough surf.

With the sun at their backs, they came nearer and nearer to the breaking surf, which was fairly close to shore, and Kenji could see that they might have trouble with the raft. The seaward end of the raft had to be held back to prevent a breaking wave from shoving it around ahead of the front end of the raft. He would have to do this himself. He waited until they were close to shore, knowing that the water was frigid and guessing he couldn't last more than ten minutes in it.

"Watch me," he ordered Hideke as they came near to the shore, "and do just as I do."

Kenji slipped over his side of the raft, grasping the perimeter rope attached to the raft, and eased himself to the rear. Hideke did the same thing, and at the rear of the raft, they acted as sea anchors holding the rear seaward where it belonged. Soon, they'd be safe on land.

The boys could now see the raft and its paddling occupants. George had made Luke stay down behind him. Luke, an experienced hunter, knew how to do that. The sun had nearly passed out of sight, but their rifle scopes still gave them visibility. The boys had carefully concealed themselves, but now they emerged in prone positions just above the grassy edge of the little sand dune. They brought their rifles to bear.

David quietly said, "There are only three in that raft. Jason, you take the guy on the left; George, you take the guy in the middle. I'll take the guy on the right."

Jason, in a subdued voice, said, "These guys look different—more like they know what they're doing."

Kenji's and Hideke's feet were touching the sandy sea bottom behind the raft. "Shove," Kenji ordered, and they started to push the raft ashore. Over the sound of the surf, they heard gunfire on the beach. Ahead of them, all three men in the raft collapsed. One of them called out something indistinguishable as he fell. Then nothing else was heard from inside the raft.

Kenji shuddered in the cold. The men in the raft had obviously been killed. Someone onshore was a deadly shot. He didn't want to die here. He had seen death this close up before, but Hideke hadn't, and he was now next to Kenji, babbling incomprehensively and shaking in cold and fear. Kenji grabbed Hideke with his left hand and shook him until Hideke focused. They had to move.

Kenji told Hideke that they must immediately move down the surf line with only their heads out of the water. They kept their bodies in the choppy surf, and soon, they had distanced themselves from the raft. It was dark enough now that they could creep from the frigid water. They needed to move to the vegetation line so that they would be concealed in the trees. Kenji spotted a large piece of driftwood mired in the sand halfway to the vegetation line and decided to use it as a hiding place. He darted to the drift log. It had a huge root wad attached to it, which concealed him well. When he saw one person and then two more appear to be carefully walking to the raft, he signaled Hideke to stay down. Hideke looked freezing in his wet clothes as he lay in the frothy surf, and Kenji was nearly as cold.

David cautiously walked to the silent raft with his rifle to his shoulder. Jason and George were close behind him. Still wary of what he was about to confront and grasping the fact that there was probably no life in the raft, he edged his rifle barrel over the raft before looking in himself. He saw three men lying in a huge amount of bloody water, which sloshed as each little wave passed under its rubber bottom.

"Jeez, this is awful," George said, gasping.

"Yeah. And what the shit are we going to do with them?" Jason asked.

David said, "We're doing nothing with them. Grab that rope on the side of the raft, and we'll pull this mother up on the beach and leave."

"This is the worst thing I've ever seen," George said, turning away. "I think I'm gonna be sick." He dropped to his hands and knees and started to gag, but it was a dry heave.

Jason put his hand on George's back. "It's an awful sight," he agreed.

"I don't blame you for feeling sick," David said, "but just grab the rope on the raft and help me pull it up away from the ocean."

Once they'd done that, the boys took off, half walking and half running, to George's house. They hoped that they would run into Henry's summoned help, but they saw no one.

They found Henry on the porch at George's house with George's mother and sister, who looked a bit afraid of what the boys might tell them. Henry demanded to know what had happened after he left. "I thought I heard some shots."

David said, in as deliberate a manner as he could, "We just killed three Japs, and this time, we have the bodies to prove it."

Mary Williams immediately slumped into a chair and uttered, "Oh my God."

Lisa said, "You didn't!"

All three boys were standing, shaking and exhausted, and they simultaneously said, "We did." They didn't know what to feel or what else to say.

"Has someone called the Coast Guard or the police or something?" Jason asked.

"I called the Bandon Coast Guard," Mary said. "They'll be right down."

Kenji had watched from behind the drift log as three people and a dog had slowly walked to the raft, engaged in some conversation, and then pulled the raft higher on the beach. When they left, Kenji signaled

Hideke to come to him. It was now dark, and Kenji and Hideke made it to the cover of the shore pine trees without a problem.

Hideke was stunned and cold and said he didn't feel like moving. Kenji was shocked that the mission had instantly gone bad, but he knew they must proceed as planned. This was war.

He spoke to Hideke, "We must get to the raft at once and salvage our gear and bags of explosives, as well as anything that would reveal our presence and the objective of our mission."

They made their way through the shore pines to a point opposite the raft, and from there, they ran to the raft. It was a bloody scene. One of their comrades had taken a shot to the head. Hideke broke into tears and looked like he would be sick. Kenji was able to put aside the scene. It would have been worse in broad daylight.

They picked up their gear: two canvas bags, each containing about twenty kilograms of high explosives. They each had electric detonator caps in their shirt pockets and about a hundred meters of insulated detonator wire in their jacket pockets as well as a dry flashlight battery in a pocket separate from the detonator caps. They stripped all the same explosives gear from their dead companions as well as the small map each had, then took all of it to the edge of the trees, where they buried their companions' gear deep in the sand.

Kenji remembered that each of the five men was to have carried a canvas bag of explosives to their target building. He and Hideke quickly returned to the raft and took the other three satchels of explosives and buried them near the other gear. There should be no evidence left in the raft that more than three persons came ashore, and no evidence giving up the secret of their mission.

Kenji and Hideke decided to leave the beach to be clear of any search effort that the Americans might mount. Besides, they needed to keep warm and get their clothes dry, and moving around would help. They set off to the east directly opposite the shoreline, each carrying a satchel of explosives. As they walked, they observed no light coming from any buildings in the area and felt reasonably safe, at least for the present, in the deserted trees. After an hour, it was totally dark and they could see nothing. The brush was getting thick, and they were exhausted and needed rest. Tomorrow they could decide what to do. They found a spot in the trees and sat down, each leaning against a small tree trunk. They would stay there until dawn, but would remain very cold and get little sleep.

"Tomorrow we need to try and move completely away from this area," Kenji said as they settled in for the night. "There will surely be a search. Then in a day or so, the event will begin to fade in the minds of the Americans, and we can move to the Coquille separator manufacturing plant and do our job."

The headlights of numerous vehicles appeared and made their way down the Williamses' long driveway toward the house. The boys sat on the edge of the porch beneath a couple of bare lightbulbs while George's mother greeted the eight coastguardsmen. Captain Avery was not with them, but George saw Seaman Ron Freeman.

"Where's Captain Avery?" he asked.

"Captain Avery is back in our Seattle headquarters office," Freeman said, "and we understand that Master Chief Petty Officer Art Spears is returning to us."

"Good," George said.

The visitors insisted that the boys accompany them to the beach, and the boys agreed. The search would be more thorough without the use of vehicles. They walked down the beach with flashlights, looking in all directions, as though snipers were lurking in the darkness. The boys heard one coastguardsman say to another, "I hope this isn't another one of those fucking wild-goose chases."

"Are we going to have to put up with that shit again?" David asked. "You guys probably don't even believe your mothers!"

The whole mixed platoon, including Luke, moved south down the beach, being careful not to spread too far apart. Soon, they reached the beached raft. The coastguardsmen started talking all at once.

"My God, what a mess!"

"They're Japs alright."

"Jeez, this one is shot square in the head."

"There must be three gallons of blood in this raft."

The boys eschewed looking again.

Freeman started poking around in the raft in an effort to find something that would be a clue as to what the Japanese seamen were doing there but found nothing. Another man searched the clothing on each body and also found nothing. It was dark and cold, though; they needed a better look than their flashlights could provide.

Freeman took charge reluctantly and told two apprentice seamen to return and bring two of the jeeps to the raft. They left immediately. Then he asked two other seamen to search the area with their flashlights for anything unusual.

Jason, George, and David retired from the scene at the raft to their now-familiar sand dune, where they sat on the seaward edge and watched the silhouettes of the men in the beams of the flashlights.

Jason said, "Is this shit ever going to end? Here we sit in the dark and cold. We ought to be home in bed, and we probably won't get there until after midnight."

"What the hell," David answered. "We don't have anything else to do, so why not this? Besides, who knows what trouble we may have prevented? At least we saved our own asses—and maybe someone else's."

The two searching coastguardsmen told Freeman that they'd found nothing of interest up or down the beach.

"Any footprints?" he asked.

"Yeah, footprints everywhere because we've been walking all over the place."

Freeman realized that the situation was partly beyond his control, but nevertheless he raised his voice. "Everyone, get over here!" he called. "Listen, it's critical that we determine what these Japs were doing here and whether or not there are any more of them." The other men nodded their agreement. "I know we need the light of day for any further investigation of this scene, so we've got to secure the area until our search is finished. I think we need some men to stay the night and some others to volunteer relief at sunup. I can't order it, but I'm asking you." Three men volunteered, and Freeman thanked them.

The headlights of vehicles appeared to the north down the beach, and two jeeps arrived, shedding more light on the scene. From their dune, the boys saw the three bodies loaded on top of one another in the rear of one jeep. The men pulled the raft high onto the beach near the boys.

Freeman said to his men, "We'll take the bodies to the station tonight, but we'll leave the raft here until tomorrow."

Two coastguardsmen turned the raft over, and the bloody water poured out onto the dry sand and disappeared.

Freeman turned to the three men who had said they would stay. "I'll send a couple of men back with some snacks and warm jackets." The men were already carrying sidearms.

Then Freeman ushered everybody, the coastguardsmen and the boys, into the jeeps, some with the Japanese bodies, and drove north to the Williamses' residence. The boys rode in the jeep without the bodies.

It was six a.m., half-light, damp, and cold. Kenji was awake. He didn't know if he had slept or not. Hideke was awake too. The night air of the southern Oregon coast was laden with moisture, and the low early-morning temperature had caused it to settle on everything, including Kenji and Hideke. They were slightly warmer than they had been when they fell asleep, but their clothing was still very damp.

Kenji stood up, brushed himself off, and said, "We should have left everything in the raft except the explosives that we need for the Smith Wood Products plant. The Americans will surely conclude from the absence of any equipment that other seamen are onshore. Surely three men without a trace of supplies or equipment wouldn't come ashore. It would be meaningless. They know that we are smarter than that."

Kenji sighed and continued, "It's too late to remedy the situation at the beach. The Americans will already have been there. We'll have to be especially careful."

Hideke said, "The Americans might think that the three men came ashore to find out what happened to the shore party in June and, if they are around, rescue them."

"No, no, the Americans know that we wouldn't risk a submarine and its crew to find four men."

Kenji and Hideke knew that they had to leave the immediate area. They decided to move toward the highway numbered 101 on their American road map. They would need food, and they would be on the lookout for it. They had some hardtack and raisins in watertight bags stuffed in the large pockets of their pants, but it would not last. At some places, the underbrush was nearly impenetrable, and they moved on their hands and knees. The trees grew larger the farther they moved inland, and the underbrush became less dense.

For a while, they walked along not seeing any evidence of habitation. Eventually they came to a small clearing and could see foothills rising to the east. The hills were inviting, covered with grass meadows and stands of larger trees. Now they could hear the noise of a motor vehicle, probably a truck, which meant they were near the highway. If they could get across the highway and up those foothills, they might be safe.

The noise of the vehicles grew louder. They peered from a tree line at the edge of a clearing and saw a collapsed barn and a one-story building, probably a deserted farmhouse, that was covered in vines. Near the house were several trees, each bearing red apples that must be ripe. They backed into the woods and made their way to the house, which was almost in the trees, then sneaked out to fill their pockets and mouths with apples. They were better than any apples they had ever eaten.

There was an unused driveway from the house reaching to the east in the direction of the noise of the highway, but it was crossed with wind-felled trees and some brush. They stayed near the edge of the driveway and remained silent as they moved.

When they reached the highway, they were certain it was the one numbered 101, so they ran across it and into the forest on the other side. By Kenji's reckoning, they were two miles from where they had landed. There were few if any pine trees, but they were now seeing deciduous trees that were foreign to them. As they climbed sharply upward, more daylight shone through the canopy of vegetation overhead. They eventually rested at the edge of a clump of wind-shaped trees. They could look down and view the area where they had come ashore. They could also see where they had crossed the highway and the farm where they took the apples. They could not see any farmhouses or buildings on their side of the highway, but they could see the foothills to the south and to the north. To the east, the hills rose higher and were covered with huge fir trees as far as they could see. The morning sun was at their back, making visibility of objects on the beach to the west clear, though the objects were very small. Again, they saw their landing place, where several vehicles and many men had arrived and had started walking around. It was nearly three miles distant, and Kenji and Hideke couldn't see if the men wore uniforms, but the vehicles were all the same color, a light gray.

Kenji said, "We'll stay here for a while. Maybe in a day or two, the excitement of our visit will die down and vigilance with it. We can live on apples for a while."

CHAPTER 20

AUGUST 1942

The authorities were on the beach. This was the bailiwick of the United States Coast Guard, and the ranking officer at the Bandon station, Chief Boatswain's Mate Fred Cummings, knew there was little or no question about the fact. He did wish that Art Spears had returned, but his own eighteen years in the Coast Guard had given Fred the experience and the maturity to direct the investigation. His large size and arresting voice helped too.

Fred had notified the Coos County sheriff, Zeke Weathers, who hadn't seen this much excitement since Bandon burned in '36. He was a one-man sheriff's office, with a single secretary to answer the phone and show him how to fill out forms. He had no one in the county jail except a drunk, whom Weathers needed to paint the sheriff's office. Now that he thought about it, he'd love to grab some Japs and hold them in his jail.

Fred had also notified the Bandon chief of police, Al Simons, who also ran a one-man office. He didn't serve civil or other process and therefore needed no secretary. He was there because the intruders, if any, might come to his town over this beach, and he, too, would like to throw them in his jail.

It was a surprise to Fred when Rink showed up at the Williamses' place that day. He hadn't met Rink but knew who he was. "I didn't invite you here," Fred said.

Rink smiled and said, "It's a public beach, and Mary Williams called me after the boys came back. By the way, I would like photos of the bodies you hauled out of here last night." He wanted photos for the newspaper.

Fred, not knowing how to respond to requests from a newspaper, said, "The photos belong to the US Coast Guard."

He'd turned to walk away when Rink said, "The boys should be here. They might prove helpful." Fred did not respond.

Fred yelled for his men to come near, and when they did, he said, "You are to search the foredune areas, and the brush and tree areas, for signs of anything that might tell us if anyone else came ashore. There were no equipment and supplies found, and because of that fact, we think other Japs might be ashore. If so, they would be up to no good."

Six men walked south and six walked north. When the party to the south arrived at the drift log with the root wad on it, they saw footprints heading east to the trees. The intervening high tide had eliminated all prints seaward of the log.

"Could be the guys who searched the area last night," one man suggested.

"Better look anyway," another said. Several men searched the brushy area and walked into the trees for some distance, but they reported nothing of interest.

Up the beach, Rink again approached Fred. "How about the boys?" he asked. "How are they? Where are they?"

"I figure they're home in bed," he said. "It's only seven a.m."

Rink knew he'd need to interview each one of the boys before he left town. He wanted to leave in a matter of hours so that he could arrive back in Marshfield before his deadline. His publisher would hold the presses for this story, but Rink needed to work fast. Pictures of the dead Japanese would be matchless newsprint. He would follow the Coast Guard back to their station in Bandon.

Word of the Japanese shore landing spread like a September brush fire in a stiff wind. The authorities were not certain if any Japanese were ashore, but everyone was urged to keep their eyes open and to report anything suspicious. The Coast Guard was in charge of the investigation, and they had three dead Japanese, plus their raft. Surely there was a submarine lurking someplace out there in the Pacific Ocean. Why hadn't it been spotted and sunk?

Fred Cummings and Linus Rink stood looking at the bodies of the three dead Japanese. They were lying side by side and faceup on a piece of canvas on the concrete floor of the storage and maintenance room where the two lifeboats were kept in readiness at the Bandon Coast Guard station.

"What happens to the bodies?" Rink asked Cummings.

"Nothing's been decided," Fred said. He let Rink take his three photographs.

Pictures taken, Rink left for the Johnsons' store, where three of the boys had agreed to meet him. He'd interviewed George at home earlier.

The boys gave Rink every detail they could think of, but Henry wasn't too much help, as he had been sent running to call the Coast Guard.

Rink cautioned the boys and Mr. and Mrs. Johnson, who, between customers, were trying to listen to what was being said. "This story will make you American celebrities, because the Associated Press and the big national newspapers will get the story. It's my story, so it'll be right, but you'll still hear about it." The boys nodded. "I don't know how you'll deal with it, but you're tough kids who have grown up in a hurry this summer. You may receive calls, letters, and I don't know what all, but my best advice is for you not to embellish your story. Do not volunteer anything, and if you don't want to talk about it, don't. Most folks will understand."

"Good advice," Bill Johnson said.

"Oh yeah. I got a picture of George this morning, and I want your picture now," Rink said to the boys. They agreed, so he got their picture, then left to write his story and achieve a little fame.

The next few days would prove troublesome for each of the four boy heroes and their families. On top of the usual face-to-face inquiries from friends and some strangers, a phenomenal thing was happening: people from their town and neighboring towns were slowly driving by their homes, trying to catch glimpses of the boys whose pictures they'd seen in the *Coos Bay Times* and the Portland paper, the *Oregonian*. George saved a copy of the *Coos Bay Times* to send to his father—when his father had an address. David's sister, Jan, and Jason's mother, Gloria, each kept scrapbooks of news articles and some letters they received from strangers.

Events were unfolding at the US Coast Guard lifesaving station at Bandon. Master Chief Petty Officer Art Spears had returned, twenty-five coastguardsmen had been added to the roster, another shack was under construction on Coast Guard Hill directly above the large lifesaving station, three army officers from the Western Defense Command had shown up unannounced, and the bodies of the three dead Japanese had been cremated in Marshfield. Three canisters of their ashes graced the top bookshelf in the recreational hall in the lifesaving station. A smattering of humanitarian common sense had gripped Spears, and although the coastguardsmen thought otherwise, he figured when the war ended, the identities of the three men would become known and their survivors would be grateful for the return of the ashes. Besides, it was a reminder to all that complacency was not the order of the day.

Roadblocks had been established by the Oregon State Police three miles south of Bandon and three miles east of Bandon. Traffic was light, and nothing of interest showed up; only one car reversed course when the roadblock came into view. When the state police chased it down, they found two men trying to conceal a freshly killed deer—a prime forked horn taken out of season. Tickets were issued, the deer was confiscated for the county poor farm, and the two men went on their way. No one stopping at the roadblocks had seen any suspicious people or any Japanese, saboteurs or otherwise.

CHAPTER 21

AUGUST 17, 1942

Kenji and Hideke remained in place on top of the large foothill east of Highway 101 for two days and two nights. It was now the third day since their disastrous landing. They had sat on their eagle's nest and watched as the roadblock south of Bandon had been established; now they were seeing it removed. They decided to wait until the next day before making a move to the Coquille River. They could move off the hill during the daylight, but as they were so close to habitation, they decided to move at night and make certain they had a secure place to rest during the day.

They also had a problem of food supplies that needed a solution. Taking food from a closed market or store would be the safest but not easy.

They each still carried a sidearm, and they had cleaned them before the salt water could do any damage, but were now afraid to test fire the guns. They were automatic pistols, and the only cartridges they had were the seven in each magazine. Kenji thought they would work just fine, but a misfire at a crucial time could be fatal. When he was on duty in the Philippines, he had killed a few civilians, and he hadn't liked it. But if necessary, he could and would do it again. Until their job in

Coquille was finished, they could leave no trail and no evidence of any kind that they were loose on American soil.

Late the next morning, Kenji and Hideke moved down a north-facing slope that they believed would place them east of Bandon and away from any concentration of people. As they moved to lower elevations, the underbrush slowed them, sometimes to a stop. Some of the brush had a yellow flower on it and impenetrable, needle-sharp foliage. Several times, they had to backtrack and find a path around the horrible brush.

By midafternoon, they were in a swamp at the bottom of a small ravine. A little stream coursed slowly through it. The traveling was miserable. Each of them was carrying a satchel of nearly twenty kilos of explosives, making travel slow and exasperating. "The Philippines was like a walk in an urban garden compared to this American jungle!" Kenji said.

Once out of the first ravine, dirty, wet, and tired, they came within sight of an unpainted structure that looked like a place where someone might live. There was a redbrick chimney, but no smoke flowed out of it. A little truck with a flat tire was parked beside the structure. The house, if that's what it was, stood in a large open area with peculiar-looking pastures or fields near it. The little fields, filled with short, reddish, bush-like plants, were lower than the house, and each little field had a dike or berm surrounding it. Near the house, there was a shack with numerous iron pipes coming out of it, and at the back of the shack, there was a large pond; the pipes extended into the pond.

"This place may be deserted," Kenji said, "but don't count on it. I think that little shack by the pond is a pump house of some sort. No one seems to be living here, but those red pastures look well kept. We'll stay in these trees until we think it is safe to move to that house, where there may be some food. If there is a family living here, we'll leave."

"Let's hope there is no dog around," Hideke said.

They had started to settle in when the door of the shack opened and an old man stepped out, buttoning his trousers and tightening his belt.

Hideke said quietly, "He just took a shit. I'll bet he's the only one living here. He's such a miserable-looking old dog that no one would want to live with him. Let's wait to see if anyone else shows. If not, he could easily and accidentally drown in that pond to keep us from starving to death. I'm sure he has plenty of food around. From the looks of his truck, he doesn't need to go to town for supplies."

"I don't like the idea of killing him," Kenji said. "If the Americans suspect his drowning is not an accident, it might help confirm that we're in the area. Too risky. The old man doesn't have to die."

They would stick to their original plan: find a food store and carefully take what they needed. Barking dogs might be their biggest enemy. They continued their rest in the trees, keeping an eye open.

A full moon illuminated ditches filled with water, old barbed-wire fences, unlit vehicles and houses, and people that could be of great peril to Kenji and Hideke as they moved about that night. They saw no light in the old man's house, and fortunately there was no dog to have a barking fit. They walked along the edge of the trees until they came to the road leading to the old man's place. Once out of sight of the house, they stepped onto it and made their way northerly. Occasionally they heard motor vehicle noise, so they figured they must be nearing Highway 101, east of Bandon.

They stayed on the old man's road for almost three-quarters of a mile, and then reached what had to be Highway 101, and behold: there was a small store on the south side of the highway with a gasoline pump in front under the edge of a wood-frame canopy. There was a house behind the service station, and lights were on in that house. Kenji and Hideke instantly moved to the store.

The latch-and-lock combination was loose and worn, so a firm twist and a shove on the door opened it. They could not read the labels, but when cars drove past, the headlights provided enough light to reveal pictures on the cans. Very carefully, they helped themselves to cans of beans and meat, filling a few stolen sacks. They were careful not to take so much of the same thing as to cause the owner to believe goods were missing. Then they left the store, gently closing the door and leaving it as they had found it. They crossed the highway to the north and were in the brush and trees again.

When they had walked far enough to be out of view, they sat down. Each cut open a can with a knife and dug in.

"American food is good," Kenji said.

"But what is it?" Hideke asked, and again, they both studied the pictures on the cans. The images matched what was inside.

"We should move a little farther from the highway," Kenji said. "Deeper into the woods."

They really didn't know where deep in the woods would be, but Kenji had a feel for such things. They slowly moved in the now-dimmer moonlight about two hundred meters to the northeast. They rested on the mossy forest floor beneath a huge, towering tree with a massive trunk. It seemed a little dryer than any other place, and they decided to stay there until daybreak.

As they tried to sleep, Kenji asked Hideke about his life before becoming a member of the 1st Kure Special Naval Landing Force.

"I was a gunner's mate on the heavy cruiser *Haguro*," he started. "My gunnery lieutenant informed the entire crew that the navy was adding to its landing forces and was looking for recruits. It looked exciting, so I volunteered."

Hideke continued, "I didn't join, I was drafted. Before that, I worked in the Tokyo Central Fish Market lifting and hauling fresh fish around. I hated the job. It stunk and I stunk, at work and away from work. You can't believe some of those fish people eat. We sold to the retail market, so it wasn't one or two fish at a time; it was dozens and sometimes hundreds of kilograms at once. We sold everything from buckets of eels to baby octopus and squid."

"I was a salmon fisherman working with my family on the Tokachi River in Hokkaido," Kenji said. "We sold our salmon locally, but occasionally a fish buyer would anchor offshore at the mouth of our river and buy large quantities of sockeye salmon. We were told that some of these salmon were taken in ice to larger cities for retail sale. I wonder if you handled our fish."

"We definitely sold salmon, mostly chum salmon, but sometimes we sold sockeye. I don't know where it came from. Hokkaido is nearly six hundred kilometers from Tokyo, and depending where your river is, it might even be farther."

Kenji agreed it was a long shot.

Hideke then excitedly said, "You should have seen some of the sharks and swordfish and monster bluefin tuna they sold, and you wouldn't believe the whale meat that was sold."

"Let's not worry about any of those things," Kenji said. "We may never see Japan again."

"The sad part is our superiors probably knew our journey was one-way," Hideke said.

"My hope is that once we get our job done that somehow we can make it safely back to the place where we came ashore. You remember Captain Toshi advising us that we needed to be back on the beach fourteen days from the day he launched us? Just before we boarded the raft with the others, he told me that if we were not on the beach in fourteen days, he would return with the sub in thirty days to wait for one night." Kenji shook his head. "The problem is twofold: one, we can't do our job and get back to the beach in fourteen days; and two, we don't have a raft. If we make it back to the beach for the pickup on day thirty, it will have to be with a boat—or something like a boat."

"Why don't we sleep on it?" Hideke said. "Maybe something will come to us."

"Yes," Kenji agreed. "Anyway, we need to keep the mission in mind before the escape."

CHAPTER 22

AUGUST 1942

News of the landing or the attempted landing south of Bandon was soon known by every living, breathing soul in southwestern Oregon and most of the rest of the state. People on the East Coast learned about it too, but weren't the westerners still fighting a few Indians and shooting themselves over rights to water and boundary-line fences? Wasn't that the way they settled things out there? In any event, the Pacific coast was three thousand miles from the East Coast, so they weren't too concerned.

Regardless of the location, the military took it seriously. The Western Defense Command immediately began beefing up numbers of personnel and various kinds of military hardware on the Pacific coast. Citizens in small coastal towns started seeing motorized guns, half-track vehicles, green trucks with canvas-covered beds, and an occasional green trailer loaded with unusual crates and small boxes. Open concrete bunkers were constructed on promontories overlooking some beaches and most harbor entrances, including the sea entrance to the Coquille River.

George Smith, general manager of Smith Wood Products in Coquille, had been greatly disturbed by news of the first attempted landing, but now news of a second attempted landing, together with suspicion that some of the landing party may have escaped inland, had him beyond disturbed. In fact, the Coast Guard supervising officer, Art Spears, had called to warn Smith about this very thing. There could be no other reason for such a move on the part of the Japanese than an attack on his plant. The Japanese knew all they needed to know about the two mills manufacturing storage battery separators, and each mill was accessible by foot.

Smith called Sam Mack, his in-house security director; John Merchant, the plywood mill foreman; Robert Harris, a separator plant foreman; and Mark Gleason, plant manager of the battery-separator plant. The meeting was held in a small, little-used, unheated meeting room adjacent to the head office. The men wore warm, well-used jackets. Smith reminded all of them of what had happened and what could happen—which, of course, they knew. Harris's son and Gleason's son had been directly involved in the attempted landing, after all.

"What's the status of the security around the mill, and especially around the separator plant, Sam?" Smith asked.

"I need more men," Sam answered. "This mill sits high on wood pilings and is most vulnerable from its underbelly. We need more lighting around the mill and some lighting beneath the mill."

Harris and Gleason suggested that security needed to be mill-wide. "Any part of the entire mill is accessible from any other part," Gleason said.

"Change of shifts—especially the changing of the swing shift at eleven p.m. with the incoming graveyard shift—is completely without control or surveillance of any kind," Harris added. "Once the graveyard shift is at their work positions, it still wouldn't be noticeable if extra people came in because there's so much wood stock stacked around and so many dark corners and places to hide. Extras would never be noticed."

Smith said, "We'll get you more lighting inside and out, Sam. And, Robert, you and Mark clean up the factory floor as much as you can. Get the jitney and forklift drivers to take care and stack the materials close enough together that a man couldn't hide among them. Sam, I'll see what I can do about getting more security people for you, and I'm making your job as security director superior in importance to your job managing the retail lumberyard. We can't furnish firearms for you or your security."

"The men have their own," Sam said.

"Then they can use them. I want you to check out each weapon and each security person. Make certain that these men have the proper weapon and know how to safely use it."

"Most people around here won't need much help in that area," Sam said.

"Also, I want you to find someone to manage security for each shift. You pick the shift you want and revolve them from shift to shift. Just let me know who you intend to employ before you actually do the hiring." He looked around. "Anyone else? I'm open to suggestions."

No one had anything to add, so Smith stood up and thanked them. They all filed out and back to their assigned tasks.

The next day, Sam was underneath the portion of the Smith Wood Products mill building that housed the plywood operation. Machinery rumbled and whined overhead, and lumber carriers and forklifts moved over the four-inch wood-plank floors. When he'd left Smith's office the day before, Sam had been scratching his head. He hadn't been given that much responsibility ever. Sam was under the floor now with Earl, one of the plant electricians, and two workers he had taken from a cleanup crew to assist.

Earl complained bitterly about the soft, muddy conditions beneath the mill. "No mill electrician has ever been forced to work in the mud and half-light," he said.

"Stop your bitching," Sam said. "Security is now a priority with this mill, and the sooner you and your two helpers string up some lights down here, the sooner you can get out of this mud."

"Why the hell are we stringing lights under the plywood mill when it's the damn separator plant the Japs think they can blow up?"

"Earl, just string the lights under the whole mill, and do the separator plant next. And don't connect them all to the same circuit, OK?"

Having said that, Sam walked through the mud alongside a small creek that ran beneath the mill. He continued until he came to a point beneath the separator plant near the railroad right-of-way. Rays of light came through the cracks in the separator plant's wood floor, creating a light pattern of straight lines about twelve to fourteen inches apart that were broken every time a vehicle or person moved over the floor. Sam was now more aware of the potential for danger to the mill and to the employees above his head. It was a made-to-order setup for a blast down here, and he worried that it was his job to stop any such thing from happening.

He walked to the edge of the river where the mill structure stopped, parted some willow bushes, and stepped onto a Douglas fir boom stick and out across a raft of logs to the place where river workers were moving logs into sawing position.

"This seems like a good route in for some bad guys," Sam told them, adding some of his security concerns about the riverside.

The river workers listened, but they didn't seem to believe there was a security problem, at least not one that directly concerned them. "We'll keep our eyes open, anyway," one promised. The log booms and rafts of logs in the river were well lit, because river workers cut and fed logs into the mill at two different places twenty-four hours a day, seven days a week.

Sam stood on a narrow plank walkway on the boom sticks between pilings. He put one leg in the river, then the other, washing the mud away from his shoes and pants. Wet shoes and pants were better than the mud. He walked on the log booms to the upriver end of the mill, talking along the way to more river workers about security matters. He walked up the catwalk along the large ramp that hauled whole logs out of the river. He stopped there and watched the large waste-wood burner shaped like a wigwam belch fiery cinders and smoke into the air. He thought that maybe, if this mill ever burned, that wigwam burner would be the culprit. He hoped.

Sam walked back by where Earl and his helpers were stringing wire and installing bare 150-watt light bulbs. Their shoes and pants were muddy to their knees, and although they were complaining about the mud and the dampness under the mill, they were getting the job done.

One day, after nearly a week of time expended on mill security, Sam returned to his office, which was more of an oversized closet with no door. He sat down and thought of everything he had done to try and secure the mill. He had spoken to all the truck drivers and all the lumber carrier drivers, as well as Southern Pacific railroad workers. He had even had the main mill office place an order at the local newspaper to have notices printed to be posted about the mill, warning of the danger of saboteurs and requesting that employees immediately report any strange occurrences.

No one had told Sam what he needed to do. He had been handed a job without a description, and so he did what his common sense told him to do. Maybe it was enough; maybe it wasn't.

CHAPTER 23

LATE AUGUST 1942

Kenji and Hideke each woke from a torturous sleep. The night was cool, and the air was filled with drizzle, which had gathered on the needles of the spruce tree canopy over them. The accumulated moisture formed drops, and the slightest breeze shook the drops loose onto the men. The night air would never be dry this close to the ocean. It was no different than the night air at Kenji's home at the mouth of the Tokachi, and Kenji wished he was sleeping there and not on the Pacific coast of the United States of America.

Kenji was telling Hideke that they should have prepared themselves better to contend with the cold and damp climate when they heard a dog barking in the distance. The barking was to the south, where they had traveled the night before and where they had broken into the highway store for food.

"We should move north now," Hideke said.

They picked up their heavy satchels of explosives as well as the canned food they had acquired and moved slowly and quietly north. If they were lucky, they would not see anyone until they reached a point above the Coquille River.

They began to find wild blackberries growing in profusion, sometimes blocking their path, but they were good eating, and the men were hungry. They ate as they maneuvered around the varying and often impenetrable brush until finally they caught a glimpse of the blue water of the Coquille River. They could see it to the east and to the west but not to the north.

There was a north wind in their faces as they came to the edge of a precipitous slope down to a gravel road. A panoramic view of the river and four or five hundred acres of pastureland spread before them. To the west, they saw a tiny village, and they consulted their maps. It was most likely a fishing village that they had been told about.

There were a dozen or so houses, mostly unpainted, on both sides of the gravel road. Houses on the riverside had docks, and many had net racks covered with drying gill nets. Small boats of all kinds were moored to the docks, and there were more small boats in the river with two or three people in each. People were fishing with poles.

Kenji and Hideke moved slightly to the west and closer to the village, staying hidden in the brush until they found a good vantage point. They moved some dead brush and fallen limbs aside and made themselves as comfortable as possible, then piled more brush and limbs in front of them to break the wind. They sat and watched the activity below. Kenji remembered that mid-August at his home had been the beginning of the fall run of salmon in the Tokachi, and he thought it must be the same here. He watched as people in one of the small boats stood up when a large salmon jumped out of the water behind them. Soon, the fish was flopping in the water beside the boat and was quickly stuck with a gaff hook and pulled into the boat. It jumped around until one of the persons hit it with a club. Kenji was surprised at the size of the salmon he was seeing. Even at a distance, the fish were three and four times the size of any salmon he had ever seen or heard about. He knew that these fish had to be another species of salmon and that their run was late in the year. The scene was familiar to Kenji; he had occasionally witnessed the same thing on the Tokachi when wealthy people from Sapporo came and fished with hook and line. People in Ōtsu thought it foolish because it was easier to catch the fish in a net.

The boat began to move, and Kenji was amazed to realize that it was moving without oars. A man was operating some sort of motor on the back of the boat, steering with an attached handle. Kenji could hear nothing from this distance, but the man could make the little boat go in any direction. There were a few other little boats on the river with the same sort of device on the back of them—no one was rowing!

He tried to get over his amazement and focus back to the mission at hand. Every once in a while, he saw a large, bright, silvery fish jump out of the water, glistening in the early-morning sun as it was caught by a fisherman. Kenji looked up and down the river to see if he could spot the cork line of a gill net in the water. There were none. Only these men with their poles were fishing. The tactical side of their venture called for commercial fishermen to be fishing so that, having captured a commercial fishing boat, they could go unnoticed. These weren't commercial fishermen but day fishermen. He wondered how the researchers had gotten this wrong—but then he decided they hadn't.

"Look at the boats moored to the little wharves," Kenji said. "They fit the description we were given."

"Maybe they fish at night?" Hideke suggested, and Kenji agreed they should wait to see.

Kenji and Hideke both knew they had to wait until dark to move. The wind was in their faces and warming slightly with the rising sun, and in their upwind lair, they were safe from the inquisitive noses of village dogs. They could see no trails or roads leading from the road below to the hill they were on.

Kenji studied the village beneath them to determine the safest route to the capture of a boat. He could see seven docks with net-drying racks, each with a boat moored to the dock. Most of the boats appeared to be about seven meters long with inboard engines. None of them looked like masterpieces of marine architecture. Two of the boats had a man working around the boat, probably doing routine maintenance. On one of the docks, a man was sitting on a box mending a racked net.

A man on the dock farthest upriver and closest to Kenji and Hideke was pouring what was probably gasoline into a long, round tank on top of the boat's engine. He looked old, with bushy gray hair. An unpainted wooden ramp extended from the dock to a wooden deck attached to a house. There were many small, bushy trees, probably willow, near the house on the upriver side. The house looked unpainted but substantial, and it rested on wood pilings. The gravel road ran within ten meters of the front door, and an old car sat in front of the house.

As they lay watching the scene below them, it became clear that the upriver house with the gray-haired man presented the choice opportunity to commandeer a fully fueled commercial fishing boat. From all appearances, the fishermen were readying their gear for night fishing. Kenji and Hideke would just have to wait.

Kenji did notice the little trail of ripples on the seaward side of each piling in the river, which meant that the tide had started to ebb. By nightfall, there would be an incoming tide and, with it, the salmon. Surely there would be gill netting on the Coquille tonight.

He and Hideke discussed their plan while they waited for the sun to set. They would move from their eagle's nest on the hill, cross the gravel road, and make their way to the house and dock where the bushy-haired man was working. They would silently dispose of him, take his boat, and under cover of darkness, they would gradually move up the river, like many similar boats. They consulted their map and calculated the distance to Coquille to be about twenty-five kilometers. It wouldn't take more than two hours to get to the separator mill.

Kenji continued to study their map. There were three places where the river ran adjacent to the Highway 101. One of those spots was about eight kilometers from where they would take a boat. The second spot was near a village with a ferryboat about seven kilometers downriver from Coquille, and the other spot was near Coquille. These would be important landmarks for their trip.

Both men looked at their navy-issue wristwatches with no numbers, a red dot at twelve and a red dot at 6, and they saw it was 1700 hours. The men on the docks had started loading nets into their boats. They would fish tonight, and Kenji and Hideke would get their boat.

When it was nearly dark, Kenji and Hideke moved to the edge of the hill and slid on their backsides for the first fifty meters down the hill. They moved slowly and quietly through the brush to the road and then crossed into the willows and other brush. A few shore pines made the going a little easier. When they reached the house, they could see an older woman inside but no one else. As long as the lights stayed on inside, and as long as she stayed indoors, Kenji knew she wouldn't see anything.

They moved around to the river side of the house and saw the old man beneath a single electric light loading a net into his boat. Kenji picked up a two-foot piece of willow limb that beavers had worked over, leaving it without bark. It was bright yellow and had caught his eye in some other drift near the riverbank. Tonight it would be useful.

Sven Clausen had his back to his house when Kenji and Hideke carefully eased up onto the dock ramp. They were on the dock when Sven first saw them. He wasn't surprised. He had many friends that visited during fishing season. When he saw them, he said, "Hello," and not recognizing them, added, "What can I do for you?"

By then, Kenji and Hideke were upon Sven, and with two blows to his head with the willow limb, Sven was down in the bottom of his boat.

Hideke, who knew gasoline engines, found the starter switch, and the motor fired up just as Kenji took the mooring lines from the cleats on the boat. The boat didn't move. Hideke looked around, still aided by the electric dock light, and found the clutch lever. He thrust it forward, and the boat moved downstream. He turned the wheel connected to the rudder by small chains, and the boat swung around and headed upstream. There was a half moon, its light diffused by numerous small clouds moving south. They could see the banks of the river covered with willow trees and an occasional large fir or spruce standing alone. There were a few other boats on the river, each with a light on at the top of a short pole in the center of the boat. They quickly found the light switch on their own boat and turned it on.

When they passed in the dark close to another boat, the fisherman waved and said, "Hello, Sven!"

Kenji waved back, not knowing what the fisherman had said. Though they didn't like being so close to the strangers, as they moved upriver, Kenji and Hideke saw fewer and fewer fishing boats. This made them jumpy too. Maybe no one fished commercially at Coquille. That thought crossed their minds and stayed there until they passed one fishing boat and then another about four kilometers farther upstream.

Before long, they saw car lights shining on the river and their boat, but the lights were moving, and soon, the river turned away from the highway. Hideke said, "That scared me." Kenji said nothing.

They motored slowly for a while, and Kenji had Hideke give him a short tutorial on the fascinating motor and how to run the boat. After nearly fifty minutes of slow running, they passed a village much larger than the one where they had taken the boat, and there was a fisherman working a long, straight drift upriver from that village. They could see a ferryboat at that place and the landing slips on each side of the river, but the ferry was not running.

Up the river, they again began to see motor vehicle traffic along the south side, and farther on, they saw similar traffic to the north. They passed some houseboats and soon came to a bridge. The bridge had a large wooden framework beneath the middle of the span. This was the bridge mentioned by the cedar-log buyer. Their destination would be around the next bend.

And then, there it was. A huge wooden structure rose from the water's edge. Nearly opposite that structure, they saw men walking on a narrow floating walkway in the river pulling logs toward some sort of ramp that was dragging the logs into the mill. Hideke stopped the boat, but the incoming tide moved them slowly toward the men.

"I see two men near us, and I see two more men upriver about nine hundred meters upstream," Kenji said. "Our best move would be to pull up to the floating walkway next to those two men. They'll think we are fishermen, and we'll motion them to come over. When they do, throw them down and into the boat and use the old fisherman's fish-killing clubs on them. You take the one on the left, and I'll take the one on the right."

Hideke moved the boat to the walkway, and Kenji tied it off as Hideke motioned with his arm for the two workers to come to the boat. They jumped, sure-footed, from log to log across a raft of logs that were stored in the river ready for processing in the mill. When they reached the boat, in a synchronized motion, Kenji and Hideke grabbed the men and threw them to the bottom of the vessel. Kenji quickly clubbed his victim into unconsciousness. Hideke killed his victim with a knife shoved between the victim's ribs and into his heart.

Kenji said, "Why did you kill him?"

"I couldn't find the club, and he was starting to yell."

They lay motionless next to Sven Clausen, who was awake and bleeding from the deep abrasions to his head. They tightly bound the river worker who was still alive with some of the many pieces of rope found in the bottom of the boat, and then they gagged him with a rag and more rope.

Each river man was wearing an orange life jacket, so Kenji and Hideke stripped the jackets from their victims and put them on. They looked around, but it seemed no one had seen the vicious maneuver.

So out of the boat and onto the floating walkway stepped the two members of the Special Naval Landing Forces carrying their satchels of high explosives. They headed for the ground beneath the mill.

To their surprise, the area under the mill was lit with electric lights—not many, but enough to make a man visible beneath the mill if someone was watching. They had no choice, so they quickly moved beneath the plywood mill to the area beneath the separator plant. Their feet and pants were caked with mud, but that was the least of their worries. There were lights there also, but the only access to the area was at the far perimeters of the mill itself. *Why the lights,* Kenji wondered, *if no one is watching?*

Kenji and Hideke began placing the explosives and stringing the fine insulated electric wire from charge to charge. Rays of light shone through the cracks in the wood floor, and the hum of plant machinery drowned out any noise Kenji and Hideke were making.

Kenji caught a movement to his left but away from their path of entry, and he motioned for Hideke to hide behind a piling. Kenji, too, concealed himself, but watched with one eye as a man approached. He seemed to be looking for something—maybe for them. Kenji saw the man turn his back and walk away, shining his flashlight from side to side.

Kenji's heart was pounding in his chest. His hand was on his pistol, but he couldn't fire a shot and betray himself. He waited, as did Hideke. In any event, neither of them were to be taken alive. They would fight to the death.

After the man disappeared, they continued their work. They easily sat the charges on top of huge timbers holding the big floor joist. Placing the detonators in each explosive charge was fast and easy, and was completed with a piece of sharp wood. Connecting the detonator wire to the main cord had to be done with care. They were especially careful to place a charge under the southwest corner of the separator plant building, where the fuel station was located.

When they were almost finished, Kenji signaled to Hideke that he was going back to the outside edge of the plywood plant to keep watch. One person under the mill would be less noticeable than two. If he saw someone that posed a threat, he would signal Hideke to hide by pointing with his arm.

As soon as Hideke was finished, he would join Kenji, stringing the detonator wire behind him. Then Kenji would take a flashlight battery from his pocket and touch the red wire to the positive and the black wire to the negative, and the separator plant would be destroyed. At least one shift of its employees would either be killed or seriously maimed.

Kenji hurried to the edge of the plant and crouched in some willows. He saw Hideke hurrying as fast as he could through the mud. That's when Kenji noticed a large man walk into view about thirty meters to the north of Hideke. The man shouted something at Hideke, and Hideke either ignored him or didn't hear him. The man yelled again then held up a rifle and fired. Hideke fell. The report of the rifle brought another man running.

Kenji wanted to get to the detonator wires, but the men were now walking carefully to Hideke's body. There would be no chance, particularly when they saw the detonator wire either at Hideke's side or in his hand. Kenji wrestled with his options, which were few. He had not been seen. He could go toward the two men, but he wouldn't get far. If he escaped, he could always return to damage the mill.

Kenji crept through the willows to the walkway and into the boat. He untied it and started the motor as Hideke had shown him, grateful that it would be difficult to hear over the noise of the mill. His escape was quick: the boat was almost instantly out of sight, and without its mast light on, it would be difficult to see anyplace on the river. Kenji passed beneath the Highway 101 bridge, and once downriver from the town of Coquille, he pulled over to a small dock. He left the old fisherman in the boat.

Now he was away from the mill, and the motor did make a noticeable noise. Kenji wished the tide was not flooding. If the tide was on the ebb, he could turn off the motor and drift silently downriver.

Kenji suddenly caught the reality of what had happened. Hideke, his new friend, was dead, and the whole purpose of the expedition was now a failure. He was halfway around the world from Japan with no real prospect of getting home. Kenji was tired and despondent, but he motored on in a slight stupor.

Surely, he thought, *the Americans will figure out that we accessed the mill from the river.* He was not going to be captured by the Americans. They would shoot him for being a spy. His uniform might not be sufficient to allow classification as a military officer, making him a spy and a saboteur—and an unsuccessful one at that. Besides, Japan was not a signatory to the Geneva convention, so even as a prisoner of war, he'd have no rights under it. He had to get out of here. He would get as close to the ocean as he could in this boat and from there try to catch the submarine.

Kenji looked at the form of the old fisherman lying on the bottom of the dark boat. He had spared the man's life so far because he reminded Kenji of his grandfather Maki. Grandfather Maki was a fisherman with bushy gray hair just like this man. He probably had grandchildren, and maybe even a grandson who revered him.

Kenji bent down and took a good look at the old man, whose eyes were open and glinted even in the darkness. His hair was matted with blood, and he was trying to move his arms and legs. Kenji wished he could communicate with him to let him know he was not going to do him any further harm.

Kenji believed that this old man had seen the killing of the river worker. Kenji wished that Hideke had not done that; though he had been involved in killing before, this felt different. Oregon wasn't a war zone, and it reminded him of Ōtsu. What should he do with the old man now?

Moreover, what was he going to do to save himself? Nine men had now died attempting to destroy the separator plants in Coquille and Marshfield, and they'd had no success. Kenji couldn't help replaying the assault in his mind. If he had only taken the detonator wire to the edge of the mill instead of leaving it to Hideke, he could have touched off the explosion and ultimate destruction of the separator plant. Going back to the far edge of the mill as a lookout hadn't been a good idea—or had it? If he had stayed with Hideke, he would be dead. He should have taken the detonator wire and let Hideke finish the connections. He would have had plenty of wire to finish the job.

The boat moved through the incoming tide, even though Kenji was running the engine at near idle speed to be as silent as possible. Surely the Americans would immediately be looking for him. He needed to figure out his next move. Kenji maneuvered the boat into a small stream's entrance to the main river and under some overhanging willow bushes. He killed the boat's engine and sat watching the darkened figure of the old man. He needed to get rid of the boat as soon as possible. The Americans would be looking for it. He could just set it adrift with the old man in it; the boat would be discovered within a day.

But then what? Should he show the Americans how skilled and fierce one man of the Japanese military could be and ravage the countryside and populace? He would never do that. The time for his landing party's escape on submarine *I-25* had come and gone. He was alone in a strange place.

CHAPTER 24

Sam Mack was sound asleep when the phone rang.

"The Japs tried to blow up the mill!" an excited voice said. "You gotta get here right now!"

"Who the fuck is this, and what in the hell are you talking about?" Sam still had a headache from having a few beers at the tavern earlier that night.

The voice said, "Sam, it's Robert Harris. Get your ass down here and get things under control!"

"I'll be right there."

When Sam arrived, many people were strolling around the railroad right-of-way. Some were peering under the mill, while others had gathered at the mill's edge. Sam ran from his car across the railroad tracks, and as he drew closer, he could see several people standing around what appeared to be a body. "Everyone, get back to the railroad tracks!" he yelled, and except for a few people around the body, most began to disperse.

Sam hastily walked over to the group standing by the body. He could see at first glance that the body was Japanese, wearing matching greenish pants and shirt, with a cap with a small embroidered anchor.

He saw Harris standing nearby and asked what had happened. Harris filled him in—it had all just happened, and they only knew that this guy had been shot by security.

Harris said, "Look at this," pointing to a long strand of insulated red and black wires leading from the body back toward the mill.

"Has anyone run the wires out to their source yet?" Sam asked. No one answered. "Well, for Christ's sake, haven't you ever seen a body before?" He grabbed a flashlight from the hand of someone he had never seen before and headed under the mill to follow the wire. Sam suddenly stopped and yelled, "Is everyone out of the mill? And I mean every part of the mill?"

Three people hollered back no.

"Get everyone out of the fucking mill! And I mean now and every part of the mill! Shut the son of a bitch down until we find out what is going on here!"

Harris immediately went to the mill to start the evacuation. On his way, he ran into George Smith, who was just arriving. Smith wanted to know exactly what was going on, so Harris filled him in as best he could. "And the mill needs to be evacuated, because it looks like some explosives might have been set."

Smith agreed. The announcements were shouted several times, and soon, one could hear the sound of mill machinery winding down. Employees streamed out of the mill.

John Merchant followed Sam to find where the wires led. They ended at the separator plant, where they branched off in a half dozen different directions. Each wire led to what was obviously a charge of explosives. Both Sam and John had previously worked in the logging woods and knew what an electric cap looked like. They slipped the caps from the charges to make sure they were disarmed. Sam knew that most people were scared to death of explosives, but nothing was going to happen to these—unless someone put a detonating cap in them and set it off, or someone shot them. Satisfied that things were clear, Sam and John emerged from beneath the mill.

"Get a couple of men and take the explosives out of there," Sam told John. "Load them in the back of a company truck for me." John agreed and went to find help.

Mill employees were now standing around viewing the body. Sam walked over. "Put that body next to the mill office and cover it up," he said. "And don't take anything from it!"

Later that evening, the mill foremen and plant managers from the swing shift gathered in Smith's office. Sam was there too, as was the Coquille chief of police but without his uniform or cap, just a badge on his wrinkled shirt. Smith held up his arms for quiet and then said, "How do we stand, Sam?"

"It looks OK for now," Sam said. "We removed the explosive charges and looked beneath the mill and found nothing. Some employees are searching the mill proper for anything unusual, but no one has seen any strangers in the mill."

Merchant said, "There may have been two of the bastards, and they probably came from the river. There are two sets of prints coming from there, but we haven't found the return prints yet. Two river workers are missing, and the dead Jap had on a river worker's life jacket."

"Maybe one of the sons of bitches is still hanging around someplace," one of the managers said.

George Smith said, "You'd better let the townspeople know that there might be a Jap runnin' around someplace."

The police chief nodded and said he'd do just that. The men quietly agreed that whoever found the guy could deal with him however they wanted, as long as they didn't let him get away.

"My God, if they came by river, they had a boat," Smith said suddenly. "Has anyone notified the Coast Guard?"

Sam grabbed the telephone and asked the operator to get him the Coast Guard in Bandon at once. He told the officer who answered what had happened at the Coquille mill, then hung up and relayed the call to the group. "They're putting a power lifeboat in the water now and heading upriver."

"Hell, they're commercial fishing the river tonight," a foreman said. "They'll see lots of boats."

"But Coast Guard boys may find the right boat," another man chimed in.

"Sam," Smith said, "take the plywood-mill headrig crew from this shift and put them under the mill until the graveyard shift shows up, and then replace that crew with the sander crew from the plywood mill. Tomorrow when it's daylight, we'll get security squared away for the rest of this goddamned war. In the meantime, this mill's going to remain idle for a day or two. I want you foremen and individual plant managers to get the word out to all employees, and put a good sign to that effect at the main entrance to the mill grounds. We will make a thorough search, inside and outside, starting tomorrow morning. And I'll notify the state police. They need to know about this; their highway patrols might spot someone or something."

Linus Rink, having heard the fast-traveling rumor of the attack on the Coquille mill, was at the mill by ten a.m. the next morning. The body of the Japanese man was still lying next to the mill office, and Rink was photographing it when Mark Gleason, manager of the separator plant, walked out of the main office.

"Rink, what's going on here?" Mark was unhappy. He did not want anything going on at the mill that did not involve plant security.

"This is news, and you know news is my business," Rink said. "And this news is also every citizen's business. They want proof, so they'll get proof."

Sam Mack was returning to the head office when he saw Rink taking photos with Gleason standing nearby.

Sam stood close to Rink and said, "Who the hell are you and what the hell are you doing here? This mill is off-limits to strangers!"

"I'm no stranger, and who the hell are you?"

"I'm head of security at this mill, and you get your ass out of here."

Rink was irritated. "This mill was attacked, so what security are you talking about?" He knew he'd made a mistake when Sam started to grab him by the arm.

Mark stepped in and told Sam to go about his work. "I'll take care of this," he said to Sam.

Mark then told Linus that charges had been set but the security people had stopped the Japs before they could detonate. And yes, they believed there were two Japs involved. "Now you know what we know, and I must ask you to leave."

Rink said, "Sure, I'll leave, but I want a picture of the explosives first."

Mark reluctantly pointed to the company pickup truck at the edge of the parking lot. Rink thanked Mark and strolled over to the pickup. He photographed the several nearly square cakes of explosives with

Japanese writing on their tough wrapping papers. Rink wanted to interview the man who shot the intruder, but he was home in bed, and no one would tell Rink who the man was or where he lived. He could only get the bare bones of the story, but he figured he had enough general information and good photos to run something that day. He would ferret out the details later.

This story was already better than anything that he'd seen in San Francisco during his twenty-five years at the *Chronicle*, and the story was far from over. Just the concept of a Japanese saboteur on the loose in Coos County would be as dramatic as the attempted attack and the killing of the Japanese. The AP would love it. *My God*, he thought, this is so good I might have to start drinking again!

But there was no time for that. He still had to go to Bandon to talk to Art Spears. While he was in town, he'd track down the boys, too, and get their take on the whole bit. This was definitely a story with legs.

Spears confirmed that a motor lifeboat had been sent upriver the night before. The coastguardsmen hadn't found anything until the sun was fully up, when they'd spotted Sven Clausen's fishing boat with Sven tied up inside. Sven had told the coastguardsmen about the men attacking him. He didn't get a good look at them but thought they were Japanese.

"Clausen?" Rink asked.

"C-L-A-U-S-E-N. He's that kid Henry's grandfather, if that helps." Rink nodded. "Sven was OK, but cold and dehydrated," Spears said. "He's at the Bandon hospital."

"Did he see two guys?"

"He confirmed that there were two Japs, and one came back to his boat."

Rink looked at Spears. "Have you notified the *brilliant* Major Allen Carlock of the Western Defense Command that you need him here to find and capture the renegade Jap?"

"We did notify General DeWitt's office, and I assume we'll have some help. My command is now at twenty-five personnel, and we can mount a search." Spears leaned forward. "Your news account of this incident should urge people to be alert and on guard; no one knows where this guy is or what's on his agenda."

Rink thanked Spears and took his leave, then headed for Bandon Hospital. As he drove, Rink mentally outlined several stories related to the attempted attack on the Smith Wood Products mill. He'd have to talk to the families of the two missing river workers, get profiles arranged. There was probably a story about the worker who shot and killed the invader, and his experience that night. He'd still have to get the reaction of the four boys to the whole incident. But now he had to get Sven Clausen's story. *It should be a dilly,* he thought.

At the hospital, Rink asked for Sven Clausen's room at the front desk.

"Well, you can't see him now," the nurse said.

"Is he alright?"

"He's fine. Tired but alert. Right now, his whole room is full of family, so you'll have to wait."

Rink didn't like the sound of that. "Do you know if Henry Johnson or his parents are in there? You think you could get one of them for me?"

The nurse agreed to check, and soon, Rink saw May Johnson headed his way down a hospital hallway. Rink was standing in the entranceway and reception area of the small hospital. There were several straight-backed metal chairs against the area walls.

"Hello, Mr. Rink," she said.

"Hello, Mrs. Johnson. I'd like to get a comment from your father for the newspaper article today."

May said that was fine and led Rink back to Sven's room. It was a two-bed room; one was empty. After exchanging hellos with Henry and his father, May introduced him to her mother, Mabel, and then to her father, Sven. Sven looked tired.

"I'm here from the newspaper," Rink said. "Just a few words on what happened would suffice."

"Well, I can tell you the whole goddamned thing if you want," Sven said. "The one thing that I want you to know is that one Jap spared my life. I saw one of those guys stab and kill one man, and the other—the one that brought me back down the river—clubbed the other man. On the way back down the river, he put the man he clubbed on a dock and dumped the other one overboard. I thought they were going to kill me, but look what the Jap that brought me back down the river gave me." Sven handed a little photograph to Rink. It was a photo of a Japanese man about Sven's age who resembled a Japanese version of Sven, bushy gray hair and all. "He showed it to me and put it in my shirt pocket just as he left me. Do you think that's his father or grandfather? Maybe because I reminded him of that person, he couldn't kill me?"

"Probably," answered Henry and Rink simultaneously.

"Would you mind telling me how they were able to subdue you?" Rink asked.

Sven said, "The light wasn't good on the dock, and they surprised me. They hit me and knocked me out, but I came to and I remember them talking. I remember the boat trip to the Coquille mill. I couldn't understand a thing they said. They kept jabbering away. When I heard the one shot, I knew something bad had happened. It's like deer hunting; you hear one shot and no others, it's usually deadly and the guy has his deer. Oh, I've wanted to know if anyone else was killed besides the Jap and the mill worker."

"Not that we know of," Rink said.

"And where is my boat?"

"The Coast Guard is holding it for closer inspection," May said. "They'll return it back to your dock soon."

All the time Rink was in Sven's hospital room, Mabel Clausen was sitting next to Sven with her left hand on her husband, first in one place, then another. Her eyes were red, and she looked tired, and Rink wondered what the night had been like for her. He decided it was time to leave. He had enough for his story—and what a dynamite story it was. He said his goodbyes but asked Henry to follow him out into the hospital corridor.

"Well, what do you think about all this?" Rink asked.

"I am glad that last guy didn't kill Grandpa."

"Have you talked to the other boys about all of this yet?"

"Yeah. They wanted to go on the warpath and find that last Jap and shoot the son of a bitch."

"That wouldn't be a very good idea," Rink said. "There will be plenty of people looking for him. Say, do you mind if I quote you for the story too?"

"I guess that would be OK," Henry said. They shook hands, and Rink left the hospital. He headed straight for his car. He already had his story outlined in his mind from start to finish.

PART II

CHAPTER 1

OCTOBER 1, 1942

Kenji woke up in daylight. He was looking straight up into dense brush and trees. He was thinking about coming down the river until he'd seen the lights of a very small village—the same village he and Hideke had passed in the boat shortly after they had taken it. He'd put the bow of the boat against a steep riverbank and had stepped out onto a grassy pasture, leaving no footprints. From there, he'd shoved the boat back into the ebbing river current with the old fisherman in it and then hurried across the pasture to the wooded hillside, which was where he was now.

He decided to make his way up the hill for a better grasp of the lay of the land. Looking to the north, he saw a familiar scene and figured he was five kilometers from the place he and Hideke had spent the night before the mission. It meant that Highway 101 was south of him, and maybe not too far. That was where he needed to go. After dark, he could take more food from that small store.

The travel was again difficult, but he soon made it to the highway. He stayed concealed in the brush and trees on the north side and watched a couple of yellow buses with black lettering on the side pass by filled with children. What were all those kids doing in those buses at this time of morning? Maybe going to school?

He watched truck after truck loaded with logs traveling east, and he saw empty trucks headed west. He wondered if some of those logs would end up at the mill he had failed to blow up. He had never seen so many cars and trucks. It seemed like they were all different. There were even women driving some of the cars. The Americans certainly liked their machines. There were a few cars with men in uniform inside; maybe they were looking for him. He still had his pistol and his knife, and he wouldn't be taken alive if they did find him.

Kenji decided to move west to a position opposite the store. When he reached the building, he made certain he was concealed, then he sat and watched the store and the vehicle traffic. He tried to focus on what should be his next course of action. First, he needed different clothes—American clothes, he decided. Maybe the Americans, after washing clothes, hung them outside on clotheslines like they did in Ōtsu. He would have to look around. He had seen a few houses on the south side of the highway before, including the house behind the station; he'd look there once he crossed the road.

Not long after darkness, the lights in the store went out. As soon as there were no vehicle headlights shining from either direction, Kenji darted across to the store. The door latch was still defective. Kenji slipped in, took a few cans, and hurried back into the trees. The trees and brush were so located that he had to stay on the west side of the store and house instead of directly behind it, but the concealment was good. He could stay here. If he didn't get greedy, the storekeeper would not notice a missing can or two. In the meantime, he'd lay low and let the excitement over the mill attack die down. The longer he remained undetected, he figured, the more likely an opportunity would present itself to his advantage.

Maybe the storekeeper's house would have laundry out tomorrow. He settled into the brush and trees; cracked open his can; ate a quick, mysterious dinner; and then tried to sleep.

Kenji was awakened at 700 hours by loud truck noises. He peered out of the bushes and saw a couple of large diesel trucks go by but nothing else. He couldn't go back to sleep. His thoughts were now on Hideke. He wanted him to be here. A good companion like Hideke would really help. What would the Americans do with his body? He should be buried in Japan.

Being alone and having to survive was a predicament that Kenji had been trained for and that he had some experience with, but it didn't erase his apprehension about the coming days. There was no Japanese warship standing offshore, and there was no Japanese Army on the ground. He was isolated and companionless. What a mess. But he was Kenji Kosoki, a first lieutenant in the Imperial Japanese Navy, and he was not surrendering.

He needed a plan, though. He wondered about the cars and trucks going by. *Should I try and take one?* Kenji pondered that for a minute and decided it would be too risky. He needed to sneak out of the area, and he needed some American clothes to help conceal his identity, if only slightly, just in case he had to show himself briefly.

CHAPTER 2

OCTOBER 1942

Linus Rink leaned back in his oak swivel chair and stared at the dirty ceiling in the newspaper office building. Rink's mind was focused on the missing Japanese soldier. Now, that was a story, but his editor had indicated that Rink needed to finish the story of the attempted explosion now and with what he had. Surely there was a conclusion that needed telling. A better story could not be found! Rink got out of his chair and stepped directly into Red Carson's office.

"Look, the unfinished business with the Jap soldier is begging to be ferreted out and told," he said. "And I, Linus Rink, am the man to do it."

Red looked up. "Do you have any idea about the time it will take and the extra help we will need around here if you are off on a wild-goose chase that probably has no beginning and no end? Just go ahead and wrap up the story you have, because that is no doubt the end of it."

"Do you know that if that Jap is not caught in ten days, the military, including the Coast Guard, has no intention of looking further for the son of a bitch? The Coast Guard chief in Bandon just told me that. The missing seaman needs to be found, and it will make a hell of a story, just like the other stories about that saga with the boys at Bandon. Just give me thirty days. I'll help with other unrelated work in the interim, and if nothing solid turns up, we'll call it quits on that story."

Red put his hands on his forehead as if he had a headache. "Jesus Christ, I must be losing my mind. Go ahead, but keep me posted. And if you come to a dead end, you are to stop and return to your desk!"

Rink already knew where he would start.

Kenji continued watching the house and store from the spot where he slept. There were no clothes hanging out, but there was a clothesline visible. Kenji's mother washed clothes once a week; maybe the American mothers did the same thing. He would wait.

Kenji was exercising the utmost care for his personal safety. Patience and perseverance were the keys to survival. He had learned that lesson in the Philippines, because, many times, when he'd become impatient and aggressive, he'd nearly lost his life. He would stay where he was. It was hard to be patient, even knowing that he had missed his chance to rendezvous with the sub. Besides, the raft was gone, there was no other boat or raft available to him, and that area would be well patrolled. So what was the use of even thinking about rescue? Maybe he could go someplace where the Americans were not looking for a member of the Japanese Special Naval Landing Forces, at least until the end of the war. Yes, he reasoned, but how?

It grew warm, and he slept without having an answer.

The next day, when the sun was high in the sky, he watched as a bus slowed and stopped in front of the store. The bus had a large, slender light-gray dog in full stride painted on, covering nearly the entire side of the bus. A man in a blue-gray uniform with a matching cap got out of the bus followed by a woman and a child. They went to the side of the bus and opened a pair of large doors. The man took out two bags and gave them to the woman and child, and then he closed the baggage door. The man then went into the store and came out with a drink in a green bottle. The woman and child sat on the bags near the side of the road. The man climbed back onto the bus, and it drove away. Almost immediately, a car drove up, and the woman and child left in the car with their bags.

Kenji reviewed what he had just witnessed. He knew that he couldn't just walk onto the bus when the driver wasn't looking, because the other passengers would see him and there would be no hiding on the bus. On the other hand, there might be plenty of space in that baggage compartment to hide a man, or even two or three men. If somehow he could get in there, he could escape the area.

While Kenji was considering his options with a bus and wondering how often the bus stopped, he noticed a woman come out of the house with a basket of clothes to hang on the clothesline. At first, she hung only sheets and towels, but soon, the woman was hanging men's pants, shirts, and maybe underwear on the lines. Shortly after the woman finished with the laundry, Kenji saw her walk toward the store.

It was warm and there was a breeze, so the clothes would dry, but they would probably not be allowed to hang out there all night. If he wanted the clothes, he would have to move in broad daylight. He could stay in the underbrush and trees most of the way. The taking would be in the open, but he could keep the house between the clotheslines and the store and remain unseen, unless there was still someone in the house. He waited, watching the house for movement. He remained until the clothes might be dry.

When he was satisfied he'd waited long enough, Kenji made his move. He took one pair of blue pants and a faded gray shirt. He made his way back to the place where he had watched the bus, then tried on the clothes. They fit well enough. He buried his old, dirty clothes beneath a log and settled in to wait.

Before dark, he saw another bus with the running dog on the side, but it was going west and didn't stop. At least it was a bus route of some sort, he mused. Kenji hated just sitting still. He was a young man forever brimming with energy and wanted to move, to do something, but his good judgment told him otherwise. The store with the gas pump was as good a place as any for an opportunity to occur.

For the next two days—during which Kenji made another nighttime trip to the store—no buses stopped. Kenji was about to abandon his bus-ride plan when a bus with the running gray dog on the side pulled up in front of the store. It was heading east. A man got off, followed by the driver, who opened the baggage compartment, handed the man his bag, left the baggage door open, and then headed for the toilet behind the store. It was very dark. The weak headlights of the bus afforded little light.

Kenji looked about and saw no one. He sneaked up to the bus from behind, then quickly slid into the baggage compartment and lay flat behind some luggage. Soon, the baggage door closed, and the bus started moving. The floor beneath him was cold and metal and very uncomfortable. He was on his way to some unfamiliar place.

After a twenty-minute ride, the bus came to a stop. Kenji could hear several voices just before the baggage doors swung open. It was very dark in the compartment, but there was some light outside. The driver took some bags out and set them down. Kenji heard the sound of a steam locomotive close by. *A railroad,* he thought. *That's my very best escape from this area.* It could go across the entire United States. He had to get out now. The bus was too risky. There would be many stops and even bus changes; a railroad would be a better option.

There were still bags around Kenji, but he determined that now was the time to leave. He crawled to the edge of the compartment. He saw people near the bus, but they had their backs turned, so he stepped out and slowly walked through some parked cars to the edge of a large gravel lot, then into the shadow of a wooden building.

His Imperial Japanese Navy wristwatch told him it was 2300 hours. The bus had stopped next to a three-story building, and he watched the people outside the bus walk into it. The driver picked up their luggage and followed them. Kenji stayed motionless in a shadow. There was vehicle traffic on the street behind the bus. He listened to a sound he recognized: the steam locomotive was stopped and making the familiar puffing noise as it held and maintained a head of steam. He had heard the same sound many times since joining the navy and traveling from base to base.

The locomotive sounded close. He looked south across the street, and between the old buildings, he could see a part of the locomotive. If he could get on that train, whatever kind of train it was, he could leave the area. He walked to the front of the building. There were no pedestrians in any direction. He headed for the train.

As Kenji made his way along from one shadow to the next, he couldn't help but peer into the buildings he was passing. He knew the window shades were supposed to be tightly drawn at night, but most of them were not fully drawn. One was obviously a place where clothes were cleaned and pressed, and two of the buildings housed restaurants.

He could only see into the kitchen of the second restaurant, and every-one in it was Asian and probably Chinese. He stopped for a closer view. Yes, Chinese. Curious, he walked to the front of that restaurant and looked in at the seating area. It was nearly empty. There was what appeared to be a white family at one table, and at another table there was a family of Asians. On closer observation, he realized they might be Japanese because of their erect posture; smoother, darker skin; and height.

"What are they doing here?" he whispered to himself. Surely after Pearl Harbor, the Americans had disposed of all the Japanese in America. He thought about waiting and approaching them but decided against it.

Kenji walked back toward the train, which was still huffing and maintaining an even head of steam. Still thinking about the Japanese family, he said to himself, "It would be most stupid to trust that family. The best move would be to get out of the area." He could see the loco-motive between the buildings, and he headed for it.

He walked between the buildings, which concealed most of the locomotive. He saw the entire locomotive, its tender, and then some weird-looking railcars on the tracks. The line of those railcars seemed endless. They weren't boxcars, passenger cars, flatcars, gondolas, or anything he had ever seen. They each had just two four-wheel trucks with a long steel connecting reach between them, and there were large chunks of tree bark scattered on the structure of each railcar. Kenji started walking toward the back of the train to see if there were any other types of car.

He eventually came to a place where the tracks crossed what appeared to be a highway. The railcars were separated at the highway to avoid blocking traffic, but it was obvious that the cars would be reconnected when the train was ready to move. Kenji slipped across the highway and continued to follow the railcars. Finally, near the end of the train were two gondolas filled with rock, and attached to the second gondola was a caboose. Kenji climbed into the first gondola, beneath the front edge of the car and out of the sight of anyone who might be in the caboose. He moved some of the rock around to make a seat, but it was still very uncomfortable. When the train began to move, it was more uncomfortable.

The train moved very slowly. Kenji edged his head up against the higher rock so that the outline of a head or upper part of a person could not be detected. What he saw surprised him. He was looking at the side of the mill where Hideke had been shot and killed. The train passed within a few feet of the rail siding where storage battery separators were being loaded into boxcars. He could see through the open barnlike doors of the mill where forklifts and lumber carriers passed. He caught glimpses of workers filling paper boxes with the wood separators; the workers were mostly women. The train started picking up speed as it passed the huge wigwam burner that was spewing glowing sparks into the night sky.

Kenji couldn't shake the image of all those women working inside that mill. He and Hideke had set about to kill them. They were civilians. They were not military people in uniform, and they were not carrying guns or swords or any weapons. They were like the women working in Ōtsu and Kure and Yokosuka and other bases and places he had been in Japan. Would the Americans kill Japanese women? He had never considered that proposition. Then it struck him, like a slam on the face: What was this war about? Wars were not just about soldiers and sailors—they were about everyone. Anyone could be killed, including Japanese families and American families. Something was wrong. He would have to think about it.

The ride on the load of rock was awful. Once past the lights of the mill, he couldn't see a thing except a light in the caboose and, occasionally, if he turned around, some lights in the distance. Soon, the train whistled several times in succession, and lights appeared on the port side. They passed under a bridge but did not stop, and before long, there were no lights to be seen in any direction. The smell of the locomotive smoke and steam was a good, familiar smell, reminding him of his travels in Japan. It made him feel a little bit free, but he knew he wasn't. The farther the train traveled, the freer he would be, but he had no idea how far this train would travel.

The train came to a stop between other railway cars. Kenji could see huge logs on either side of him. He was obviously parked between two log trains. There were a few lights around that told him he was in or near a village of some kind, so he knew he'd better stay put. He could hear the stationary puffing sound of the locomotive in what had been the direction of the train's travel.

He had not had any sleep for thirty-six hours, and he fell asleep on the motionless train only to be jolted awake by forward movement. It was dawn and he saw a sign, POWERS, OREGON, and the train was slowly passing it by on its westerly and southerly edge. He was now moving through a place he'd never heard about or seen.

Kenji looked over the edge of the gondola. He could see thirty or forty empty log railcars and the locomotive ahead. He now knew that the train was headed someplace where it would be loaded with logs and emptied of the rock in the two gondolas. The train was in a rugged forest twisting along precipitous mountainsides and across frightening wooden railway trestles. There would be no train jumping. He counseled himself to stay calm, to keep his wits about him, and to take advantage of the first good opportunity to abandon the train.

By the time the train started to slow, it was midday. Broad daylight! Keeping his head low behind the rock, Kenji peered ahead and saw the steam and smoke from the locomotive. He could also see two rows of small, wooden buildings and several large buildings.

The train stopped, and he heard voices coming closer from the rear of the train. The voices became louder and then quieted, and then he could not hear them at all. Those voices had to have come from the caboose. He had no choice. He climbed over the front of the gondola, keeping the caboose out of sight.

Once on the rails, he looked cautiously around. He saw no one. Kenji ran to the edge of the rail bed and then up a slight incline to brush and small trees, and soon, he was out of sight. He scaled the hill to find a place of good observation and then settled in. He saw men moving about near the buildings carrying what he believed were lunch boxes. A man in a white apron came out of the back of a building and put something in a large can. Kenji guessed that this large building was a kitchen or cookhouse of some sort. There would be food in that building; he would get some of it.

The sky was clear, and there was a breeze. He was much more comfortable here than on the train. Kenji was tired. Everything within his vision was unfamiliar. Maybe this was where the logs came from for the mill. He continued watching. Before Kenji dozed off, he was more certain than ever that he had taken the wrong train—at least the train headed in the wrong direction.

He was awakened by the shrill locomotive whistle. Dozens of workers were sitting on two railcars on low, bench-like seats facing outward. Apparently these trains carried the workers to where they cut trees and loaded them on the log railcars. The camp would be mostly empty now, Kenji thought as the train pulled away, and the opportunity for taking food would improve.

But after the train had pulled out, he continued to see activity around the galley. As hungry as he was, Kenji decided to wait until after dark to sneak forward. It looked as though this place might serve his purposes well, though the lack of shelter was going to be a substantial problem when things got colder. For now, the sun warmed Kenji as he lay back and again fell asleep while pondering his present purpose.

CHAPTER 3

MID-OCTOBER 1942

Henry and Jason sat in the warm sun on a wooden bench on the south side of their high school. They had just finished the sandwiches their mothers had prepared for them.

In a slow, lazy voice, Henry said, "This is one of the few peaceful moments I have had in nearly two months. Everyone wants to know what happened on the beach. If they don't want to know about the beach, they want me to tell them about my grandfather Clausen. I hate to say it, but maybe we should just stay in school all the time and avoid the questions. Did the guy from *Time* magazine come to see you?"

"Hell yes," Jason said, "but when he started to question my dad about the separator plant and its safety, my dad shut him down and told him the interview was over. He must've been there for thirty or forty minutes, though, so there will be a story in his magazine. He even wanted to know what the guy that got away looked like. How in the hell was I supposed to know that? Nobody knows that except maybe your grandfather."

"My grandfather says he can't really say for certain because it was dark, and he was lying in the bottom of the boat, and the guy didn't say anything he could understand. But he did get a good look when the Jap left the boat, and he said the Jap didn't see him do that. But don't they all look alike anyway?"

Jason responded immediately, "Jeez, Henry, the Japs don't all look alike any more than all of us Americans look alike."

George slouched on the bench and against the schoolhouse behind them. "I'm really tired of all this stuff. Sometimes I wish it had never happened to us. Our old friends are not as chummy as they used to be, and adults don't want us to be kids anymore—except when they want us out of the way."

"I know what you're saying. I probably killed a couple of guys, even though they were Japs, and together, we probably saved some American lives and at least one and maybe two separator plants. Does that mean we can't climb into the neighbor's Royal Ann cherry tree after dark and eat his cherries?" Jason asked. "I guess maybe it does mean that."

"So if we get caught in the neighbor's cherry tree or the farmer catches us stealing his chittum bark, we make *Time* magazine, is that it?"

"That's it, buddy."

CHAPTER 4

MID-OCTOBER 1942

Linus Rink sat at his desk in the *Coos Bay Times* building pondering his next move and how his upcoming syndicated story would be gobbled up by the Associated Press. He had interviewed Jason, Henry, George, and David several times, though not recently. He had interviewed mill managers in Coquille and Marshfield and even most of their underlings, and he had written great human-interest features. He had looked for leads and had reported interviews with the Coos County sheriff and his secretary, the Coquille chief of police, the Oregon State Police, and the Bandon chief of police. Rink was in continual contact with the US Coast Guard station in Bandon, and the most important news there was that they now had twenty-four coastguardsmen at that station—but no word on the Japanese saboteur at large. No one knew anything. What could one guy do with no supplies of any kind? The mills were now guarded, some of the beaches were being patrolled, and they were all on the lookout for one pesky Japanese guy. Maybe he'd died in a swamp or a mountain lion had gotten him—or, better yet, he might still turn up someplace, and then, Rink thought, they'd get him. But soon, the whole event was fading from people's minds, and the story was petering out. Soon, he, Linus Rink, would be the only bulldog on the trail.

Rink knew that tightened security was in place on the West Coast, but that was not the reason for the scarcity of information on the missing Japanese spy. He had heard rumors that an American bomber had dropped bombs on a Japanese submarine just west of Port Orford. Rink speculated that the same submarine had brought the Japanese landing force to the beach south of Bandon. He further speculated that the sub was hanging around to pick up what was left of the landing force. That would be a great story. Rink wanted to take a break from office work, so he drove to the Coast Guard station in Bandon, where Art Spears reluctantly agreed to another interview in his office.

Rink related the rumors he'd heard to Spears, including one particularly unbelievable story about a plane coming from the sea toward the coast, and asked him if they were true. "Now, don't bullshit me. I instantly recognize bullshit when I hear it. As a matter of fact, I'm an experienced master at detecting the slightest bullshit included in an answer to an easy question."

Spears noticed the grin on Rink's face and said, "There may be some truth to those rumors, and that's all I can say."

"That's a beautiful response," Rink said, already calculating the potential for a great story. With a smile on his face, he rose from his seat. "Your candor invigorates me," he said, his tone grand, "and I'll return when I am fortunate enough to hear other rumors of concern to you."

On his way out the door, Rink turned and asked, "Hey, can Jap submarines carry airplanes?"

"Some can," Spears said, his tone matter-of-fact.

Rink left the office muttering. Driving back to Marshfield, Rink considered the effect of the story he was about to publish. If he wrote about the submarine and the possible flyovers, the story would replace the search for the missing Japanese spy in many people's attention. He couldn't help it; the Japanese were raising hell in the Pacific. Hell, the United States had invaded North Africa recently. With all that going on, who the hell cared about one missing guy?

At his office, Rink, staring out his single grimy window, started to mentally frame the new story, wondering if it would be the final chapter on the Japanese invasion of Oregon, which made him think about the Western Defense Command. He wondered what it might be doing, if anything, about the missing Japanese spy. Maybe he should call that Major Carlock who had been in Bandon after the first landing. He called Art Spears for the phone number of the Western Defense Command, and soon, he was talking to Major Allen Carlock.

"So this Jap is still missing, but the efforts to find him seem to be dying out," Rink said. "I'm just wondering if the army is interested in helping out."

"For Christ's sake, we're fighting a war," the major said. "We don't give a shit about one lost Jap running around in the state of Oregon with only the shirt on his back when we've got a million of the bastards to fight in the Pacific. You want the son of a bitch, you find him!"

Rink decided that the saga of the missing Japanese was at an end, at least as far as the United States military was concerned. Most locals, he mused, still wanted to kill the guy, but the hunt would be a big inconvenience. *Screw it,* he thought, knowing that they were thinking, *We got other things to do!*

CHAPTER 5

LATE OCTOBER 1942

It had been nearly a month since Kenji had arrived at what he now knew to be a logging camp. In the past two weeks, the nights had become increasingly cold with an occasional frost. He had crept into the camp at night and taken blankets from empty bunkhouses, and he had grabbed substantial scraps of food from the garbage cans on the porch behind the cookhouse. An astonishing amount of food was thrown away. He had learned to take food once a day, at night, after the camp was quiet. This method gave him the freshest food, even if it came from the trash. It was disgusting, but he was living, he was well, and no one seemed to be looking for him here.

About every other day, he saw a man load all the garbage cans from the cookhouse onto a small truck and drive on a narrow dirt road that circled below him and around to the opposite side of Kenji's hill. One afternoon, he followed the small truck around the hill to see where it went. Maybe he'd find a new way to get food. He hadn't gone far when the truck stopped and backed to the edge of a steep draw. Kenji moved to get a better view, and what he saw shocked him. At the bottom of the draw was a dump site, and there stood at least six black bears pawing through the garbage. He definitely couldn't get his food there. The back porch of the cookhouse was not safe, but it was safer than competing with a bunch of hungry bears.

Kenji had taken a dark-green canvas from one of the empty bunk-houses and made a tent in a depression on the hillside. His camp was not visible except from directly above it or unless you were nearly standing on it. He felt somewhat safe from the Americans, but now he had to consider a potential bear problem. There were bears on Hokkaido Island where he lived, and he knew it was dangerous to have unsealed food around. He had stored little or no food at his camp, and he would stop bringing any back with him. He decided it wouldn't be a problem. The real problem was going to be the weather.

Kenji had learned from his beginning navigation class at Etajima that Hokkaido and Oregon were at nearly the same latitude and that winter weather could be horrible. The air was still warm during the days but cold at night. It had rained some, and he knew that in these coastal mountains it could rain and rain and rain. He would have to do something about shelter—and soon. He began to wonder if the logging camp operated during the winter. He decided to wait another week or so to see what happened in the camp. If the camp closed, he would move in. If the loggers left a winter caretaker, he would have to some-how work around him.

Smoke came from the chimneys on most of the bunkhouses, but no smoke came from the cookhouse. This meant there was some other type of heat for cooking and warming. Maybe there would be a large enough supply to last one man for the winter. He hoped so. Kenji's life had been miserable since leaving the submarine, and that was more than two months ago.

One morning, not long after the bear discovery, Kenji watched the workers file into the cookhouse later than usual. Upon leaving the cookhouse, no worker had a lunch box in his hand. Soon, they started carrying their bags and cases to the railroad siding. No crew train left for the woods, and the only train with a locomotive attached was ready to travel back down the mountain. The camp was closing, but Kenji couldn't decide if this was good news or bad news. If they left no food in the cookhouse, it would be bad news. If they left a caretaker, that would also be bad news. He'd have to stay put and wait them out and then decide what course to take.

The morning drew on. He became more and more convinced that the camp would close. One man walked down the row of bunkhouses and, after inspecting each one, shut its door. Kenji got a good look at the men while they waited, and he noticed something unusual: two of the workers waiting for the train to leave were not white Americans. They were standing together but talking to the other workers in a friendly manner. *What's going on here?* he thought. *Are those guys Japanese, or do they just look like they are Japanese?* He remembered seeing the captured Native Alaskan prisoners on a wharf near the submarine dock shortly before he'd departed on this mission. They had certainly looked Asian, some even a little Japanese. He knew that Alaska was a territory of the United States, and these men could easily have come from Alaska for work. Could he fool the Americans into believing he was an Alaskan Native? If his situation worsened, it was a possibility. Language would be a problem, but maybe he could figure something out.

Now he watched the workers hop onto some railway flatcars with their bags. The train tooted its whistle and slowly began chugging down the mountain. Not everyone in the camp had left, however. The cookhouse people were still at work, and two men were lingering where equipment was taken for repair. If the remaining workers didn't leave soon and the weather deteriorated further, Kenji knew he would have to risk slipping into one of the bunkhouses at night.

He was an experienced member of the Special Naval Landing Forces, and risk was his job. His career in the Imperial Japanese Navy had taken an abrupt turn after he'd enlisted, and he had given no thought to the idea that the navy would have him on land and not onboard a fighting naval vessel.

Kenji wished he were home with his family tending their gill nets. The salmon season would be nearly over now, and the easy, enjoyable part of the year would follow. Would he ever be there again? It was a question he had asked himself frequently, and he never had an answer.

CHAPTER 6

EARLY JANUARY 1943

Linus Rink was disappointed with himself and his inability to discover anything about the missing Japanese soldier. He'd thought that the Coast Guard or the army guarding the area would have given him something to put him on track; at the very least, he'd expected a name of someone to talk to. But the military had washed their hands of the case.

There was one thing that Rink had considered doing from the beginning, but he had discarded the idea as too time consuming. He'd wondered if the Japanese who'd come to shore had some contact in the area. The trouble was, there were no Japanese in the area. Any contact with a Chinese person would be unlikely because, by now, the Chinese in the area—and probably everywhere—hated the Japanese for a multitude of reasons. Still, Rink thought maybe if there were Japanese people in the area, some Chinese folks might just know about it. He decided to ask around.

There were three Chinese restaurants in the county: two in Marshfield and one in Coquille. A laundry in Marshfield employed a couple of Chinese people. It would take some time to talk to them all, but Red hadn't said his thirty days had to be consecutive, Rink reasoned. Therefore he had a little time to continue his quest.

Two weeks passed, and some workers were still in the camp. Kenji heard a train whistle in the distance. He quietly said to himself, "I certainly took the wrong train, and one to a dead-end place at that!" Soon, he heard the steam locomotive laboring up the mountain grade. He hoped this would be the last train out, taking with it all the remaining workers.

The weather had turned lousy both day and night. The wind and rain were almost constant, and his camp on the hillside was a mess. He had finally moved into one of the unused bunkhouses, but because of the other men present, he hadn't had a fire. The food situation had worsened; there were few scraps, and getting the scraps out of nearly empty garbage cans was loathsome business. He certainly wasn't getting fat on a garbage diet. *Oh well,* he mused, *things have to get better when everyone leaves this camp.* At least the constant fear of capture by the Americans would lessen.

The only weapons he had remaining were his knife and his pistol. For some reason, his arm's-length perception of the American civilians had changed him. Killing an American civilian was something he would avoid if possible. If he could continue to live in this logging camp for several months without interference, he would have time to plan a course of action. It could take the form of escaping the Oregon coast to someplace where his and his colleagues' exploits were unknown or at least long forgotten. There was also the possibility of assimilation into the workforce of the logging camp. This approach might be possible through the two workers he had seen who appeared to be Asian. He wondered if he might overcome the language barrier by feigning a mute affliction.

Of course, if he had decent clothing, good camp gear, and a rifle and ammunition, he could disappear into the dense coastal forest of Oregon and maybe live indefinitely. The war against the United States couldn't continue forever, and his experience and training would be a great asset. This latter alternative was not Kenji's first choice. Living like an animal in the forest was akin to no life at all. He had done that in the Philippines in good weather; when that sojourn had ended, his expectation had been that it would never happen again. How wrong he had been. But as soon as the war ended and Japan emerged victorious,

he would be back at the naval academy at Etajima. He would be making visits to his family in Ōtsu. He would stay alive—no matter how
difficult and arduous the course was. He was a soldier in the Imperial
Japanese Navy, and although he hadn't swallowed all the dogmatic
crap about dying for the emperor, he would still do his duty as best he
could. Staying alive for the emperor would be more helpful than dying
for him.

The sound of the locomotive was getting closer. Kenji hurriedly
straightened up the bunkhouse and exited through the back window.
No one should suspect he was in the camp. He crawled beneath the
bunkhouse, where he was fully hidden unless someone looked with a
flashlight. He would wait there until dark and then venture out to see
what had happened. He would wait even if he heard the locomotive
depart, because that wouldn't necessarily mean everyone had left the
camp.

From time to time, he heard people walking on the plank sidewalk
between the rows of bunkhouses, and occasionally he heard voices
and doors closing. According to Kenji's still-working waterproof wristwatch, the train had arrived at noon. He knew it would leave that day
because he could hear the pulsating metallic sound of the excess steam
escaping. The train would leave, but when?

Finally, around five o'clock, as it was getting dark, the train sounded
its horn a few times and began to chug away. Soon, he would be able
to emerge from hiding to discover whether or not he was finally alone.

CHAPTER 7

LATE JANUARY 1943

David, George, Henry, and Jason met in downtown Bandon, then walked to the Coast Guard station. They had questions about their encounters with Coast Guard patrols on the beach. Following the recent events nearby, enhanced security at the station had been ordered. After much wrangling at the entrance door with a coastguardsman who had never seen them before, he went to check with Art Spears. At last, the four of them were allowed to enter. They found Spears in the large upstairs recreation room overlooking the Coquille River. In a friendly but curious tone, Spears asked the boys what he could do for them.

David said, "Well, every once in a while, when we walk the beach, we run into one of your men on horseback who tells us it would be better if we stayed off the beach, and from the expressions on their faces, they don't like the looks of the guns we're packing. I told the last guy that my father said we had a constitutional right to pack a gun and that the guy could go screw himself."

"David, I've told you before that you boys shouldn't use such foul language."

Jason interrupted the impending lecture. "Why don't you tell your guys who we are and what the hell would have happened if we didn't carry guns on the beach?"

Spears sighed. These boys—though he liked them—could be a real pain in the ass. "Alright, most of my men have been raised in the city and are not used to seeing boys walking around with high-powered rifles. I'll instruct them to ignore you all. I may as well tell you that we're getting a bunch of dogs to help with beach patrols. Those dogs will be kenneled down by Bradley Lake on the ocean side near the beach, so try and stay clear of that area. We don't want anyone injured by a dog. If we'd had dogs at the time of the last incursion by the Japs on our beach, we sure as hell would have found all of them and their supplies."

"We were wondering about that too," David said. "Linus Rink wrote that the two Japs that tried to blow up the separator plant had about all the explosives—or whatever it was—that they could carry. Five Japs came ashore. If there were enough explosives for five Japs to carry, did you find the rest of them?"

Spears slowly looked from one boy to the next. "As far as the phantom supplies are concerned, we think as you do, but we haven't located anything. The dogs will help once we get them. You guys satisfied?"

David was looking north out of the windows at a sea lion in the river tearing up a steelhead trout. "If I had my rifle, I'd shoot that son of a bitch," he said. He turned. "When we're on the beach, we'll look for their supplies of explosives and stuff."

Oh shit, Spears thought, *here we go again. If the boys find explosives, no telling what would happen.* "OK, wait a minute. I can't stop you from looking, but if you find anything, you leave it alone. Don't touch it, and call me at once. It could be very sensitive and dangerous, and the country doesn't want to lose any of its most famous boys."

David grinned. "Don't worry," he said. "We'll just keep on performing the work of the US Coast Guard. And we'll stay away from your dogs."

Spears shook his head and looked at Henry, who was smirking. "You still not gonna let us have some submachine guns for patrol?" Henry asked.

"This conference is officially over, and the exit is right there," Spears said, mock-serious, and the boys filed out. Well, he thought, they annoyed him, but he liked these boys more than ever. They already seemed older in some ways—the two beach incursions had taken care of that. Yet, in many ways, they were still teenage boys.

CHAPTER 8

FEBRUARY 1943

It was the first cloudless day in two weeks. About the time the Earth's northern hemisphere turns as far away from the sun as it can, storms in the eastern Pacific punish the Oregon coast with wind and rain—and bring Japanese glass fishing floats high onto the beaches. George Williams knew this, as did most of the boys living on the coast. He called David, Henry, and Jason, and they agreed to meet at George's place near the beach as soon as possible to beat any other scavengers.

By ten o'clock, they were all at George's place ready to go. They headed for the beach with Luke, the black dog, leading the way. Henry was carrying a gunnysack for floats; David and George carried rifles.

When they hit the beach, Henry broke into a dead run. About a hundred feet ahead, high in the new drift, was a beautiful green glass float at least ten inches in diameter. He proudly held it high and dropped it into his gunnysack. Soon, Jason sprinted ahead and held up a small green glass ball, and then all of the boys were on the lookout for floats. Luke romped in the surf, disappeared in the brushy green plant life behind the foredunes, and occasionally rolled in a dead seabird.

When they reached the place where they had repelled two Japanese shore parties, they stopped.

"Look, some of our little dune is still here," David said, "but that big driftwood log down the beach is gone."

"I keep thinking," Jason said, "if the Japs had any extra supplies, they have to be close by." The other boys agreed.

"But we've been up and down this beach. I've never seen anything," David said. "Come on, let's go on down the beach and find some more floats."

They walked south on the beach for a half mile but found nothing, so they turned around and headed back toward George's place. Somewhere around their little dune, they noticed Luke was no longer with them. George looked back and saw Luke's heavy black tail above the dune grass. Frequent bursts of sand flew out of the grass.

"Hey, Luke's got something," George said.

They all dropped to their knees and dug with Luke. Soon, some clothing showed up: three green jackets with little anchor insignias on their left. Next came three military leather belts, each with a scabbard and knife and a holster and pistol. This was obviously the cache, and surely the explosives were buried there. The four boys dug up eighty pounds of high explosives loaded in several satchels, along with a satchel with hundreds of feet of detonator wire and many electric detonator caps.

Henry asked, "How in the hell did that dog know where to dig?"

"Because he's smarter than you and remembered why we were here," George said proudly.

During the past eight months, starting with the first incursion by the four Japanese soldiers and the explosion of their raft, the boyish character of each young man had diminished. Nor were they easily intimidated by anyone, adults included. Even Henry had changed.

They sat looking at the stuff they had dug up and talking about what to do with it. Luke was resting by them, panting, with sand clinging to his wet coat.

Jason said, "Well, we told Art Spears that we would notify him if we found anything, so I guess we better do that."

They all agreed, but David added, "We're not packing this stuff to them. They can come and get it. Art Spears will be notified, alright. I'm walking down the beach with one of these satchels. You guys stay here." David picked up one of the satchels containing explosives and walked south on the beach about 150 yards and sat it down on a small drift log. When he returned, he said to George, "You were wondering if the scope on your rifle had been knocked out of whack. Now's your chance to see if it still shoots straight."

George was prone on the beach behind a slight rise in the sand. He fired, and a tremendous explosion ensued. "Holy shit! How much stuff was in that sack? I bet my mom could feel that all the way at the house."

North of the boys and trotting in their direction on horseback were Coastguardsmen Ron Freeman and Sam Gibson. Sam and Ron had been watching the boys on the beach for some time and had been speculating whether or not it was David, Jason, Henry, and George. The explosion told them it was.

Freeman's horse reared and almost threw him to the ground, and Gibson's horse whirled in circles. Their riding experience in Kansas allowed them to quickly regain control of their mounts. They raced toward the boys.

Freeman said, "What in the hell do you think you're doing? I should have known it was you guys!"

David calmly said, "We just notified Art Spears that we found the supplies the Japs left on the beach. It was the easiest way. Besides, George needed to see if his rifle scope had been knocked off-kilter. It turned out to be OK."

"Is that the stuff you found?" Sam asked, pointing at the stack of things that Luke was again sniffing.

"Yes, what's left of it, and you can have it," Jason offered.

Everyone there went down the beach to see what the explosion had done to the log and the beach. A small crater in the beach was still smoking, and the drift log was gone.

George said, "Gee, that was fun. Let's do it again. We'll set off all that's left, and we'll really make some noise. But we'll need to get farther away from it."

Before the idea went any further, Ron stepped in. "Jeez, are you guys nuts? Just stop!" He told Sam to go back and tell Spears and to send a vehicle. Ron led his horse back to the stash of goods after Sam had left at a near full gallop. They all sat in the sand looking at the pile of Japanese goods.

At last, Ron said, "Those bastards had their nerve. How'd you guys find it? We thoroughly searched the area, and we couldn't locate it."

"Luke found it. When are you guys getting dogs?" George asked.

"Pretty soon. You know, this has been one hell of a day for us."

"Friday is always a good day. Besides, we have to go to school Monday. What the hell do you guys care anyway?" Jason said.

About an hour later, a light-gray jeep arrived with Art Spears and Sam in it. Art stepped onto the beach, looked at the boys' smiling faces, and said, "So you found it. I guess you just had to explode some of it to see if it worked, right?"

"Right," Jason answered. "But we wanted to make sure of what it was, and we wanted to talk to you about something."

George stepped forward in front of Art Spears and said, "Look, during the past six or seven months, we have taken a lot of crap and have put up with more talk and baloney than we should have. It was unbelievable that the second landing happened and we had to go through everything again. David even had to fight one person over the deal."

Henry moved up next to George and said to Spears, "Some people even thought one of my buddies had shot me, and all of our parents had to get involved."

Spears gave the boys a quizzical look. "Yes, I understand all that, but what are you trying to tell me?"

Jason explained to Spears, with Ron and Sam listening, "Just before Sam and Ron arrived, we talked and decided that there's been enough talk about us, and we want it to stop. If anything is going to be said about this find, the Coast Guard should take all the credit for it and not mention us. We would really appreciate that. Will you do it?"

Spears said, "Yes." He looked at Ron and Sam. "You heard them, and you heard what I said, so you keep this to yourselves, OK?"

They both nodded in agreement.

Ron and Sam loaded all the stuff into Spears's jeep, and Spears gave the boys and Luke all rides home.

Spears and the US Coast Guard kept their word. The find of the Japanese supplies remained unknown to the public.

CHAPTER 9

MARCH 1943

Kenji Kosoki sat warming himself on a wooden bench in front of the large black cookstove in the camp cookhouse. The propane stove was a welcome convenience. He had seen stoves like it aboard the naval vessels he'd traveled on. There had even been one on the submarine that had brought him to the Oregon coast. The gauge on the propane tank between the railroad tracks and the cookhouse showed the tank to be nearly full when the last of the crew and train had left months before.

It was then that he had moved into the cookhouse. Burning firewood in one of the bunkhouses might have betrayed his presence in the camp—never mind the fact that the cook's quarters adjoined the kitchen and were furnished with a good bed with sheets and blankets stowed in a mouse-proof wooden chest. Not only was the pantry well stocked with canned goods, but there were five-gallon tins of rice, beans, and pasta, all ready for cooking.

Kenji had taken full advantage of the shelter and food, but had been careful not to create any kind of mess or disturbance that could not be eliminated on short notice. He felt sure that there would be winter inspections of the camp, and he was right. Whenever he heard the locomotive puffing up the grade, he would clean up what little disorder there was and disappear beneath the cookhouse. The train, with one or two men on board, had so far made only two inspections, and both times, he had had time enough to open and then close the doors and windows in order to cool the kitchen. The bed was always stripped, the dishes and utensils clean, and the garbage can empty. No one would suspect a person was living in the camp.

During the last week in December through the first of March, the camp had been frequently buried in snow. It was a wet, miserable snow. Then, when it was nearly gone and the mountain weather warmer, another storm would arrive, bringing freezing temperatures and more snow. He would not have survived in the forest. He had seen rain and snow on Hokkaido, but it was nothing like the Oregon winter. In mid-January, the accumulation of snow reached the eaves of the bunkhouses, making it impossible to walk anywhere. Deer were starving to death in the sheltered spaces between some of the bunkhouses.

Walking around outside in the snow was not a good idea. His footprints would be obvious. Getting rid of the empty cans and the other little garbage he generated was difficult. He had to wait for a day with little or no snow to empty the garbage, and then he was always sure to try to brush out his tracks, even though the next snowfall or rain usually took care of them. Every time he walked to the camp dump, he was fearful of bears, until he remembered that Japanese bears hibernated in the winter and American bears likely did the same.

In February, he heard a disturbance down among the row of bunkhouses. The growling and near screaming was fierce. He stepped out on the covered porch of the cookhouse and watched two huge reddish-brown long-tailed cats fighting over a deer carcass. He stepped back into the cookhouse and closed the door, then said, "That is one more reason not to go outside. There are lions in America!"

Kenji could do nothing except stay near the big stove in the cookhouse. The railroad tracks were also buried. The two times the train showed were in January and February, when the snow was less than two feet deep on the tracks at the camp. Each time, he was fearful that someone would stay. He never emerged from his hiding place until the day was almost dark and he was half frozen.

Kenji was lonely. From time to time, he would talk to himself. There were occasions when he would ask himself out loud, "What am I doing here? Why did I have to take a train that brought me to this place?" He had no answers. He would consider what may have happened to the old commercial fisherman he left adrift in the boat and how the fellow he left on the dock had made out. There were books in the place, but none he could read. Boredom was his persistent enemy. Pleasant thoughts of his family were his only relief.

Kenji did not know exactly what the date was, but he had found calendars hanging in the cookhouse for the years 1941, 1942, and 1943. The days had been marked off from April through the beginning of November every year. Kenji was glad for the mathematics background that allowed him to read the Arabic numerals. From the markings on the calendar, he was able to approximate the current date. That knowledge, along with the warming weather and the letup in storms, led him to believe that the locomotive would soon be coming up the railroad grade again with workers.

He had given months of thought as to what he would do and how he would conduct himself when the train did arrive. He had determined that he would somehow move in among the many employees getting off the train, and then he would find the Alaskan Natives and feign the inability to speak. However, it seemed probable to him that the train would first bring people to set up the camp and make it operational. Maybe some mechanics would come to tend to equipment and get it running. If that happened, he would have to stay away until the regular logging workers were brought to the camp. He could not live beneath the cookhouse while that happened; he would have to reestablish his hillside camp, from which he could readily observe the comings and goings of the workers.

He had no understanding of the English language, excepting a few proper nouns, and he would somehow need to speak some English. How he would do that, he didn't know, but surely it could happen if he spent enough time with the Americans.

But maybe he would be caught. When that idea nagged at him, he avoided thinking about it. He stuck to his assessment of the situation as being a thorough, rational plan, and he would not consider failure. If the plan were to fail—well, he probably should have been killed months ago. Kenji's morale ebbed and flooded every day, like the tide. Memories of his family and his fishing days continued to bolster him, as did those of his time at the naval academy. Of course, he envisioned a favorable outcome to the war, with Japan emerging victorious. He could do what he had to do, regardless of hardship, in order to be able to embrace in reality all of those happy times and future events.

He was going to have to exercise better care than he had two weeks before. That day, he had fallen asleep after his noon meal of rice. Fortunately he had cleaned the kitchen and stowed the blankets and sheets from the bed, but the kitchen was still warm when he was awakened by the sound of the locomotive. He looked out the window, and it was coming to a stop in the camp. He turned off the cookstove and slipped out the back door. He held the door open very briefly to cool the kitchen, but within a minute, he had to dart under the cookhouse. He immediately heard footsteps above him, and voices. The back door opened and closed, but the footsteps retreated from the cookhouse, and there were no more voices. The only sound was the noise of the locomotive idling while maintaining steam. He was sure he heard the train leave, but he waited for more than an hour before exiting the crawl area under the cookhouse. The train had parked a small boxcar on a siding at the camp. It no doubt contained camp supplies for the summer. All the train's crew had left with the train. The train had made its way back down the grade.

CHAPTER 10

MARCH 1943

Linus Rink was driving away from the second Chinese restaurant he'd visited that day, and he had accomplished nothing. The Chinese man he'd spoken to had known nothing about any Japanese people in the area, and one man in the first restaurant had had no idea that a few Japanese men had come ashore south of Bandon. *Talk about a wild-goose chase.* Rink muttered to himself, "Oh, what the hell. I'll run this out and then call it quits."

His next stop was the laundry. Inside, there were half a dozen Chinese employees. The owner gave him permission to talk to the workers, but most of them couldn't speak English. One Chinese lady who spoke English suggested that Rink go to Coquille and talk to Tommy Shu. If anyone knew anything about the local Chinese or Japanese people, it would be Tommy Shu.

Rink had heard of Shu before. A select few people in Coquille knew Tommy Shu truly well, and among those, Tommy was immensely liked and respected. Tommy had worked hard, lived on nothing, saved his money, and bought a falling-down shack on Highway 101 in Coquille. He had repaired the shack and turned it into a successful Chinese restaurant.

Rink parked his Ford V8 in front of the restaurant with the TOMMY SHU sign above the door. He went in and was welcomed by the proprietor. Tommy was very personable and spoke broken English. He sat with Rink in an uncomfortable painted wooden booth. Rink looked around with an approving nod and told Tommy that his restaurant was a very nice place as they drank weak tea from tiny cups. At last, Rink told Tommy what he was looking for.

Tommy said, "You know that business about the Japanese trying blow up separator plant? It happened right over there." Tommy pointed to the southeast.

"I know," Rink responded in a quiet voice. "Please tell me, do you know of any Japanese individuals or families living in this part of the state?"

"All Japanese were moved to camps, but I can tell you this: the army never came here to get Japanese because there are none. I tell you I hate Japanese military. They are devils. So I tell you something, but it is about good Japanese family that lives here. Fred Shobara and his family all born here and are good citizens loyal to United States. The army must not know about them, but I sure they come and take them soon. They move here some time ago, and have many friends and no enemies here. No one reports them. Don't you report them."

"OK." Rink nodded.

"About a week after attempt to blow up separator plant, one night after Fred Shobara and his family ate here, I see a man, I sure he Japanese, follow the Shobara family. I think him probably a friend or relative come to stay with them. I not see anyone with the Shobara family since then. I forgot about it. Maybe he that Jap you look for?"

"Maybe. Tell me where the Shobaras live."

"Fred not home now. He work for highway department."

That evening at about seven o'clock, Rink knocked on Fred Shobara's door. One of Fred's children answered and invited Rink in.

Fred's demeanor, and that of his wife, became a little uneasy and fidgety as soon as Rink walked into the room. They clammed up and seemed suddenly frightened, and Rink felt uncomfortable. Rink said, "I'm with the newspaper, and I'm working on a story about a Japanese—"

He saw that he was frightening Mr. and Mrs. Shobara, so he stopped talking.

Fred and his family were understandably nervous and upset. This was a stranger in their home. They had dreaded deportation to a Japanese internment camp since it started happening. First his and his wife's parents in Orange County, California, then Mrs. Shobara's brother and sister-in-law living near Monterey, California, had been taken. Each family sustained a loss of property and business. Mr. and Mrs. Shobara were now thinking that their time was at hand.

They needed time. They knew about the Japanese landings on Bandon Beach and the Japanese man on the loose. Maybe the authorities were trying to connect them in some way with that Japanese man, and that could be even worse.

Fred said, "Before we talk about this, I need to discuss some things with my wife and children. If you can come back in a couple of days, we can have this conversation."

Fred knew that his wife, without saying a word to one another, also believed that any discussion with a newspaperman involving a Japanese person could do nothing but hurt them. If named in a newspaper, they could be the focus of attention. Deportation to an internment camp would become reality.

Rink thought for a moment. If he pressed them for information now, they wouldn't talk. "Sure," Rink said. "I'll come back in a couple of days."

He left knowing he had stumbled onto something. The Shobara family might very well point him in the right direction. The problem Rink had was that they might think they'd done something wrong and would not talk. He was still sure he, Linus Rink, could convince them otherwise.

CHAPTER 11

APRIL 1943

It was early spring, and there were some windless, sunny days. The snow was almost gone, and surely a train would soon be in camp. Kenji was ready. He had disposed of the little bit of trash he had left in his initial location on the hillside above the logging camp, and he had established a better, more concealed campsite. He hoped he would need to use the new site for only a couple of days. He would stay in the cookhouse until the train came.

While he was waiting for the sound of the locomotive, three days passed in good, clear weather, and he continued to review his plan. The more he considered and reconsidered it, the more uneasy he became. He had always been careful and measured in his actions and thoughts, and he was now overanalyzing the situation by conjuring up all sorts of fateful situations. Kenji knew he had to stop tormenting himself. Besides, he wanted to know how the war was going.

While aboard the submarine, he had been told about the battle of the Coral Sea. Though the battle had ended in a standoff between the Japanese and the Americans, Japan had lost some hard-to-replace naval vessels, and Port Moresby—the Japanese stepping-stone to Australia—was not then taken. Worst of all, there were rumors aboard the sub that the Japanese Navy had lost four aircraft carriers at Midway, that the Midway Islands were not taken, and that the battle was a devastating loss to the Japanese Navy. They were only rumors, but they sounded real. Certainly these losses, if the rumors were true, would be only temporary setbacks. Kenji remained a member of the armed forces of Japan and would continue to conduct himself accordingly.

Kenji was sitting in the sun on the front steps of the cookhouse so that he might enhance his chance of hearing the train as early as possible. If things went as planned, he knew that he must learn to read and speak the English language. It would be difficult, but he could gradually pretend to overcome his muteness. He was considering how important it would be to learn about what was happening in the war against the Americans when he heard the sounds of the locomotive in the distance. He immediately grabbed his bundle of supplies and went to his hiding place on the hillside above the camp.

The train came straight to the camp and stopped. Immediately behind the tender was the familiar flatcar with seating along each side. At least seventy-five or eighty workers alighted and walked around the camp. Some headed to bunkhouses and disappeared inside. Others walked directly to the cookhouse.

Kenji was eager to spot the Alaskan Native workers. He spotted one, and it was the one whose appearance was less like Kenji's appearance than the other's was. One would do. His plan would go forward. He did not want to spend the night on the hillside. It was after one o'clock, but there was plenty of time for the cook, if the cook was there, to prepare a dinner for the camp. Kenji figured he may as well make his way to the camp and start milling around, acting like a worker. He eased himself down the far slope out of view of the camp and then up through the brush to the open area behind the row of bunkhouses. He felt confident his maneuver had not been seen.

He stepped out between bunkhouses near the cookhouse and walked over to the Alaska Native and indicated to him that he was unable to speak. Kenji did not draw much attention. Some workers looked him over more closely than others, but they knew that the company, like all mill and logging companies since the beginning of the war, was having difficulty hiring workers. Another Alaskan was not unusual.

Kenji followed the Alaskan to a bunkhouse, where the man commenced to make up his bunk bed and take personal things from his duffle bag. The Alaskan had likely seen more than one down-and-out logger with no personal possessions, so Kenji's lack of any belongings was probably not unusual to him.

Kenji could see that he made this man uncomfortable. Kenji pointed to himself and said, "Kenji."

The man pointed to himself and said, "Lawrence," and motioned for Kenji to sit down on one of the empty bunk beds. The bunks were unmade, but each bunk had a neat stack of sheets and blankets stacked at the foot.

Kenji had just sat down when another worker walked in with his duffle bag. He held out his hand, and Kenji shook it as the worker said the name Mike Dodge. Dodge lived in Coquille and had grown up there with two brothers. One brother was dead. Kenji knew that Mike Dodge was greeting him and telling Kenji his name. Kenji feigned muteness and said nothing. He hit himself on the side of his head with the heel of his hand to indicate it was a blow to the head that caused him to be mute.

Mike immediately commenced talking to Lawrence. Mike and Lawrence seemed to know each other, and Kenji could tell that the conversation was about him. It seemed to Kenji that Mike was asking the questions, to which Lawrence mostly shrugged his shoulders. When Mike finished making up his bunk bed, he left the bunkhouse.

Sitting at one of the large tables inside the cookhouse was Ray Sampson, the camp's senior foreman in charge of managing one of several logging operations on the company's forested mountain timber and property holdings. He was sorting through a small pile of papers and taking notes on a notepad with a cup of coffee in front of him. Ray had worked for several logging outfits, but years ago, he had settled on the logging operations of Smith Wood Products. The company liked him. He had not graduated from high school but was smart, innovative, and a beneficial mentor to young loggers. He had a good rapport with his workers, and his sense of humor was the best in camp.

Mike Dodge walked into the cookhouse and sat down opposite Ray. Without looking up, Ray asked, "Anything bothering you?" Ray knew Mike was a complainer. If it wasn't the weather, it was the equipment or the way his steak was cooked. But Mike was a good logger, so Ray tolerated his complaints.

Mike asked, "What in the hell were you thinking about when you hired that guy that can't talk? Jesus Christ, Ray, a logger that can't talk is useless. He might get someone killed!"

"Mike, there are times I wish you couldn't talk, but as long as you're talking now, what in Christ's name are you saying?"

"I'm saying one of the guys you hired can't talk."

"I didn't hire any son of a bitch that can't talk. You think I'm nuts?"

"Well, some asshole must have hired him, or what the fuck is he doing here?"

"With the war going full bore, we can't help but hire an asshole once in a while. Would you like me to cite you some examples? Where is this man?"

"He's in the bunkhouse with Lawrence and me."

"OK, as soon as I finish here, I'll see about it. In the meantime, do you think you could find something to do?"

An hour later, Ray walked into Lawrence's bunkhouse, where Kenji was seated on the edge of an empty bed. Ray asked Lawrence, pointing at Kenji, "Who is this man?"

Lawrence looked at Ray and said, "I don't know. He was just here. Indicated his name, but I didn't understand it. He can't seem to talk. I think he just wants a job."

Ray looked at Kenji, and Kenji mumbled the words "Attu" and "Alaska." Kenji said nothing else.

Ray glanced at Lawrence and asked, "Was he on the train?"

"I don't know; I didn't see him until I got to camp."

Ray thought that if this man was from Attu, he must have escaped somehow. Ray looked at Kenji and said "Attu, Attu" several times, and Kenji made a rowing motion with his arms, then hit the side of his head with the heel of his hand. Ray motioned for Kenji to follow him.

Ray and Kenji walked into the kitchen, a place most familiar to Kenji. The big cook, Marge, was at the island counter making something.

Buster, the bull cook in charge of the cookhouse and Marge's husband, greeted Ray.

"I know you're short of kitchen help," Ray said. "This is your helper. He can't talk—something haywire with him, maybe a knock on the head or something—but he looks plenty strong." Ray pointed at Buster and said, "Buster." He pointed at the cook and said, "Marge." He pointed at himself and said, "Ray." He then pointed at Kenji, while making it obvious that Kenji was to tell them his name.

With apparent difficulty, he uttered, "Kenji."

Ray then went from individual to individual, pointing at each and again saying their names, believing it might help Kenji remember. Ray spied a sink full of dirty pans and utensils. He took Kenji by the arm and led him to the sink. Then Ray found a broom and dustpan and showed them to Kenji.

Kenji realized what had happened. He had just been hired, but not as a logger.

Before Ray left the kitchen, he told Buster to set up Kenji in Lawrence's bunkhouse and to get Kenji's full name and Social Security number as soon as he could.

At five thirty p.m., Kenji sat down in the kitchen with Marge and Buster and ate the best meal he had eaten since living on the submarine that had brought him to this predicament.

Later that evening, Buster took Kenji to Lawrence's bunkhouse and pointed at the bunk as Kenji's. Kenji mused that this was nearly as good as life at the naval academy. Buster wanted some information. Kenji said his name, "Kenji Kosoki," and wrote his birth date in Arabic numbers, but he couldn't understand what Buster was saying about a Social Security number. Kenji had mimicked the phrase "Social Security number" aloud but had no idea what it meant or what Buster wanted.

Buster told Lawrence to try and explain to Kenji about a Social Security number and left the bunkhouse. Lawrence didn't like being told what to do, but he figured that Buster thought because Kenji and Lawrence looked a little bit alike, he might get the job done.

Everyone in the camp thought Lawrence was a Kodiak Indian, and he'd seen no need to correct them. Lawrence was Athabascan, from southeast Alaska. He couldn't say what Kenji was; he could be Athabascan, Yupik, or Aleut, but what the hell difference did it make?

Lawrence had few friends. He was snaggle-toothed and ill-tempered, and he pissed everyone off when he fingered through the pancake stack at breakfast to find the hottest ones. He would walk away from everyone at lunchtime when on the job. He was a choker setter but thought he should be a riggin'-slinger, a step up in authority and pay. When working, he complained about anything and everything, and he was always on the verge of walking off the job. His fellow workers kept telling him that the log train left camp twice a day and it was easy to catch, just jump on and wave goodbye.

Lawrence at first considered Kenji a nuisance, but Kenji was quiet and expressed no opinions—or anything else. It might be an interesting venture to actually help someone. Lawrence was barely literate, but he did speak English and he knew the logging business, at least from the lower echelons of the labor force. After much difficulty, he made Kenji understand about the Social Security number. He showed Kenji some old paycheck vouchers. About that time, Buster returned with an application for a Social Security number for Kenji to sign. Lawrence taught Kenji how to write his name, and for the first time, Kenji did it in English rather than Japanese.

CHAPTER 12

LATE APRIL 1943

Linus Rink pulled up in front of Fred Shobara's house and parked. Rink had been unable to return to the Shobaras' when he said he would. He found that the Shobaras had a phone, and he had called to say he would be delayed, but there was no answer. Nine days had elapsed rather than two. Fred's house was dark. Obviously no one was home, but he knocked hard on the door anyway. There was no response.

Rink walked to the house next door and inquired about the Shobaras. The man answering the door said that the army had come several days before and had removed them to an internment camp. He said, "One of my kids asked a soldier where they were taking them, and he said he didn't know."

Rink knew there were many internment camps in the West. There was one at Tule Lake, California, and another at Ontario, Oregon, but camps were also located in New Mexico and Arizona as well as Nevada. Rink drove back to Marshfield cursing himself for not pressing the conversation with the Shobaras. He was at a dead end. The army wasn't about to talk to him, and he wasn't about to drive all over the western United States trying to get into Japanese internment camps. Besides, he didn't have the gasoline ration coupons to do so.

On the return trip to Marshfield, Rink was considering writing another feature article for his paper assailing the violation of the constitutional rights of US citizens by the US Army and the United States itself.

CHAPTER 13

MAY 1943

It was only a matter of weeks, and the camp was in full operation. All sides of the logging show were functioning, sending trainload after trainload of logs to the mill—the same mill Kenji and Hideke had tried to blow up. Kenji could not forget the night the train he was hiding on had passed slowly by that mill, where he had witnessed all the female employees busily manufacturing battery separators; nor would he forget the regret he'd felt about his attempt to injure or kill them. Maybe war against civilians was not proper.

Buster and Marge were at first frustrated with Kenji because he didn't understand anything and he couldn't speak. It wasn't long before Kenji knew what "wash the dishes" and "clean the kitchen" meant. He also learned the meaning of "sweep the floors" and "change the linens in the bunkhouses." When Buster pointed at the garbage cans on the rear porch and said, "Take the garbage to the dump," Kenji also knew what that meant. He would load the cans on the back of an old truck with no windshield and drive to the dump. There were always black bears at the dump, and he would wonder which ones had frightened him during the past winter. He was beginning to gain a slight comprehension of what people were saying, especially if some ongoing activity was being mentioned. He toyed with the idea of beginning to utter more sounds, as if his voice were returning or he were getting better. He would have to think about it for a while. Things were going very smoothly for him, and there was no reason for him to change—at least not yet.

Kenji usually finished his work in the cookhouse at about 1900 hours and would then walk to his bunkhouse, where he was able to spend time with Lawrence. Lawrence was helping Kenji learn English by identifying objects in magazine pictures. If Mike was present, he would lie in his bunk reading while shaking his head at the exercises that Kenji and Lawrence were performing. He was learning to tolerate the two Alaskans, but sometimes he got annoyed quickly.

On one such occasion, Mike said, "Jeezus, Lawrence, what the fuck's wrong with him?"

Lawrence stood up and said to Mike, "If you'd been through what he's been through, you couldn't talk either. When the fuckin' Japs took Attu, artillery shells exploded around him, and his hearing got all screwed up. Besides, he could only speak Yupik and hardly any English. That's about all I can get out of him."

Lawrence sat back down next to Kenji, who thanked him.

CHAPTER 14

AUGUST 1943

It was now the middle of August, with clear skies and hot sunshine, but a northwest wind made things tolerable. The breakfast mess had been cleared, and Kenji was on his way to his bunkhouse for rest. The kitchen help rose at 0400 hours every day and rested for an hour or so prior to lunch. Ninety percent of the lunches and lunch food for the day was prepared immediately following the breakfast service and set out on tables. Loggers picked what they wanted and stowed it in their lunch boxes. Only the kitchen help, a couple of mechanics, and maybe a visitor or two were served lunch. Now he could rest.

Kenji's attention was drawn to the long, continuous blast of a locomotive whistle coming off the mountain to camp. It was the wrong time of day, and the whistle blast was one he had not heard before. He went to see what was happening. The locomotive and its tender arrived with two severely injured men. One was on a dirty canvas stretcher on the floor of the locomotive cab. The stretcher was brought to the lunchroom in the cookhouse and placed on a table. Buster asked the locomotive engineer why he hadn't kept going into Powers. The engineer said that the man was tortured by the rough train ride and had insisted on stopping. Buster told the engineer to get the locomotive to

Powers at once and to get a doctor to camp as soon as possible. The train left with the ambulatory injured worker.

Buster had seen many an injured logger and a few dead ones. They always brought them to the cookhouse if they didn't go straight to town. This logger had a head injury but was conscious. Kenji saw the pulsing of blood coming through a tear in the man's pants. It was a sure sign of serious bleeding. A mechanic and a saw filer had come to the cookhouse to see who was injured, and one of them said, "I guess there's nothing for us to do but wait for the doctor."

Kenji made some guttural sounds and pointed to the pulsing blood. No one moved, and nothing was said. Kenji ran to the kitchen and fetched a clean dish towel. He tore it up to make a compress. He motioned for someone to take the injured man's pants down, then Kenji applied the compress and then a tourniquet with the man's belt, wrapped it firmly, and tied it off. He had been trained to do it at Etajima as emergency first aid. He completed the entire operation without a misstep or wasted motion. Once finished, he sat back and wondered if he'd just blown his cover.

It was three hours before the train returned with the doctor from Myrtle Point. Kenji went to the cookhouse when he heard the train arrive. Dr. Black walked into the cookhouse and said, "It's a good thing you didn't bring him straight in. The rough train ride might have loosened the tourniquet, causing more blood loss. He has a concussion, I don't know how serious, but he's awake. That's encouraging. However, his leg is broken almost exactly where he was bleeding. The compress probably saved his life. Without it, he would have been dead by the time he arrived in Powers." Dr. Black paused, then asked, "Anyone know how this happened?"

"A strap on a haulback block broke, and the line threw a wad of brush and heavy logging debris into the choker setters," the locomotive's fireman said.

While the injured man was being loaded up, Buster drew Dr. Black aside to the table where Kenji was sitting. He told the doctor about Kenji's inability to talk and how Kenji was trying to utter some words. The doctor asked Buster, "Has he ever had a serious head injury or a stroke?"

Buster looked at Kenji and then the doctor and said, "He indicated to me that he had a head injury, but it is difficult for me to communicate with him."

"This is probably a form of aphasia, but loss of speech or power to use words is usually associated with stroke and not head trauma. This man's symptoms seem more in line with what we call 'global aphasia,' which is the result of a stroke and is usually permanent. Is this man's behavior abnormal in any other way?"

Buster told him no. The locomotive whistle tooted, and Dr. Black headed for the train. When he was almost to the train, the doctor turned and called, "Buster, your man that can't talk seems a little strange to me. Where's he from?"

"We think Alaska. Maybe he was run out of Attu by the Japs, but we really don't know. He's a good worker."

"He looks a little like a Native Alaskan, but more Oriental than Alaskan," he mused. Then he added, "If he's the one that spotted the injured man's bleeding and applied the compress, then there's more to him than meets the eye." Dr. Black hopped onto the locomotive for the ride down the hill.

By the time Buster got back to the cookhouse, he had forgotten the conversation with Dr. Black. He was intent on seeing that dinner was produced on time.

The only empty bunkhouse in the camp had been set up by some of the workers as a poker room, complete with a large round table with an old gray blanket spread across it. Every evening after dinner, six or seven workers, usually the same men, played poker with a one-dollar bet limit. At that limit, there could be some sizeable winnings—and losses. One evening in late September, Kenji walked into the poker bunkhouse for the first time to see what was happening. Lawrence was standing watching, and Kenji moved to his side. One of the players was obviously having a good night, considering the amount of money in front of him.

Soon, the big loser, also a big man, looked up at Lawrence and Kenji and said, "What the fuck are you two weird assholes looking at?" A bit of a smile crossed Lawrence's face, showing his four remaining brown teeth. The big loser growled, "You think it's funny? I'll show you what's funny." He shot up, grabbed Lawrence, and dragged him outside. Kenji and some of the other poker game observers followed them.

It was nearly dark. The guy started to pummel Lawrence, and Lawrence was having trouble defending himself against the bigger, stronger man. Kenji stepped in. With two swift blows, one to the throat and one to the underside of the nose, the big loser was writhing in pain on the ground, clutching his face and throat. Kenji's work was so quick and so sudden that the few observers couldn't tell what had actually happened. Kenji's hand-to-hand combat training at the academy had served Lawrence well.

Kenji took Lawrence by the arm and led him to their bunkhouse. Lawrence had some bruises and an abrasion on his face but was otherwise unhurt. Lawrence thanked Kenji, but he was especially happy that he did now, in fact, have a friend he could count on. He would help Kenji as much as he could. No one else in camp counted Lawrence as a friend.

Kenji had now administered first aid to the bleeding worker and swiftly cut the big poker loser down to size. The two events were more than a month apart, but Kenji hoped no one was putting two and two together. He would have to be more careful. He would avoid the poker room, and he would tell Lawrence to stay out. Fortunately the fight had lasted but seconds, and it was not clear to the men whether Lawrence or Kenji had inflicted the damage to the poker player. The poker player was too embarrassed to talk or complain about the incident. His sore throat and bruised nose were his constant reminders to stay clear of Lawrence and Kenji.

CHAPTER 15

OCTOBER 1943

The days continued to become cooler and shorter. Kenji was following his plan to gradually regain his ability to speak. The plan actually aided Kenji by concealing his ignorance of the English language. Buster had helped him in a limited way, and Marge, the big cook, had become fond of Kenji because of his kind and gentlemanly ways and also helped him with his speech difficulties. She had taken the time to make hand-lettered cards of the alphabet, which Kenji quickly mastered. He was sounding out simple words but making a disaster of sentences because of his lack of understanding about English verbs and tenses. He could verbalize a newspaper headline, although he usually didn't know what he had read. But he was gaining ground. If Buster told him to split fire-wood and see to it that each bunkhouse was well supplied, Kenji knew what to do. After the job was finished, he would practice his speaking skills by repeating to Buster the task that Buster had assigned him.

Kenji was earning $1.50 per hour and was paid for eight hours each weekday. Saturdays and Sundays, he was paid $2.25 per actual work hour. He didn't know what the paychecks he received amounted to or what to do with them; he couldn't equate the numbers with yen, and didn't dare ask about the difference, so he saved them in a small box on the shelf by his bed.

One afternoon, the train brought a man to camp that Kenji had never seen. The man walked into the dining hall. Buster seemed to know him on sight. Buster called Kenji out of the kitchen and said, "This is Mr. Purvis, the company bookkeeper in charge of payroll. He wants to talk to you about your paychecks. It seems you have not been using them."

Kenji sat across a dining table from Mr. Purvis, who explained to Kenji that he must take the paychecks to the bank. Kenji wasn't sure what was being said to him. Buster, sitting beside Kenji, said, "The checks represent money, and they must be taken to a bank."

Kenji knew what a paycheck was and he knew about banks, but not in the English language. He soon understood and told the bookkeeper that he would go to a bank.

Mr. Purvis, while looking at both Kenji and Buster, asked, "Where you from, Kenji?"

"Attu. Japanese soldiers chase me out, take others with them."

Buster thought, *I'll be damned. He's learning pretty good.*

That evening in the bunkhouse, Kenji asked Lawrence if he would take him to a bank, saying, "The bookkeeper told me to."

Three days later, Kenji and Lawrence were on a train from camp to Powers. Lawrence took Kenji to a tavern and café, where Lawrence announced that they needed a ride to Myrtle Point and to come back the same day. An old man with a tattered straw hat got up from a table and walked to the cash register. As he was paying for his meal, he gave Kenji and Lawrence the once-over and said, "My name's Wallace. You can ride with me. I'm picking up some grain, and you can help load it. But I may not get back until dark, OK?" Lawrence and Kenji hopped in the cab of the big farm truck, and they were immediately headed north along the river on the dusty gravel road to Myrtle Point.

Kenji marveled at the countryside. It could have been a scene on Hokkaido. Most of the fields were green with subterranean irrigation, with cattle all grazing in the same direction into a cool breeze. The river was clear, with many gravel bars showing—obviously a good place for salmon to spawn. Kenji asked if salmon ran in the river, and farmer Wallace assured them that within a month or so, after the rains started, the river would be full of salmon.

Forty-five minutes passed, and they crossed another stream and were traveling on a hard-surface highway. Soon, they were in Myrtle Point, and the truck was backed up to a loading platform at the large feedstore. Wallace told Kenji and Lawrence to help the store clerk load the sacks of grain. As he walked away, Wallace said, "Be here at four o'clock if you want to go to Powers!"

Lawrence took Kenji uptown—a five-minute walk—to Security Bank, the only bank in town. He said to Kenji, "Tell them you want to open a savings account, but you want to hold out fifty dollars." This was Lawrence's test for Kenji, who did as he was instructed.

It took a long time at the teller's window. The communication was difficult for both. Kenji now had a little black book that said he had $1,967.24 in the bank. He also had $50 in paper money in his pocket. The best part was that Kenji had been able to communicate with a strange American. Finally, after more than a year in the United States, he could speak a little English. He hadn't actually used the words as Lawrence instructed, but the words "open account" and "savings account" and "fifty dollars cash" had done the trick. Kenji had signed his name as "Kenji," and after a brief conversation with the bank teller, just "Kenji" was good enough.

They left the bank, and Lawrence said, "Now we're getting you some new clothes." They walked across the street to a clothing store, where Lawrence bought a new white cotton snap-brim hat. Kenji bought one too, along with two pairs of pants, socks, shirts, and underwear. Now he had about $40 left.

Lawrence headed to a restaurant, with Kenji following. They sat at a window table. Lawrence ordered a chocolate milkshake, and when the waitress looked at Kenji, he said, "I'll have a chocolate milkshake." He didn't know what he had ordered, but in a few minutes, he was enjoying his first milkshake. The main street in town was also the main highway through Myrtle Point, and Kenji watched as large trucks hauling logs drove by. Some of the logs were so immense that there was but one log on a truck. The vehicles he saw were not the same as Japanese vehicles. They were larger, more varied, and seemed to be in a hurry. He was fascinated by what he saw in the small town. The people seemed happy and well fed, and had business to attend to. He even saw a large yellow bus filled with smiling, happy schoolchildren. Didn't these people know there was a war on?

They left the restaurant and headed for the feedstore and the truck. They would be early, but there was nothing else to do. There was a boy on the main street selling newspapers, and it sounded as though he was saying something about the war in his effort to sell the papers. Kenji held out some coins in his hand to the boy, who took a dime and gave Kenji a paper. When they sat down on some feed sacks at the feedstore, Kenji asked Lawrence to tell him what the paper said about the war.

The paper was dated Friday, October 15, 1943. Lawrence read the paper out loud, tracing each line with his forefinger, with Kenji following and repeating the words as they were spoken by Lawrence. They were reading a front-page article about the Americans having struck the Japanese-held Port of Rabaul, destroying 177 Japanese planes and wrecking 124 Japanese ships in the harbor. Kenji knew that Rabaul was on the island of New Britain, near New Guinea. He asked Lawrence, "Is that a true story about Rabaul?"

Lawrence was a little puzzled that Kenji would ask about Rabaul, a place no one had ever heard of, but Lawrence didn't care what Kenji might know. "Of course it's true. Our news is exactly what is happening—not like the propaganda handed out by the Japs and Germans to their people at home."

"Anything else about the war in that paper?"

There was an article about the United States Army Air Force bombing Frankfurt, Germany, and an article about the Russians driving the Nazis out of the Caucasus. Kenji again followed Lawrence's finger across the page, and as he did, he was beginning to understand the import of the news articles. The war might not be going well for Japan.

Kenji carefully framed his question. "Are we winning the war with Japan?"

Lawrence had given no thought to the fact that Kenji probably had no idea what was going on in the world. Apparently the only thing he knew was that the Japanese had run him out of Attu, which was only a remote territory of the United States, and if the United States was bombing the Japanese, there must be a war going on. Lawrence thought he should educate Kenji on events that were happening in

Europe and in the Pacific. He told Kenji about Pearl Harbor and how the United States had declared war on Japan and Germany. He told Kenji about the Battle of Midway, where the United States Navy had sunk four Japanese carriers and numerous other Japanese ships, and how the earlier Battle of the Coral Sea had saved Port Moresby and Australia from the Japanese. Kenji was shaken but hid it well.

Kenji vowed to himself that he must learn to read English and asked Lawrence to continue to assist him. There were always newspapers lying around the bunkhouses and in the cookhouse. He would stay informed. It might help him decide how to handle his situation.

Wallace took them back to Powers, but there was no train leaving for the logging camp until morning. They stayed in town at a rooming house known simply as "The Hotel." The next morning, before the train left, Lawrence took Kenji to the town library. Lawrence said something to the lady in charge, who soon brought him three beginner reading books. He could have them for two weeks. After leaving the Powers library, Lawrence took Kenji to a barbershop, where Kenji lost his long hair to a very short haircut.

It was Saturday afternoon when they returned to camp. Most workers had departed on the train that brought Kenji and Lawrence back to camp. Kenji was wearing his new clothes. Buster and the cook looked him over, and Buster commented, "Your new clothes and haircut make you look more civilized." Kenji didn't know exactly what Buster had said, but it gave him a good idea. He would get busy with his library books and hone his English.

It was nearing November, and the camp would soon be closing. Two sides of the logging operations had shut down, and it became apparent that the camp would close by the week's end. Kenji had made up his mind that he would try to make arrangements to stay in camp and be a winter caretaker or some such thing. He would volunteer to do it without pay, and the company could leave tins of food for him and maybe some beans and rice. He revealed his plan to Buster and the cook, and Buster promised to talk to the logging superintendent, Jon Jensen, about it. Jensen was to be in camp for the closing in a few days.

While Jon Jensen was in the cookhouse finishing his coffee after the noon meal, Buster took Kenji to Mr. Jensen's table. "This man," said Buster, motioning toward Kenji, "wants to stay and live in the camp as a winter man or caretaker or something, and he would do it without pay. I think it's a good idea, and he's a good man for the job."

Jensen looked at Kenji and said, "Aren't you the guy nobody hired, but we hired you anyway?"

Kenji knew what the question was and replied, "I think so."

Mr. Jensen turned and faced Buster. "I've considered doing this very thing for a number of years, but I didn't think I could talk anyone into doing it. Now I have a volunteer, but we'll pay him something and leave food for him. We have already planned on being here three or four times during the winter, and he might even come out for a break once or twice, depending on the weather. With the war on, we need a little security in our camps. The military is buying much of the lumber we produce, and you all know what we are using the white cedar for. So, Kenji, you stay."

Without anyone needing to look at a calendar, the late-October weather told all loggers in western Oregon to go home, rest, and reacquaint themselves with their families. All the logging sites had shut down, and most of the workers had left camp for the winter. Buster, three mechanics, Ray Sampson, and Kenji remained. Soon, Kenji would be alone for the larger part of five months.

Ray Sampson sat at a table in the cookhouse reviewing his checklist for closing the camp. Buster was in the kitchen and saw Ray fussing with his papers. He asked Kenji to take Ray a cup of coffee.

"Sit down, Kenji," Ray said. After a while, without looking up, Ray said, "Looks like you're staying for the winter, and I'm not so sure you weren't here last winter. You obviously took care of the place if you did stay here. According to Buster and Marge, you're the best help they've ever had in all the many years they've been cooking. So if you claim you were run out of Attu by the fuckin' Japs, that's OK by me. I want you to understand that Lawrence isn't the only Alaska Native we've employed. Lawrence's friend Virgil was here last year, and we've had others. They all speak slowly and very deliberately, as well as softly. Their skin color is dark like yours, but they're usually much shorter. You do not speak like them, you are taller, your teeth are good—you do have the right coloration, but I am hard-pressed to make you out as an Alaska Native. Incidentally, I have not shared these thoughts with anyone, and I don't intend to share them so long as you continue the way you have been."

Kenji understood what Ray had said, and a thousand thoughts passed through his mind. He only replied, "Thank you."

"Another thing, Kenji. There's a .30-30 Winchester rifle in the kitchen with some cartridges. We'd like you to thin out the black bear population before spring. Buster says they've been on the back porch of the cookhouse, and the dump is getting a little dangerous with a dozen or more bears hanging around the place."

Kenji's first reaction to the rifle request was that Ray must harbor no suspicion whatsoever that Kenji was a member of the Japanese Special Naval Landing Forces that had come onshore at Bandon fifteen months ago. Ray's trust in Kenji may have been intuitive, but it would prove valid. Kenji had already made up his mind that the war was over for him, whether Japan won or lost.

Several days later, the last logging locomotive eased out of camp on the downgrade across the high wooden trestles and onward to Powers, Myrtle Point, Coquille, and Marshfield. It would soon return to the huge covered railroad shop in Powers for annual maintenance and a few runs to the Eden Ridge Camp.

Kenji couldn't believe his good fortune. He was evidently safe, with ample food and shelter, and he was even being paid a wage. But he was assisting indirectly in the supply of Port Orford white cedar logs to the battery-separator manufacturing plant in Coquille, the plant he was commissioned to destroy. Was his conduct treasonous? He instantly vowed not to torment himself over that ethical dilemma. He would live through the winter, take care of the camp, and whet his language skills. He now had a dictionary and copious reading materials that Buster, Marge, and Lawrence had left him. By the time the camp closed, he was speaking and understanding English at an acceptable level, at least according to Buster and Marge, but there was much room for improvement.

Reading the old summer newspapers and magazines gave Kenji a view of the war with the United States. Things weren't looking all that good for Japan. Not only that, the Russians were on the offense against the Germans, England was not going to be invaded by the Germans, and the Americans were pounding the Germans from the air. Germany was Japan's strongest and most important ally, so what was happening here?

Worrying about the war was meaningless. He was out of it. Kenji decided to worry about shooting a few bears before they hibernated for the winter.

Between Christmas and New Year's Day, Kenji heard a locomotive laboring up the railroad grade. The camp was in order, as it always was, but this time, Kenji was able to meet the train. It was a locomotive and tender with four people in the engine cab. The fireman handed Kenji a large pasteboard box filled with fresh food, including a baked ham. Buster was aboard, and so was Mike Dodge, who had bunked in the same house with Lawrence and Kenji. They came to wish Kenji a happy New Year. Kenji didn't know how to respond. He thanked them when Buster handed him another box full of magazines and newspapers.

There remained about a foot of snow on the ground from the last storm, and the weather was clear and cold. They all left their footprints in the snow as they walked to the cookhouse, where Kenji brewed coffee for them and tea for himself.

Kenji's visitors anxiously told Kenji how the United States was hammering the Japs in the Pacific. Kenji acted excited about that news, but he would rather have heard something different. After coffee and tea, the four men boarded the train and went back to town.

It took Kenji some time to read the magazines and newspapers. As he waded through them, he was confounded by the Americans' obsession with what appeared to be sporting events called basketball and football. Teams from all over the country were playing as though there were no war. Additionally, Kenji was puzzled by articles about movies, books, musical plays, and all sorts of cultural events he hadn't heard of before. The Bears beat the Redskins, 41 to 21, for the football title—what was that? Obviously the war was not interfering with American recreation and pastimes, and whatever the rest of that stuff was.

By February, the snowstorms had left drifts reaching the eaves of the bunkhouses, just like last winter. Deer were again dying near the bunkhouses. Their forage was either covered or nonexistent. The train had not yet returned, but it would come as soon as the warmer rain started. Kenji was lonesome. Maybe next winter, he would live in town. He had reread the last batch of magazines and newspapers until they were nearly worn out. He wanted fresh reading material.

Buster had brought him a 1944 calendar. He was turning the page to March when he heard the distant whistle of the locomotive. He would soon know the plans for the spring opening of the logging camp—it couldn't be far off. Again, it was only the locomotive and tender, but there were four people aboard the engine cab besides the engineer and fireman. Ray Sampson was aboard with Buster, Mike, and Lawrence. Lawrence had persuaded Ray to let him aboard. He had missed his friend. Kenji met them halfway to the cookhouse. Kenji's English was good. His winter of reading out loud had done wonders for his language acquisition. He asked Buster if he had any newspapers for him. Buster not only had newspapers but a book and some magazines.

Kenji found out that the camp would be opening in less than a month. Lumber was in sharp demand, and their camp was where it originated in large quantities. Buster and Kenji made coffee, and they were all sitting at a table in the cookhouse when Ray announced that they would be operating one additional logging side. More workers would be arriving, many of them young and inexperienced. The war and the military draft had taken most men, and few remained who had experience and could do the strenuous work. It would mean more work for the kitchen and camp crew, but there was a pay raise in the works.

After the men left on the train, Kenji was again alone. He dove into the box of newspapers and magazines, and after an hour of reading, it was apparent to him that Japan was losing the war. In February, US battleships had shelled the Kuril Islands, which were part of the Japanese homeland, and the Americans were headed to the Mariana and Marshall Islands. The Imperial Japanese Navy was gradually going to the bottom of the ocean. Kenji had no options. Barring any serious blunders on his part, he should remain undetected.

CHAPTER 16

APRIL 1944

George and David rode their bicycles into town. It had started to rain lightly, so they headed for the confectionery store, where they found Jason and Mary Lou Petersen, a classmate, each with a five-cent Coke in front of them. Jason had walked into the place alone, as had Mary Lou. Without an invitation, the two boys sat down at the same table and wanted to know what was going on.

"What you see is what's going on," replied Jason.

"This is the first day of Easter vacation, we have a whole week, and there's nothin' to do except watch it rain," George complained.

"Well, the wind's blowing west southwest, and some Jap floats should come on the beach. You could hunt floats to stay out of trouble, but," added Jason, "whatever you do or we do, let's not make the newspapers with it."

David said nothing. He was looking at two girls sitting on stools at the counter. David was almost a year older than his friends, and it showed. He would be sixteen in June, and he was uncommonly handsome, with blue eyes, perfect teeth, and the body of the athlete he was. Glass balls, beach hikes, and bumming around with the boys were no longer his main interests.

The blonde girl looked over her shoulder at David, and he saw her quickly return to conversation with her companion, Sally, a girl David knew from class.

Mary Lou saw the exchange and said, "That's Anne Hall. She just moved here with her family from Redmond. Pretty, isn't she?"

All eyes at David's table were now on Anne Hall, and she noticed. David was embarrassed and admonished his friends. "What the hell is the matter with you people anyway? I look at a person I've never seen before, and you make her uncomfortable and embarrass me. Now I need to let her know that we're not weirdos."

As Anne and Sally were leaving, David walked over to them and said, "I apologize for my friends' bad manners, but more than that, Sally, please introduce me to your friend."

Sally did, and David asked if he could walk with them. It had stopped raining, and surely they didn't have far to go. He took a close look at Anne; she was a beauty with a body to match. If she was as bright as she looked, he had to have a date with her.

Anne looked him over and said, "We're not going far. Maybe some other time."

"I want to call you sometime. Is that OK?"

David's question went unanswered for a moment, but she told him that would be OK and told him her four-digit phone number. He embedded it in his brain.

David went back and seated himself with his friends. George asked, "Well, what the hell happened?"

"Nothing," David said.

They finished their Cokes, and Jason said, "Let's go visit our friends at the Coast Guard station. We haven't been there in a while. They may need some help, and they probably miss us anyway." Jason asked Mary Lou if she wanted to go with them, and she responded by moving in her chair with an exasperated look.

The three boys walked to the Coast Guard station. David said to Jason, "You shouldn't have left Mary Lou sitting there."

Jason said nothing until they walked up to the sentry. "We're here to see Master Chief Petty Officer Art Spears," he announced.

The sentry looked them over and murmured, "Oh, it's you guys again. Go on in. I probably couldn't stop you anyway. Spears is around someplace."

They found Art Spears in his office, and he invited them in. They sat down after once again looking the place over as if they had never seen it.

Spears asked, "Alright, what is it this time?"

Jason said, "We got some time on our hands, and we talked it over, and we're here to help you iron out any problems you may have. So do you have a job for us, something that requires application of our cognitive powers?"

"I see you've learned some new words since I saw you last. Are you here to practice them on me?"

"Nah, we just missed you," David said, "and we wanted to visit in case you weren't doing anything."

George said, with an expressionless look, "We've stayed away from that bunch of cur dogs you have down at Bradley Lake, and we've all done well in school so far this year, but I suppose we still can't get any submachine guns from you."

Spears laughed.

"There is one favor we wanted to ask," George said, "and that is: Will you please tell your sailors on horse patrol to stop taking those glass floats? They cover ten times the territory we do. They're on the beach all the time, and after they get through, there are no floats left for us poor boys."

"I'm not telling them anything. They're all hundreds if not thousands of miles from home for the first time in their lives, and they need diversions. Do your cognitive powers cause you to understand what I'm saying?"

"I guess so," Jason allowed. "By the way, we want to thank you for keeping us out of the newspapers with that explosives find. Things have settled down for us, and we like it that way."

"We see your reporter friend, Linus Rink, once in a while," Spears said. "He's still on the search for anything dealing with the missing Jap, the one that beat up Henry's grandpa. We looked, the army looked, and even the FBI looked, and nothing turned up. We do check in on Mr. Clausen once in a while. He's the only person that could identify the

Jap. If that Jap were smart, and we think he is, he would have left this area for a new location where no one remembers or even knew about the incursion on the beach and the attempt at the separator mill. No one cares about that Jap anymore, and he's certainly on no official's priority list. Unless—don't tell me you guys are going to embark on a search."

"We're through with beach patrols and anything else having to do with the lost saboteur," David said.

George added, "David's got that right. He and Jason both have their minds on girls, and Henry and I are probably not far behind."

"That's when boys start not being boys," Spears said. He stood up behind his desk. "Thanks for the visit. You're always welcome here," he said in a friendly manner.

When they left, George asked the sentry if he had shot anyone yet with his Garand rifle. The sentry closed his eyes and winced in disgust but said nothing.

That evening, David called Anne Hall and, after some verbal fumbling around, asked her for a date. They agreed to meet at the confectionery store the next afternoon.

Five days later, on Saturday, Jason, George, Henry, and David were all at George's house doing as little as possible. It had been raining, the wind was blowing from the southwest, and it was a good day to be inside. George's mother and his older sister, Lisa, were in the house someplace.

George said, "David, I saw you with Anne Hall the other day. How are things going anyway?"

David bristled and said, "None of your damn business, but," he calmed down and said, "I may be in love."

George said, "In love? Are you nuts? You can barely tie your shoelaces!"

David immediately changed the subject and told his friends that he had talked to his father about getting a job in the logging woods the coming summer and that his father thought he could get on with Smith Wood Products. They had logging operations at Sitkum on the East Fork of the Coquille River and at Eden Ridge up from Powers on the Coquille River. If he got a job, he would be living in their logging camp during the weekdays. David figured he could see Anne Hall on weekends.

Jason thought he might also get a job with Smith. "Maybe we could work at the same place and live in the same camp," he suggested.

David would be sixteen, and though Jason would still be fifteen, workers were scarce, and they were both physically strong. The state of Oregon was issuing work permits for children under sixteen years of age. Jason would get one. George, whose father was still deployed, would not leave his mother and sister at home during the summer or any other time. Henry knew his parents wouldn't allow it because of the dangers common in the logging industry. They wanted him to work in their store if he really wanted to work.

Before school was out for the summer, David had acquired a learner's permit and had learned to drive. On the day he was sixteen years of age, his mother, at his insistence, drove him to Coquille to take the driver's exam and driving test. He passed and again insisted on driving his mother home with his temporary driver's license in hand. As soon as they arrived home, David was on the phone to Anne. She accepted his invitation to a movie that night at the New Bandon Theatre. It would cost him fifty cents for the movie and ten cents for a Coke afterward, but he thought it was worth it.

After the movie and Coke, David drove to the state highway gravel storage area east of town on Highway 101 and parked behind a large stack of crushed rock. He put his arm around Anne and kissed her lightly, and she kissed him back aggressively. David then suggested that they get in the back seat of the car.

"No way," Anne said. "Not with you or anyone else!"

David hastily retreated from his suggestion by claiming he was uncomfortable with the gear shift and emergency brake handles coming out of the floorboards between them. Anne relaxed, thinking she had overreacted. She did not know that she had not overreacted or that David's youth was giving way to manhood. They kissed again and again and again.

After he had taken Anne home, he decided that she was the woman for him. At sixteen years of age, he was sure of everything. It was a clear-cut case of him and Anne together for the remainder of their lives. The reality of the situation skipped over David's intellect and reason. But next time, he would try harder.

CHAPTER 17

MAY 1944

The Eden Ridge Camp above Powers had been open for about a month, and all sides of the logging operations were in full swing. Kenji's winter job had finished up nicely with one more bear kill before anyone arrived. Its skin was nailed to the bunkhouse.

Ray Sampson was short of loggers because of the increase in the number of logging operations, and he'd offered Kenji a job setting chokers. Kenji's pay in the kitchen was less than that of the lowest logger's pay, but he turned it down at Buster's insistence. He'd received a small pay raise because of Buster's and Marge's objection to taking Kenji away from them.

On Sunday in the first full week in June, the late train brought more workers. Six of them were high school boys from various towns in the county. When the older loggers learned about the "kids in the brush," as they called them, they were generally disappointed because they needed training to do the work and to keep from being injured or killed. Teaching them to know what was around them, what might be moved into them, what might happen if a line broke, and to stand clear of everything moving was a daunting task. One of the boys from Coquille was given a bed in the bunkhouse occupied by Kenji,

Lawrence, and Mike Dodge. Mike was heard to say, "Jesus, I sure hope this one can speak English."

Meanwhile, at the Sitkum logging camp of Smith Wood Products, miles from the Powers camp, David and Jason alighted from the logging company's crew bus and were told to stay where they were with their duffle bags. As soon as the bull cook, Gus Olson, returned from depositing two other boys in a bunkhouse, he led David and Jason to a bunkhouse occupied by two old poker-playing loggers who worked on the falling crew. On the way to their summer quarters, Gus asked where they were from. David said they were from Bandon.

When they arrived at their designated bunkhouse, David and Jason found the two older men resting on their bunks. The two had worked at every job in the logging woods and were now at one of the top-paying jobs falling big old-growth timber. They were not going to be bothered with teaching the new boys about logging because the boys were not going to be on the falling or bucking crews. The oldest faller was Ed and the other faller was Vern. Vern and Ed had paired up as fallers years before. They were both heavy chested, chewed Copenhagen snooze, smoked cigarettes, and could be profane, depending on the aggravation. They did shower and shave daily, played poker nightly, and went home on the Wednesday-evening train to their families in Powers. They returned Thursday morning in time for work. Ed and Vern had married their high school sweethearts after graduation and were through raising kids. They sure as hell weren't going to raise these two kids from Bandon. In fact, they might even torment them.

When David and Jason had finished making their beds and emptied their duffle bags into the old wood dovetail-jointed powder boxes, Ed said, "You boys' job is to get a fire going in that barrel stove each morning. Gets cold as hell around here at night. And if the place gets dirty, you need to sweep the floor."

David looked at Jason and then looked at Ed and said, "Who was doing that before we arrived?"

"Whoever got up first. Don't argue with me, boy."

Both Vern and Ed had slight, toothy grins on their faces that revealed a lack of determination to follow through on Ed's direction, and David saw it. David looked at Jason and said, "These guys are changing the rules just for us. Whadda ya think of that?"

"What I think is that this is a democracy, and we should vote on all rule changes," Jason said. "All those in favor of David and Jason making the fire and sweeping the floor, raise your right hand."

Neither Ed nor Vern knew how to deal with the situation. Neither raised a hand.

"That motion sure as hell didn't pass," David said, "so I guess we're back where we started: first guy up builds the fire, and the first guy that complains about the floor sweeps it."

Jason and David had never experienced such exhaustion on a daily basis. Toward week's end, they were debating whether logging was for them. Ed and Vern overheard their complaints, and they both lectured the boys on the finer points of traveling the royal path of life. Number one rule was: Finish whatever you start, and don't start something you can't finish. Vern squared off at the boys, first one, then the other, each one sitting on the edge of his bed, and intoned, "There is no one worth his salt that can't be a logger. If you give up on this, you'll give up on other things not half as difficult. You started logging this summer, and you finish it."

Ed added, "And when you finish the summer in this camp, you will be stronger and better persons for it. Besides, you'll have some money in the bank!"

"Yeah, you're probably right," Jason said. "We're going home for the weekend, so we'll think about it."

Ed said, "I better see you both back here Sunday night, or my first day off, I'll come to Bandon and whip your asses red."

David and Jason arrived home that Friday evening. They had taken a logger's bus called a "crummy" to Coquille and then caught a ride with Jason's father to Bandon. The return trip—if they went back—would be the same.

David was home in Bandon for about five minutes before he called Anne Hall. It was after seven p.m., and she wasn't home. He wanted to ask where she was, but he knew better. Manners were everything when a guy was trying to impress a young lady with his maturity. Her mother probably wouldn't have told him anyway. He'd been thinking about her all week in the logging camp, and now this obstacle. Another reason not to be a summertime logger. He couldn't even remember the details of his plan to seduce her.

Jason called Henry and George. They had done nothing all week except hang around town. Henry had worked one day stocking shelves in his parents' store. George had helped his mother around the house. Neither had made a nickel. The summer looked bleak for them. *They should have real jobs*, Jason thought.

David talked to Anne on the phone the next day, and they arranged to go out that night when he had his parents' car. A sickening love story starring Esther Williams, the Queen of the Surf, was the movie that Saturday night at the New Bandon Theatre, and David didn't want to see it. Instead, they took a car ride to Coquille to see what movies were playing. The movies had already started at both theaters, and the second features were too late to get Anne home before her appointed curfew of eleven p.m. So they went back to the gravel storage area and behind the large pile of crushed rock. Anne and David lost sight of the fact that they were too young to be acting like adults. David did not make the mistake of suggesting that they repair to the back seat. He skillfully moved around the stick of the gearshift and the emergency brake handle arising from the floorboards and, soon, was as close to Anne as he could possibly get.

She held him tight, and he held her tighter. They both knew what was happening. They were both physically mature beyond their years. Until now, Anne had demonstrated significantly more mature judgment in most matters. David was less mature, but as he had demonstrated in the past year or so, he could act with maturity in any crisis situation, and so it happened.

As David walked Anne to her doorstep, he vowed to himself that he would never return to the logging camp, no way, never, never. He was in town to stay. Nothing else mattered. On the doorstep, he told Anne of his decision, and he had no sooner said it than he realized he didn't actually mean it.

Anne shoved him back and said, "You, a quitter? I don't believe it. I don't have any friends that are quitters, and I don't plan on having any, no matter how much I like them!"

David was stunned. His first love was evaporating before him. "Anne, I was just saying that to let you know how much I adored you.

I won't quit my job, but I'll see you weekends for sure, OK? Besides, I need the money to take you out."

"Well," she said, "for a moment, you made me think poorly of you. Don't do that again."

As he drove home, he thought about Ed and Vern's rule about finishing what you start. He decided that those two old bastards were right. The rule applied to all things.

CHAPTER 18

JUNE 1944

Monday morning during breakfast in the camp cookhouse, Kenji was busy serving platters of hotcakes, fried ham, bacon, fried eggs, toast, and bowls of hot cereal. Kenji now had a helper, a young overweight girl who bunked in a separate room in the cookhouse. Her appearance didn't turn the head of any logger. Her name was Bertha, and she had worked in log camp kitchens before this camp, and she knew what she was doing.

The increase in the number of workers in camp taxed the cookhouse to the limit. Kenji still had unspoken rank above Bertha, but no one really noticed or cared. The two of them did their work, and no one paid much attention to them.

One of the new workers, Clint Jennings, helped himself to a third round of hotcakes while asking a logger across the table from him who Kenji was and where was he from.

"I don't know much about him," was the answer. "Ask Lawrence, the other Alaskan, or Mike about him. They bunk with him. He's been here for a couple of seasons, and Buster, the bull cook, says he's the best help he's ever had in the kitchen and cookhouse. Their bunkhouse is across the walk from you and four houses down."

Clint Jennings wasn't about to go looking for Lawrence or Mike, whoever that was; he was just curious, that's all. The only Asian-looking people he had seen were dead ones, and this guy was a little darker than one of them.

Kenji was speaking good English, and by now, it was noticeable to everyone in the cookhouse. The better English he spoke, the less likely anyone would guess that he was born and raised in Japan and was a member of the Japanese Special Naval Landing Forces. He had continued to eagerly read news accounts of the war, which had recently taken some horrible turns against Japan. Not only did it appear that the Japanese had lost more than four hundred planes in the Battle of the Philippine Sea, but Americans were bombing Japan using a long-range bomber called a B-29. He had also read that a General MacArthur had taken some islands from the Japanese that were only nine hundred miles from the Philippine Islands. Kenji knew that if the Americans retook the Philippines, the war might be over for Japan. He had read about the Allies landing in France and that Germany had failed to stop that invasion. Germany was surely doomed, and certainly that country was not going to be any help to Japan.

He had read articles in some news magazines claiming that the United States now had nearly thirty aircraft carriers in the Pacific. Kenji asked himself how that could be true. If it was true, he knew that support vessels for the carriers would be numerous. The war was lost. His essential thought and purpose would now be to survive and somehow return to Japan and his family. How was his family? The thought was ever present for him.

Kenji had no idea what he would do when he learned of the war's end, if it ever came. Would the Americans treat him badly if they learned who he was and what he had done? Kenji knew that he would make himself miserable if he dwelled on those negative thoughts. He would concentrate on his work and maintain his identity as a Native Alaskan from Attu.

CHAPTER 19

AUGUST 1944

Jason and David had worked themselves into prime physical condition and no longer complained about aches and pains or any of the difficulties of setting chokers in a big-time logging operation.

Ed and Vern were proud of their lectures to the boys. They were also happy to see the boys' return and told them so.

Jason and David marveled at the power of the yarding machine. With chokers properly attached, the lines spooling onto the yarder could pull two forty-four-foot logs five or six feet in diameter up a steep hill, destroying everything in their path. It soon became a game to see how fast they could attach the chokers to the logs and get them on their way to the landing, where they would be loaded onto a railcar or be decked in a monster pile of logs. The work was agreeable to David and Jason, but they were always happy to spend the weekends in town. They were nearing the end of their summer vacation period, and they were looking forward to it.

It had been nearly three weeks since David and Jason had left the logging camp to spend a weekend at home in Bandon. They had been offered eight hours of overtime work each Saturday, and at one and a half times regular pay, they couldn't turn it down. Three straight weeks in camp was enough.

David's thoughts were mainly focused on Anne Hall, making the decision to work on Saturdays most difficult. He had written Anne to explain his absence, and she had responded with a letter that was in agreement with his decision, but the letter had had a chilly quality to it. David didn't understand. He'd immediately fired off another letter to her. Mail left camp on Wednesdays and Fridays. It was a week before Anne's reply reached David. The succinct message was that she and David needed to talk at once, and the sooner he came home, the better. David did not share with Jason, or anyone, the details of his relationship with Anne. Now there was something apparently infecting the relationship that David did not understand. Maybe she was dating someone else. David reasoned that if that were the case, Anne would have told him.

David did something he thought he would never do. One day while working on the job, he related his confusion with Anne and her recent letters.

Jason examined David and said, "Did you have sex with her?"

"That's none of your business, and it has nothing to do with what I'm telling you."

There was one other thing that was truly complicating David's and Jason's lives: the military draft. Shortly after they turned eighteen, they would be taken into a branch of the military, whether they liked it or not. If the United States was still at war, they were eager to get in it, but if the war was over, they didn't know what would happen. They discussed it on the job, at meals, and in the bunkhouse. Ed and Vern finally told them to shut up about it.

Meanwhile, they were eating like horses, putting on a little muscle, weight, and height. Thursday was steak-dinner night, when monster porterhouse steaks were served. David and Jason each ate two steaks and drank a quart of milk, then finished with pie or cake. Every Thursday following the evening meal, they would develop a painful gut ache and spend forty-five minutes on their bunks getting over the discomfort. They agreed it was worth it.

David and Jason returned to Bandon on the weekend following Anne's last letter. David called Anne as soon as he entered his home and before he said hello to anyone. They met in the city park that was close to Anne's house, where they sat side by side on a picnic table bench. It was a bright, sunny, unusually warm day in Bandon, and they were alone for the first time in weeks.

Anne looked around and then focused on David and said, "I've been upset simply because I miss you, and I'm not sure if you care or not."

David was surprised. He moved close to Anne and said, "You are the only girl that I ever got crazy about—actually, I think it's a lot more than that, and I have no idea what to do about it."

Following a long pause, giving each of them time to ponder what was happening, Anne said, "Maybe we're in love and don't know it, and that's too complicated for people our age."

They again sat silent. Then David whispered to Anne in a clear but affectionate voice, "You're right, we can't get so serious with each other that we start considering marriage. If that's what we're thinking, or anything like it, we must stop. It's easier to end this now than later. We can still see each other and date whoever we want. Besides, I'll soon be eligible for the military draft, and I may really be gone."

Anne put her head on David's shoulder and admitted, "You've just said what I've been thinking. Our affection for one another isn't over. We'll be OK."

The fact that David and Anne were able to set aside their emotional entanglement was remarkable and, if it lasted, substantiated their emerging maturity. David had, of course, directly participated in the killing of seven men on the beach, and his maturity was miles ahead of other teenagers. They were happy that they had talked their way through a mutual problem. David took Anne's hand and walked her home. At her door, Anne said, "You know what they say, David: You never forget your first love." They parted as lasting friends.

As he walked away, David mused, *We'll be together again, sometime.*

David and Jason headed back to the logging camp that Sunday afternoon. David was silent. Jason had asked him about Anne and what the problem was. David told him that they got it straightened out.

David decided to work that following Saturday while Jason went home. For some reason, he knew he would feel comfortable in camp; besides, he would get in eight hours of overtime pay.

CHAPTER 20

AUGUST 1944

The logging camp had been a very busy place all during the summer. There had been few visitors to the camp, but every visitor and every new employee was disconcerting to Kenji. Surely the search for him was over. Still, he couldn't be too careful. He did, from time to time, think about the night in Coquille when he'd seen a Japanese family in a restaurant and had started to follow them to talk to them and how totally stupid that would have been. Instead, he had turned away and returned to the train, and he hoped no one else remembered that night.

One night, Kenji was serving platters of meat and potatoes to the hungry loggers. He reached across the table opposite the men and set down a platter of beef roast, and as he did, his shirtsleeve slipped up, revealing his wristwatch.

Clint Jennings looked at the watch. The picture of a watch flashed across his brain, telling him that he had seen this watch someplace. He made no mention of it, but the image wouldn't disappear. That evening after dinner, on the way out of the cookhouse, Clint went to talk to Lawrence.

"Where did you say Kenji was from? Attu?"

Lawrence nodded, and Clint asked Lawrence if Kenji had ever said anything about his family and living on Attu. Lawrence told Clint that he knew very little about Kenji, and that when Kenji first came to the camp, he couldn't speak because of some head injury or something.

Lawrence was puzzled by Clint's questions. "Why are you interested in Kenji? He's a good man, and he helped me when I was in trouble."

Clint looked at the floor for a moment. "I don't know, Lawrence. I guess I'm just being stupid or something. He seems to be more than he is. But what the hell do I know?" He told Lawrence good night.

That night, Clint lay back on his bunk and, looking at the ceiling rafters, said to no one in particular, "He looks more like a Jap than Lawrence does. Maybe he's a Japanese American avoiding the internment camps, but a Japanese American wouldn't come from Attu, Alaska!"

One of Clint's bunkhouse mates was lying on his bunk reading, but he rose up when he heard Clint. "What the hell makes you think you know what a Jap looks like?"

Clint quietly said, "I've seen a few."

"Where, in the movies? There's not a Jap in southwestern Oregon, and if there was, he's probably only half Jap anyway."

Clint sat up and looked over at his housemate. "I worked in the salmon and tuna canneries in Astoria several seasons. Most of the fish workers were Filipinos and Chinese, but there was one group in the Union Cannery that was Japanese. None of them could speak English except their leader. They all returned to Japan after every season with a steamship full of canned salmon and cured salmon eggs."

Another bunkhouse mate said, "What the hell does that have to do with anything? Most of us that have been around much have seen Japanese people. There's been a Japanese family living in Coquille for years."

"The point is," allowed Clint, "this Kenji guy claims he is an Alaskan, and I don't think he is. When I first saw Kenji's wristwatch, something clicked in my brain, and now I remember seeing a couple of watches on those Japanese fish workers that looked nearly identical to Kenji's watch. Those watches have a unique face and are unusually thick. The face had no numbers, just a dot for twelve and six o'clock."

The bunkhouse mate said, "Didn't those fuckin' Japs sell those things all over the world?"

Clint lay back down on his bunk. "I don't know, but those are the only ones I've seen." It was late, and someone turned the lights out. It was time to sleep.

CHAPTER 21

SEPTEMBER 1944

The camp would be closing in about two months, and Kenji would remain in camp as the winter man, assuming the company wanted him.

Lawrence had told Kenji about his earlier conversation with Clint and about a breakfast-table conversation Lawrence had overheard between Clint and another logger. It sounded as though the other logger had lived in Bandon until about a year ago and that he'd known the boys who had shot and killed three Japanese men who had tried to come ashore in a raft just south of Bandon. Clint had appeared surprised by the information, according to Lawrence, but it seemed to Kenji that the logger had failed to connect that information with Kenji. Nor had anyone else made the connection. Kenji now spoke the English language without difficulty.

Kenji was beginning to be aware that his perceived security in not being identified might be getting frail. He would be on guard, but wasn't sure how he'd respond if events went sour.

Lawrence wasn't the only person who had overheard that conversation. Ray Sampson had been seated close enough to hear what had happened in Bandon a couple of years ago, and he began to recall the Asian-looking man who, more than a year ago, had appeared in camp at the beginning of the season. No one seemed to know who had hired him, and the poor devil couldn't talk, and if he could've, it would've been some Native Alaskan tongue that no one could understand anyway. Ray knew that soon there would be the matter of rehiring Kenji for the winter job, and he decided to question him at the time of his rehiring. In the interim, Ray would keep his thoughts to himself. Ray hadn't forgotten that Kenji had saved a logger's life.

Meanwhile, Lawrence's affinity to Kenji was something Lawrence himself didn't quite understand, but the two were immensely loyal to one another. It could have been the Native Alaskan status or Kenji's protection of Lawrence from the aggressive logger after the poker game. He wasn't sure. He just liked having the guy as a friend. He had no other close friends.

Lawrence was beginning to hear conversations at the dinner table about the Japanese soldiers that had invaded Bandon Beach. Lawrence had been unaware of these Japanese incursions, but the more he thought about those events, true or not, the more he worried about his friend. He had not as yet heard any talk or any rumor connecting Kenji to the Japanese, but Kenji's lack of knowledge of the Aleutians and its people, coupled with Kenji's disinterest in discussing anything about those matters, left many questions.

Lawrence was a Native Alaskan. He had lived in the Territory of Alaska, a possession of the United States, and yet he did not know whether or not he was a citizen of the United States. He had worked in the logging woods in the states of Washington and Oregon, and on many occasions had been treated in a disrespectful manner. Loggers and others had derisively called him "Chief" rather than "Lawrence." He had become callous to such cruel and cutting remarks and nearly always ignored them, but he could never forget such treatment.

Lawrence vowed that if Kenji was the Japanese man who had escaped, he would not reveal him. He would protect him. Kenji was a good man. He was—with the possible exception of his identity—an honest, hardworking man who seemed to get along with everyone. If Kenji Kosoki had a secret, then so did Lawrence.

Kenji, for the past two months, had developed an increasing interest in world events, particularly those events unfolding in the Pacific regions. His reading skill had improved exponentially, and by late summer, few words were a mystery to him. Kenji knew the geography of the western Pacific, and in July, when he read about the conquest of Saipan and the retaking of Guam, he knew Japan was in trouble. The recent news was confirming it. The news stories about horrendous losses of Japanese soldiers and few if any of them surrendering bewildered Kenji. How could the Japanese military permit such losses to occur? You couldn't fight a war that way and win! To make matters worse, Saipan was now an American air base that was launching air strikes on the Japanese homeland, and the Americans were attacking Formosa. Surely they would soon mount an invasion of this Japanese island and take it like they had taken all the other islands. This war would be over soon. No issue was greater in Kenji's mind than what the Americans would do to the Japanese and, in particular, what they would do to him.

CHAPTER 22

OCTOBER 1944

The 1944 logging season on Eden Ridge above Powers was nearing an end. The production of logs was at an all-time high from that operation, and yet there had been no major injuries and no deaths. Ray Sampson was a master logger. He could spot potential trouble and avoid it. He could set up log yarding operations that reduced danger to his workers and at the same time produce logs for the mill.

The lesser of Ray's job tasks was the function of the camp. He was responsible for its operation, but Buster actually ran it—which meant that, as it was late October already, Ray needed to talk to Buster about closing.

He met Buster in the dining hall. They sat alone, sipping coffee, to discuss winding down. They agreed again on a winter man and winter provisions and talked about some upgrades for the kitchen.

Then Ray, looking deep into his coffee cup, asked, "Buster, what do you know about Kenji? Is he who he says he is, and do you have any questions about him of any kind?"

"I don't think I know any more about him than you do, and that ain't much. He's been an excellent worker, is a self-starter, and seems to get along with everyone. I don't want to lose him. Why do you ask?"

"I don't want this conversation to go any further than right here. Do you understand?" Buster nodded, so Ray continued. "Do you remember a little over two years ago when there was some commotion on the beach south of Bandon, and then there was the attempt to blow up our separator plant in Coquille? Remember that they killed one Jap and the other Jap escaped?"

"What are you getting at?"

"Well, Kenji showed up here the spring after that happened, and there was some slight evidence that someone had been around the camp that winter. With all that has happened with him and his speech problems, it occurs to me that we may have a Jap on our payroll. I can't be certain."

Buster took a deep breath and said, "He's a good worker. I can't believe he's dangerous."

Ray continued, "I talked to Lawrence about him, and he backs Kenji up one hundred percent. So, piss on it, I'm hiring Kenji again for the winter job, and if he's still here in the spring, his job continues. You got any problem with that?"

"Nope. We'll have killed half the fuckin' Japs in the world by then anyway, and the war will be over. Besides, I can practically guarantee you that Kenji is no threat to us or anyone else."

Ray hired Kenji for the winter season, and at Kenji's request for a day off, Ray gave it to him. Kenji had not been to the bank in Myrtle Point all season, and he had accumulated more than a dozen paychecks that needed to be deposited. He and his buddy Lawrence once again made the trip to town. The little towns were peaceful and active. The people on the streets seemed happy and appeared to be occupied with all things except war. Meanwhile, his homeland was being demolished by American bombs, and its troops were being killed by the tens of thousands. Was this the way wars were fought? Of course, it was. One nation wins and one nation loses. In the newspapers he took back to camp, Kenji would read that the Americans were at that moment landing their armies in the Philippines and that the Japanese Navy was suffering the most crushing defeat of the war.

The camp was closed to logging on Friday, October 27, and on the first of November, Kenji was once again alone in the logging camp. Before leaving, Ray had asked Kenji if there was anything Kenji would like to tell him about Kenji's family and some of the things Kenji had been doing before he came to work in the camp. Kenji told Ray that there was nothing worth talking about and that he was just happy to have a job and a place to live. Kenji saw that his answer did not sit well with Ray. He knew Ray was a man who gave straight answers and expected to receive straight answers, so he hurriedly added, "My life has been a mess, and I'd rather not talk about it."

Ray liked Kenji's second response and accepted it.

Kenji decided that this answer was the truth. He hadn't had to leave his family on Hokkaido, and maybe he wouldn't have been drafted because of his work in an important fishery. Beyond that, he hadn't had to accept the assignments that took him from the Etajima naval academy. The Philippine assignment had required the performance of terrible tasks he'd never dreamed he'd perform at all, let alone execute with deadly skill and without remorse. He had done those things only three years ago, yet now he was convinced that he could not kill another human being unless in self-defense. Killing the mill worker had been part of the assignment, and even though he hadn't stabbed the man, he felt just as responsible for the man's death as if he had done the killing himself. He was glad he had spared the life of the old fisherman. He had now been out of the war for more than two years.

His only plan was to survive until the war ended. He was uncertain about what would happen then, but it would undoubtedly be better than being caught prior to the end of the war. He would be lonely for the next four or five months, but he was accustomed to loneliness, and there would be a few visits via the train from Powers. He would have newspapers when the train showed. He was ever anxious to learn the war news. The faster things went to hell for Japan, the sooner the war would end.

The newspapers Kenji received late in January 1945 showed that the demise of the Japanese Empire was near. Kenji saw his first picture of a B-29 bomber in a newspaper called *Coos Bay Times*, which was published in the town of Marshfield, where the Evans Products separator plant was located—the second separator plant they were to destroy, but they didn't get close. He studied the picture of the huge airplane, but when he read the article beneath the picture, he couldn't believe it. These bombers were flying 2,500 to 3,000 miles round-trip to bomb Tokyo, and they were destroying the city and killing tens of thousands of Japanese. To make matters worse, American troops had landed on Luzon, just 172 kilometers from Manila. Once the Philippines were secured, Japan would be cut off from nearly all sources of oil. Kenji had landed in December 1941 in the Lingayen Gulf, about a hundred and fifty kilometers from Manila. The Americans had probably landed in the same spot. All of his difficult work in that area was a waste.

All the war news made Kenji weak. His mental strength was waning. How long could his charade last? What difference would it make if it ended before the war was over? The Americans were busy killing Japanese everyplace they could find them: in a city, on an island, on a boat, or in an airplane. It made no difference. It seemed that the Americans would only stop killing Japanese when the war ended. Surely all Americans felt that way. He would rely on that and hold out until the war's end.

CHAPTER 23

FEBRUARY 1945

Clint Jennings was suddenly wide awake in bed in total darkness. He heard rain on his window. In a flash of a dream, he saw dozens of wristwatches with no numbers on the dial, only a red dot at twelve o'clock and a red dot at six o'clock. The watches were the same as the wristwatch he had seen on the fellow waiting tables in the logging camp. Or were they? Anyway, the only watches he'd seen like that were worn by Japanese or Japanese-looking people. He wondered, *Why in hell am I having such a dream? It must be that Kenji guy. He's a nice guy, but there is something haywire there.*

"Jeez, what the hell's wrong with me?" he whispered as he slammed himself down on his pillow. Here it was the middle of February, he thought, and he hadn't been in that logging camp for more than three months. He continued to lie on his bed, listening to the rain but thinking about the wristwatches. Surely there were thousands of wristwatches that were identical. But if the ones he was thinking about were all made in Japan—and maybe they weren't—then maybe someone should check it out. It certainly wouldn't hurt anything. The last thing he was going to do was make a big deal out of his suspicion. He would talk to someone about it. Clint wasn't a real self-starter.

About a week later, Clint Jennings was sitting at the bar in the Pastime Tavern in Coquille. It was one of a half dozen taverns in town. It was illegal to serve hard liquor drinks in Oregon, and Clint was having a beer or three or four when Buster, the bull cook, walked in and sat next to him.

"Lemme buy you a beer, Buster," he said. After a few pleasantries, Clint said, "I want to talk to you about something that happened in camp last year." Buster nodded. "You know the guy Kenji that worked for you may be Japanese, if my suspicions are right." Clint continued to tell Buster all about the watches, leaving out the part about the dream.

Buster said, "You could be right, and you could be wrong. If you think you're right, what are you gonna do?"

"I don't have the foggiest idea, but I may do something," he said. He tipped his glass and drained it.

Buster wasn't keen on anything being done for several reasons, the least of which was that Kenji had been in Buster's employ and presence for about two years, and that would be embarrassing. Buster said, "Well, if you think you are onto something, why don't you call the army and navy?"

Clint, picking up a fresh glass of beer, said, "I might just do that. You got a phone number?"

They both laughed and had another beer together, then called it an evening.

Clint returned to his room in the downtown rooming house in Coquille. He sat in his chair and pondered the day's events and his conversation with Buster. He would do something about it tomorrow. Yes, he remembered the involvement of the Coast Guard at Bandon with the Japanese landing. He didn't have anything else to do, and he wasn't working, so he would drive to Bandon. He hadn't been there but once.

The next day, Clint Jennings pulled his car up to the US Coast Guard station in Bandon, got out, and was stopped by a coastguardsman with a rifle. Clint was tall and lean, cleanly shaven, but normally he was unshaven. He was ever ready with an opinion and enjoyed asserting himself, sometimes in other people's business. He liked doing what he was now doing. Clint, on this overcast day, said in a loud voice, "I want to see the guy in charge here."

"Just stay where you are." The sentry walked toward the front door of the station, and out stepped Art Spears. "That fellow wants to talk to you."

Spears said, "What can I do for you?"

"I have something to tell you about the Jap you were looking for at one time. It may or may not be important, but I need to tell someone with authority."

Spears invited Clint Jennings to his office, where they both sat down. Clint related the whole story about the wristwatches and the Japanese-looking man at the logging camp. He decided not to tell him about the watch dream. Clint was about to ask about any watches that might have been taken from the dead Japs when Spears said, "Well, let's go look and see what we have in the way of Japanese wristwatches."

They went to a locker downstairs in the lifeboat garage. Spears unlocked it and pulled out several sacks, one with pistols, one with belts, one with knives and coins, and one with three wristwatches.

Spears and Clint examined the watches. Clint said, "This is the same watch I saw on Kenji."

"Who the hell's Kenji?"

"He's the Jap you may be looking for." He told him about Kenji and the logging camp.

"Do you know where he is now?"

"Yes, he's the winter man at the logging camp up above Powers."

"What kind of a person is he?"

"He's well liked, and he seems to be a good worker. He's not a logger; he works in the cookhouse and helps the bull cook."

Art Spears thanked Clint Jennings for the information.

Clint hesitated and asked Spears, "So what actually are you going to do with this information?"

"I'm not going to tell you or anyone else except the FBI. Is that alright with you, or do you have a better plan?"

Clint Jennings left the office, and Spears reminded himself that if there was a person who might identify this Kenji fellow, it was Sven Clausen. Spears knew his business. The FBI had jurisdiction in all cases involving foreign enemies on US soil. Within minutes after Clint left the Coast Guard station, Spears was talking on the phone to a secretary in the office of the Federal Bureau of Investigation in Eugene, and then soon to Agent Mark Weathers. Spears related the case to the agent in detail.

Weathers asked, "Is this Kenji a present threat to anyone or anything?"

"He doesn't appear to be, no."

"Look, we get reports of suspicious persons and events all the time," Weathers said, "and if they appear to be no threat, we pretty much ignore them and pursue what we believe to be real threats and real dangerous people. Your case is a little out of the ordinary because your Kenji guy may be a Jap. Nevertheless, he seems harmless, and our case priorities are not with him, at least not at this juncture. If our more serious caseload dwindles, we may pursue this Kenji guy, but until then, I can't promise you any action. In the meantime, you should probably stay away from him. Any clumsy efforts to get him might fail and drive him away or underground where we could never find him."

Spears protested. "If this Kenji is our man, he's killed one person and attempted to blow up an entire section of a mill housing an essential-war-material manufacturing plant, and God only knows how many people would have died in that explosion. He was dangerous less than three years ago, and he is probably still dangerous."

"I agree, but the man's nearly two years of working and living in the logging camp in apparent harmony with everyone around him does not convince me that he is still dangerous." Weathers quickly added, "He's probably intending to hang out there in that camp until the war is over, and if that's his intent, he's not going to cause any trouble."

Weathers was no dummy. This was not a case to get excited about when his present cases involved everything from capturing a violent escaped murderer to developing a case against a defense contractor who was cheating on quality and double billing the US Navy. The US Coast Guard officer on the phone might not understand, but that was the way it would stand. No action now, maybe some later on.

When Spears hung up, he was disappointed, and he was having trouble accepting it. He wondered if this was going to be like dealing with the Western Defense Command and that Major Carlock. He decided to let things ride. He had a huge section of Oregon coastline to patrol and thirty-four men to manage, as well as boats, vehicles, horses, and now dogs to care for.

CHAPTER 24

MARCH 1945

When Clint left the Coast Guard station in Bandon, he wandered into the nearby Slough Tavern and ordered a glass of beer. The Slough Tavern was a dump, unpainted inside and outside, with a concrete ditch of running water stretching the entire length of the bar on the floor just behind the rail. You could spit in it, pee in it, and throw cigarette butts in it.

The man seated on the stool next to him said without looking up, "This is lousy beer. Haven't had a good beer since the fire."

Clint tasted his beer; it was no worse than any other wartime beer.

The man said, "You new here?"

"No, I live in Coquille. I had some business with the Coast Guard today. I gave them some clues to the whereabouts of one of those Japs that came ashore here awhile back."

"Well, I'll be damned," the man said. "I'd forgotten all about that. I know the parents of one of the boys that was shot by them Japs."

Clint said, "Well, the Coast Guard wasn't going to do nothin', but they were calling the FBI."

They moved to talking about other things. Clint finished a second beer, then said goodbye and left for Coquille. He was finished with the wristwatch thing.

The man at the bar was Bob Stroud, a friend and customer of Bill and May Johnson. He walked from the tavern directly to Johnson's Emporium to share the news.

Mr. and Mrs. Johnson were both in the store. It was midafternoon, and there was one customer in the store, when Stroud said to them, "Your son was one of the boys that met the Japs on the beach south of Bandon. I think you should know that the missing Jap, the second one that escaped from the beach, has been found. The Coast Guard here has been informed about him, and they called the FBI. I don't know what's going to happen."

The Johnsons were surprised to gain information about an investigation regarding a suspected Japanese soldier in this manner. The Coast Guard or the FBI should have alerted them.

"I can't believe any of the boys or their families are in any danger," Bill said. "We all hope that they catch the guy, whoever or wherever he is."

May thought about the danger Stroud mentioned. "None of us ever thought that Sven Clausen was in danger from the escaped saboteur," she said. "First, clearly the saboteur was no dummy, and if he had wanted to eliminate Sven as a witness, he would have done so. Second, the man gave my father a family picture and seemed kind. And third, Dad told my mother that just before the man finally jumped out of the boat, he'd looked him over carefully—even put his hand to Dad's bushy hair and smiled in a friendly manner. Dad knew he was not in danger."

The Johnsons immediately shared this news on the phone with the other boys' parents. Henry's mother wanted to tell him the news and found him at home, got his attention, and said, "Henry, they may have found the Japanese man that hurt your grandfather. That's all we know."

"Wow, where is he?"

"We don't know, but we should know soon. The FBI is on the case." Henry was excited and could barely wait to talk to Jason, George, and David.

The other parents told their sons, and that the FBI would take care of the problem sooner or later. Henry, George, David, and Jason were excited by the news, and each wanted to know what would happen. No one had the answer. The boys and their parents talked to each other on the phone. There was nothing they could do but wait for the situation to develop.

That evening after dinner, Bill, May, and Henry Johnson drove to the Clausen home on the bank of the Coquille River. They discussed the news that the missing Jap may soon be arrested.

Sven and his grandson, Henry, had both suffered at the hands of the Japanese landing parties. "You know, we both could have been killed," Sven said, "you by a bullet and me by a knife. But it didn't happen. I was intentionally spared, and you were accidentally spared."

Henry, sitting close to his grandfather in the small living room, asked, "What does that mean?"

Sven looked at Henry and said, "How are you going to feel about the Jap if they capture him? I saw him in his uniform, so they tell me he could be treated as a prisoner of war and not be executed. You know that he looked me in the eye and smiled when he could have killed me, the only witness that could identify him. He should live."

Henry said, "Whoever shot me was blown up in that first raft. I think your Jap should live."

Sven said, "Do you know that we may be the only persons in this war to be assaulted on American soil and injured? One thing I want you to remember from all of this is that you may become a soldier before this war is over, and if you do, be honorable and merciful."

CHAPTER 25

JULY 1, 1945

It was late Friday afternoon. The day shift had ended at three thirty, and inside the Casino, a bar and tavern in Coquille close to the Smith Wood Products mill, there was standing room only. Not only were some of the day-shift mill workers tossing down beers, a few loggers were doing the same. After three and a half years of war and the surrender of Germany, spirits were high. It was the summer solstice; the days were warm and long, and Japan was on the ropes and slipping to the canvas. Why not have another beer before going home to dinner?

Clint Jennings was standing at the bar complaining to the bartender—who wasn't listening—that the punchboard he was punching had no winners in it. It was crooked, and he should have his eight dimes returned.

Sam Mack was downing his seventh or eighth beer when Jim Potter and Willie Daggett joined his table with beer glasses in hand. They leaned heavily on the table in Sam's direction, almost in his face. They looked agitated.

"What the hell do you guys want?"

Jim said, "My wife's cousin was the river worker that those two fuckin' Japs killed!"

Willie said, "And the other worker that was clubbed was my uncle, the rotten bastards. Luckily he didn't die, but he sure has a nice scar on his forehead."

"So what the hell good is that information to me?" Sam demanded. Both Jim and Willie started to talk, and Sam said, "One at a time, boys."

Clint overheard the nearby conversation and immediately turned around, with his back to the bar, to listen to every word spoken.

Jim said, "Here it is, the first of July 1945, almost three years since that boy was killed, and nothing has fuckin' happened. The FBI has had the case damn near three months, and they haven't done a fuckin' thing about it!"

"So what the hell am I supposed to do? Wait a minute—why don't we just go and tell the Coast Guard?"

Clint rocked forward from the bar and, in an exasperated tone, said, "I have told the Coast Guard, and they are not going to do a damned thing!"

Jim Potter looked at Sam and said, "Well, that does it. You're head of security at the mill, and that one remaining bastard might try and blow up the separator plant again if you don't stop him."

John Merchant, foreman at the mill, was seated at the next table, trying to concentrate on the five-card poker game he was playing. He overheard Jim's and Willie's loud assertions. "Deal me out," he told his partners and scooted his chair around. He knew Jim and Willie; they were employees in his division. "What's going on here?"

Sam gave him the summary. Merchant said, "I was in the mill office the other day, and I heard some talk about the same thing. It's a long shot, but it seems that we may have the missing Jap on our payroll." He told them what he'd heard about the supposed Attu survivor at Eden Ridge. "It's all very suspicious, but no one seems to care."

Willie, who by now had quaffed twelve glasses of beer, stood up and said to the entire Casino crowd, "Did you hear that? These fuckin' smart-assed loggers have been working with the missing Jap in the Eden Ridge Camp for nearly three years and have done nothing about it."

One of the loggers jumped to his feet and yelled, "You stupid rummy-assed drunk, you wouldn't know a Jap from your own rabid dog that probably bites you daily!"

Jim stood up from his chair and shouted at the logger, "Why don't you go home and take a bath, you red-mouthed son of a bitch?"

The Casino bartender came over and yelled, "You all shut up and sit down or get the hell out of here. Jim, you and Willie are cut off at the bar, so you might as well leave peacefully."

On the way out of the Casino, Willie shoved the loudmouthed logger. The man fell out of his chair but was up in a flash. He caught Willie with a left hook that knocked Willie to the floor. Jim swung at the logger and missed, but the logger's companion knocked Jim to the floor. A melee followed, with logger pitted against mill worker (with some mistakes as to identity being made). Chairs were broken and poker games disrupted as poker chips fell and men ran for the door. The bartender was wielding an axe handle with good effect, connecting directly with heads. Jim Potter, Willie Daggett, and Sam Mack left during the fray. By the time the two Coquille police officers arrived, the brawl was nearly over.

Jim, Willie, and Sam headed for Greg's Place, a popular beer and pool joint, two blocks away. Jim had a bloody nose and Willie sported a cut on his cheek, but Sam was unscathed. They took a table near a pinochle game and across from a snooker table, and Jim and Willie formulated a plan. It was simple. Sam would supply the information as needed, Jim and Willie would enlist more men, and they would go to the Eden Ridge Camp and "capture the Jap." Then they would enroll a firing squad and execute the guy.

Sam demurred. "You will not execute anyone, you crazy bastards! Just capture him. He needs to be identified. Even if he is the Jap, if you killed him, you would be guilty of murder. Do you understand what I'm telling you? Because if you don't, I'll abort your whole plan!"

"OK, OK—we'll just catch him and hand him over to the sheriff. Is that what you're telling us?" Willie asked.

"Exactly, but I'm not certain I trust either one of you."

Before Sam could expound on this, the owner of Greg's Place walked up to their table. "I heard what happened at the Casino, and if you start anything in here, you'll feel like Chicken Licken!" He walked over to a pool table in the rear where a few young teens were playing pool. "You kids get out of here. Your dads called me, and they don't want you in here." He stopped by Sam's table on his way back to the bar. "Is there anything you boys don't understand about what I told you?"

"We all understand," Willie said. The bartender walked away.

Sam said, "OK, now tell me exactly what you are going to do to get the guy, and then tell me how you're going to handle him if you get him."

"We know some guys in Powers that'll help us, especially if we tell them who we're after," Jim said. "If we get him, we won't shoot him, but we'll fetch him to the sheriff in Coquille."

"Yeah, that's it," Willie said.

Willie Daggett and Jim Potter woke the next morning, a Saturday, and later that morning, drove to Powers in Jim's 1940 Chevrolet sedan. The weekend was the perfect time to go to the logging camp and capture the saboteur. The loggers were all in town, and there would be a minimal crew hanging around the camp. Willie had a friend who he figured would let them take one of the company's several railroad speeders to reach the camp, particularly if they told his friend some phony story. An important message about a death or serious injury should do the trick. Jim and Willie were pleased with themselves.

When they arrived in Powers, they drove straight to Red's Tavern and walked into the joint. It was a large room with booths along a wall, a couple of tables with chairs, and a long, much-used wooden bar with a footrail and no stools. Willie and Jim found the loggers standing at the bar, each with their hands grasping a glass of beer as if to say, "No one's getting this away from me." Willie asked them to join them at a table and ordered another beer for all. Willie and Jim told the men that they needed their help and explained the problem and the plan. The five of them left Red's with a sack of cold beer in quart bottles.

They went directly to the railroad machine shop and maintenance shed and found mechanics working full time on a locomotive and some broken-down log cars. Joe, one of the men they had recruited at Red's, knew two of the mechanics. When Willie and Jim told them that they needed to reach a man in the camp because his wife had been critically injured in an automobile collision, they got the use of a speeder. All five of them jumped on the speeder before the mechanic could ask why it took five men to deliver a message. They were soon headed up the railroad grade to the camp. The single-cylinder gas engine was burdened with the extra weight, but the speeder forged on up the grade anyway. Crossing a hundred-foot-high wood trestle scared all five of the riders so much that it gave some of them second thoughts about their venture.

Jim had worked as a logger and had lived in the camp until he was seriously injured in a logging accident. Willie had never been to the logging camp, but the three men recruited in Red's Tavern had lived and worked there from time to time. One of them knew who Kenji was and where he bunked and worked, but he had never suspected he was a killer and a wanted man, especially a Japanese military person. Joe started asking questions that Willie and Jim had difficulty answering, particularly how the man had been identified. "We heard people talk who knew who and where he was," Willie said.

As soon as the speeder reached the camp, Joe split off from the group. Maybe he had a drinking problem, but he wasn't ignorant. He went directly to the cookhouse and found Buster. "Buster, I have to talk to you." Joe had his attention, so he continued, "You have an employee here that is not who he says he is. We understand that his name is Kenji and that he is the missing Jap that killed a man and tried to blow up the mill in Coquille. Tell me where he is."

Ray Sampson was sitting at a table in the cookhouse reviewing logging equipment and supply requirements for the next month. He watched Buster and Joe, whom he knew. "Hey, what's going on?" he called.

Joe told Ray about the other four men and why they were here. Ray stood up and asked, "Buster, is Kenji in camp?"

"Yes, he never takes a weekend off. I think he's in his bunkhouse with Lawrence."

Ray motioned for Buster and Joe to follow him, and they headed for Kenji's bunkhouse. As they passed Jim, Willie, and the other two loggers, Ray said to them, "Go to the cookhouse, have some coffee, and stay there." Ray didn't like what he saw in their eyes and demeanor.

Buster remembered Jim as the logger with the injured leg that Dr. Black had come to see. Buster also remembered that Kenji had, according to Dr. Black, saved the man's life. The rest of this crew knew who Ray Sampson was, so they followed his instruction.

The bunkhouse door was open. It was the usual four-man bunkhouse with a bed in each corner and a woodstove in the center. Lawrence and Kenji were awake but resting on their bunks. Joe stood in the doorway, and Buster and Ray took a seat on the empty bunks opposite Lawrence and Kenji.

Kenji sat up and put his feet on the floor. The serious look on Ray's and Buster's faces, plus the man standing in the doorway half blocking it, told Kenji that something serious was about to happen, and it was probably his unmasking. He had easily made it through the past fall and winter, and he had nearly forgotten his immediate past and who he actually was. Was the day at hand that the masquerade was over, or was it something else?

Ray looked at Lawrence, then focused on Kenji. "Kenji, the time has come for you to tell us exactly who you are and where you came from. Several men have just arrived in camp claiming that you are one of the Japanese soldiers who tried to blow up our separator plant at Coquille. You've been a very good employee, and as far as I am concerned, you have not engaged in any mischief or caused any trouble since you've been here. I'm asking you to level with me. If you are who some people think you are, I will see to it that you are handed over to the proper authorities, but we will see that no harm comes to you."

Kenji sat on the edge of his bunk, obviously in heavy thought. His employer had been fair and honest with him, and his fellow workers had trusted him and had treated him almost as an equal. Newspaper accounts of the war had related accounts of the retaking of the Philippines, the taking of Okinawa, and the bombing destruction of every major city in Japan. Japan had lost the war, and he had lost his false identity.

Kenji gradually rose to his feet. His stance was that of a Japanese naval officer at full attention with his right hand and arm in a smart salute. Kenji's move and his direct focus on Ray brought Ray involuntarily to his feet facing Kenji.

Kenji moved his arm down to his side and said, "I am First Lieutenant Kenji Kosoki of the Imperial Japanese Navy assigned to the Special Naval Landing Forces deployed on the West Coast of the United States. I am the only survivor. I apologize for my deception. Everyone in camp has been fair to me. I have nothing to honor you with except the truth that may kill me."

Ray and particularly Buster were visibly stunned. Standing before them was a young commissioned officer of the Japanese Navy showing exceptional courage and character.

Ray said, "I am personally taking you to the state police office in Coquille. If I have your word that you will not attempt to escape, you will not be bound."

"You have my word."

Ray looked at the big logger in the doorway and said, "Joe, you heard everything. Do you have a problem with it?"

"No problem, boss."

"OK, then, can you keep those two nitwit mill workers out there under control?"

"I think so."

Ray told Kenji to pick up whatever personal items he wanted to take with him. Kenji walked over to Lawrence, who was now standing, and hugged him. They might not see each other again. Tears appeared on their cheeks. Kenji picked up a few things, including some accumulated paychecks. He endorsed them as he had learned and gave them to Lawrence. "My friend, come see me sometime. I live in Ōtsu on Hokkaido."

They all walked down the wood-plank sidewalk from the bunkhouse to the cookhouse where Jim, Willie, and the two other loggers were seated having coffee.

Ray walked over to Jim and said, "Stand up. I want to educate you about something. That man standing near Buster is Japanese. He is a lieutenant in the Japanese Navy, and he is the missing Jap that you came for. What you don't know is that, according to Dr. Black, he saved you from bleeding to death right here in this very room. Buster just told me that you were all but unconscious and that you wouldn't remember what had happened. But remember this: if you harm this man, you'll answer to me, and you'll never work for this company again."

Jim was shaken and sat down. "Jeez, Willie, what the hell are we doing here?"

When the seven men alighted from the speeder in Powers, Ray asked Joe to come with him and Kenji in Ray's car. Jim and Willie followed in Jim's car. The two loggers went back to Red's Tavern.

Ray drove north toward the Oregon State Police station in Coquille, where a crowd was waiting. At Willie's insistence, Willie and Jim had stopped in Myrtle Point so Willie could phone his wife and tell her that the man they had come for was being delivered to the state police in Coquille. She had made a few calls, and word spread.

The crowd at the station was unruly, but Ray, with the help of the state police sergeant and Joe, ushered Kenji through the crowd and into the small station. The crowd hurled hateful remarks about the Japanese. Some wanted to "lynch the Jap." Others just wanted to see what a Japanese soldier looked like.

The police sergeant was familiar with the Coos County Jail and the Coquille City Jail, but he approved of neither as a proper place for what might be a prisoner of war. He called the North Bend naval air station. The best place for this guy was on a military base. There would be no funny business there, as might occur in Coquille. The military police from the base agreed to come and get him.

Ray Sampson and Buster stayed until the navy military police arrived from the air base.

Ray stood before Kenji and, after a thoughtful moment, said, "I wish I knew more about you. You may be a warrior, but I have a feeling that you are also a good person. Good luck to you."

Buster stepped over to Kenji, who now had a uniformed military policeman standing on either side of him. "You were the most dependable worker I ever had. Whatever happens, good luck to you."

CHAPTER 26

JULY 1945

The capture of the Japanese man who had killed the mill worker and had attempted to destroy the separator mill in Coquille was sensational local news. In other areas of the United States, it was just part of the general news. It bore no newsworthy resemblance to the capture and execution of the five German saboteurs caught on the East Coast. Linus Rink had written the story for the AP newswire and had great plans for a feature article that his paper might sell.

The United States naval air station at North Bend held Kenji Kosoki, but the personnel there had no clue about what to do with him. They had made an inquiry to their superiors without response. The Western Defense commander in charge of the Fourth Army defending the West Coast declined to comment or offer advice. The United States Coast Guard headquarters, 13th District, in Seattle wasn't interested.

So the FBI dispatched Agent Mark Weathers from its Eugene office to investigate and determine exactly who Kenji Kosoki was and what he was doing in the United States. The issue was plain, and it was serious: Was Kenji Kosoki a Japanese military person to be treated as a prisoner of war, or was he a spy or a disguised saboteur? If not a prisoner of war, he would be subject to a military execution.

Kenji was confined at the naval air station in a makeshift room that could hardly be called a jail. It was what the navy called a brig, a place where miscreant sailors spent a night or a couple of days. There were a few iron bars on the door, there was a window without bars facing the airstrip, and the walls were plywood painted typical navy gray. The bed was no worse than the one in the logging camp, but the food was not nearly as good. The commanding officer at the air station was uncertain about Kenji's claim that he was a commissioned officer in the Japanese Navy, but nevertheless presumed the claim to be true. A certain but unwritten comity had always existed with the officer class of wartime combatants, and as a result, the commanding officer of the naval air station had extended a few courteous gestures to Kenji in the form of daily newspapers and outside exercise.

Agent Mark Weathers sat at the small wooden table in the room that confined Kenji. Kenji sat on the edge of his bed facing Mark. A sailor with a rifle stood outside the room watching and listening through the barred door. Mark had brought an interpreter with him and was surprised, if not a little unnerved, to learn that Kenji spoke good English. He told Kenji who he was and how very important it was that Kenji tell him what he was doing in the United States. Kenji had concluded some time ago from reading the newspapers that Japan was beaten and it was only a matter of time before the war would end. He also knew that he possessed no information that would aid the Americans in the war. He had decided he would tell what he knew, and he did.

Following the interview, Weathers concluded that clearly, up to the point when Kenji had set the old fisherman adrift in his own boat in the Coquille River, Kenji had been a Japanese sailor in uniform. He would need the old fisherman to confirm the uniform. Kenji had shed the uniform to conceal his identity, but after that, had he been doing anything other than hiding? Was he gathering information for the Japanese or plotting some manner of espionage? Kenji said no. He had done nothing but live and work in the logging camp. He even had a bank account with more than three thousand dollars in it, and there had been no withdrawals from it.

Weathers called Sven Clausen and asked him to come to the air base to identify the Japanese prisoner. Sven called his daughter, May, to ask her if she would drive him to Marshfield. When Henry found out about the proposed trip, he insisted on going, and he pleaded with his mother to take Jason, David, and George too. The Johnsons had a large sedan, so she agreed.

Mark and the commanding officer of the air base met May's car at the front gate and let them in. As the little group walked down a hallway to the place where the Japanese soldier was being held, Sven became agitated and nervous. The boys were also nervous and a little afraid. Weren't the Japanese soldiers and sailors fanatical people? No telling what they might do.

David recognized what was happening. "Come on, guys. We've been through stuff a hundred times worse than this." They relaxed a little.

Soon, they stood in front of the confined Kenji Kosoki. Mark pointed at Kenji. "Mr. Clausen, is that the person who kidnapped you, then turned you loose?"

Sven nodded and said, "That's him."

"Was he wearing any kind of a uniform?"

"Yes, he and the other one had on green uniforms. There was a little anchor on the pocket and the same little anchor on their caps."

Kenji said, "The anchor is the insignia of the Japanese Special Naval Landing Forces." His voice and demeanor were calm and courteous.

It inspired Sven to ask, "Why did you let me go? I saw your fellow soldier kill the mill worker. I think I'm the only one who could identify you."

Agent Weathers said, "That's right. The other mill worker who survived told me he didn't remember a thing."

Kenji paused and looked at the boys. He said to Sven, "Do you have grandchildren?"

"Yes."

"Are these boys your grandchildren?"

Sven pointed at Henry. "This one is."

"The main reason I didn't kill you is that you look like my grandfather, and I figured you might have grandchildren. I really didn't need to kill anyone else. Besides, my grandfather is also a fisherman. Salmon fishermen are special people."

David faced Kenji and said, "The four of us are the ones who shot up the raft with our rifles. We thought that maybe there were others that escaped but didn't know what to do." No one said anything about the previous raft.

Kenji was surprised to learn that four young boys had shot up his raft and killed three of his companions. He said to them, "You have no idea how many people and how much property your rifle fire on the beach that evening may have saved."

The air base commander said, "Kosoki hasn't held anything back. We're pretty certain there are no others like him on our shore and that there are no remaining caches of explosives or other gear. He wanted to know what was done with the bodies of his fellow soldiers; he now knows that they were cremated and their remains kept by the Coast Guard. He says that if he gets home to Japan, he'll see to it that their families have that information. He realizes that he may never get home."

Kenji spoke up. "I have read your newspapers, and I do know what is happening in the war. Germany has been beaten, and Japan is nearly beaten. It won't last much longer. I can think of a lot of reasons I might not see Japan again, but I think I will."

Jason asked, "Why wouldn't he see Japan again?"

"It hasn't been determined whether he should be treated as a saboteur or an enemy soldier. If he's a saboteur, he'll face a firing squad; if he is a soldier, he'll be a prisoner of war to be released at war's end."

When leaving the brig area, Sven said to the boys, "Did you notice how strong and erect this fellow Kenji stood, how direct and straight he spoke, and how, not knowing his fate, he showed a kindness to us? But most important, he did not make any apologies because he had none to make. Always make sure you judge a man by his own acts and not the country he comes from. He is an honorable man, and that is character worth having."

CHAPTER 27

AUGUST 1945

A navy military policeman walked to Kenji's cell and, with a smirk engulfing his face, dropped two newspapers through the bars. The MP stood back to watch Kenji return to the edge of his bunk and open one of the papers. The front page was covered with a picture of a large mushroom cloud. "Atomic Bombs Fall on Japan." Kenji dropped that paper and opened the other, which trumpeted the same picture under the heading "Hiroshima Japan Destroyed by Atomic Bomb." Kenji looked at the date of the newspaper and then started to read. The article set forth the basic facts of the bombing:

> The first atomic bomb to be used in a military operation was dropped on the City of Hiroshima, Japan, on August 6, 1945, at 8:16:02 a.m. Hiroshima time. A B-29 bomber carried the bomb, that exploded 1,900 feet aboveground with a force of 12,000 tons of TNT killing approximately 80,000 outright. The bomb killed indiscriminately. Hiroshima was a city of considerable military importance. It contained the 2nd Army Headquarters, which commanded the defense of all southern Japan.

The second atomic bomb was carried by a B-29
bomber that dropped it over Nagasaki, Japan, at 11:02
a.m. Nagasaki time on August 9, 1945, and it exploded
at 1,650 feet with a force of 22,000 tons of TNT killing
approximately 70,000 outright. The city of Nagasaki
was one of the largest seaports in Japan.

When Kenji finished reading, he knew that hundreds of thousands
of people had been killed and maimed in his country, and two cities had been completely destroyed. Kenji was stunned, and he uncon-
sciously dropped the second paper to the floor.

The MP had been watching and waiting for Kenji's reaction to the
news. Now, when Kenji looked up, the MP took a short step toward
Kenji's cell. Looking directly at Kenji, he said in a subdued yet mean-
ingful tone, "That'll teach you bastards to suck eggs!"

Kenji looked up at the guard, and in Kenji's eyes, the guard could
see a combination of shame, regret, and loneliness. The guard, who had
seen nothing of the war, had embarrassed himself.

After the guard left, Kenji pondered what he now knew would be
the unmerciful march of events. If the war ended—and he had little doubt that it would—what was going to happen? Had Hokkaido
been bombed? If so, had his hometown of Ōtsu or the nearby town of
Toyokoro been bombed? And what of his family? Were they alive? Was
there a chance he would see them again? Maybe joining the navy was
no mistake. Surely most of the Japanese Army was dead by now. He
had two things to worry about: Would he be shot, and if not, would he
see Japan again? Salmon fishing on the Tokachi River sounded like a
pretty good life after all.

The next day, Saturday, August 11, 1945, Japan offered to surrender.
Kenji would not learn of the surrender for four more days. No one
bothered to tell him, not even the unpleasant guard. On the fourth
day, the air base commander came to Kenji's cell to tell him that the
war was over and that all that remained was the formal, unconditional
surrender. He looked at Kenji and said, "Of course, your war was over
years ago, but you'll be treated as a prisoner of war and sent to Japan

when conditions permit. But you won't be released until we're ready to ship you out."

This was the first time in nearly four years that Kenji was almost assured of surviving the war. If the news articles in the American papers were accurate, millions of Japanese soldiers, sailors, and civilians had died in the war, and the major cities of Japan had been devastated by American bombers. What would it be like in Japan? What of his family? His hopes and thoughts blossomed. "Maybe I didn't take the wrong train after all," he said with a smile.

Japan officially surrendered on September 2, 1945, and Kenji learned of the event from the sailors on the base and from the *Coos Bay Times*. A writer for that newspaper by the name of Linus Rink had authored a commentary on the reach of the Japanese military into the heart of Coos County. Kenji read it with interest because he was the focal point. Rink had not interviewed Kenji, and Kenji thought the story lacked about 90 percent of the facts. Maybe someday he would supply all the facts. It would be a story worth telling.

ACKNOWLEDGMENTS

Helen Slack Miller helped with reference citation, invaluable computer skills, and reading. Joe Slack helped with reading. Jennifer Kepka, Elizabeth Guenther, and Laura Berryhill helped with some initial corrections. Author Jeremy Darlow introduced me to Girl Friday Productions and put publishing in motion for me. My editor-in-chief, Kristen Hall-Geisler of Indigo Editing, provided excellent professional editing advice, revisions, and sharpening of scenes and dialogue. Michelle Hope Anderson, the copyeditor at Girl Friday Productions, expertly guided me away from all the continuity and grammatical errors I managed to commit.

REFERENCES

The internet provided unlimited access to information related to World War II in the Pacific theater. Combatant's names, places, ships, and events helped give this book some factual substance. Without it, this book would not have been written. Not every website is included.

Port Orford Lifeboat Station, "www.portorfordlifeboatstation.org," 7/27/2005

Japanese Special Naval Landing Forces, "en.wikipedia.org/wiki /Japanese_Special_Naval_Landing_Forces," 4/17/2006

Louis Morton, *HyperWar: US Army in WWII: Fall of the Philippines*, "www.ibiblio.org/hyperwar/USA," 3/7/2006

Tech Sights, *Collecting and Shooting the Arisaka Type 99 Rifle— Ammunition*, "www.surplusrifle.com/arisaka/ammunition.asp," 8/2/2005

Advanced Japanese Destroyers of World War II, "www.friesian.com /destroy," 3/11/2006

Stetson Conn, Rose C. Engleman, Byron Fairchild, *Guarding the United States and Its Outposts*, "www.army.mil/cmh-pg/books /wwii/Guard-US," 3/14/2006

World War 2 Atomic Bomb, "www.world-war-2.info/atomic-bomb," 3/18/2009

Imperial Japanese Navy Page, "www.combinedfleet.com," updated 2/19/21

Oregon History—World War II, "bluebook.state.or.us/cultural/history /history26," 2005

Slavic Research Center News, No. 10, December 2002, "src-h.slav .hokudai.ac.jp/eng/news/no10," 2/9/2009

The Tokachi River, "www.ob.hkd.mlit.go.jp," 2/5/2003

Hiroshima Prefecture Guidebook, "apike.ca/japan," 4/12/2006

Battle of the Coral Sea, "en.wikipedia.org/wiki/Battle_of_the_Coral
    _Sea," 3/15/2006

Commander Fleet Activities—Sasebo, "www.cfas.navy.mil/History,"
    5/10/2005

California State Military Department, The California State Military
    Museum, *California and the Second World War,* "www.military
    museum.org/HistoryWWII," 3/14/2006

An Overview of Coast Guard History, "www.uscg.mil/hq/g-cp/history,"
    3/14/2006

Battery Council International, *How a Battery Is Made,* "www.battery
    council.org," 2/18/2006

Japan-guide.com, *Taisho and Early Showa Period (1912-1945),* "Japan
    -guide.com/e/e2129," 2/23/2006

Earl Miller, *Cowboys in the Surf, Bandon Western World,* 2005

Amos L. Wood, *Beachcombing for Japanese Glass Floats,* 1967

DK Publishing, Inc., *20th Century Day by Day,* 1967

ABOUT THE AUTHOR

Harry Slack is a retired lawyer with a degree in political science from the University of Oregon and a law degree from Willamette University College of Law. He owned a commercial-fishing enterprise in Alaska for twenty-five years and served on the board of directors of a community bank for twenty-five years. He now lives in Bandon, Oregon.

Harry grew up in Coquille, Oregon, and was a teenager during World War II. During his school years he worked each summer in a sawmill or lived in a logging camp and worked as a logger. He hunted and fished along the Oregon coast. During the war, he and his childhood friends often speculated about what they might do if the Japanese attacked their shores, but thankfully no plan ever needed to be put to the test.